WHITE
OUT

WHITE OUT

DANIELLE GIRARD

THOMAS & MERCER

Text copyright © 2020 by Danielle Girard, Inc.
All rights reserved.

Published by Thomas & Mercer, Seattle

www.apub.com

Amazon, the Amazon logo, and Thomas & Mercer are trademarks of Amazon.com, Inc., or its affiliates.

ISBN-13: 9781542000109
ISBN-10: 1542000106

Cover design by Shasti O'Leary Soudant

Printed in the United States of America

For Meg Ruley,
friend and agent extraordinaire.
I'm grateful that you saw something in this one
from that first (long ago) draft.

CHAPTER 1

Cold sliced her skin like a thousand tiny blades, and pain beat its thunderous drum in her right temple. Her feet were damp, her toes frigid. She opened her eyes to pitch black and had the sensation that her body, pain and cold and the distant heartbeat, hovered in midair. Something slid down her neck with the thick, heavy texture of turkey gravy rewarmed the day after Thanksgiving.

In the darkness, her memory conjured a pool of scarlet blood, thickening on the floor. In the blood lay a man with a pale, round face and a patchy beard. The air smelled of yeast, vinegar, and pennies.

She recalled an older girl who had held her protectively. "It's over," she'd whispered through tears.

She blinked, a red light behind her eyelids, and searched for more memories—of the girl and the dead man—but none came. Who were they? Where were they?

And more importantly, where was she?

As her fingers explored the dark, fabric rustled. Not the familiar cotton of bedsheets but the whispered hush of a windbreaker or a parachute, as though she were buried in it. She pushed the fabric aside and touched her face, palpating until she reached the epicenter of the pain above her right ear. There was no bump. A bruise, maybe. She reached out and touched a hard, cold wall. Too close.

Adrenaline flooded her limbs. She was in some sort of box. Trapped.

As she shifted, a hideous noise erupted beneath her, the wailing of some massive cat. But the sound was too loud and mechanical to be an animal.

Panic reared her upright, but she rose only inches before something halted her. She blinked furiously, willing her eyes to adjust. A moment later, the piercing stutter of metal on metal filled the space.

She touched the bar against her chest, fingered the hard fabric edge across her shoulder. Not a bar—a seat belt. As realization struck, she clasped the fabric. It was not a parachute but an airbag. She was in a car. She felt a moment of pure relief. She was the passenger in a car. She thought of the pale man in the pool of blood. Was that man the driver?

After a moment of fumbling around on the ceiling, her fingers found the reading light. She blinked against its brightness and studied the driver. Eyes closed, hands limp in his lap, chin dropped to his chest. He wore a heavy down coat, and on his right wrist was a bulky gold watch, like for scuba diving. He was attractive but not at all familiar. And he wasn't moving.

She closed her eyes. *Mine eyes are ever toward the Lord; for he shall pluck my feet out of the net. Turn thee unto me, and have mercy upon me; for I am desolate and afflicted.* Psalm 25. The words felt natural in her mind, offering a brief calm.

Reaching for the sleeve of his coat, she followed the arm to a hand and broad fingers. She gripped his wrist. *Palmaris longus. Flexor carpi radialis.* Then the radial artery, where she felt the steady thump thump of his pulse.

"You're alive." Her own voice was unfamiliar, loud in the tight car.

He did not respond.

She shook his arm. "Wake up."

Nothing. She squinted through the windshield but saw only blackness. Inside, everything was foreign to her. The seats were leather, the dash inlaid with wood. Expensive. A man's billfold sat in the console between them. She palmed the pebbled texture and fingered the *LV* embossed across the brown leather. Louis Vuitton.

She opened it and read the driver's license. Brent Alexander Nolan from Fargo, North Dakota. She surveyed his unconscious form, then the wallet, her pulse a steady thrumming in her neck. The pain subsided slightly as a nervous throb rose below her ribs. A voice, male and angry, spoke in her head. *"Always take what's easy. Quick. Then get back. Nothing bad happens when we're all here, together."*

A warm rush of adrenaline spiked in her chest as she ran her fingers along the line of credit cards. Several Visas, two AmEx. *Take what's easy.* A stack of bills—crisp bills, meaning high denominations. How did she know? She slid the bills from his wallet and folded them, their hard edges sharp against her fist. A few hundred dollars, maybe more. She imagined a bottle of whiskey, something sweet. She was filled with pride. She'd done well.

"Now, get back. Don't leave me here with him." She imagined green eyes behind too-long bangs, felt the warmth of recognition. A name flashed in her head. *Abby.* Where was Abby?

The car lurched and pitched her forward, and the seat belt cut across her sternum. She froze, panting tiny breaths to avoid big motions. Through the windshield, she made out the twisted guardrail beside the car, the dark void beyond it.

The car rocked forward, and she held her breath. They had crashed on an overpass. The front of the car jutted over the edge. It would be— what—thirty or forty feet to the ground below? Or more? They would not survive the fall.

Her breath came in ragged chunks like violent hiccups that she tried to hold in. *Stay calm. No big motions.*

She leaned back against the seat, using her body weight to keep the car from tipping.

She had to get out. But Brent . . .

"Don't help nobody. Don't stop for nothing." The voice again, angry and male.

She shook her head. No. She had to wake him up. Get him out. "Brent," she said, her voice rusty in her throat. She gripped his forearm with all her strength, afraid shaking him would tip the car over the edge. "Come on."

Nothing.

Fingers trembling, she pressed the button to unfasten her seat belt. The belt didn't release. She jabbed harder, using only two fingers, keeping the motions controlled and small. Still, it stuck.

Terror clamped her throat and squeezed. Trapped. "No!" The word was sharp in her ears as she wrapped the belt around her hand for purchase. Clenching her jaw, she jammed three fingers into the release and jerked hard on the belt. It sprang free. The car tipped several inches, then slowly righted again.

She slapped Brent's cheek, then pinched. "Come on. Come on. We've got to get out!"

He didn't respond.

Get out; then go around and get him.

She edged toward the door, gripped the handle, and said a prayer that it would open. When the door cracked, she cried out in relief. The door swung open, and the car's underside let out another howl as it slid forward an inch or two, then stopped, swaying gently. She froze until the car steadied.

"Brent!"

Setting her right foot on the icy pavement, she shifted her weight off the seat. Her foot was wet inside the boot, and the chill in the outside air cut straight to her toes. She was almost out of the car when her boot slid on the ice. She landed hard, slamming her head on the asphalt. The car tipped forward, and the door swung closed on her left foot. The nose of the car teetered over the edge.

Grunting, she kicked to free her leg, but the door was heavy, the boot caught. The ground was too slick; she couldn't get traction to hold on. The car slipped forward, dragging her across the road. Panic scalded her lungs as she twisted, clawing at the ice. The cawing sound of the car sliding over the guardrail escalated into a scream.

"No!" she cried, fighting to cling to the passing ground as the car tipped, every second gaining momentum. She cried out and bucked upright. Her fingers caught the edge of the door. She wrenched it open. Her foot came free.

The door fell closed, and the car wrested through the guardrail with a deafening screech. She scrambled backward as the car tipped into the night.

A beat of silence passed, and a sound exploded from the blackness, the rippling crunch of the car landing below.

CHAPTER 2

She swiped at her tears and listened for sounds from below—Brent calling out or the whisper of fire from the car. There was only the hush of wind blowing ice across the asphalt like the scurrying of so many mice. Above her, stars dotted a moonless black surface like reverse freckles. Around her lay road and darkness. There was no sign of a house or building. Where were they? She patted her pants pockets for her phone, but they were empty. The wind cut through her blouse, and she shivered. Where was her jacket? She couldn't remember how she'd gotten there. Or why she'd been with Brent. Why she had stolen from him.

It was more than that, she realized now. She couldn't remember *anything*.

Scrambling onto her hands and knees, she crawled to the broken guardrail. Below, the car lay upside down, its cabin crunched to half its normal height. The front bumper hung from one side, flung out like a limp arm, and the rear right tire spun slowly, as though trying to find purchase in the air. "Brent!"

No answer.

He couldn't have survived that fall.

He *had* to have survived.

"You get back home. You don't come back, you know what happens."
Pain sliced her shoulder—the sharp edge of a blade. She spun around, but there was no one there. Nothing touched her back. And yet there was something there, some lingering pain. Her fingers dug beneath

her shirt, finding the hard edge of her scapula and, below it, a series of narrow ridges, like thin worms beneath the skin. She scratched them, though they didn't itch.

The wind howled, and she shivered against the cold and pressed her palm to her chest, struggling to draw a full breath. The cuffs of her jeans were damp against her legs, her shoes wet, as though she'd walked through water somewhere. But there was no standing water in sight. She had to get moving. On her feet, she took a step. Her left ankle throbbed, the pain a metal taste in her mouth. She stepped forward, slipped and fell, then rose again, sliding her boots slowly across the ice.

When she reached the place where the overpass met the sloped ground, she studied the icy hillside. She wouldn't make it down without falling. Sitting on the frozen ground, she inched down: butt, then feet, using the heels of her boots and her fingers to keep from sliding. *Come on, Brent. Be okay. Please.* She needed him—to tell her who she was. Where she was.

Her fingers burned with cold. She stopped partway down the hill and blew onto them, rubbing them roughly as though to beat the warmth back in. Her own hands were unfamiliar, the red polish uneven on her thumbs and forefingers. A messy job, done in haste. She pressed them into the denim fabric of her pants, willing the heat to return.

When she made it to the car, she went straight to the driver's side and dropped to her knees at the blown-out window. Brent hung upside down from the seat belt. Small abrasions covered his face, but she couldn't see any external trauma. It would be internal. The internal damage was what would kill him.

She located his pulse—palpable, consistent. He was not dead. "Oh, thank God," she said, pressing her forehead to the cold car door. *Get him out.* She flattened herself to the ground and stared up into the car. The window opening was crushed. Would he even fit through?

You have to try.

7

With her head inside the car window, the top of the frame cut painfully into her spine. She stretched for the seat belt, then hesitated. If he fell wrong, he could break his neck, or his weight might pin her, and they'd both be stuck. And what about his back? If he was injured, the drop could paralyze him. She drew a breath, trying to decide. Beneath them, the ground vibrated. She backed out of the car and saw the black lines that ran under them.

The car was on a railroad track.

There was no decision to make. Moving might paralyze him, but a train would kill him.

The vibrations dulled, and she wondered how long they had before the train arrived. Was there a train actually coming? It was suddenly quiet. *Get him out.* She slid back into the car, headfirst. The rearview mirror against her tailbone, she jabbed the seat belt's release button. The strap loosened, and Brent dropped. Arms extended, she guided him down so that he landed shoulders first.

Brent's knees caught under the steering wheel, and she struggled to move him, her back aching with the effort. But the steady beat of his carotid reassured her—he was alive. She managed to maneuver him so his head was closest to the window.

Hard ice and gravel dug into her knees as she muscled her hands beneath his back. She gripped under his arms, then tugged him through the window. He was heavy, the space narrow. Every inch of progress was slow.

Halfway out, he caught on something. Tugging, she struggled to free him but couldn't. Not strong enough to lift him, she set his torso down and moved to one side. There—his belt was hooked on the plastic window seal. She tried and failed to free it. Beneath her knees, the earth vibrated again. She froze and listened. A train? Why couldn't she hear it? *Move him.* She lifted his jacket and unbuckled the belt. With the belt loosened from his pants, she tossed it aside. A long final yank freed him from the car.

She dragged him down a small hill to softer ground, safe from the tracks. Sweat slid between her shoulder blades, collected at the waist of her jeans.

"Brent," she whispered, crying. A tear fell from her chin and landed on the side of his face.

As she reached to wipe it off, a man's voice sounded from the car. "OnStar has recorded your accident, Mr. Nolan."

She leaped backward, striking her elbow on a rock. Yelped.

"Mr. Nolan? Can you hear me? We are contacting the authorities."

She clamped a hand to her mouth. Why didn't she answer? What was wrong with her?

"You don't talk to anyone. Ever."

She waited a moment, silent.

What she needed was her phone. She crawled back to the car and scanned the backseat, spotting a canvas purse on the ceiling, almost in the rear window. The passenger-window glass was shattered but still in its frame. Using her uninjured foot, she kicked the toe of her boot at the glass, flinching as it collapsed into the car.

"Mr. Nolan, can you hear me?"

She said nothing. Her belly on the cold earth, she crawled over cubes of tempered glass and retrieved the purse, returning to Brent.

"We have police and emergency vehicles en route, Mr. Nolan."

The word *police* took her breath.

"A response team is seven minutes out."

"Never talk to the police. No matter what. You know what he'll do."

"No!" she cried out and clasped her hands against her ears, willing the voice away. They'd had an accident. They needed the police. An ambulance, too.

But every fiber inside her screamed one thing—*run.*

She turned to the bag but felt a rush of dread. Why? What would she find in her own purse? She drew even breaths. A minute passed. The voice from the car spoke again, muffled by the roaring in her ears. The ambulance was coming. The police.

She would go to the hospital. With Brent.

Beside her, Brent's expression was still, lifeless. His pulse was still palpable. She drew his eyelids open, one at a time. The darkness made it impossible to see whether his pupils were uneven. Surely he had suffered a concussion. But that fall—there would be other damage as well. Gently, she lifted the hood of Brent's coat to cushion his head from the hard ground. She zipped it up to his chin and pulled the sleeves over his hands to keep him warm. Rubbed his shoulders through the heavy down.

On the dark horizon lay a dull-orange glow. Civilization beyond the hill. Again, the instinct to run overwhelmed her. Dread collected like sharp stones in her belly.

She would wait for the police and tell them what had happened.

"Don't forget the rules." A boisterous laugh. *The same green eyes, an older face.* "Abby." The name was swept into the darkness.

Do something. Find your phone. She turned to her purse and took hold of its zipper. The thread was frayed, the pocket on one side torn at the corner. Nothing like Brent's Louis Vuitton wallet. She emptied the bag's main compartment. A light-blue zip-up fleece. A makeup bag containing powder, lip gloss, and mascara, the labels worn off. She pulled on the fleece, saw the broken stitching on the blouse she wore. Her jeans were dark but worn thin at the knees. It was all a far cry from Brent's expensive jacket and wallet. Maybe they didn't know each other.

At the bottom of the bag she found a pink-and-red polka-dot wallet. It all looked so innocent, so young. She ran her fingers over the inexpensive vinyl, worn at the edges, and waited for some memory, some sense that the wallet belonged to her, or she to it.

None came.

She cracked it open and squinted at a state-issued ID card from Arizona. The name was Lily Baker. The woman didn't look familiar, but she guessed from the dark hair in her peripheral vision that she was this woman. *Lily.*

She studied the ID. Born July 2, 1994. But what year was it now? Was she twenty years old? Or thirty? The address on the ID card was Phoenix, Arizona. She looked around the dark, cold night, thought of Brent's North Dakota address. This was not Phoenix.

"Mr. Nolan, your response team is four minutes out."

Lily Baker. *You are Lily Baker.* She drew another breath and sifted through the contents of the wallet. A debit card for the Paradise Valley Credit Union. A frequent-shopper card for Safeway and a couple of other loyalty cards. The billfold held seven dollars—a five and two ones—and a folded photograph. The image was old, the photo finish cracked where it had been folded, the paper softened from wear. Two girls—one blonde, one brunette. The brunette was her, a younger version of the woman in the ID photo. The blonde was older, her face thinner, her expression more a wry twist than an actual smile. Those same green eyes. Abby. Her sister?

She shivered and looked through the rest of the wallet, but it was empty. There were no receipts, no credit cards. A debit card and seven dollars. She returned the wallet to the bag and unzipped the side pocket. She reached in and drew out a hard metal column, four or five inches long. A flashlight? She held it in her hand, squinting at the black object. Through a slit in the center, she eyed the copper circles of primers, one on top of the other. Bullets.

Not a flashlight. She was holding the magazine for a gun. Tentatively, she fingered the cloth bag and felt the outline of a pistol. She drew it out slowly. Her hands came together, the magazine sliding into the gun with a firm click. She drew the slide back, chambered a bullet.

The pale, fat face, surrounded in blood. "You did it," *the girl whispered.*
What had she done?

"Mr. Nolan?"

She jumped, the gun slipping from her hand and cracking against the frozen earth. The sound of a bullet echoed in her mind. Had she killed that man?

"The ambulance is two minutes out, Mr. Nolan. Can you hear me?"

Two minutes. And then, in the distance, she heard the muted shriek of a siren.

"Run," the voice shouted, sharp and angry. *"What are you waiting for?"*

She could not be here when the police arrived. She touched Brent's face, whispered, "Don't die, Brent. Please don't die."

She pulled back the slide to release the chambered round. The bullet dropped to the ground and disappeared from view. She scanned the snow-dusted shrubs underfoot but couldn't locate it.

Forget the bullet, she thought. *Two minutes.*

She rose quickly, facing the orange light that blinked beyond the hill. Looping the strap of the bag over her left shoulder, she hurried down the train track as the pitch of the sirens grew louder.

A line came to her. Romans 6:23.

For the wages of sin is death.

CHAPTER 3

KYLIE

At the first vibration of her mobile phone, Detective Kylie Milliard was wide awake. Her father used to say she slept like a cat, one eye open. She'd given Santa Claus a run for his money, but it was a useful skill in her line of work. As she sat up in bed, her fingers found the phone, which spent nights at the edge of her mattress. The main department number showed on the screen. She answered at the second buzz. "Milliard."

"Hey, there, Kylie, it's Steve."

Good humored and easygoing, Steve Cannon had the broad-shoul-dered, narrow-waisted physique of a swimmer. Not that bad to look at. On occasion, when the cuff of his dress shirt had slipped too high, she had spotted a tattoo. In her opinion, most tattoos were men's attempts to look tougher than they were, and she suspected Cannon's was no different. He had started in the department a few months before Kylie, the only other outsider. Everyone else had been born and raised in Hagen. Steve had joined as the department's mechanic, but the small size of the police fleet meant he did a little of everything. Still, middle-of-the-night Dispatch wasn't usually in his list of responsibilities. "What are you doing at Dispatch?"

"Marjorie's out. Called me a couple of hours ago. Her back again. Sorry to bug you."

The clock on the bedside table said 5:27. "No worries. What's going on?"

"Dead woman in a dumpster." That was something she liked about Steve. Hagen was full of people who liked to talk. Steve got to the point.

"Who's the victim?" she asked.

"Don't know yet. Late twenties, no ID."

"Where?"

"Skål," Steve said. "The bar."

"I know it." She stood from the bed and stepped out of her flannel pajama pants, the wood floor icy on her bare feet. She grabbed the tan Carhartt pants she'd tossed over her chair last night and pulled them on, phone tucked under her chin. "You call Sheriff Davis?"

"Patrol called him direct. Ambulance, too."

She zipped her pants quickly and put the phone on speaker. "When was that?"

"Maybe thirty minutes ago."

She eyed the clock again. Patrol should have contacted her, too. Now she was a half hour behind them. What good was being the town's only detective if no one called her to the damn scene? Such small-town BS.

This wouldn't happen in Fargo. She'd be respected there. She just had to *get there*.

"Sheriff wanted to make sure you got word," Steve added.

She'd gotten word of it, all right—the last word. "I'll be there in fifteen." She could make it in twelve.

"I'll let them know. Stay safe," he added, something he always said. It had seemed odd at first, but it had sort of grown on her. Or maybe he had grown on her. Not that she would admit that. Never. Plus, in this tiny town, safety wasn't supposed to be an issue.

Kylie pulled a blue button-down over the T-shirt she'd been sleeping in, put on a blazer, and zipped her canvas department jacket over it. She was out the door in three minutes.

As Kylie had suspected, the full response team was at the bar when she arrived. The sky was pitch black, sunrise still hours away. Two patrol cars, a fire engine, an ambulance, and the sheriff's personal car—an old Ram truck—were parked in the lot. Three construction lights, mounted on tripods six or seven feet above the ground, illuminated the rusty dumpster as though it were at the center of a movie set.

Kylie drove to the far side of the gravel lot. There had been no new snow in the past twenty-four hours, but the winds were strong. Any tire tracks from the night before had been blown clean. The ones that remained led directly to the vehicles in the lot now—parked a little too close to the dumpster, considering it was the scene of a crime.

Keep your opinions to yourself, she thought.

Eleven bodies—all men—huddled around the rusty dumpster, and a ladder was propped against the outside, but otherwise, no one seemed to be doing anything.

The bar was maybe ten yards from the dumpster, to the north. To the south was a gap for access and, beyond that, parking. To the dumpster's east, maybe fifteen yards, a patch of thick woods began. She'd been called out to Skål before—or rather she'd joined Patrol on a few of the drunk-and-disorderly calls. There were very few real crimes in Hagen—a few accidental shootings, mostly hunting related, but no murder in almost a decade. With the low crime rate, Kylie spent a fair amount of her time helping Patrol and getting to know the town. So she'd been to Skål.

In the summer months, couples disappeared into the woods here for privacy. Patrons regularly used the trees to piss if the bar was full and the weather warm. But with the temps below freezing, she wasn't sure they'd find much traffic now. They'd have to take a look around.

Stepping out of her car, she pulled down the flaps of her hat to cover her ears from the bitter wind and adjusted the fingers on her heavy work gloves. The men were surprisingly still and quiet in the cold air as she grew close, their faces turned to hers. The artificial lighting cast them in strange shadows, hollowing their eye sockets and cutting across their cheekbones. For one short moment, she was staring at almost a dozen skeletons.

A hand touched her back, and she whipped around, swallowing the sound that rose in her throat.

It was Sheriff Davis, phone to his ear. Though it had been fifteen years since he'd been on a team, Davis's appearance screamed football star. The broad shoulders, the thick neck and sandy-blond hair, plus that easy, charming smile. Even the way he walked was like he was coming off the field. Not her type. But that was as far as it went for Davis. He didn't have the asshole jock personality or the bravado. Though she had expected to have to work around a big ego, Davis was surprisingly humble.

"Of course," Davis said. "I understand, sir."

The mayor, she guessed. This would not be happy news for the mayor, who was already battling unfavorable press over his girlfriend, about whom his wife was none too happy. Davis covered the phone with one palm and said, "We're waiting for the crime scene team."

Hagen's "crime scene team" was two patrol officers who had completed a twenty-hour training course on evidence collection in Bismarck, training Kylie herself was halfway through. Hardly a mighty forensic team. She greeted the group and noticed that everyone wore gloves. It was bitter cold, but the layer also meant they were preserving the evidence.

Carl Gilbert, the patrol officer she worked with most, approached. A couple of years older than her, Gilbert was lanky and a little awkward, like there was too much limb to control. He always jangled—a full ring of keys on his belt that rang like wind chimes when he moved and the change in his pocket he constantly worked with one hand. And he had a habit of sucking on hard candies—one after another. He didn't gain a pound, but she did wonder about his teeth.

Gilbert had been a patrol officer for only a few years, having taken some detours outside Hagen after high school before getting his degree. She wondered if he aspired to detective and whether her appointment had stepped on his toes. If so, he never let on. "Victim's mid- to late twenties, Caucasian," he said, his gaze drifting toward the dumpster without quite reaching it. "That's all we know right now."

This was Hagen, where everyone knew everyone. "Who is she?" Kylie asked. As she surveyed the men, her pulse galloped under her heavy coat. What weren't they saying?

Kylie reached her thumb across her index finger and pulled it down, popping the knuckle in a rush of pain and release. The action was like a reset, and she was herself again. She was a professional. "Hold the ladder. I'm going up."

"Are you—" Gilbert started.

"Hold it, please."

Gilbert gripped the ladder as she climbed. She pounded her feet into each rung, willing them to hold her up, keep her strong. By the fourth step, the inside of the dumpster was visible, more than halfway filled with black trash bags, stray beer bottles, and plastic cups. And the woman.

Kylie flinched at the blue-white skin, her gloved hands clenching the hard metal edge. She had imagined the dead woman lying peacefully on a bed of trash bags. As though she might have been asleep.

Instead, her body was splayed with violence. Her limbs struck unnatural poses, her head too far back, chin too far to the right, the right arm too far to the left. Kylie's gaze traveled up her arm until it met with a bony shoulder cocked so strangely that it had to be detached.

She noticed the broken angle of the opposite arm. The woman wore black jeans, a spaghetti strap blouse, and no shoes. Her only jewelry was a wide red leather bracelet, its color dingy from wear. A generic puffy coat hung off one arm, worn shiny in places and dotted with little strips of black duct tape to cover the holes. The victim was oddly beautiful in her violent death. Her eyes were open, and the skin around them had the same soft green tint as her irises. Petechiae were visible in the whites of her eyes—small red blood vessels that had burst, often caused by strangulation. Kylie tried to think of them as clues, of the dead woman as a puzzle.

Behind the victim's head was a dark shadow, maybe something or maybe a trick of the bright lights. Kylie shifted on the ladder, noticing for the first time that the back of the victim's hair was dark and matted.

Blood.

She took a moment, not sure she trusted her voice, then said, "Has anyone checked the woods?"

"I did a cursory look, but it's too dark to see much," Gilbert said. "I'll go back when it's light." He took her hand to help her back down, and the touch gave her chills. On the ground again, she shook out her arms to get the blood moving and searched for the sheriff.

Sheriff Davis was ending his call when Kylie approached. "We have any idea who she is?" Kylie asked.

He shook his head. "I've never seen her before." His eyes flashed back to the street, and she caught in them something unusual. Fear. "We've all looked. She's not familiar to any of us."

Someone had to know her. Kylie glanced around the parking lot. "Any sign of her car?"

"None. Nothing in a four-block radius—it's all warehouses out here."

Hagen was not an easy place to get around without a car. Someone had brought her there. "No one knows her," she repeated.

Davis met her gaze but said nothing.

Over in Fargo, it wouldn't be so strange if a dozen people didn't recognize someone. But in Hagen, even with the influx of oil workers, an unfamiliar face was rare. There was no main highway within twenty miles of Hagen. People who drove the 1804 were either coming to Hagen or leaving it. They didn't just happen through.

Another pair of headlights turned into the parking lot. Kylie recognized the squared shape of the department car's lights. The evidence tech. Now at least they could move the body. Maybe that would help them figure out who the mystery woman was.

And how she'd ended up murdered in Hagen.

CHAPTER 4

—

IVER

A slant of bright light cut across Iver's face, and he opened his eyes. As he scanned the familiar living room, his heart drilled a violent beat into his ribs. He blinked a single time, and a bomb exploded in his head. Pitching forward off the couch, he vomited. Puke splashed across the hardwood floor. Cal stood, the dog's hind legs trembling as he moved away from his owner. Iver wiped his mouth with the back of his hand and caught sight of the Jack bottle on the floor.

It was empty. Iver groaned.

"The alcohol messes with the medications," his ex-wife's voice shouted in his head. *"You have got to get smart, Iver."*

The familiar pressure weighed on his chest. All the fighting. He'd hated how angry she always was. He exhaled, trying to relieve the pressure. She was his ex-wife now. No more fighting. He saw the flash of an angry face. Had Debbie been in the bar last night? Had they fought? Damn, his head hurt.

Iver closed his eyes and breathed past the steady drill of his pulse in his eyeballs, swallowing carefully as though he could lure his stomach into calmness. The saliva met with a lurch in his gut, and another wave rose in his throat. Cupping a hand over his mouth, he sprinted to the bathroom. Hands gripped the porcelain as bile and brown liquor splashed into the bowl.

He imagined the scene from Debbie's perspective. How hard it must have been for her. Every time he'd woken up hungover. Every time she'd had to come get him at the bar when one of his friends had called to tell her that he couldn't drive. Every time she'd woken up to him coming home drunk. "I can't live like this," she had said. "You have to quit the drinking."

He had tried. He really had. Like that was so easy.

That bar was his business. Now that Debbie had left him, the bar was also his life.

He splashed water on his face and rinsed his mouth, then found his way back to the couch, a damp towel pressed to his cheeks. He should clean the vomit. At least it was on the hardwood floor this time. He'd clean it. Soon. He just needed a little more rest. The morning light was so damn bright. With the towel across his face, he closed his eyes, tried to find his way back to the empty bliss.

No more Jack. The Jack always made the pain worse. He could quit the Jack. *Promise,* he thought, as though he could barter away the pain in his head. But it wouldn't let up. The agony built, like a vise clamping his optic nerve. Squeezing his eyes closed against the ache, he palmed the table for his meds and noticed a sharp pain radiating from his hand. A long red scratch stretched across his knuckles, oozing blood. He shook it as though it might loosen the sting.

What the hell had he done? He cupped the hand to his chest and reached out the other one for his meds. They had to be on this table.

But his hand struck wood and nothing else. Shit. Where were his damn pills? He sat up, his stomach rolling again. He squinted against the assault of the dim lights, reached across to the coffee table, and pushed aside the pizza box that held last night's dinner. No pills. He patted the pockets of the jeans he was still wearing. No pills. He forced himself to his feet, then shuffled toward the kitchen, stepping around his own vomit. He made it as far as the doorway, leaned against the jamb, and blinked as gently as he could, every motion of his eyelids a jackhammer. From the doorway, he scanned the countertops. No pills.

"Think," he said, stumbling toward the bathroom. The air was sour. The nausea returned. Holding his breath, he opened the medicine cabinet and searched the line of bottles. No headache pills.

He'd been at work last night. He'd taken a couple of pills in the bar. He remembered that. He'd been in the office, trying to finish up an order. Kevin had brought him a Jack and Coke. Then another. And one more. Was there a fourth? Doubles, probably. Kevin always made him doubles. The sugary film still coated his tongue. Kevin had been complaining about his girlfriend. They'd been talking about exes. He must have left the pills there.

Closing his eyelids, Iver pushed the knuckles of his index fingers against the pain behind each eye. *You can do this,* he told himself. *Pull yourself together and get in the car.* He opened his eyes and noticed a thread caught in the band of his watch, pulled it free.

The thread brought back the night air, the sting of hard wind. He felt a bruise on his shin as though it had just happened. Reached down to finger it through his pants. There was something hard and crusty on the denim. It looked like blood. Damn. He unbuckled his belt and stepped out of his jeans, kicked them toward the laundry room and grabbed a pair of sweats off his bedroom floor. His head throbbed like a mother now.

He dropped the hand towel on the vomit.

Get the pills from the bar, come home, and clean this shit up. Clean yourself up.

As he walked toward the front door, a wave of debilitating fear swept over him. He didn't remember coming home. Had he driven? What if his truck wasn't there?

When he reached the front door, he was relieved to see the white pickup parked in the driveway. He opened the front door, and Cal stood, making his way toward the sunlight, nails clicking on the wood floor.

"You coming, boy?"

Cal answered by moving past Iver and down the front stairs, toward the truck.

Iver opened the passenger-side door and stooped to lift Cal into the cab. An Australian shepherd–collie mix, Cal had been a gift from his ex-wife after his second tour in Afghanistan. His second and last tour. The accident had ensured he wasn't going back.

Cal had been wandering the streets of town, abandoned, when he'd been hit by a car on the 1804. Thankfully, the roustabout who hit him had brought him to the local vet, who set his broken leg and got him back to health before turning him over to the Hagen pound. When his wife had brought Cal home, the dog's leg had still been in a cast, and Iver had still been battling vertigo and nightmares and a dozen other symptoms of his brain injury. She'd brought her crippled husband a crippled dog. She must have taken one look at that pathetic beast and thought immediately of Iver.

The beginning of the end.

Iver rounded the truck, shivering against the cold, and pulled himself into the cab. He grabbed the ball cap from the bench seat and lowered it down over his eyes. The morning light was a killer, and he'd lost his sunglasses somewhere. *Just get to the bar. Get to your meds.* If he'd been smarter, he'd have stashed some pills in his car, some in the house, some in the bar. Hell, he'd have them on every surface. But they were hard to get, and the doctor only prescribed so many.

Iver found the keys, still in the ignition. As the truck whined once, then coughed to life, Cal made a couple of awkward circles on the passenger seat before settling down. Iver revved the engine.

On the drive through town, the early-morning light reflected brightly off storefront windows, the side mirror of an oncoming car, even the dash of his own truck. Every glare made Iver wince. Since the accident, sunlight was painful. Doctors couldn't explain it. "The brain isn't fully understood," they'd said.

Sunglasses. He had to get new sunglasses.

He turned down the gravel road to his dad's bar. His bar now. Snow clung to the curled shingles on the roof and the rounded wooden sign that hung from a rusted iron arm. Once upon a time, the ring over the *a* in *Skål* had been painted bright cobalt blue. Iver wasn't sure if he could actually remember the color or if he had just heard about it so many times that his memory had filled in the blank. Either way, the color had faded decades earlier, like most aspects of the bar, which sat like a stubborn reminder that the thing his father had been most proud of was not his son.

By the time Iver pulled up to the bar, a blind spot had formed in his left eye, and it hurt to blink. His father's bar. The place had been giving him headaches for as long as he could remember, but this was no regular headache. He knew from experience that he'd have a full-blown migraine in a matter of minutes. He lifted Cal to the ground and made his way to the front door. When he reached to unlock the bolt, the door was ajar. Who the hell had closed last night?

He pushed through the door and into the dimly lit space. The smell of rancid beer made his stomach turn. Seated at one of the low tables was his bar manager, Mike Hammond. Next to him was Sheriff Jack Davis. Both men looked like they'd been up all night. Only then did he notice a woman in a blazer on the far side of the table.

"What's going on?"

"Hey, buddy," Jack Davis said, standing from the table.

The sheriff crossed the room and reached out to shake Iver's hand. Forgetting about the cut on his knuckles, Iver shook, wincing at the pain. The sheriff still had the same grip he'd had in high school. Three years ahead of Iver, Jack Davis was big, with a wide neck and a thick head of blond hair. Varsity quarterback from the time he was a freshman, played varsity basketball as a sophomore. He'd gotten some kind of scholarship to college. When he'd come back to Hagen, he'd become deputy sheriff at twentysomething. Sheriff by thirty and married to a gorgeous woman. The guy was perfect. Until Mrs. Davis had up and left for no reason. No one stayed perfect forever. At least Jack Davis had had a turn at it.

Davis glanced down at the hand.

"Cut myself," Iver said as Davis's gaze sliced across the room.

Davis motioned to the table. "This is Detective Kylie Milliard," Davis said. "She joined us from Fargo PD a few months ago."

Iver didn't need to see her expression for more than two seconds to know Jack was bullshitting him with the whole "Hey, old buddy" routine. Iver sank into a chair, legs suddenly weak as a new wave of nausea crested in his gut.

CHAPTER 5

LILY

Lily shivered in the dark shed, shifting against the hard concrete ground. Bright light shone from under the door. Her bare feet were cold in the open air, her ankle stiff, painful with even the slightest motion. She looked around the small space as the memories of the night flooded back.

After walking on and off for two hours toward what she'd thought were city lights, she'd come upon a huge flare, its flame hissing like an angry snake. Beside it, two oil pumps had cranked up and down in the night sky. Steel machines, like something from a *Star Wars* movie. She had walked past the pumps and stared out into the dark.

Beyond the flare, the night sky was an extensive swath of blackness. She was still miles from civilization. A small shed sat beyond the pumps, its door unlocked. She had heaved the door open and entered to take refuge from the cold night air. A small voice in her head had reminded her to remove the wet boots—a half-remembered lesson about frostbite. A generator of some sort was running inside, and the machine kept the space almost warm enough to be comfortable.

She tried to think back further, shuffling through her mind for memories.

The man from the car. Brent. With the nice clothes and the cash in his wallet. Cash she had taken. What was he to her? Was he the one who had told her not to go to the police? To hurry back to Abby?

To fight the spinning thoughts, she recounted what she knew. First, her name was Lily Baker. She had an inexpensive bag with cheap makeup and a wallet with seven dollars. She had been driving with a man named Brent Nolan. They'd had an accident. She'd taken his money but had tried to save him. Then she'd left. The lines repeated in her head. *Never talk to the police. Never give anyone your name.*

She had a gun. She closed her eyes and tried to remember something about that gun, about herself before waking in that car. She shivered at the memory of standing in the snow with the other girl, Abby. Only she wasn't a girl; she was a woman. The two had huddled in the dark, frozen, as they'd listened. Lily could feel her own terror. Then there was the slashing sound of boots crunching through the snow. "He's coming," Abby had said.

Lily squeezed her eyes closed, searching for more images. Nothing came. She opened her eyes and shifted in the tight space, taking stock of the pain that radiated through her. Neck, face, back, ankle. The tender scratch on her hand, thin slices along her neck that disappeared into her shirt.

But aside from her ankle being caught in the car door, she could recall none of those injuries happening. The final moments were hauntingly clear—the shrieking of metal as the car had tipped over the edge, the hot rush of fear. Had Brent survived the night? She'd heard the ambulance. The OnStar operator had said the response team was two minutes out. If she'd stayed, she would have been in a warm bed right now. But then there was the money she had taken from Brent, the gun, the sense that all of this was wrong. That *she* was wrong.

You don't make good choices.

Start, she thought. *Start to make good choices.*

First, she needed to get out of here. Then she needed to make sure Brent was okay. Find Abby.

Leaning across the space, she cracked open the shed door. The sun was a bright fiery ball in the sky. Immediately she felt the warmth of its rays on her skin. Her stomach growled, and her mouth was tight and parched. She also needed food and water.

She had to move. She needed something to wrap her ankle. With her bag emptied onto the floor, she pushed past the makeup, looking for some piece of fabric to use as a bandage. Only then did she notice that the bag had an inside zipper as well. She pulled it open, slid her hand inside, and felt a small, thick book.

The book was a paperback, its exterior covered with a brown paper bag, like a high school textbook. Intricate black pen designs covered the paper, flowers and vines in and around the lines. The drawings had been sealed with clear packing tape that was worn at the corners. Bits of dirt ran in lines where the tape had come up off the paper.

Had she done that? And why? She was an adult, and this looked like a child's schoolbook. She flipped the book open. A Bible. The book of Job, chapter fourteen: *Man born of woman is of few days and full of trouble.* The words were familiar. She held the book by its spine and shook it, letting the pages flutter open in hopes that some clue would fall from its pages. None did.

Setting the book on her lap, she opened to the inside cover and found small, square handwriting. *I. Larson, 416 4th Street*, followed by a seven-digit phone number. Someone's name was on the inside of her Bible. What did the *I* stand for?

She pulled the picture from her wallet and studied the two women. The name she remembered was Abby, but maybe the woman's name was something else—something that started with an *I*. But if they were sisters, why would they have different last names? Unless Baker was a married name? And she had a husband? The questions pinged across her brain like a pinball, striking hollow, empty notes.

She tucked the Bible back into the bag and searched the other pockets. Had she overlooked anything else?

But there was nothing else. She felt in her jeans pockets, back and then front. In her right front pocket, she found something about the size of a wadded tissue. She pulled out a folded strip of newspaper. She held it in one hand, afraid. What else? What. Else.

The thin newsprint felt like it might dissolve in her grip. Unfolding the strip with careful hands, she laid it out against her leg and scanned the page. An image, severed three-quarters of the way down, showed the bottom edge of a mattress. Below, in bold, it read, *EVERYTHING MUST G—* The edge of the *G* had been torn off.

On the flip side of the page was a single headline. *Police Still Investigating Possible Second Suspect . . .* She skimmed the words, her vision blurred by the too-rapid beating of her heart. Her gaze froze on the words *second suspect.* Why did she have this article? Was she the second suspect? Her sister?

She drew a shaky breath to calm herself. She had a Bible, an address and phone number, a wallet with seven dollars, some piece of a newspaper article, and a picture of herself and another woman. Even with these things, she could not answer the most basic questions about who she was and why she was here, in this place.

Teeth chattering from the cold, she rubbed her ankle gently, trying to work out some of the swelling. She had nothing to use as a wrap, and there was nowhere for her foot to go but back inside the boot. Her eyes teared from the effort of getting back into the damp boots. After quickly repacking her bag, she rose and pushed the door open, squinting in the bright sunlight as she filled her lungs with cold air.

For a moment, she considered leaving the gun behind. Why did she have it? Surely there was some reason. What if she needed it? In the end, she kept it. With a last look around, she left the shed behind and set out into the day, hoping town wasn't far.

CHAPTER 6

—

Iver

The bar felt dank, the way it did when the old wood floors were swollen from the moisture in fall and spring. But it was the dead of winter now. The table had gone quiet. Iver kept his gaze on Jack Davis while, across the table, that detective's eyes bored into him like a drill, which only added to the sensation that his head was about to explode. As though sensing trouble, Cal sidled up close.

"Sheriff." Iver rubbed Cal's neck and tried to hide his own fear. "What's going on?"

"Can you tell me what time you left the bar last night?" Davis asked.

Iver glanced at Mike, who sat motionless in the chair beside Davis, avoiding his eyes. Mike held a notebook in his hands, the one he carried to keep track of tasks he had to accomplish for the bar. Iver could picture his friend's small block print, the cramped way he held his pen— the same way he'd been holding it since kindergarten. Fear expanded in Iver's chest until it felt like he couldn't breathe. A stab of pain, excruciating behind his left eye.

"Iver?" Davis repeated.

He shook his head, pressing his palm against his eye. The pressure eased the pain only slightly.

"Are you all right?"

He turned to the woman's voice. She had removed her blazer and now leaned forward on her forearms, shirtsleeves rolled up above her elbows. Dark hair pulled back, a woman ready to get to work.

"I need to get my medication. Excuse me, Sheriff." Iver stood and pushed past Jack Davis, fumbling with the keys to unlock the office. The vision in his left eye was all but gone. He flipped on the overhead light and flinched at the brightness that usually seemed too dim to work by. He staggered to the desk and scanned its surface. *Come on. Come on.*

He spotted the empty drink glass and slid it into the open drawer of his desk, still scanning for the meds.

Panic built in his chest as he pushed aside paperwork. Where were the meds? His fingers found the bottle beneath the pages of an order fulfillment. He sank into the chair, unscrewed the top, and shook two of the small white pills into his palm, then into his mouth, where he chewed them and swallowed them dry, wincing at the bitter taste. They worked faster when he chewed them. Or that was what he told himself. His cell phone was on the desk, too.

The screen was filled with notifications of missed calls and texts.

Where are you?

The police are here.

Sheriff Davis stood in the doorway. Iver had seen Davis around—in this town, you saw everyone around—but he hadn't talked to Davis since they'd played high school football together. Or, more accurately, since Iver had sat on the bench while Davis had starred in the games. Iver had been a freshman, Davis a senior. Since then, Iver had talked to Davis exactly once—at the Christmas tree lot before his first tour in Afghanistan. Iver and his wife had been picking out a tree, as had Davis and his wife. They'd had some stupid exchange about which was better—the Scotch pine or the balsam fir.

How things had changed.

Davis looked at him long and hard. "I heard about the accident. You were lucky."

"Yeah," Iver said. Lucky to survive the IED that had hit his Humvee. His head pounded harder, and his vision faltered. Luckier than his four buddies, anyway.

Not wanting to be cornered in his office with the sheriff, Iver forced himself out of the chair. Back in the main part of the bar, he sat down next to Mike and across from Davis, leaving an empty chair between him and the detective. The pain in his head was no better, but he was momentarily distracted by fear. Fear of what, he didn't know. He absently touched the scratch on his knuckles, the vague memory of anger at the periphery of his mind.

"What's going on?" Iver asked again.

"Just a few questions," Davis said. "Can you tell me what time you left the bar last night?"

Iver swallowed the bitter aftertaste of his meds and looked at Davis. He didn't actually remember when he'd left the night before. "I usually leave about ten thirty," he said carefully. "That sound about right?" he asked Mike.

Mike rubbed his face, the middle finger on his left hand a little shorter than on the right from an accident with an ax when he was a kid. "I don't know. Maybe." He looked up at the sheriff. "Like I told you, Sheriff, it gets nuts in here. I've got fifty or sixty people plus the bartenders and the girls. I can't keep track of everyone." The way Mike said "everyone" made Iver sound like a child who'd gotten lost.

Still Mike wouldn't meet his gaze. What the hell had happened?

Mind racing, Iver struggled to put the night back together. Panic mounted in his chest, the kind he'd felt when he'd woken in the hospital and remembered the accident. Or rather, remembered that he couldn't remember the accident. They had told him what had happened, that the others had died. Brolyard and Wykstra and Sanchez and Garabrant—his closest friends over there—were all dead. Everyone but him.

This wasn't the same. No one had died. There had been no accident. Last night, he'd done what he always did—he'd arrived at the bar around three to help the guys restock. Mike had been there early, and they'd already finished it, so Iver had hung around at the bar and shot the shit with the first patrons, who usually arrived before four. And he'd started drinking. A beer or two first, usually. Not like he was doing shots or anything. Well, not usually.

When things got busy, he typically settled in his office and blasted Springsteen or Zeppelin or, when he was really amped up, Nirvana or old AC/DC and dealt with the paperwork—orders and payroll and taxes, the mindless shit of running his father's bar.

He remembered the bottle of Jack on the floor in his living room. He must have brought it home from the bar. God, he hoped that bottle hadn't been full last night. But it couldn't have been. That much alcohol would have killed him. He'd probably grabbed a half-empty one from behind the bar on his way out. For the drive home . . . he had driven home. That was an asshole move. He'd been doing that a fair amount lately.

Not that lately, he thought. He'd been doing it since Debbie had left him. A year.

"Iver?" Davis asked.

Iver rubbed his face in an attempt to force his brain to focus. "Sorry. What were you asking?"

Davis glanced at the detective, then back at Iver. The message between them was clear. Iver was a shit show. But so what? He hadn't done anything wrong. Well, there was the driving. Shit, had he hit something? He opened his mouth to ask but snapped it shut.

"Sheriff Davis was asking what time you left the bar," the woman said, that gaze of hers like a laser into his brain.

"Like I said, I think it was about ten thirty, but I didn't think to check my watch." Iver swallowed what little spit he had. "What is this all about?"

"We need to get a sense for what happened in this bar last night," the woman said.

"A sense," Iver repeated.

The detective added nothing, and her piercing stare intensified Iver's returning nausea. What had he done? Nothing. He hadn't done anything. No one spoke for a minute. Iver looked back at Mike. "Kevin and Wyatt were with you last night, right? And Nate?"

Mike nodded. "And Donnie helping on the door. We were busy, so if any of the guys had gone missing for more than the time it took to piss—" Mike looked over at the lady and cringed. "Excuse me, ma'am. Any longer than a bathroom break, I'd have noticed."

Iver ran a hand through his hair, the strands bent and fanned out from sleep under his fingers.

"We've talked to them already," Davis said and turned to Iver. "You got any cameras in here? Any monitoring of any kind?"

Iver shook his head. "No. Whoever's at the door keeps an eye on the lot, and we've always got a couple guys inside. We haven't had any issues." As he said the words, he wondered why, then, Sheriff Davis was here at this hour of the morning. He glanced at the detective, who studied him with a furrow between her brows. She reminded him of those head doctors, the psychiatrists. "You going to tell me what's going on?" he asked Davis.

The sheriff's jaw worked a moment before he spoke. "A woman was murdered last night."

The rush of memory made Iver flinch. His neck taut, his voice hoarse from screaming. The cut on his hand. He'd been angry. Shouting. He glanced over at Mike, but his best friend was doing a damn good job of not meeting his eye.

"Murdered?" he said. "Where?"

"We have yet to find the crime scene," the detective said. "But her body was found in your dumpster."

Your dumpster.

Your anger. Your violence. Off your meds.

"Something bad is going to happen, Iver," Debbie had told him the day she'd moved out. "I can't be here when it happens." His ex-wife's parting words.

Iver shook his head. "I don't—" He had to cough the words out. "I don't know anything about a dead woman."

And he didn't.

Or maybe he did, and he couldn't remember it.

CHAPTER 7

LILY

Lily lasted ten minutes down a dirt road before the pain in her ankle was too debilitating for her to continue. She was about to sit down on the shoulder when she heard the spit and crunch of tires on the icy gravel road coming up behind her. She scanned the area for a place to hide but found only low grasses, nothing higher than her ankle. The driver slowed, and adrenaline washed through her belly. As the pickup stopped, Lily adjusted her hair to hang across the right side of her face, unsure if there was bruising at her temple.

The window was down. The driver, an older man in a flannel shirt and a trucker hat with a gas-pump logo on the front, was alone in the cab. His hat read *Hills Drilling, North Dakota*. His face was stern, but something about it was reassuring. "Where you heading?"

"Town," she said, pulling her gaze from the hat. North Dakota. Had his license plates said North Dakota, too? She hadn't thought to look. Her identification card was from Arizona, but Brent Nolan's license was from North Dakota. How the hell had she ended up in North Dakota?

"You're in luck," he said. "Hop in."

She pried the door open and used her arms to lift herself so that she didn't have to put weight on her ankle.

"Name's Jim," he said. "And what's your name?"

Never tell anyone your name. She searched her mind for another name.

"Well, I'll be damned," he continued before she could respond. "You're little Lily Baker."

Lily felt her lips part in a rush of breath, as though she'd been punched in the gut. She looked outside. Surely this wasn't Arizona, so how did this man know her?

"Wow," he said, staring alternately between her and the dirt road. "Look how grown up you are. I remember when you were knee high to a grasshopper."

Still, she said nothing. Questions swirled in her mind, but how could she ask? Where did she start?

The truck idled loudly as Jim removed his hat as though to give her a better look at his face. "You probably don't remember me. It's Jim Hill. I was a friend of your parents."

The word *parents* made her chest swell. Tears burned in her eyes. She did live here. She searched the landscape for something familiar, but it was low hills and grasses in every direction.

"You look just like your mom did at your age—you're, what, twenty-five, twenty-six?" Jim grinned, and Lily felt her own angst lessen. This was home. "The trouble your dad and I used to get in. We were the same class, did you know?" Jim glanced over conspiratorially. "We used to ride our bicycles right down the main hallway of school, and your father would leave these huge skid marks. He could stop that bike on a dime."

Lily smiled. Her father was funny, a clown.

"Another time, your dad loosened the joints on the math teacher's chair. Mrs. Penderson, she was a fussy, uptight thing who liked to slam herself into her chair when we misbehaved. Sure enough, your dad got her all frustrated, and she slammed down, and her chair just collapsed." Jim laughed.

Lily looked out the window as Jim told stories about her father, and she found herself smiling at the antics. Even the pain in her ankle seemed to abate. Within ten minutes, they arrived in a small residential area and then a single street of businesses. As Jim turned onto Main Street, a sign welcomed them to Hagen, North Dakota. *Population 864.* She read the numbers again. Eight hundred and sixty-four people.

"Don't know when they'll fix that sign," Jim said. "Got to be near fourteen or fifteen hundred by now, don't you think?"

"Yeah," she said. Fifteen hundred people. It was so small.

"Where am I taking you?" he asked as he headed down Main Street.

"I might just go home," she said.

"Sure thing, Lily. Where are you living these days?"

Her ID had an Arizona address. Where was she living?

She cleared the dust from her throat. "Actually, I need to visit a friend at the hospital."

"Oh no. Nothing serious, I hope."

She clamped her mouth shut.

Jim shook his head and raised a hand. "Sorry," he said quickly. "Starting to sound like my wife, Annie, asking all sorts of questions. None of my business. I'll drop you at the hospital straightaway."

"That would be great. Thanks."

Lily watched the streets, the small houses, the businesses. *Home,* she thought to herself. *This is home.* She would go to the hospital to check on Brent, and then she'd find her own house. Contact her parents.

She searched the truck's dash for a clock. "Do you happen to have the time?"

Jim turned his wrist to look at his watch. "Just about nine fifteen now."

"Nine fifteen," she repeated.

"Yes, ma'am."

"And what's the date today?"

He glanced over at her.

"I should know," she said quickly. "I've been on the road a few days, and I'm afraid I lost track."

He glanced at her again before answering. "This here's the seventh."

"The seventh," she repeated. "Sure."

"January seventh," he said, eyeing her.

"Of course," she told him.

A beat passed in quiet, Jim watching her from the corner of his eye. "I was at your dad's service last year," Jim said, his tone softening. "Guess it's been almost two years now."

Service. She blinked back the well of tears. Her father was dead.

Jim shook his head. "I should have come up to say hello, but there were so many folks, you know," he went on. "I was sorry about his passing."

She nodded mutely, trying to stir up memories of her father's funeral. But it was blank.

"Oh, jeez," Jim said, patting her awkwardly on the shoulder. "I didn't mean to upset you. You surely been through enough not to have to listen to an old man prattle on."

Lily shook her head. "I'm fine."

Jim turned into a parking lot and pulled to the front of the hospital, a small, single-level brick building. "You sure you can get inside on that ankle?" he asked. "Looks like you hurt it."

"I'll be fine," she assured him. "Thanks again."

Jim turned to face her. "Your dad was a good man, Lily, but he never did recover from losing your mom. She went way too early."

Lily barely heard the words, her hand on the handle of the door. She couldn't escape the truck fast enough.

"You be careful," Jim called after her. "Call on us up at the house if you need anything."

Not just her father. Both of her parents were dead. A tear slipped down her cheek, burning against her skin. She wiped it away and hobbled toward the hospital door.

CHAPTER 8

—

IVER

Cal whined, and Iver put a hand on the soft fur of his neck in an effort to calm the dog—or maybe to calm himself. Davis pulled out his phone and placed it in front of Iver on the table. "Does this woman look familiar to you?"

Iver set down the pill bottle and drew breath through his teeth, filling his lungs before lifting the phone. The vision in his left eye was still blurry, and he couldn't quite make out her face. He used his fingers to zoom in until he could see her features. She was about the right age to work in the bar. He tended to employ women in their mid- to late twenties and always from somewhere other than Hagen.

The girls who grew up in Hagen were sisters or cousins of guys he'd known in high school. No one wanted their sister or cousin working in his bar. Mostly he hired from the community college two towns over—the students were better workers, more focused. But she was not familiar. He shook his head. "No," he said, the word catching on something in his throat. Not something. Fear.

"You've never seen her in here?" Davis said again.

"No. Never." He looked up at Mike. "You seen her?"

"No. And Nate and Kevin and Wyatt neither."

Iver felt the slightest bit of relief. If no one had seen her in here, then he hadn't seen her either. Right? "Nate would know," Iver told the sheriff. "He's good at faces. Or Donnie, since he's at the door. I spend most of the night back in the office."

"And the office doesn't have a door to the outside?" the woman detective asked.

Iver's pulse seemed to beat directly through his left eye.

"No," Sheriff Davis said to her and turned back to Iver. "Only way out of the office is through the bar."

Iver thought about the small window above the desk. As kids, he and Mike used to climb into the bar through that window to steal liquor. Until his father had caught them.

Iver nodded. "Right." He could barely hold her gaze, the way his head was pounding. Maybe these were routine questions. Maybe they asked everyone. The pain was escalating. He felt like he might throw up. He needed to lie down.

"What time did you come in yesterday?" Davis asked.

"Around three," he said. "Nate and Mike were already here."

"And you left at ten thirty, you said?" Davis asked.

"About then," Iver said, unable to get rid of the bitter taste now caught in his throat. Maybe they were right to ask him. He tried to remember what he'd been doing before he'd left the bar. The night would have been in full swing. Sometimes, he stood behind the bar and watched. Other times, he stayed in his office and drank alone. Most nights it was all a little fuzzy. Last night, it was a black hole. He recalled that Nate had come in at some point to tell him they were running low on Seagram's Seven. He'd made a note. Or was it Beam?

"And you didn't come back for any reason?" Davis asked.

He shook his head, willing the words from his mouth. "No." It sounded like he was choking.

"Anyone corroborate your story, Iver?" Davis asked. "Was your wife home?"

The word *wife* jolted his insides. Every damn time. Iver forced himself to look Davis in the eye. "She moved out," Iver said. "Almost a year now."

Mike shifted beside him, his gaze aimed at the floor, as though uncomfortable hearing Iver talk about his divorce. They didn't talk about stuff like this. They weren't that type of friends. Not anymore, anyway. Somewhere along the way, they'd stopped talking about things that mattered.

Maybe it was him. Maybe Afghanistan had made him into someone who was hard to talk to.

"I'm sorry," Davis said, and the table was quiet a moment. Perhaps Davis was thinking about his own wife. Iver couldn't remember her name now.

What was the right response? *I'm sorry, too. I'm sorry and pissed and angry, and most nights I'm so lonely that I stay at my bar until I'm just buzzed and tired enough that I can go home, take my meds, and not even know that I'm in my own bed, let alone that no one is there with me.*

"You see any new faces in the bar last night?" Davis asked. "Guys from the camp or anything?"

The "man camp," as they called it, was a Quonset-hut-like building on the north side of town that housed the fracking workers who'd come to Hagen when the drilling had started. The building contained tiny single bedrooms and communal showers where the men who worked the drilling could live on the cheap. Drilling in Hagen wasn't a huge operation, nothing like the Bakken area. In Hagen, drilling jobs were more highly prized and scarce, so the camp residents tended to keep to themselves and stay out of trouble. But Iver hadn't noticed anyone new last night.

"Don't think so," he said.

"Me neither," Mike agreed.

"Doesn't mean there wasn't someone from up there in the bar," Iver added, thinking it would be good to have another suspect. *A suspect,* he corrected. There was no suspect here. Not unless he was one.

Davis was still watching Iver. "Mike said he and Nate, Wyatt, and Kevin all left at the same time, around one forty-five," Davis said.

Iver shrugged. "Last call is twelve forty-five, bar closes at one, so that's about right."

"But no wife at home?" Davis asked Mike, and Iver could see from his friend's expression that it wasn't the first time he'd asked.

"No wife." Mike's gaze was nailed to the floor, as though not having a wife were deeply shameful.

"He lives in an apartment above his parents' garage," Iver said.

Mike shot him a look of surprise.

"Your mother still a light sleeper?" Iver asked, remembering how hard it used to be for Mike to sneak out. His mother woke if he hiccupped in the night. "She would have heard you come home."

Mike shifted in his seat. "True. She does sleep pretty light."

Davis looked like he was about to say something but closed his mouth.

The pain swelled in Iver's brain until his head threatened to explode. He bent over and gripped his temples between his palms.

"Can I ask what you have?" the detective asked.

"A headache," he said, holding his breath and trying to sit back up.

"Migraine?" Her gaze shifted to his pill bottle.

She was definitely like one of those head doctors. He tucked the pills in his pocket. "Something like that," he told her.

"You okay?" Davis asked.

"Yeah. Sure," he said.

"What happened to your hand?"

Iver looked down at his knuckles. He'd forgotten about the cut. There had been blood on his jeans, too. How the hell had he hurt himself? "Cut it on a piece of metal."

Davis looked around. "Here?"

"No. At home. Garage," he added in an attempt to sound more confident. But it was a lie. Why would he lie? Because they were acting like he'd done something. He hadn't done anything, had he?

The room was still and silent again. Cal rose, shuffled in a circle, and settled back down.

Jack Davis motioned to the picture of the dead woman. "And you're positive that she doesn't look familiar to you? To either of you?"

"Nope," Mike said.

Iver took another look at the woman's photo. When he shifted the image under his fingers, he noticed a line of fringe stitched along the front of her top. Suddenly hot, he enlarged the photo with two fingers, his eyes watering, until the silver threads came into focus. The pain chose that moment to whip its metal tip against the flesh behind his eye. He pressed on the eye, fighting against the sense that he was about to black out.

Shaking his head, he passed the phone back to Davis. "I've never seen her before," he said, and it felt like the truth.

His vision throbbed in and out as he recalled the thread he'd pulled off his watchband an hour earlier. He'd assumed the sparkly string had come from one of the waitresses.

Only now he wasn't sure.

Because the thread in his watch looked a whole hell of a lot like the ones that lined the dead woman's top.

CHAPTER 9

KYLIE

The noon sun cast long shadows as Kylie Milliard walked toward the wooded area beyond Skål bar. It was well past noon but still dark among the trees. The morning had vanished in a series of unending interviews with the bartenders and waitstaff. Kylie had personally spoken to the five waitresses who had worked last night.

A smarter bunch than she'd been expecting, the women had arrived at the police station in jeans and sweatshirts, carrying book bags on their way to or from class. None of them had stepped outside the bar between the start of their shift at four p.m. and closing time at one a.m. They carpooled for safety—three in one car, two in another—so they'd left together as well. None had any complaints about the job, which paid well, or about management. They thought Mike, who managed the bar, was awkward but harmless, and Iver was generous if aloof.

None of the women had ever been assaulted by any of the customers. There were always two or three male employees who kept an eye out for rowdy guests and escorted them from the bar when they drank too much. Although sex was always a consideration in a death investigation, nothing so far indicated that sex had been the primary motive for this particular murder.

None of the bar patrons who'd been interviewed recognized the dead woman. If the victim hadn't been in that bar, the next logical place she might have been killed was the adjacent woods. Wet, frozen weather and snow would make it tough—maybe impossible—to locate the scene of the killing, and that was if the crime had actually happened outside.

But Kylie wasn't convinced that the crime hadn't involved the bar itself. An army brat, Kylie had learned to do two things exceptionally well: lie and know who else was lying. Iver Larson had been lying this morning—maybe not about all of it but about something. And in a murder investigation, something could well be everything.

According to Sheriff Davis, Larson was a responsible citizen—a veteran who'd been handed a raw deal, blown up, sent home, and then abandoned by his wife. Maybe that was all true, but there was something about him that itched a spot Kylie couldn't scratch.

She wanted a warrant to search that bar, but for now, she had to settle for looking in the neighboring woods. Pausing at the edge of the trees, Kylie cracked her knuckles through her gloves and aimed her flashlight at the snowy ground. The surface of the snow was dimpled—spots where ice had fallen from the trees or small animals had traversed the snow. Or perhaps larger animals.

When she was four or five steps into the woods, the sunlight faded from view. The shadows and snow were grayer; the temperature dropped. It wasn't much lighter here than it had been at five in the morning.

She scanned left to right, trying to measure the width of the woods. It was a small area, she knew from driving. From inside, it felt larger. No new snow in Hagen in the past twenty-four hours meant it should be easier to spot any evidence the perp might have dropped. Not easy but easier. She crept along, searching for a clue that she had no idea even existed. Still, she made her way, gaze tracking. She found a set of boot prints heading from the bar. She followed them until they seemed to make a circle and go nowhere else.

Instinctively, she looked up and studied the trees overhead. "Right. Like the killer just up and flew away," she muttered to herself.

She moved on, discovering another set of boot tracks, then a large area where something might have bedded down—likely deer, but there were some larger animals in the area, too.

She took a step, and her boot struck something hard. Feeling a rush of excitement, she reached down and pulled out a clear beer bottle, the label long since disintegrated. She set it upright beside a tree and kept moving, searching the snow for anything that didn't belong.

Halfway across the patch of woods, she found a trail that had been used by more than one person. This deep in the woods, she wasn't sure how long it took the snow to filter to the ground. Overhead it was still thick in the trees, making it impossible to say if snow from the last storm had touched the ground here. There were other businesses on the far side of the woods and houses on the streets a mile or so beyond. It was conceivable that some of the bar's patrons walked home this way, though from what she'd seen, Hagen residents didn't worry much about driving under the influence. Hagen's motto was more "Why walk when you can drive?"

The woods grew darker as she walked. Her eyes were getting tired when the flashlight beam struck something. She blinked, and it seemed to vanish. Then she saw it again. She studied the shadow. In one area, the snow was packed down and tinged a pinkish shade. But what would tint the snow that way? Blood? She looked around. Way out here?

Kylie bent down, aiming the flashlight. It could definitely be blood. She leaned over to take a picture with her phone, but the image was too dark to see the pinkish shade. Using the flash made everything white. She shoved the phone back into her pocket and freed her hands to collect some of the snow. She needed a way to mark the spot in case it was the scene of the killing.

As she reached to retrieve an evidence bag from her pocket, something rustled nearby. A shadow crossed her vision. She twisted around, but there was nothing. She turned back, and the light from her flashlight blinked twice and went dark. She slapped it against her palm. Tried flipping it on and off. No luck. Loosening the bulb section and screwing it tight again didn't help either. These flashlights never just died.

Returning her attention to the ground, she tried to find the pinkish tint again. Still squatting, she whacked the flashlight on a nearby tree, tried the on/off switch again. Not even a flicker. "Damn it."

She closed her eyes and opened them, as though rebooting her vision. It was too dim. She pulled out her phone again to use the flashlight, but the device caught on the edge of her pocket and flew from her hand.

Another crackle of shifting branches made her scan the woods, but the shadows of the trees made the forest feel like dusk rather than noon. A shadow darted from her left. Gasping, she went to duck when a large white-tailed deer leaped between the trees, then slowed to a trot.

"Damn," Kylie whispered, trying to catch her breath. She patted the ground in front of her. Where the hell was her phone?

Her pulse began to beat a haunting drum.

You're just in the woods. Thirty feet from your cruiser, from backup. If she had to, she could go back and get another flashlight. She patted the snow, everything hard and indistinct under her gloves. She pulled them off and patted again, feeling the cold crunch of snow.

She thought she saw the black phone when a light shone full in her face.

She cried out and covered her eyes with her hand. "What the hell?"

"There you are." The light shifted, and Carl Gilbert's face appeared in the beam of the flashlight. "You drop your phone?"

She scanned his face, her heart still racing. "Yeah."

"It's there," he said, stepping past her and reaching into the snow right where she swore she'd been searching.

She picked it up and put it back in her pocket. Pulling her gloves back on, she was still fighting to calm her racing heart.

"Find anything?" he asked.

"Some blood, I think." She waved him over. "Shine your light right here."

The two of them located the pinkish spot. "I think we'll want to collect some snow," she said.

"I can do it," Gilbert said. "Vogel was trying to reach you on the radio."

She hesitated.

"I got this," Gilbert said again, pulling a small plastic container from one pocket. Almost like he'd known he'd need it. She'd brought an evidence bag, she reminded herself. But he had a container.

Hesitant to leave, she watched him scoop snow into the container. He held it out to her, the pinkish tint visible through the clear plastic under the bright beam of his flashlight. What did the DA want? Glen Vogel was mostly a pain in her ass. A big man in his late fifties, he was an old-fashioned misogynist. The only redeeming thing about Vogel was his wife, who liked to show up at the station with baked goods, her demeanor cheery and kind. But Kylie had to admit the thing that endeared her most was Mrs. Vogel's raspberry–white chocolate scones.

"We should mark the spot, too," she said. "So we can find it again."

"Good idea," Gilbert said. He looked around for a second, then pulled a large pocketknife from his pocket. He thumbed a button, and the blade released. On the nearest tree, he carved an *X* into the bark. Then he did the same to another tree. "If you want to wait a minute, I can walk you back out," he said. "It's kind of dark." He reached for a third tree, and Kylie turned to leave.

"I'm fine," she told him and started walking before he could argue.

At her car, she climbed inside and brought out her phone to call Vogel. She felt light headed and winded, as though she'd run a long distance. Gilbert had startled her, was all. She stared down at the worthless flashlight, tossed it on the passenger seat, and turned on the engine.

The first thing DA Vogel said when her call was patched through was, "We're going to hold off on searching the bar."

Danielle Girard

Kylie clenched her phone with an iron grip and forced herself to use her nice-lady voice. "Sir, it's urgent that we search the premises as soon as possible if we want to avoid losing potential evidence. We found blood in the woods."

"Blood?"

"Yes. In the snow."

As soon as the words were out, she recalled the white-tailed deer. Surely animals died in those woods all the time. But then where were the bones?

"We're collecting a sample for the lab," she told him.

"Good," DA Vogel said, and she could hear the squeal of his big leather desk chair. Every time he leaned back in that thing, it shrieked like a pig about to be slaughtered. With all 230 pounds of him on the worn-out springs, the chair would surely fail. How she wished it would happen while she was watching. "We're still going to wait on the bar," he said. "There's nothing to indicate the crime happened there."

Hagen had a murder—an actual murder—and the first real crime since she'd arrived from Fargo eight months ago. As the town's only detective, if she solved this one, she had a chance at a spot in Fargo. And damn if eight months in this place wasn't seven months and twenty-nine days too long. "Sir—" she began, formulating a plea in her mind.

"You interviewed how many people who were in the bar?" Vogel interrupted.

Kylie gritted her teeth. A bunch of drunkards being wooed by women in short skirts. Not a reliable source.

"Miss Milliard?"

Miss Milliard. He always called her Miss Milliard. It was Detective Milliard. She was a detective, not a four-year-old. She spoke carefully, calmly. "Nineteen, including staff," she answered.

"And not one of them remembered Ms. Jensen from the bar?"

Kylie halted. "Wait. Jensen is her name?"

"Yes," Vogel said. "Abigail Jensen. We were able to ID her with prints."

Prints meant a record. "She had a record?"

"Not exactly," Vogel said.

"What do you mean? Who is she?"

Vogel sighed. "Miss Milliard, can you confirm that no one in the bar saw the victim last night?"

Kylie tried not to scream. "That is correct."

The DA let out a long breath that sounded, in her head, like flatulence. "You understand that this isn't just any case, Miss Milliard," he said after a moment's pause. In her mind, his fat hands rested on his fat belly, stubby fingers interlaced.

"No, sir. It's a murder case."

"That's not what I mean," Vogel said, his voice dropping. For a moment, the pause made her wonder if he was considering a warrant.

"What do you mean, then, sir?"

"You remember Derek Hudson?" Vogel asked.

Even the name gave her chills. Images flooded her mind of the torsos of thin little girls, ribs showing from starvation, the strange cuts that covered their backs. "Of course." But Hudson was dead, shot twice in the chest and once in the face. She recalled the case from a criminalistics course in college—Hudson lying in a pool of blood, left where one of his prisoners had shot him. Served the bastard right.

"This victim," Vogel said, "Abigail Jensen—she was one of his."

Detective Kylie Milliard's shiver had nothing to do with the cold.

CHAPTER 10

—

LILY

Doing her best not to limp noticeably, Lily Baker entered the hospital through the main entrance. The hallways were painted a deep purple the color of boiled eggplant. If the choice was meant to be soothing, it had failed on her. It felt dark and unusual for a hospital. Then it occurred to her that she might not know what a hospital should look like.

Framed drawings of wildflowers lined the wall to her left, black-and-white photographs of old men on the right. In one corner was a fake tree. She recognized it as a ficus. How odd that she could recall the name of a plant but had no memory of her own life—not her sister or her parents.

Making her way toward the desk on her tender ankle, she experienced a sense of déjà vu, and yet nothing was familiar.

Behind the information desk, a receptionist typed on a keyboard, her fingers slow, her head down as she hunted for letters on the keyboard. The hair was a little too red to be natural, cropped in a straight line at her chin and parted in the center. A pair of reading glasses dangled from her neck by a long line of purple stones, as though she'd made an effort to match the decor of the hospital. She looked to be in her late fifties.

When the receptionist looked up, her eyes went wide. She rose from the chair, and Lily stepped back instinctively, pain searing her ankle.

"My God, are you all right?" The woman rushed around the desk. *Sandra*, her name tag read, the word blurred through the tears that filled Lily's eyes.

"Lily, sit down. What happened?" Sandra tried to take her bag and lead her to a chair, but Lily clasped the strap in a clenched fist.

Before Lily could answer, Sandra was shouting down the hallway. "Tim! Beth! Lily has been in an accident."

Two nurses ran down the hall, their uniforms the same blackish purple as the walls.

"I'm fine," she argued as Sandra pressed her into a chair.

Then there were three faces staring down at her. The man pushed her hair off her face to look at her temple as the woman palpated her ankle. All of them talked at once.

"Were you in an accident?" the woman asked.

"Bike," she whispered, the first thing that came to mind.

"What were you doing biking in this weather?" the woman asked.

"Christ," the man muttered. Tim. His name tag read *Tim Bailey*. "What does the bike look like?"

She studied his face as he watched her, his mouth cracking into a smile that was a little too wide. He raised his brow. "Get it? What does the other guy look like?"

Lily couldn't think of what to say.

The two nurses exchanged a worried look. "You think she's concussed?"

Tim pulled out a cell phone and shone its flashlight in her eyes, his fingers pulling her lids open. "Doesn't look like a concussion."

Beth stood. "I'll get some alcohol and gauze. We can clean her up. This ankle's going to need an x-ray."

"I'll call down to radiology," Sandra said.

After the others left, Tim studied her with concern in his eyes. "Are you sure you're okay?"

She hesitated, wondering how well she knew him. Well enough to tell him the truth? *Never talk about yourself.* She noticed the wedding ring on his finger. He was married. Did she know his wife?

"Lily?" he pressed.

"I'm okay," she lied, swallowing the dry knot in her throat, along with the thoughts of the car accident, the cash, the gun.

"It seems like—" He was cut off by the unmistakable shriek of an alarm. "Code CPR," a voice said over the loudspeaker. "Code CPR."

Tim ran for the doors. Beth dropped a bin of supplies at Lily's feet and followed. As though by an instinct she didn't recognize, Lily rose and went after them.

Two doctors from the code team passed, moving into the emergency room, and Lily followed.

Behind the doors was a giant room with a circular island at the center, where nurses in purple scrubs buzzed around a small cluster of desks. Yellow curtains divided the outer ring into individual rooms. A doctor ripped open one curtain to reveal Brent Nolan on a gurney. Quickly, he was surrounded by the doctors and Beth and Tim. Beth placed the bag valve mask while Tim started compressions, counting out loud. "Two, three, four . . ."

The monitor above Brent's head showed a flat, straight line. He was in asystole. He was going to die. He couldn't die. She clenched her fists, shifting her weight off her bad ankle as she studied the monitor.

Come on, Brent.

When Tim reached thirty, Beth administered two breaths, pumping the bag against Brent's mouth. The doctor applied gel to Brent's chest and pressed the ultrasound wand to his skin. There was the whooshing sound of the machine as the doctor studied his heart on the monitor.

"He's got tamponade," the doctor said, sounding discouraged.

"Pericardiocentesis?" Beth asked.

The doctor gave a brief shake of his head. "He's got no cardiac activity."

"Should we try?" Beth asked.

The doctor paused, then said, "Give him one milligram epi."

"I'm on it," Beth said and looked to Lily. "Can you bag him? Do you feel well enough?"

Lily hesitated. She had no memory, but she could perform CPR. Two breaths administered at every thirty compressions. She was a nurse. That was why she knew how to do it, why the people here recognized her.

"I could call someone else," Beth said, looking around.

"No, I can do it," Lily said, moving in beside Beth to stand at Brent's head as Tim continued compressions.

Beth returned with a syringe and pushed the epinephrine into Brent's IV.

Tim reached thirty again, and Lily pumped two breaths. All eyes watched the monitor. The line was still flat.

"Come on, buddy," Beth said to the man on the table.

Lily closed her eyes and prayed from the book of Isaiah. *Fear thou not; for I am with thee: be not dismayed; for I am thy God.*

The doctor moved in with a long syringe, and Beth swabbed Brent's chest. The doctor inserted the needle and drew out the stopper. The syringe filled with blood.

Lily gasped, and Tim stared at her. "You okay?" he whispered.

Nodding, she averted her gaze. Brent had blood around his heart. The fall had done it. If she could have gotten him out before that . . .

"Twenty-eight, twenty-nine . . ."

Lily administered two more breaths.

The doctor drew more blood from his chest. Beth prepared a second syringe of epinephrine. Tim and Lily continued CPR. Beth pushed more epinephrine. Three minutes passed on the clock. The monitor showed no P-waves, no sign of QRS complexes. The line remained flat. Lily understood the monitor easily. Brent was dying. Brent was dead.

Again, they went through the motions, driven by some tiny thread of hope. The doctor pulled the syringe and watched the monitor.

Slowly, the room fell quiet. The doctor shook his head.

"One more," Beth said and nodded toward the hallway. "For Brent's family."

Tim looked at the doctor, who nodded.

They continued CPR and breaths, pushed another dose of epi.

No change.

Tim's motions slowed. Beth turned her back to dispose of the needle in the sharps-disposal container. No one spoke. Tim stopped compressions. When Beth turned back, her eyes were glassy.

"Time of death," the doctor said. "Ten forty-seven."

Beth reached up and shut off the monitor.

Lily set down the bag mask valve on the table and turned for the door.

Brent was dead.

"Let's get you cleaned up and have that ankle looked at," Beth said, looping her arm in Lily's.

Lily allowed herself to be led through the double doors.

As she entered the hallway, the front doors hissed open, and a petite woman ran in, out of breath and crying, her reddish-blonde hair loose and wild around her face. Another woman trailed behind her, a hand on the woman's back. "It's going to be okay, Pamela. We're here now."

But Pamela halted in the middle of the hallway, gripping her stomach, looking like she might double over. "I got a call—an accident. Brent Nolan." Her words came out in bursts like air leaking from a tire. "I'm his wife. In from Fargo."

The receptionist, Sandra, crossed to them, but the doctor stepped forward, raising his hand. "Mrs. Nolan, I'm Dr. Morrison. If you will follow me, please." The doctor pushed open a door across the hall, and Lily saw a couch and chairs. He was about to tell Pamela Nolan that her husband was dead. Lily could feel the fear coming off the woman, raw and sharp. Brent Nolan was dead, and Lily had been in the car with him.

Lily stood in the hallway, frozen and numb, as Brent's wife sat on the couch. The woman focused on the doctor's face, her eyes wide and hopeful. His voice too soft to hear, Lily studied the shift in the woman's expression, watched as it crumpled.

Lily pressed her hands to her stomach as some piece of her twisted back onto itself. Suddenly light headed and short of breath, she stumbled backward until her knees hit the bench and she sank, fighting back her own panic.

Brent Nolan was dead because she'd let him die.

CHAPTER 11

—

KYLIE

Seated at her desk in the station, heavy down coat over her shoulders, Kylie worked through the to-do list she'd written on a yellow legal pad: *FB pictures, sex offender registry, research on Derek Hudson, survivors, coroner report.* She was still cold from that morning. There had been something unnerving about being in the woods. Even in the bright light of day, it had felt dark and dank, like a cave. And then her near heart attack when Gilbert sneaked up on her. Had he sneaked up on her? Or maybe she was simply unsettled by the fact that the dead woman had been a victim of Derek Hudson's house of horrors. Five girls kidnapped and held for sixteen months. Blindfolded and tortured, a block of each of their backs covered in tiny wounds.

Only three girls had come out of that cabin alive. One of them—Abigail Jensen—was currently at Dahl's Funeral Home, awaiting the coroner. Then there was Hagen's very own Lily Baker. The third woman, Jenna Hitchcock, who'd been injured in the escape, now lived in Glendive, in eastern Montana.

No one knew exactly what had been done to them. The three survivors had been unable—or unwilling—to talk about it. But there remained a nagging question: How had Derek Hudson managed it alone? The police had never discovered an accomplice, but had there been someone else who was finally resurfacing after a decade to kill off the survivors?

Why now?

The most common reason criminals reemerged after periods of dormancy was release from prison. If she could get her hands on any suspects, the first thing she would do was check their records. There was also the possibility of a traumatic event—the death of a loved one, loss of a job, or divorce. Any big stressor could cause an offender to become violent again. But most criminals didn't have the self-control to stop once they had started, which made her wonder if she was dealing with a copycat, someone who'd discovered Hudson's crime and had become fixated on the survivors.

After finding no new registered offenders in the area and no recent prison releases with records that linked to Hagen, she shifted to social media. A search for photos taken the night before that had tagged Skål yielded nothing, which was unusual since there seemed to be images every other night.

Kylie wondered if the three survivors had stayed in touch. She dialed the number she had for Lily Baker, but no one answered. Anxious to get hold of her, she requested Dispatch send a patrol car by the house. Gilbert had been in touch with the police in Elgin, who would notify Abigail Jensen's family. When she texted the local coroner to check on the status of the autopsy, the reply read, Everest first. Your gal next. Mr. Everest was a resident who had died of old age, but he was being buried today, so his embalming took priority. The frustrations of a small-town coroner.

Kylie pulled phone records and called Hitchcock next, holding her breath as she punched the final digit. How badly she wanted one of these women to answer, to know they weren't all . . .

"The number you have dialed has been disconnected or is . . ."

Kylie ended the call and dialed the Glendive police, requesting a welfare check on Hitchcock.

What if he had killed them all?

A call on her desk phone interrupted her thoughts. "Milliard," she answered.

"No one's home at the Baker house," the officer told her. "But the car out front is registered to her."

It was rare to go anywhere in Hagen without a car. "Any sign of disturbance?"

"None," he said. "We walked around the house, and everything looks fine."

Kylie thanked him and ended the call, returning her attention to records on Derek Hudson. Hudson had grown up on the outskirts of a town called Molva, North Dakota, sixty minutes southwest of Hagen. Hudson's father, Frank Hudson, had been an alcoholic and a recluse who lived off the grid, using money from his wife's family to buy a parcel and set up a sort of commune. Hudson and his older brother were among six or seven kids who had grown up on the land, though most were long gone when Hudson had kidnapped those girls. Allegedly kidnapped. A lot of the language in the records suggested that no one had conclusively determined that Hudson was behind the kidnappings. Derek Hudson had never been in trouble before he was found dead on the floor of that cabin, a gunshot to the face.

The first girl to go missing had been a thirteen-year-old from the tiny town of Bowman in westernmost North Dakota. She had vanished after performing in a school play in 2007. Between then and 2010, four other girls between the ages of nine and fifteen had been kidnapped from the southwest corner of the state. Police hadn't found any link between the cases until the day, almost exactly ten years ago, when two young girls had come tearing out of the woods near Elgin, one town east of Molva, and flagged down a trucker. The trucker had called for the police, who'd found the cabin where the girls had been held. There, they'd found Derek Hudson dead in a pool of blood. One of the girls had told police that a struggle had ensued between Lily Baker and Hudson over a gun, and two girls were injured. One of them had died.

Her phone rang again. "Milliard."

"This is Deputy Sheriff McIntosh from Glendive. We did a welfare check on Jenna Hitchcock."

Kylie felt herself stiffen.

"No one was home. We went in, in case she was harmed, but it doesn't look like she's been there for a while."

"Like she moved?"

"No. Just like she left in a hurry. Place was pretty torn up, but no telling if there was some sort of disturbance or if that was how the place always looked," he went on. "Last opened mail was stamped December 29."

Today was January 7. Nine days.

"We've got an APB out on her car, so we'll let you know if she turns up."

As she hung up, the hope of finding Hitchcock alive and well faded. Because something about the deputy sheriff's words made Kylie imagine a dead woman in a shallow grave.

CHAPTER 12

―――

LILY

For Lily Baker, it seemed the hospital fell into a strange sort of slumber after Brent Nolan died. Eventually, Beth and Tim returned their attention to her. She was whisked to radiology for x-rays to confirm there was no fracture in her ankle. Beth wrapped her foot, and Tim cleaned the scratches on her hands and face and neck.

By then, Lily felt an overwhelming need to get away from the hospital. The moment they stopped fussing over her, she excused herself to the bathroom and found a side exit. Only outside the hospital could she catch her breath. Brent was dead. He had died. If she'd gotten him out of the car before it had gone over, he would be alive. But she hadn't. She couldn't. If she hadn't been worried about his wallet and stealing his money . . .

It was like someone was sitting on her chest. She bent over and tried to breathe. She touched her purse, still looped over her shoulder, and pressed her hand protectively against its bulk. The Bible. The gun. She needed to get home. Standing tall, she shivered in the cold air, staring at the mostly empty parking lot. Did she have a car? It wouldn't be here. Maybe it would be at her house, which was . . .

She had no idea.

The doors opened behind her, and a burst of warm air rushed across her back. She shivered against the startling contrast to the icy outside air. A hand touched her shoulder. She spun. Tim clasped the back of her neck and pulled her toward him, his voice against her ear. "You scared me," he whispered.

She thought of his wedding ring, then the way he had pushed the hair off her face when he'd approached her in the hospital. The gesture seemed suddenly so intimate, his fingers on the back of her neck almost proprietary. But if they were together, why didn't she remember him? Stepping back to put space between them, she shook her head. "Brent," she whispered.

He frowned. "The guy from Fargo, you mean?"

She nodded.

"You know him?"

She shook her head. An instinct to lie. But it was true. She didn't know him. At that moment, she didn't know anyone.

"I guess it was a bad wreck," he said, running the pads of his fingers gently across her cheek. "It's amazing he made it to the hospital at all. Are you okay?"

She studied his face. Brent was dead. "I'm fine."

He stared down at her, taking hold of her shoulders. "Are you sure? You need a little bump?"

"A bump?" she repeated. She couldn't think what he meant.

He nodded back to the hospital before she could respond. "Let me get my jacket and keys. I'll take you home. I assume you didn't bring the bike?" He laughed loudly. "Joke."

She faked a smile as he turned back to the building.

Home. Her home. She had a home. The answers would be there. She would find her sister, call her.

Tim jogged from the building a minute later, wearing a jacket and hat and spinning his keys around one finger. Brent Nolan had just died. Tim's reaction to it, his lack of emotion, was chilling. He stopped beside her and kissed her forehead before nodding toward the parking lot. "I'm parked over here." With a hand on the small of her back, he led her into the lot. "Pretty sure I've got something in the glove box."

Was it possible that *she* was married to Tim? That it was her ring he wore? She should tell him about her memory. About the accident. But she hadn't come home last night, and he hadn't noticed—but maybe he'd been at work all night? Obviously, they had a relationship. He was worried about her. He wanted to drive her home.

They approached a white Ford Explorer, and Tim unlocked the doors. "Can I borrow your phone to call my sister?" she asked.

Tim stared over the top of the car, frowning at her. "Your—" He stopped talking as his gaze shifted to a black sedan driving toward them. "Ah, shit," he whispered.

Lily's first thought was that it was a police car. The instinct to run rose like acid in her throat.

The car stopped beside Tim, and the driver's window lowered. The woman behind the wheel didn't look like a police officer, and in the backseat was a young child in a car seat. Not the police.

"I got called in to work," the woman said, eyeing Lily, though she was talking to Tim. "You need to take Skyler."

"I just finished my shift," he said. "I was just going to drop Lily at her house and head home."

The woman's gaze met Lily's again. "What the hell happened to you, Baker?"

Lily said nothing.

"Well, take her home, then," the woman snapped, cracking the driver's door. "But you have to take Skyler now." She stepped from the car. A long coat with a hood trimmed in faux fur covered a blue postal uniform. She pulled the girl, now crying, from the back and handed the child to Tim, casting Lily a hard stare.

Tim wrapped his arms around the little girl and bounced her gently. "Where's her jacket?"

"It's at home," the woman said. "And they're coming to look at the dishwasher at four, so you need to be there," she told him. "I can't go another damn day without a dishwasher."

"I'll be there," Tim said.

The woman glanced at Lily again, saying nothing, then climbed back into the car and drove away.

"Sorry," Tim said to Lily as he loaded the child into the backseat. "She wasn't supposed to work today."

Lily sank into the passenger seat of the car and watched as Tim belted the little girl into a car seat, murmuring softly. His child. His wife. She crossed her arms and shivered. So what was she? She searched her memories, the vague fragments that had come to her last night. She'd had the sensation of someone holding her down, the warnings. *"Get back. Nothing bad happens when we're all here, together."* Was that voice Tim's? It had sounded like a man talking to a child. Was that how she let herself be treated? He was a married man, she reminded herself.

Tim climbed in the front seat and grabbed Lily's leg, his hands splaying across her thigh. "You know it's just temporary. Housing's too expensive for me to move out now."

Lily nodded.

"I'll come by later and make it up to you. I'll get my mom to watch Skyler."

Lily shook her head, crossing her legs to get away from his touch. "It's okay."

He reached around and took the back of her neck again, his grip just a little too tight. "Come on, baby. You're not mad about last night, are you?"

She froze in her seat. "Last night?"

"I tried to get away," he went on, lowering his voice. "Trisha was just all over my ass. I worked three nights in a row, and it was my turn with Skyler. She'd have gone apeshit if I'd left."

She had talked to him yesterday. Yesterday she'd been having an affair. No. He and his wife were separating. Divorcing? Did that still make it an affair? It felt like it did. That wasn't important. What mattered was that yesterday she had spoken to Tim, which meant that she hadn't vanished for days or weeks. Whatever had happened to her memory was less than twenty-four hours old. Maybe it would come back by tomorrow. A one-day amnesiac episode.

His fingers dug between her legs, pinching the thin skin of her inner thigh. She flinched and shifted, but his hand was like heavy machinery breaking through earth. "I need to see you. Know what I mean?"

She grabbed hold of his hand to stop him, the images that flipped through her mind assaults of their own. Her reality—the gun, the money, the dead man in the pool of blood, another woman's husband. And Tim's wife was not fooled—she knew that Lily had been sleeping with him. Were they really splitting up?

He reached across her and unlatched the glove box. Her fingers found the place where his hand had been on her neck, and she rubbed gently. As he rifled through the glove box, a thin pack of baby wipes fell to her feet, followed by a diaper and a manual for the car. "Damn it," he muttered, his torso in her lap as he stretched for a closer look. "I'll bet she took them."

Tim slapped the glove box closed and slammed a fist on the dash. "Damn her." He patted his jacket pockets. "That was all I had."

"It's okay," Lily said to calm him, then stooped to pick up the fallen items from the floor.

"You're not quitting," he said, scoffing at her. "That's bullshit. You say that like once a month."

Quitting what? What was she doing? She placed everything back in the glove box.

"The buzz is so good," he said, pressing his nose to her neck.

She held a fist to her stomach, fighting off the nausea.

"The sex is so good."

From the backseat, the baby began to cry.

Lily felt a wave of relief.

"Hush now, Sky," he said as he sat back upright and started the car. "We're going home now." He pulled out of the parking lot with a rough turn and spun out briefly before his wheels gripped the road.

Lily drew even breaths. She would be home soon. There would be answers there. She would sort this all out. Her gaze drifted sideways to Tim.

He looked over and smiled at her, displaying a row of nicotine-stained bottom teeth. "Almost forgot," he said, and she stiffened as he reached into his pocket. He handed her his phone. "You wanted to call someone?"

The word *sister* was on the tip of her tongue, but she held it back. Instead, she shook her head, tucking her hands under her arms.

He made a turn without signaling, the car fishtailing slightly on the slick road. "What were you doing on a bike in this fucking weather?"

"Being an idiot, obviously," she said, her pulse a deep, insistent bass under her ribs. Would he believe her? She scanned the streets for something familiar. How far was the damn house?

Behind them, the girl shrieked in protest, her foot kicking the back of Lily's chair.

"Sky, we'll be home in a few minutes. Keep quiet, you hear?"

Lily kept her eyes on the road.

"I can't do anything about the crying, Lily. She's a kid."

"I know," she said, trying for a soft voice. "Your daughter."

He eyed her, and she forced a smile. He had a daughter. And a wife. What was she doing? Was this who she was? A thief, a cheat . . . but also a nurse?

"You sure you're okay?" Tim asked as he turned off the main street. "You seem off."

"Little headache is all," she lied.

"You need a little fix. I got you."

Tim drove straight for several blocks, then turned again and slowed to a stop in front of a small gray bungalow. She exhaled. Her house. The house was in need of paint. One of the shutters on the front window hung askew, and a thin layer of frost covered the small lawn. But her relief was short lived. The house felt cold and unfamiliar.

A white Volkswagen Passat was parked at the curb. It had to be her car, but it, too, looked strangely wrong. Then she remembered the contents of her wallet. There had been no driver's license—only a state ID issued in Arizona. Maybe it wasn't her car at all. Tim would know, but she felt the weight of his stare on her. She didn't ask.

Beside her, he had shifted the car into park and turned in the seat to face her. "How the hell did you do that?"

"What?"

"You've got scratches all across your forearm." He pointed to the place where she had rolled her sleeve back to help with Brent. "And on your chest, too," he added, reaching to pull her collar down. "What were you wearing on that bike ride?"

She yanked her sleeve down and held her shirt closed.

His breath was hot on her cheek. "Sorry. They made me think of the other ones," he whispered. "Freaked me out."

Other ones?

His hand gripped her leg. "I'm sorry. I know you don't like to talk about what happened." But the force of his fingers was anything but comforting.

She stared at him a moment, wanting to ask what he was talking about. What other ones? Other what? What had happened? Her breathing felt ragged and shallow. She had to get out of this car. Lily opened the car door.

"I'll call you later," Tim said. "I need to see you, you hear? I'll bring something, too. Get your mind off all this. We'll relax," he added with a twisted smile that gave her chills.

Lily nodded, wanting nothing to do with him. How had she ever? She stepped from the car and walked toward the front door. She didn't turn back as the car drove away.

Only standing on the front porch did she realize that she didn't have keys. She waited until Tim's car was gone, then squatted beside the single pot on the porch to lift it up. No key. She checked in the pot's frosty dirt, under the doormat, and beneath the cushion on the small wooden chair. When she scanned for another hiding place, she came up empty. She sank down on the chair, which creaked beneath her, the wood cold and wet. She could break in. It was her house.

She stared in through a small living room window. The answers were inside. All she had to do was go in. But she couldn't shake the fear about who she was. About what she'd done. Why hadn't she asked Tim about Abby? Or about the name in her Bible? Because she didn't want anything to do with Tim, with his nicotine-stained teeth and his drugs and his wife and daughter.

She caught sight of the coffee table, glasses and bowls on its surface as though it belonged in a fraternity. *This is who you are. Where you live.*

She wanted nothing to do with that either.

Then she remembered that there had been an address in the Bible. She found the book in her bag and opened the front cover: 416 Fourth Street. The sky was growing darker, and she had the sense that it had to be close to dinnertime. She would go there first.

Shouldering her purse, she walked off the porch and down to the corner, where she checked the street signs. She was at Eighth and Townsend. She continued, walking slowly. The wrap on her ankle helped support the injury, but it was tender. The next block was Seventh Street. Whether by some buried memory or dumb luck, she was headed in the right direction. She rubbed her arms, noticing the light snow that had started to fall, and continued to walk toward Fourth Street.

She arrived at 416 Fourth Street and climbed the stairs. A small white note was taped on the front. *Come on in. Back by 6. Xo, I.*

The small block lettering was the same as in the Bible. Relief flooded through her.

Lily gently pulled the note off the door and stared at the familiar handwriting as though it held a promise that everything would be fine. The note pressed in her hand, Lily reached for the doorknob and, when it turned easily, stepped inside.

CHAPTER 13

KYLIE

At just past five, the sheriff pinged Kylie to come to his office. She hoped it was to tell her he'd decided to get a warrant to search the bar. Davis rarely made decisions quickly, and when he'd decided on a course of action, he preferred to do things in person. She was getting used to going to forty-five-minute meetings in his office that would have taken two minutes over the phone.

As she emerged from the stairwell on the second floor, she passed Steve Cannon. He stopped when he saw her. "Scene this morning go okay?" he asked. "Heard it wasn't pretty."

"It wasn't."

He nodded quietly. Murdered girl. What was the right thing to say? A beat passed, and he said, "I'm calling for a tow truck now."

She had no idea what he was talking about.

Just then, Carl Gilbert entered the department.

Cannon swung around. "How many keys do you have, Dilbert? You sound like a kid carrying a damn piggy bank."

Frowning at Cannon, Gilbert took hold of his keys and quieted the clanking. The two men regarded each other, but neither said anything else. Cannon headed off down the hall. She noticed he hadn't said *stay safe*. Maybe he'd been distracted by Gilbert and his keys. Gilbert ducked into the kitchen, and Kylie came in after him.

"Don't mind Cannon," she said.

As Gilbert topped his coffee with cream and lifted the bright-green-and-yellow mug to his face, Kylie waited for him to sniff it the way he always did. A pause at his lips, and then he smelled it, not like inhaling an aroma—more like making sure it didn't smell rotten. Kylie felt annoyed for no reason. She turned to leave the room when Gilbert said, "He doesn't bother me."

As she approached Davis's office, she was surprised to see two other men sitting across from him. One was District Attorney Glen Vogel, but she didn't recognize the other. He was about Vogel's age—maybe midfifties—and dressed in a pair of khaki slacks and a button-down shirt. He sat with one foot propped on the opposite knee, and something about him made Kylie think he represented one of the drilling outfits. Probably here about Brent Nolan. The big drilling companies often sent their senior folks—always older white men—to make nice with local law enforcement and politicians. Those meetings never included her.

She paused in the doorway until Davis spotted her and waved her inside. She greeted Vogel and Davis. The third man stood and reached out his hand. "Gary Ross," he said.

"Nice to meet you, Mr. Ross," she said, shaking his hand before glancing at Davis.

"Ross is a special agent out in Saint Cloud, Minnesota," Davis said.

FBI. She looked to Davis. What had changed? She gave Mr. Ross a smile. It took an effort, that smile—like chiseling stone. "What brings you to Hagen, Agent Ross?"

"I worked the Derek Hudson case for about six years. I joined the investigation about a month after the girls escaped, when we were investigating the possibility of a second perp. I thought I'd come down for a few days, help out."

She studied his expression, wondering if this was more of Vogel's bullshit. Her thumb crossed over her index finger, and she felt the satisfying release as the knuckle cracked.

"We sure appreciate your help," she said.

He nodded. "Happy to be of service."

"We get any word on cause of death?" She eyed Davis and Vogel to test how much they were willing to share with Ross. People in this town tended to get testy when outsiders stepped in. But now—when it was supposed to be her case—they seemed all too happy to share.

"Actually, yes," Davis said. "Coroner said there was blunt-force trauma to the back of her head—either she was hit by something or she struck her head on something. But she was also strangled."

"Did she struggle?" Kylie asked, thinking of the evidence that might entail.

"Yes," Davis confirmed. "They found skin beneath the nails."

"What about time of death?"

"Estimate is between nine p.m. and one a.m.," Davis said.

So she had died while the bar was in full swing.

"Body's en route to the ME in Bismarck," he told her. "They'll collect DNA evidence from under the nails and confirm cause of death. Results will trickle in over the next few weeks—four to six on the outside."

In four to six weeks, Kylie wanted this case closed so she could put in for a transfer to Fargo. "I spoke to the deputy sheriff, Pete McIntosh, over in Glendive, last known residence of Jenna Hitchcock. She was—"

"The third survivor," Ross said.

"Right. Police did a welfare check. No sign of Hitchcock."

"They have any idea how long she's been gone?" Vogel asked. "Possible she just moved or took a trip?"

Kylie nodded. "I'll follow up."

"Let's find out if Iver Larson's been out of town anytime recently," Vogel suggested. "Glendive's, what, an hour from here?"

"Just about," Davis agreed.

Kylie studied Vogel. Was he finally taking the possibility of Iver Larson seriously? Did that mean they'd get inside Skål?

"You check that out, Miss Milliard?" Vogel asked.

"Yes, sir."

"What's next, then?" Ross asked.

"Think the next step is to get a look inside the bar where Jensen was found," Kylie interjected, holding back her smile. "I believe DA Vogel was working on getting us a warrant."

Vogel's lips vanished into a thin line of pale mouth.

"That sounds like a good place to start," Ross said, either clueless to Vogel's displeasure or ignoring it.

Davis nodded to Vogel. "Let's get a couple of the crime analysts over there. If you can't get a warrant, I could probably call Iver Larson. I think he'd give us permission to look."

Vogel sat up in his chair. "I can get the warrant," he said, a little edge in his voice.

Kylie turned to Davis. "Great. I can head over—"

"Actually," Davis said, stopping her, "right now, I'd like you to go out to the scene of Brent Nolan's car accident."

"What?" Kylie made no effort to hide her frustration, realizing now why Cannon had mentioned a tow truck.

Davis raised a palm. "Highway patrol is sending an officer to inspect the scene. Someone from our department has to be there."

"So send Patrol to meet them. Abigail Jensen's death is a murder investigation. She was held in captivity for nearly sixteen months and escaped almost ten years ago to the day. We need to find whoever killed her."

"We'll get the crime team into the bar," Davis said calmly. "In the meantime, we want to make sure that the accident was an accident."

Kylie stared at him. Was this just about kissing ass, or did they know something? "Why wouldn't it be an accident?"

Davis and Vogel exchanged a look, and Ross rose from his chair. "I'm going to refresh my coffee." He crossed the room and paused at the door. "If you don't mind an old man tagging along, Detective, I'd like to join you at the scene of the accident. If you end up going, of course."

Kylie fought her frown. Why would he want to come to the scene of a car accident? She eyed him as though she might be able to uncover some hidden agenda.

Vogel cleared his throat.

"Sure," Kylie said. "You're welcome to join."

Ross nodded and left the room.

The moment the door clicked closed, she asked, "What's going on?"

"Brent Nolan died in the ICU this morning."

"I know. I was sorry to hear it. But it *was* an accident—he hit a patch of ice and drove off the overpass."

Vogel leaned back in the chair. "Before we rule it an accident, we want to be damn sure we're not overlooking something."

"Is there some reason to believe that it wasn't an accident?" she asked.

"Just a precaution," Davis added with a little shake of his head.

Bullshit, she thought. She could read between the lines. If Vogel and Davis didn't want to tell her what they knew about Nolan's accident, there were plenty of other ways to find out. Information in Hagen leaked like a sieve. You wanted to hear gossip, all you had to know was who to ask. And she did.

CHAPTER 14

LILY

Lily took another look at the note in her hand, the neat block letters. *Come on in. Back by 6. Xo, I.* As she entered the foyer, a medium-size black dog rose on stiff hips and made his way to greet her, the wagging tail instantly reassuring. With his dark hindquarters spotted white and the splotches of brown on his underside and across his muzzle, the dog looked a little like an Australian shepherd, mixed with a lot of mutt. She squatted down as the dog pushed his nose into her hand. He knew her. Of course he did. She had been here before. She belonged here.

She didn't allow herself to think about how her brain recognized an Australian shepherd but couldn't pull her own name from her subconscious. She was safe now. In the entryway, she removed her wet boots and left them beside a pair of men's Pumas and a pair of Blundstone boots. She started to lift the strap of her bag over her shoulder but thought twice. There was something comforting about the weight of her things. Even if one of them was a gun. Or maybe because one was a gun.

The house felt warm, and she shivered off the cold she'd been carrying. She moved slowly through the foyer, pausing at a table against one wall, its surface piled with mail and keys, catalogs and magazines. In a wood frame was a photograph of a man standing between an older couple—his parents, likely. The man wore a military uniform. She studied the young soldier, feeling hopeful.

But there was nothing familiar about him.

Panic rose in her chest and throat, and she fought to calm herself with breath. It made sense that he didn't look familiar. No one was going to look familiar. *You've lost your memory. It's just amnesia. It could be over in minutes.*

Or it could last.

"No."

The dog peered up at her as though startled. She couldn't focus on what would happen if she never remembered. *Focus on this, on now.* She was in a safe place, where she was meant to be—the note on the front door said so.

She studied one of the envelopes in the stack of mail. *Iver Larson.* She spoke the name out loud, watching as the dog wagged his tail. At least one of them recognized the name, but not her. Was Iver her husband or boyfriend? Had she been cheating on him with Tim? The thought of Tim made her a little ill.

How odd to wonder at her own behaviors, her own reality, as though maybe she wasn't this Lily Baker at all. As she moved through the living room, she studied the pictures and books on the shelves. There were no images of her, and the home definitely belonged to a man. So they weren't married. Were they dating? If they were, wouldn't there be some sign of her in his house?

The dog followed her around the room as she went. Past the living room was a long hallway. The first door opened into a bathroom, and she stepped inside, averting her gaze from the mirror, and used the toilet. As she stood at the sink to wash her hands, she finally met her own gaze.

The face—her own face—was unfamiliar. But it was the same face she'd seen on the Arizona state ID, though a few years older. So she *was* Lily Baker.

"Lily Baker."

The name was foreign as it drifted through the empty room. A fine enough name, even if it meant nothing to her. Her appearance, though, was startling. Dark circles formed inky blue-purple smudges beneath her eyes. Her face was red, windburned, and her cheeks dry, her lips cracked. Thin scratches lined the left side of her face. Along her neck were several deeper cuts.

"The other ones," Tim had said. The ones she didn't like to talk about. What did that mean? To her, it looked like she'd run through brush somewhere, but where?

She'd been in a car. Staring at the scratches, she didn't see how they could have been made in the car accident. They were on the wrong side of her face. Across her right shoulder, a deep bruise was forming where the seat belt had been. She thought about what might be under her clothes but was afraid to look.

Instead, she ran the tap until the water was warm and washed her hands with soap, her sleeves rolled up to keep them dry. She averted her gaze from the scratches Tim had pointed out on her forearm and gently washed the tender skin of her scraped palms. Even after the cleaning at the hospital, the water that slowly drained in the sink basin was dirty. She added more soap before turning and scrubbing her hands. On the inside of her left wrist was a raised pink ridge she hadn't seen before. Her first thought was that it, too, had happened in the accident. In the dull light of the bathroom, it had the same size and sheen as an earthworm. Glistening, moist. Not a new injury. She touched it. A scar.

Shivers hummed down her spine like small electric shocks. She knew what this was. The placement on the inside of the wrist, the orientation of the line parallel to the veins of her arm.

She had tried to kill herself.

She pushed the thought aside. Not necessarily. It might have been something entirely different—an accident, a defense wound. *You don't remember enough to judge who you are.* But she did, didn't she? The stolen cash, the gun, the married man, whatever Tim had been trying to get her to take—some sort of drugs, surely.

Trembling, she yanked the sleeve down over her wrist and pressed her wet palms to her cheeks. In the mirror she glimpsed a streak of dried blood partially hidden behind her right ear. She lifted the hair and turned her head, probing gingerly. A small knot, painful to the touch. Not actively bleeding.

Eyes closed, she found the stream of warm water and brought her face close, cupping the liquid between her palms. She washed out her mouth, then drank deeply and finally splashed her face, cleaning her neck and ear. She needed a shower, but that would have to wait until Iver got home. Surely he would be home soon. She rinsed her face again, then shut off the faucet and patted her face and neck with carefully folded toilet paper so she didn't get blood on the light-colored towels.

She rolled her hair into a ponytail and tucked the long end down the back of her fleece. Her eye was swollen and she was scraped up, but she looked better. Less like a criminal.

The wad of cash in her bra argued otherwise. She pulled out the bills without looking at them and shoved them down into her bag. Her head throbbed, and she opened the medicine cabinet to find some Advil or Tylenol.

Medicines and prescription bottles lined the glass shelves of the cabinet, over-the-counter ones like Advil, Motrin, Excedrin, and Aleve, as well as herbs and naturopath solutions she'd never heard of. The labels all included headache and pain relief. Ibuprofen would help with her head, but her fingers moved to the prescription bottles, a solid row of them.

Many were familiar to her: Neurontin for seizures, Ambien for insomnia, several SSRIs, two antianxiety medications, and also a host of ones she'd never heard of—Maxalt, Sumatriptan, Axert, Zofran . . . good God. What was wrong with him? She thought of Tim, his offer to get her something to make her feel good.

She pulled her fingers away from the bottles, glancing at her hand as though it might tell her what it had been looking for. But some part of her knew. Pain meds. Tim had given her pain meds. Was she addicted?

She closed the cabinet door firmly, then went to open it again. At that moment, the room went dark. Outside the bathroom door, the dog started barking. She froze, listened. Other than the dog, she could hear no sounds. Maybe a breaker had flipped. Could the snow have done that? But what if it wasn't a breaker? She palmed her way across the room and sat on the edge of the bathtub, her heart pounding. She would stay where she was. She would wait. Iver would come home and fix the power.

Without a window, the room was pitch black. On the other side of the bathroom door, the dog whined, his nails clicking on the hardwood as he paced. A few more barks were followed by more whining. Soon, he was scratching at the bathroom door. She remembered the kitchen light had been on when she had arrived. Maybe the dog was afraid of the dark. Damn it.

She ran her hand along the cloth of her bag, feeling the shape of the gun inside.

You don't need a gun.

But her fingers had already slipped inside to find the hard metal column of the magazine and slid it into the slot at the base of the grip. The click vibrated up her arm, and she froze.

God, no. She was not going out there with a loaded gun.

She released the gun back into her bag as she drew a shaky breath and stepped toward the door. *There's nothing to be afraid of,* she told her pounding heart. *It's just the lights. Be smart.* She stepped toward the door and gripped the bag. The dog scratched more furiously. *Okay,* she thought. *I'm coming.*

She cracked the door and took one step into the dark hallway, her own breathing loud and raspy. The dog pressed his muzzle to her hand,

and she gasped at the sensation of his wet nose. He let out a whine, and she breathed, her body pressed to the wall.

"It's okay, buddy," she whispered, squatting beside him, listening to the silence.

The dog whined, pushing against her. "It's just the dark," she whispered. There would be a flashlight somewhere. Or candles.

Hand gripping the edge of her bag, she pivoted toward the living room. Then a single human grunt came from the darkness, followed by the smell of something reminiscent of herbs and liquor.

"Iver?"

No response. She took one step back, ready to run, and heavy hands grabbed her shoulders and brought her to a halt.

Pain knifed across her injured ankle. She reached into the bag for her gun. Drew it out and swung it toward the figure. An electric current seared the back of her neck, and she dropped to her knees. The gun clattered to the floor as she swayed forward, unable to lift her arms. Heavy fabric covered her head. She fought to breathe, to move. The smell of hay and mold burned her eyes. Her muscles had seized and were frozen, useless.

The dog barked again—angry, frantic barking.

She slammed facedown into the floor, the breath forced from her lungs. She gasped, reaching out a hand to fight him. Her fingers grazed his skin and the uneven surface of hair or a piece of clothing before he wrenched her hand to her side.

"Let me go." The words came out weak and feathery. Her pulse punched at her ribs, but her limbs were numb. Something constricted her chest, pinned her arms. His knees, his weight. She fought to free an arm, to use her elbow to push herself up, but his hold was too tight. The sensations of being trapped, of her own panic, were instantly familiar. The scent of dank sweat heightened her terror as the man's weight pressed onto her back.

She kicked a foot up, trying to strike him. Her injured ankle twisted painfully in the air, and she let out a strangled cry. Her attacker straddled her. His hands closed on her neck from behind.

"Let go of me," she screamed. "Help!"

The dog was so close, barking, then growling. The hands loosened on her neck. She stole a frantic breath and tried to roll. The dog let out a sharp yelp and went silent.

"Help!" she screamed. "Help me!"

The gun. It was somewhere nearby. But she couldn't lift her arms, couldn't use her hands at all. Still she stretched her fingers across the hard floor, searching for the cold metal.

His hands tightened on her neck again. Her breath halted as pain filled her throat. In the darkness under the fabric, lights spotted her vision. He was choking her. She was going to pass out. She threw her hips upward again, bucking against his weight. A moment later, he slammed her to the floor. Her pulse pounded in her temples. The white spots went gray and melted into the black. Her own voice screamed inside her head—begging, shrieking. *Preserve me, O God: for in thee do I put my trust.*

The din in her head softened. A part of her remembered where those words came from. Psalm 16:1. Then everything grew silent.

She was going to die. This man was going to kill her.

CHAPTER 15

KYLIE

Kylie Milliard found Gary Ross waiting in the department lobby, leaning against a cement pillar, phone in one hand, thumb flicking upward. Social media, probably, though he wore a pretty serious expression for a guy looking at images of people he hadn't seen since high school. God, she hated social media. No single woman in her thirties was supposed to ignore social media, but Kylie hated it with a scathing fury that she held for few other things. Cats, she thought. She really hated cats, although that was partly because she was so allergic. She hated social media most.

Ross caught sight of her and pushed off the pillar. "You okay if I join you?"

She paused and narrowed her eyes at him. Away from Vogel and Davis, she wanted Ross to know that she wasn't keen on sharing the limelight on this case.

"It's just something to pass the time," he said, both hands raised, though one was still cupping his phone. "And I could probably give you some insight into Derek Hudson that might be helpful after I'm gone."

"And when is that, again?"

Ross let out a belly laugh. "Not one to mince words. I like it. Thought I'd stay the weekend, leave on Monday." He slid the phone into his pocket. "What do you think? Can you suffer through the company of an old bureau guy for two days?"

Since today was Thursday, it was technically three and a half days. "I've got to make a stop on the way to the scene," she said and headed for the door.

It was snowing hard as Kylie drove the three blocks to the diner. She parked on the curb and left the engine running against the cold. "Just have to touch base with my roommate," she said. "Back in five."

"Your roommate," Ross said.

"Roommate," she repeated. Not that she cared if he believed her or not. What she was doing in the diner was none of his damn business. She jogged through the snow and pulled the door open, stomping her boots on the welcome mat before stepping inside and sliding onto a stool at the counter.

Amber *was* actually her roommate. Not that Kylie had expected to have a roommate at thirty-one, but a detective job in Hagen, North Dakota, did not pay enough to afford a place of her own, not while Hagen was in the middle of an oil boom and Kylie was still paying off student loans. And Amber had a cute little house, walkable to town. Kylie had been skeptical of how things would work between them, but she enjoyed Amber.

Amber was absolutely everything Kylie was not. For one, she was blonde and tall and smiled way too much. She wore her hair in a high, messy bun perched on top of her head, wisps of it flying left and right as she turned and talked, both of which she did nonstop, even during the diner's midafternoon lull. Kylie raised a hand to get Amber's attention. With a quick nod, Amber grabbed the coffeepot and made her way down the bar, refilling cups as she headed for Kylie.

"You here for the banana cream?" Amber asked.

Kylie had a total failing when it came to banana-cream pie. She shook her head. "Heading up to the scene where Brent Nolan died."

Amber made the sign of a cross in a tiny motion over her heart. Something else Kylie wouldn't have been caught dead doing.

"I heard about that," Amber said. "He was such a dear man. Always so sweet to William." At the mention of her son, Amber glanced to the corner behind the counter where her son's playpen was usually set up for at least a few hours of her shift, when Amber's mother wasn't watching him.

Kylie followed her gaze. At the moment, all Kylie could see was the top of the toddler's head, a mass of blond hair just like his mother's.

"Asleep," Amber said.

Kylie had also never expected to room with a child, but she'd signed the lease before she'd known about William. Well, that part was on her. For a detective, she had missed a lot of clues that there might be a baby living there. At the time, she'd been too desperate for a place to live to care.

Amber poured a few inches of coffee into a mug for her as Kylie leaned forward, lowering her voice. "You know anything about Nolan?"

"He came in from time to time."

"Any reason to think someone wanted to hurt him?"

Amber's expression remained totally neutral as she pondered the question. It still amazed Kylie to watch Amber process questions like this, questions other folks would have pretended were shocking and inappropriate. For all that blonde hair, Amber was refreshingly no nonsense.

Amber checked her surroundings to be sure no one was too close before answering. "There was some talk about a woman in town."

"Mistress? Any idea who?"

"No. And I never saw him with anyone here. Not that folks come to the diner for privacy." Amber took another look over her shoulder. "Bethany Stevens mentioned Nolan is Pike Drilling's number two guy."

Pike Drilling had the largest drilling contract in Hagen. That alone could have made him unpopular with some. Drilling brought money with it, but not everyone shared in the windfall. For many residents, the drilling companies had done nothing for Hagen except make it more expensive for regular folks.

"Bethany also mentioned that she and her husband attended a dinner party with Nolan at the mayor's house last month."

So going to the site of the accident *was* about brownnosing. "Nothing else?"

"Not that I've heard." Amber poured her another inch of coffee and nodded outside. "Who you got in the car?"

"Visiting FBI agent, here on the Abigail Jensen murder."

Amber shook her head and made another cross. "That stuff ain't supposed to happen in Hagen."

"Vogel and Sheriff Davis just threw him at me."

Amber scanned the room. "Wanda was just in here."

Kylie frowned. "Who?"

"Mrs. Vogel. I guess Vogel's sister died a few weeks ago."

Kylie took a sip of the coffee. "I didn't even know he had a sister."

"Well, she's gone now." Amber took a few steps down the bar and filled a couple of coffee cups with a smile at each customer. Sometimes she was like a scary Tinker Bell robot.

When Amber returned, Kylie leaned forward and lowered her voice. "Listen, I couldn't find any pictures on Facebook from the bar last night. Think you can put out feelers about who was there? I could use pictures."

"Oh, I know some hos who were there last night. I'll check Insta, too." Amber pulled a couple of paper cups off a stack and turned them right side up to fill them before handing Kylie lids for each.

To Amber, *ho* was a sign of endearment, one she better not ever use on Kylie. *Insta* was short for Instagram. Sometimes it was hard to believe she and Amber were anywhere close to the same age. "Thanks," Kylie said.

"I'll get you a piece of banana cream to go." Amber narrowed her gaze through the window as if studying Gary Ross, though she couldn't have seen him for the falling snow. "And cherry for your friend."

With that, Amber was on the move again.

While Kylie waited for their pie, she texted Carl Gilbert and asked him to find out if any of the bartenders from Skål had been out of town in the last week. Kylie scanned the faces in the diner. If Iver had been out of town, someone in this room would know. There was something unsettling about how easily people found things out in Hagen.

A couple of minutes later, Kylie left the diner with coffee, pie, and some useful insight into Brent Nolan. Maybe the accident would be interesting after all.

CHAPTER 16

——

IVER

With another swig, Iver set down the bottle he'd picked up on the way to the high school and backed up to the three-point line. He dribbled the ball on the worn gymnasium floor, the sound echoing in the empty space. He pitched the basketball in an upward arc. The moment it left his fingers, he knew it was short. The ball hit the edge of the rim and bounced back. Skirting the bottle of liquor wrapped in a brown paper sack, he caught the ball, dribbled twice, and shot again. This time the ball vibrated against the backboard with a thunderous rattle and flew toward the empty bleachers.

He lifted the bottle to his lips again, comforted by the burn of liquor in his throat. He walked to retrieve the ball, Mike's voicemail playing in his head. Why had Iver listened to it? He'd been avoiding Mike's calls, so why play that damn voicemail?

Because he had to know what Mike knew. What Iver had done. He couldn't get his friend out of his mind, the way Mike had refused to meet his eye at the bar that morning. Mike was his best friend. Sure, they'd given each other hell, but they covered each other's asses, too. The time Mike had drunk his father's whiskey when they were sophomores in high school, it was Iver who'd taken the blame. Mike had confessed to spray-painting a locker when that had been Iver's doing, taking the fall so Iver, who was already on probation, wouldn't get expelled. But this . . . this was not boys raiding a liquor cabinet or vandalizing the school. Iver stared at the phone, Mike's words playing back in his mind.

"Hey, man. Listen, first I want to make sure you're okay . . ." The awkward start of Mike's message had made Iver wince, and a knot had grown in his gut. Something was definitely wrong. He and Mike went all the way back. They'd been babies together. Mike never tiptoed around him.

"Last night . . ."

Iver had held his breath, waiting for Mike to go on. The strain in Mike's voice was so clear, so gut wrenching. What about last night?

Finally, Mike said, "I mean . . . shit."

Iver stooped for the basketball and turned back to the court, trying to shake the memory, but it was right there, dribbling inside his brain. "I don't know if you want to talk about it," Mike had said. "Or if I should never mention it again."

It.

Iver thought of the silver thread in his watchband, the dead woman. It couldn't be that. There was no way. Except there was. He felt that anger, the memory of it. He'd been angry last night.

He launched the basketball up toward the hoop and missed. Fighting back the panic, he leaned over and pressed his hands to his knees. So he'd been angry. That didn't mean he'd hurt someone. Or killed her.

"I'll play it however you want," Mike's message had continued, his voice cracking. "But I'm here if you want to talk."

When Mike stopped talking, Iver had thought the voicemail was over. Just as he was about to delete the message, Iver heard Mike say, "Okay, man. I'll see you later." Then the voicemail ended. Iver swiped to delete the voicemail, then went to his deleted voicemails and cleared them. There could be no record of that call.

Except the recording that looped in his mind. He'd done something. Mike wouldn't rat him out. But something bad had happened.

Iver grabbed the bottle and made his way across the dull floor. In high school, the gymnasium had always felt magical. The bleachers, the shiny wood—it was the biggest indoor arena in Hagen. He'd sat on that bench for three years, hoping for a turn to play. As a senior, he had finally gotten his chance to play—and it had been every damn thing he'd ever imagined. Man, he loved the noise of a crowd, the ball, the satisfying hiss of the ball through the net, the thump thump of a player dribbling before a free throw.

A door opened on the far side of the gym. Iver swung around, feeling the alcohol hit him. He reached for the bleachers to catch himself and fell hard onto a wooden slat.

Alan scooped up the ball that had bounced across the gym and walked toward him. "Yo, man. You okay?"

"Fine," Iver lied.

Alan glanced at the bottle, then averted his gaze as though pretending he hadn't seen it. "I've got to lock up in about ten."

"Sure," Iver said, his tongue awkward against his teeth, like they were just meeting for the first time. "I'm heading out." He took a step toward the basketball but felt gravity shift beneath him.

"You okay, man?"

"Yeah. Fine." Iver took a breath and stood.

Alan reached for his arm as though to help, but Iver shook him off. "Said I'm fine."

Iver grabbed the ball from Alan and took a shot, which bounced off the rim. On the first bounce, Alan caught it easily in one palm as Iver turned toward the door to leave.

"You forgot your stuff," Alan said, palming the ball as he nodded at the bottle in the paper bag.

Iver thought about the fifth he'd bought on the way over. He'd told himself he wasn't going to drink today, but then he'd passed the liquor store. Damn. "Think I'm okay," he said.

"Sure." Alan lifted the bottle and gave it a shake. "Seems like you did a good number on it." He crossed to Iver. "You mind taking it with you? Be bad for me if someone found it here."

"Yeah, sure." Iver reached out, but his fingers somehow missed the bottle. Alan took his hand and pressed the bag into it.

Iver raised a toast. "Thanks, man. Appreciate you letting me in."

"Anytime," Alan said. "You okay to get home?"

"Yeah. No problem. I'm walking," Iver said, raising a hand as he left.

He made his way down the long dark hallway of the high school. How many times he'd walked across these floors. He hadn't especially liked high school, but something about the place was comforting. Since returning from Afghanistan, he occasionally came to the gym when the school was empty. He liked the smell of it—the rubber scent of gym shoes and dodgeballs, the underlying stink of young-kid sweat, the squeak of his shoes on the floor, the way every noise was both hushed and amplified.

Stepping out of the school, Iver curved his shoulders against the full force of frigid air and driving snow. He'd left the house in only a flannel. Thankfully, he had the alcohol to warm him. The sky was darker than he'd expected, and he wondered what time it was. He had intentionally left his phone at home—half because he didn't want to be bothered by the bar and half because . . . He slowed his step and scanned the empty street. Half was because he was scared that the police would show up at his house. That woman detective in particular. She would show up with more questions that he couldn't answer.

He remembered the note he'd left on the door for his mother. How long had he been inside that gym? He picked up the pace, wondering if he'd missed her. What a shit son he was. A shit human. Iver had spent most of the day half dozing on the couch, staring at the television. Unfortunately, the flashing lights and movement—even from something as slow paced as the damn golf channel—left his head pounding, so he had gazed at the black screen. By midday, the migraine was gone, at least the blindingly painful part of it. His phone rang all day, but Iver had ignored it. Mike. His mother. A couple of other guys from the bar. Not Debbie, he noticed. Had she heard that a woman was murdered at the bar? Did she wonder if he'd done it?

But Debbie had no reason to think he would kill someone. Iver was the only person alive who knew that he was a killer. The people who'd known about that day were all killed in the Humvee accident.

That he had killed, he told himself. It wasn't the same as being a killer. War was different.

But that hadn't exactly been war. It wasn't a sanctioned kill, anyway. Debbie knew something traumatic had happened. With the nightmares, there was no way to keep it from her, but he'd never told her the details. Never let her know just what kind of a man she'd married. She knew he'd shot people, but killed a woman with his bare hands? How did you tell your wife that? How did you hear that from your husband? How did you ever love someone who had committed that kind of violence?

And now?

A dead woman at his bar.

But it was more than that. He couldn't remember exactly, but he had a sense that there'd been a fight. He remembered the anger. He rubbed a thumb across the scabs on his knuckles. Had he punched something?

He bunched his fist, and the anger rushed through him. His hand near her face, her eyes closed in fear. He stumbled on the sidewalk, slipped, and caught himself. But the bottle inside the paper sack dropped from his hand, shattering against the pavement.

He didn't reach for it but kept moving. The vision of that woman nudged at his subconscious. He'd been so angry—not afraid, not like with the Afghan woman. What he remembered was pure rage, his fingers trembling with the desire to strike, the skin on his hands vibrating with it. But why would he hurt a total stranger?

The cold was piercing, cutting through his skin and drilling into his bones. He ran a few yards, but the snow turned slick under his tennis shoes, and he fell. The sidewalk struck hard, his skull slamming on the concrete slab. For a moment, he felt nothing. Then the alcohol churned in his stomach, and he turned sideways to vomit across the layer of slush on the ground. He wiped his hand across his mouth and heaved himself onto his feet.

He staggered a few steps before his footing felt firm again and he could walk at a normal pace. He ought to have felt better after purging the alcohol, but his head began to thunder again. The snow drove hard and thick. He waved a hand through the air as though to clear the flakes from his path, but the clumps caught on his eyelashes and fell into his eyes. It felt like he might never make it home.

He reached the corner and tried to read the street sign. His eyes wouldn't work. He crossed and made it another ten or fifteen yards before he heard the sound of Cal's barking. But this wasn't Cal's normal bark. Cal sounded scared. Iver ran, slipping and catching himself as he approached the house. The whole place was dark. Cal hated the dark. Had Iver forgotten to leave lights on? He stumbled up the stairs and shoved the front door open.

Cal's barking didn't stop.

A gust of snowy wind followed him into the house, and Iver pulled the door closed, palming the wall for the light switch. Nothing happened. He turned it off and on again. Nothing. Cal ran toward him, still barking. A shadow shifted in the hallway. Someone was in the house.

Without pausing, Iver ran across the room and tackled the shape to the ground. He smelled wool as the shape splintered into two, one part throwing weight at Iver as the other dropped. Iver spun and slammed face-first into the wall, then fell sideways and landed hard on his left elbow before knocking his head again.

For a moment, Iver felt like he was in a dream. A sound punched through his stupor—someone pounding from somewhere far off. "Police!" someone shouted, the voice growing closer. "Open up!" He opened his eyes and blinked in the darkness. Cal's face was pressed to his. The pounding continued, and Iver tried to sit up. "Police! Open up!"

He was barely upright when he heard the creak of the front door opening and boots on his floor. He raised a hand. "Here. I'm here."

A beam flashed across his face, passing him before coming back. He caught the light as it landed on a shape across from him. The head dropped, eyes averted. The intruder.

Iver pressed himself up with one hand as Cal nudged against him, barking again. The shape on the floor turned its head, and the police officer's flashlight caught the sheen of eyes beneath the heavy cover of a wool blanket—his wool blanket. The intruder was a woman, her eyes wide and terrified, black looking in the sharp beam of the flashlight. Iver gasped at the thought of the woman in the bar, but this was not that woman.

At the sight of him, she backpedaled, scooting away until her back hit the wall.

Iver saw broken glass on the floor. A picture must have fallen. "Watch out. There's glass."

The woman raised her hands with only a cursory glance at her palms as though afraid to take her eyes off him. She glanced over her shoulder, hands shaking, shivering at the wave of cold. Iver saw that the back door was open. She must have come in that way. But why was she here? What had happened?

The officer crossed the room. "Neighbors called to report a fight."

Iver looked up at the shadowed officer, his face unreadable behind the bright light in Iver's eyes. "I just got—" He shook his head. She'd been here. She'd broken into his home. But something kept him from speaking.

Something about her.

He closed his mouth and turned back to the woman huddled against his hallway wall. Only then did he recognize the woman as Lily Baker.

But she stared at him like he was the devil.

What if he was?

CHAPTER 17

KYLIE

After a fifteen-minute drive on Highway 1804, Kylie and Gary Ross reached the scene of Brent Nolan's accident. The two-lane highway was the most popular route in and out of town. A highway patrol car had already parked on the side of the road, lights flashing in the deepening twilight. Down on the tracks below the overpass, the highway patrolman moved around Nolan's overturned car. The snow wasn't falling here, and the roads were mostly dry. Crazy how ten miles could mean a whole different weather system, but that was North Dakota.

Kylie left her headlights on high and flipped on her police lights, parking opposite the patrol car in the other direction. Common sense would suggest that two sets of police lights were sufficient to make drivers slow down, but out here there was no guarantee. After removing her flashlight from the trunk, she sidestepped down the hill to join the officer below the overpass beside Brent Nolan's totaled car. It had landed on its roof. The crash had caved the window opening on the driver's side to barely a foot.

"How the hell did he get out of there?" she asked.

The officer turned to her. "Been wondering the same thing. He must've been conscious after the car landed. Pretty amazing, considering that fall."

Ross joined them and introduced himself to the patrol officer. Feeling chagrined, Kylie shook hands as well. "Will Merkel," the officer said.

"You find anything?" Kylie asked.

Merkel motioned up to the highway, where the darkness was softening the details of the road. "Tread marks on the road are consistent with a driver reacting to hitting a patch of ice. He braked late, and the car spun. Looks like it made a one-eighty-degree turn, then another ninety before the car rammed into the guardrail."

Heading out of town. She looked back up at the twisted metal above, squinting in the fading light. "What's surprising is that the car had enough momentum to break through," Kylie said.

"You may want to get an engineer to look at that rail," Ross said, pointing back toward the road. "Lot of these haven't been updated during my lifetime. In Minnesota, at least."

The metal looked as flimsy as a twisted bike fender.

Merkel nodded. "Yeah. We've got someone from state transportation coming out tomorrow."

"But no sign of a second car?" Kylie asked.

"No second car, no," Merkel said. "Looks pretty straightforward."

Kylie flipped on her flashlight and ducked to study the car's interior. "Both airbags deployed. Does that mean there was someone in the passenger seat?"

"No," Merkel explained. "If the impact affects the passenger side of the car, that airbag is automatically triggered."

Shining her flashlight, she studied the tiny space inside the car. How had Brent Nolan gotten out of there after that fall? She stood back. From the corner of her eye, she caught sight of a long slender form a few feet away. At first, she thought it was a snake, but it was the wrong time of year for snakes. The shiny buckle caught the beam of her flashlight. A man's belt. She stooped to look more closely.

Merkel joined her, hands on his knees as he bent to study the item. "That his belt?"

"It's someone's belt," she said, trying to imagine why Nolan would have taken off his belt while escaping the car. Had he used it as a tool of some sort? Maybe he had broken the window with the buckle. It looked heavy enough.

"You notice the hair on the passenger seat?" Ross called from the other side of the car, where he was on his knees, shining the light from his phone through the window opening.

Kylie and Merkel joined him, and Kylie squatted to get a better look. Sure enough, there was a handful of dark hairs caught in one of the metal posts between the headrest and the seat.

"Didn't see those," Merkel said. "No saying when they got there, though."

Tiny bits of tempered glass littered the interior, but there was no trash. No marks on the ceiling or seats. The outside, too, was clean, a feat in a town with as many dirt roads and as much dust as Hagen, especially with the snow and mud of winter. Brent Nolan obviously took pride in the car. How long would it have taken before he'd noticed and removed the hair? Not long, she thought. Scanning the car, she noticed a shadow. She looped a ballpoint pen under the seat belt and drew it out, pulling the fabric until the dark stain was clear in the light of Merkel's high beam flashlight. "Take a look at this."

Ross pulled a handkerchief from his pants pocket, tented it around his index finger, and rubbed the spot. When he removed the handkerchief, there was a deep-copper stain on the white cotton. "Looks like blood."

"So there was someone else in the car," Kylie said. From the long hair, Kylie's first guess was the passenger was female.

"Starting to look that way," Merkel agreed.

If someone else was inside that car when it had gone over the pass, where the hell was she now?

CHAPTER 18

—

IVER

Iver closed his eyes against beams of light that bounced off the walls as the first police officer was followed by a second, flashlights swinging across his living room. The effect was dizzying. Even with his eyes closed, he felt like he could see the beams pass over him, as though he were in a disco. The sound of boots pounded across the wood floor toward him. He opened his eyes as both officers crouched beside Lily Baker. Iver felt instantly sober, the alcohol buzz hardening into an immediate hangover. She had broken into *his* house, not the other way around. Plus, she had slammed him into the wall. Or someone had.

But she looked injured. And terrified. *You did that. Again.* He couldn't look at her, couldn't sit there. Pushing himself off the floor, he crossed to the foyer.

"Where do you think you're going?" the officer yelled.

The voice was familiar, but Iver couldn't place it. "To get a flashlight and try to figure out why the damn lights are off," he snapped.

He found his flashlight in the drawer of the front-hall table and shone the beam at the three people in his living room. One of the officers looked up. The voice Iver had recognized came from Larry Sullivan. Sullivan had been a few years ahead of Iver in school, the type of guy who was meaty from birth, broad without having the coordination to do anything athletic with his mass. To make up for the lack of athletic prowess, Sullivan had made himself memorable by being loud and a bully.

Iver walked past them to the laundry room, where the main fuse box was. The lights of neighboring homes were visible through the windows, so whatever had happened wasn't a general outage. The fuses were all on in the box, so he exited the house through the back door and checked the main. There, he found the main switch flipped off. He turned it back on and felt the glow of the lights streaming from the house. He squinted against the brightness, his head starting to throb in a single point behind his left eye, like a nail. He hesitated, not ready to go back inside.

Eyes closed, he raised his face to the dark sky and let the snow fall on his skin. What the hell was happening? The last time he'd seen Lily Baker . . . no, that wasn't the last time. He'd seen her recently, around town. But he hadn't talked to her. Not since the night she'd been taken. How many times the sight of her in the aisles of the grocery store had brought him back to that time. But she'd ignored him, so he'd ignored her, too.

He wiped the melted snow from his face. They had been best friends once, in middle school, tossed together in a church youth group of all places.

Iver's father had believed that attending church youth group kept kids out of trouble, which meant Iver's twice-a-week attendance was nonnegotiable. Mike had come a time or two and had grown bored. Mike's parents had enforced no such rules. Lily's mother had died by that time, and they'd never talked about why she came. It was possible that her father, like his, had required attendance. It was equally possible that she came of her own volition, because things at home were more miserable than at youth group.

Iver and Lily found each other by process of elimination. Most of the group were what he and Lily called Jesus freaks, kids from very religious families. Hagen had a strong Lutheran foundation. Lily's father had been raised religious, but he'd let it go—in hindsight, he'd let most things go—after Lily's mother had died. And Iver, for his part, wasn't sure how he felt about God back then. He was less sure now.

Every Wednesday night, every Sunday morning, they were inside that church building for youth group. Singing, reading scripture, and listening to one of the two assistant pastors on a shifting schedule. Iver and Lily spent much of that time passing notes, written on torn bits of napkin or the tissue paper from the doughnut box. Occasionally, when they were stuck in the chapel, whole conversations could be had on one of the church offering envelopes—first the outside, then ripping it open and writing on the inside as well.

And then the friendship spilled over to other days as well. They did homework together and watched television—both had an affinity for anything superhero. And then there was that Wednesday night when they went from church to his house to watch one episode of *Smallville* before she had to get home. He would have happily spent time at her place, but she preferred his. Her father was usually drunk, and the house had the strange smell of unwashed clothes and burning plastic. And Iver's mother had taken a liking to her as well, so that was where they usually ended up.

The last night he saw her before she disappeared, he gathered all his courage. Focused only on Lily, he barely paid attention to the TV. Instead, he was busy gearing himself up to kiss her. With hindsight, he had realized that his timing couldn't have been worse, as Lana Lang and Clark Kent were splitting up for the last time. Looking back, what he'd taken for rejection had likely just been surprise. But when she asked him what he was doing, he was embarrassed. Humiliated.

And she told him she wanted to go home.

And he told her she should go.

She didn't ask him to walk her.

So he didn't offer.

And that was the last time he saw her for sixteen months. Somewhere between his house and her own, on the six-minute walk they'd done hundreds of times, she had been kidnapped. When she'd returned to Hagen, he'd gone to see her. He had wanted to apologize, to be sure she was okay.

But her father had never let him inside the door.

Only years later did Iver recognize that Mr. Baker had surely been blaming himself more than anyone else. But Iver couldn't shake it. Although Iver had been a fourteen-year-old boy, he should have walked Lily home that night. He'd held on to that guilt for a long time, let it lead him to a dark place. A place where Debbie had found him and eventually led him out.

The next thing he'd heard, Lily Baker was living in Arizona, and the first thing he'd felt was relief.

"Iver?" Sullivan shouted out into the night. "We've got some questions for you."

Iver headed back inside. As he rounded the house, he saw the side gate was open. He went to close it and noticed footprints on the walkway beyond the fence. They were large and fresh, not yet covered by the falling snow. "Sullivan!" Iver shouted.

Larry Sullivan appeared at the back door. "What?"

"Did someone go out to the street this way?"

"What?"

"There are footprints here, leading from the house to the street."

Sullivan walked outside and stared at the tracks in the snow. He said nothing for a minute, then eyed Iver. "You think some fake boot prints are enough to convince me that you didn't just beat the shit out of her?"

"Larry, those aren't my tracks." Iver lifted one foot to show the tread of his sneaker. "Those are boots."

Sullivan surveyed the back of the house like maybe Iver had a pair of boots hiding somewhere.

"Someone else was here," Iver said.

"Maybe it was your neighbor, the one who called it in."

"Who called?"

"I don't know," he said. "We can find out from Dispatch." With that, Sullivan returned to the house, and Iver took another minute to stare at the tracks in the snow. Was he foolish to think maybe someone else had been in his house? That maybe he wasn't the one who had hurt Lily Baker?

When he walked back inside, Sullivan stood with his hands on his hips while the other officer sat beside Lily Baker on his living room couch. The other officer looked a little like another kid he'd gone to school with, maybe a younger brother. The officer glanced at Iver and looked away. Yeah. Someone's younger brother. That was Hagen. Iver ran a hand over his face. Why the hell was he still in this town?

Sullivan eyed him and then turned back to Lily. "Ms. Baker, you sure you don't want to press charges?" He motioned to his face. "Looks like he beat you up pretty good."

"I didn't—" Iver snapped his mouth closed. There was no use fighting with Sullivan. Plus, Sullivan was calling it like he saw it. And there was a chance Sullivan was right. Adrenaline, the sound of Cal's barking, the alcohol. Iver had come sprinting into the house ready to attack. But the marks on her neck. Christ, had he really done that?

She shook her head again, her gaze flitting to Iver and then away again. "I had a bike accident."

"A bike accident?" Sullivan asked, clearly doubting the story.

"I'm not pressing charges," Lily repeated.

Sullivan moved back toward Iver. "That your gun?"

Iver's gaze went to the place Sullivan pointed. A pistol on the ground. "No. I don't own any handguns."

Sullivan looked at Lily Baker. "Is it yours, then?"

She hesitated. Her eyes met his, and he read something there. Only he didn't know what it was. There had been a time when he'd thought he could read her thoughts clearly. But that was a long time ago.

"You can go, Larry," Iver said, looking away from Lily. "We're fine here."

"What about the gun?"

"Take it. Pull prints off it. Maybe you'll figure out who attacked her." It felt like bluster, but it made him feel better to say it, to put another sliver of possibility out into the universe, another chance that he wasn't guilty of beating up a woman who had once been his dear friend. Of beating up any woman. *Again,* he added.

Sullivan collected the gun with a handkerchief while the other officer went to collect an evidence bag. Once the gun was bagged, Sullivan started for the door. He paused at the threshold and turned back, eyes on Lily. "We've got to call it in, so we'll be outside for a bit if you change your mind."

Iver trailed behind them and bolted the front door. When he turned back around, Lily had pulled a blanket over her shoulders.

"I remember you," she said.

He stopped moving.

"I remember that night when—" She shook her head. "We had a fight. The night I walked home from your house." She nodded slowly, her gaze distant. "There was a van," she said, as though realizing it for the first time.

Iver moved forward slowly. "Lily?"

"She was crying in the back."

He shook his head. "Who was crying?"

"The girl in the van."

He tried to follow what she was saying. "What van?"

Tears flooded her eyelids and trailed down her face, but Iver didn't move. Her words made him afraid to move. None of this made sense. Coming home to Cal's barking, the open door, finding her, taking her down. But she'd slammed him into a wall. He'd felt her power. Hadn't he?

"Lily?" he asked. "What's going on?"

Lily turned to her purse and dug inside until she pulled out a pink wallet. He still had no idea what she was doing. She removed a photograph, printed on plain paper and folded in half, and held it out to him.

He took it and stared down at the faces. One was clearly Lily, thinner than he'd ever seen her and younger. It had been taken some time after she'd escaped, he guessed. But it was the face beside hers that caught his attention. "Who is this?"

"Abby," she said. "I think. She's my sister."

He didn't answer. Lily didn't have a sister. They were both only children. Twenty-four hours ago, he would never have recognized the woman in the photo. But he knew her now. Had seen her on Sheriff Davis's phone that morning.

The woman in the photo with Lily was the dead woman in the dumpster.

CHAPTER 19

LILY

The way Iver stared at that picture told Lily he did know Abby. Where was she now? The look on Iver's face made Lily terrified to ask him. She touched her neck, fingered the tender flesh to assess the damage. Someone had attacked her, right here in Iver's house. She tried to recollect the details of her attacker. The jolt of electricity, the strange texture under her fingers, the smell of cigarette smoke. Tim Bailey had smelled like smoke, but there was something else to the smell. When she'd started to black out, an image had come to her. Blonde hair splayed across the snow, a beautiful face, lifeless. She pressed her hands to her throat and looked up to see Iver staring at her.

He ran a hand across his mouth, blinking hard. "Did I do that?"

She looked down.

"Your neck," he said. "It's . . ."

She fingered the skin. It felt hot to the touch, welts like ridges.

Iver set the photograph on the table and sank into a chair across from her before dropping his face in his hands. "Christ. What happened?"

She tried to remember the details. "I read the sign on the door and came in. I was in the bathroom when the lights went out. The dog started barking, so I came out, and he grabbed me . . ."

"Who?" Iver's eyes were wide with fear and something else. Hope? "I swear, I don't remember touching your neck. I heard Cal barking and ran up the street. The house was dark, and I saw a figure." He looked at her. "You, under that blanket," he said. "Only you seemed bigger, and I ran toward you."

"It wasn't you. That man had a Taser. He smelled like cigarettes and . . ." She couldn't identify that other smell.

Iver stared at his hands. "I'm so sorry, Lily."

She watched him, sensing that the apology was bigger than this night. But she shook her head, too many thoughts winging through her mind. "You interrupted him," she said softly. "You saved me."

His gaze darted up to meet hers, scanning her face for signs of a lie. She could read how much he wanted it to be true. But then he broke eye contact and stood, looking around the room. "Who would have been here?"

She shook her head, unable to find a way to tell him all that had happened, all she had discovered about herself. She started to shiver, huddling in the blanket.

Iver rose from the chair and disappeared into the kitchen while she remained on the couch. What now? She had to go home, face her house, her life.

She'd pushed the blanket off, preparing to stand, when he returned with two mugs. He set one down in front of his chair and carried the other to her. He set it on the table and wrapped the blanket back across her shoulders where she sat on the living room couch. The house wasn't particularly cold, but she couldn't stop shivering. He squatted in front of her and offered the steaming liquid. She stared at his face, matching his features to the image on the front-hall table. He had nice hazel eyes and brown hair that, despite its buzz cut, seemed to have a mind of its own. When their gazes met, his smile was tentative, not quite reaching his eyes.

"What is happening?" he whispered.

She shook her head, unable to answer.

He lifted the mug again. "It's peppermint tea."

She let him put it into her hands, but her fingers trembled, hot liquid sloshing over the white ceramic edge, and he took it back. She gripped her hands together. She didn't know who she was. A man had attacked her. What was happening to her?

Her stomach heaved, and she stood, dropping the blanket from her shoulders. Pain seared through her ankle as she half hobbled, half ran to the bathroom. She vomited into the toilet, a thin stream of water and bile. When had she last eaten? More bile released in a second wave, and she waited for another.

When it didn't come, she wiped her mouth with toilet paper and flushed without moving from the toilet.

Instead, she laid her head on the arm that rested on the toilet seat, too ill to consider how dirty it might be. She deserved to be there, face in the toilet. She squeezed her eyes closed and swallowed through the tenderness in her throat.

The Lord is my rock, and my fortress, and my deliverer; my God, my strength, in whom I will trust; my buckler, and the horn of my salvation, and my high tower.

The door creaked open, and from the corner of her eye, she saw the dog nudge his way in. He approached her, sniffing, and after a short time, he settled onto the floor beside her.

She heard the water running in the sink, and Iver handed her a wet washcloth. "Thanks," she whispered, pressing it to her mouth. Then she lowered her head again and closed her eyes. She could sleep right there.

Iver removed the washcloth from her hand and wiped the edge of her face. "Feel better?"

"Yes," she said, trying to lift her head. But that meant facing what was happening, and it was so much easier just to rest there.

"I didn't mean to hurt you. I would never—" He cut himself off with a shake of his head.

"I know," she whispered. "You didn't hurt me, Iver."

He gave her a tight smile. "But you don't know that, not really."

"It feels like it's all I know," she told him. She thought of Tim Bailey, but he had smelled of Old Spice cologne and stale breath. Her attacker had smelled of something else, earthier. It was some sort of spice. What was it? Iver continued to stare at her, so she explained being in the bathroom, the lights, Cal's barking. When she'd finished, they were both quiet for a few minutes. It felt comfortable, safe.

"Why did you come here?" he asked.

A sound escaped her mouth without consent. A gasp, pitched high at the end. She lowered her face, pressed her palms to the heat in her cheeks.

"I mean, it's good to see you," he said quickly, "but it's unexpected. Which I guess is why I might've—" Again, he stopped talking.

She looked up. "The note. The one on the door."

From his expression, she understood the note was not for her.

She was not supposed to be here. Of course she wasn't. "I found your address in my Bible."

"Your Bible?"

She found her bag in the hallway, just outside the bathroom. Retrieving the Bible from inside, she handed it to him.

"I can't believe you still have this," he whispered, sitting back on his heels as he turned the book in his hands.

The Bible, the writing. It was a young person's writing, she realized now. "It's old."

Nodding, he handed the book back to her. "From before you were—" He halted, clenching his fists against his thighs as though fighting back anger.

"Before I was—"

"We were in the eighth grade," he said. "Confirmation class."

"Eighth grade." She squeezed her eyes closed. Half a lifetime ago. "We aren't friends now."

"Of course we are," he said, though the awkward tone of his voice revealed the lie.

"And my sister?"

Iver watched her before slowly shaking his head. "You're an only child. We both are." He touched her arm. "Are you okay?"

Where did she go from here? What was left? Her home. She could go there, find a key. There would be answers. She thought about the woman in the picture, the attack, the gun. Her memory of a man in a lake of blood. She could empty her bank accounts and run. Did she have savings? She was a woman who emptied an unconscious man's wallet and dated a married man with a small child. She put her face in her hands and squeezed her temples.

"Lily, tell me what's going on."

She stood and walked delicately to the sink. Running the water, she washed her face and drank from the faucet. Her stomach had settled. The discomfort now was in her chest, her neck. She wiped her hands on the towel, leaving the water on her face. "Thank you for helping me." She turned to the door, but Iver caught her hand, put the toilet lid down, and motioned for her to sit.

"You need to tell me what's going on, Lily."

Her eyes filled with tears, and she blinked in an effort to clear her vision. "When was the last time I saw you?"

Iver touched her arm. "What do you mean?"

"I—" She closed her mouth and sat down on the toilet seat, defeated.

"Lily, you're scaring me, and it's already been a scary day."

She narrowed her eyes. "Scary how?"

"You first," he said.

She said nothing.

He rose and shook his head. "If you won't tell me, I'm calling the police back in here, making them take you home."

"Please," she whispered. "I can't talk to the police."

"Then tell me what's going on," he demanded. "Why are you here?"

"I had nowhere else to go."

Iver held her gaze. "What the hell is happening?"

"I don't know, Iver. I don't know anything."

"But you know me," he said, his eyes searching hers. She looked away, and he touched her leg. "Don't you?"

A momentum built in her chest, a driving force that she couldn't contain. The words burst out of her. "I don't even know myself."

"What do you mean, you don't know yourself? Like you've done something you're ashamed of?"

That, too. She shook her head. "No. Like I don't know. I have no memory. Well, it's just images and fragments. When I saw you, I could remember bits of something. Walking home, that girl crying in the van—I remember that. I thought she was my sister. Abby."

She had other memories, ones that didn't make sense. After the accident, Lily had recalled standing in the snow with the other girl, Abby. Only Abby wasn't a girl. She was a woman. The two had huddled in the dark, frozen, as they listened to boots crunching through the snow. Someone was coming.

"Lily?"

She shook her head, unable to repeat those memories. "That's all I can remember. I only know my name because it was on my ID." She pulled out her wallet and withdrew the ID card.

His expression softened. "You have amnesia?"

"I guess."

"Since when?" He shook his head. "I mean, what is the first thing you remember?"

"Nothing. I woke up . . ." She wasn't ready to tell him about the car accident, about Brent. Was that her fault?

"You woke up . . . ," he prompted.

"And I had no memory." She shook her head. "But I still knew how to do things. Like how to check for concussion. I could remember the names of the tendons of the hand but not my name."

"They're different memory systems," Iver explained. "Declarative versus nondeclarative."

"Are you a doctor now?" she asked.

He smiled. "No. I've got firsthand experience after a brain injury in Afghanistan."

"You were in Afghanistan? The war?" He laughed, and she stared at him. "What's funny?"

His smile slid away. "You might be the only person in Hagen who doesn't know I was in Afghanistan."

"That must've been awful."

"It was."

They sat a moment in silence. Then Iver got up, left the bathroom, and returned after a moment with her mug of tea. She took it from his hand without comment, the smell of mint calming.

"Was there an accident?" he asked. "Do you remember?"

She thought about the car. It must have crashed through the guardrail before she'd woken, but was that serious enough to cause amnesia? She hadn't even realized that amnesia like this was a real thing outside of TV and movies. She couldn't remember ever watching a movie. She let go of his hand and cupped her face. "I don't know."

"It's okay," he said. "We'll figure it out. Do you remember anything?"

Lily shook her head. "But maybe Abby remembers." She had to remind herself that Abby wasn't her sister. But they were close; Lily could feel it. "I could talk to her."

Iver made a sound like he'd been punched. "Oh."

"Do you know where she is?" she asked, an uneven thumping in her throat.

"We should really speak to the police," he said.

"Why? What did she do?"

"She didn't do anything, Lily. She was murdered last night."

Lily closed her eyes and pictured the face in the image. Murdered.

The warm tea in her mug spilled over the edge onto her thumb. The floor was shaking. Then she realized the trembling was in her hands. Iver took the mug from her as the vibrations shuddered through her limbs, the panic building in her chest. She had been attacked in this house. A man had tried to kill her. And her friend was already dead.

Someone wanted her dead. He hadn't been successful tonight, but surely, he would try again.

CHAPTER 20

KYLIE

The call on Kylie's radio came in as she was approaching town, her headlights cutting a swath through the dark and reflecting on the falling snow. It was Marjorie at Dispatch requesting Patrol at an address on Fourth Street. "Woman attacked in the home. Sullivan and Damonza are there now." A woman attacked in her home in downtown Hagen. Damn. What the hell was happening to Hagen? Such a quiet little pissant of a town. Until now.

Kylie dialed the station. "Heard the call on the attack. You have an address?"

"416 Fourth Street. Name's Larson."

"Iver Larson?"

"One and the same."

Kylie popped the knuckles of one hand and took a left, heading toward Larson's side of town. "Interesting."

"And I got an anonymous call about thirty minutes ago—woman saw Iver Larson driving in town last night, around two a.m."

"Any idea who Anonymous is?"

"Nope. Called from a burner phone, if you can believe that. Actually, both these last two calls came from burners."

"Same burner?"

"No. Different numbers—one a woman, one a man."

Burner phones in Hagen. Maybe she didn't know sleepy little Hagen as well as she thought. "Okay, I'm heading over to Larson's."

Kylie navigated the quiet streets until she reached Iver Larson's address. Patrol officer Larry Sullivan sat in his cruiser in front of Larson's, his face illuminated by the car's interior light, and Kylie parked on the curb behind him. A text from Amber came in as she was getting out of her patrol car.

Sarah Ollman was in the bar that night. That's why no pics.

Kylie stared at the name. Tobias Ollman was pastor of the Lutheran church. His daughter, Sarah, was in high school. If her father found out she'd been in the bar . . . Kylie glanced at the clock. It was only seven p.m. She'd have to pay Sarah a visit after she got some answers from Larson.

Sullivan rolled the window down as she approached.

"What happened?" she asked.

"Someone called in a fight. Woman looks pretty beat up, but she's not pressing charges. Power was off at the main, and Larson's saying there were some boots tracks in the backyard, like someone else attacked her. But we only found the two of them inside. No sign of anyone else."

Kylie studied the house. "Larson is there?"

Sullivan nodded. "He's there, all right."

She patted the top of the car. "I'm going to go in for a little chat."

"You want company?"

She shook her head. "Thanks, though."

When Iver Larson opened the door, his eyes narrowed at the sight of her. Fine. They weren't going to be friends. Across the room, a woman came out of the bathroom, her eyes red, her skin sallow and bruised. She looked like hell. But she also looked vaguely familiar.

Kylie entered the house without asking for permission. "You should have someone look at your injuries."

With a quick glance at Larson, the woman shook her head. "I'm fine."

"You were attacked. You should be looked at by a medical professional."

"I am a medical professional."

"We've already answered all of these questions," Larson interrupted. "And Lily has said she's fine. You should leave."

"Lily?" Kylie repeated, remembering where she'd seen that face, though a much younger version. "Lily Baker?"

The woman looked terrified. "Yes."

"You know that Abigail Jensen was killed last night?"

Neither one spoke.

"The woman in the dumpster," Kylie said to Larson. "Her name was Abigail Jensen. Does that name sound familiar, Iver?"

"No."

Baker said nothing.

Kylie turned to Baker. "She was one of the girls who was taken when you were. You must know the name."

Baker shifted her gaze to Larson.

"Iver?" Kylie prompted, wondering what was going on there. Why wasn't Baker reacting?

Larson rubbed his face. "I didn't recognize her from back then."

Even from four feet away, she could smell the alcohol on him. "You've been drinking?"

"What does it matter?"

"I'm just wondering if alcohol is the trigger that makes you violent."

"I'm not violent," Larson said, the cut of his jaw more pronounced as he clenched it. He rubbed his face.

Kylie scanned the room. "Broke a picture frame. Looks like it got a little rough."

"Someone was in the house," Baker said from across the room, her arms wrapped around herself. "He attacked me. Iver saved me."

She nodded, and Kylie noticed the way she glanced at Larson again.

"There were boot prints in back," Larson said. "I showed them to Sullivan."

"Boot prints?"

"Fresh tracks in the snow that don't match my tread. I can show you—" Larson took two steps and halted. "They'll be gone now, but they were there. You can ask him."

"So someone broke in and attacked Ms. Baker here, in your home?"

"I think so," Larson said.

There was something unexpectedly earnest in Iver's expression. Either he really believed someone else might have been there, or he wanted to believe it so badly he'd almost convinced himself. "Someone knew you were here?" she asked Baker.

Baker hesitated and shook her head. "Maybe. I don't know."

Kylie turned back to Larson. "Is there someone who would want to hurt you?"

He blinked as though in surprise. "No."

"The front door was unlocked?"

"Yes. My mom was supposed to come by." He seemed to only now remember his mother.

"Is it common for her to show up when you're not home?"

"My mom?" he asked.

"No, Ms. Baker."

He shook his head without looking at Baker. "No."

"You two aren't dating?" Kylie asked.

"No." He crossed his arms, and she made a note of the reaction. "Old friends."

"Does it seem weird that she was attacked in your house?"

"Very."

"You two had plans tonight?"

"No."

"You weren't expecting her?"

"No."

"You might want to be more forthcoming, Mr. Larson. In the past twenty-four hours, you've been in the same place where two women were attacked. One of them is dead. And it looks like Lily Baker was on her way."

Larson straightened up and uncrossed his arms. "I am being forthcoming. I don't know anything."

"Sullivan told me that the power was cut off to the house. Pitch black. Ms. Baker never saw her attacker. Could have been anyone . . . but when the officers arrived, it was just you and her on the floor."

Larson said nothing, the muscle in his jaw a knot beneath his ear.

"Odds seem to suggest the attacker was you," Kylie said.

Larson clenched his fists. "Why would I want to hurt her? Why would I want to hurt either of them?"

Larson had said they weren't dating, but there was something there, strained and awkward.

Baker stood motionless, watching Larson. Was Baker afraid of Larson? Or dependent on him? He'd said they were only friends. Why, then, were their interactions so strange?

"It's almost like someone's coming after Hudson's survivors—first Jensen, then you," Kylie said, studying Baker's expression. "Any reason you can think of for that?"

"No," Larson said.

"You don't seem to have much to say, Ms. Baker. Your fellow hostage was killed, and then you were attacked. Mr. Larson at the scene both times." When Baker said nothing, Kylie added, "You do remember Abigail Jensen, don't you?"

"Of course she does," Larson said, an edge to his voice. "You know what they went through together. You don't need to ask that."

Baker said nothing, her focus on her hands, as though she were translating from a language she rarely spoke.

"I do," Kylie said, turning her attention back to Baker. "In fact, I was trying to reach you earlier today to talk about Abigail Jensen. Was she staying with you? It didn't seem like she knew anyone else in town."

"It's been a long night, Detective," Larson interrupted. "Maybe you could ask your questions tomorrow."

"A woman is dead, Mr. Larson."

Baker shook her head. "I really don't feel up to talking tonight."

Kylie wanted to scream. She didn't feel up to talking? A woman had been murdered and thrown in a dumpster. Lily had been attacked. Kylie didn't give a shit that she didn't feel up to talking. But what could she do? There were no grounds to arrest Larson, not if Baker wouldn't press charges. Kylie drew a slow, steady breath. "Just one more question for you, Mr. Larson," Kylie said.

Iver nodded.

"You said you left the bar at about ten thirty last night, and then you were here, alone, for the rest of the night?"

He licked his lips, and she wanted to pounce on him. She knew he'd been lying, the bastard. What else had he lied about? There had to be something going on between him and Baker, too. Had he threatened her? Was she being held against her will?

She poised her pen. "Is that still your statement?"

"I—"

The room hummed with tension. She could almost hear the low bass of it, a tap tap tap in the background of the quiet.

"He wasn't alone," Baker said.

Larson looked at her, surprise on his face.

Baker kept her gaze on Kylie as she moved across the room toward Larson. "I was here," she said.

"You were here last night?" Kylie asked.

"Yes."

"Really?" Kylie glanced between Larson and Baker, waiting for one of them to crack. Was this the thing he'd been lying about? The fact that they were together? People were so stupid. But it seemed like there was more. "What time did you get here?"

"About eight, I think. I fell asleep at some point, but I woke up when he got home."

"And what time was that?"

"I didn't look at the clock," she said.

"So it could have been three in the morning?"

"I left the bar around ten thirty," Iver said. "I already told you that this morning."

Kylie thought about the anonymous call that Iver had been driving around town at two in the morning. She wasn't ready to play that card just yet.

Baker squeezed his arm. "I think I need to lie down."

Without giving Kylie the chance to ask anything else, Baker retreated down the hallway.

"Whatever you're not telling me is going to get you in a shitload of trouble, Larson."

"I've told you everything I know," Larson said. "You can let yourself out."

CHAPTER 21

LILY

Lily Baker sat on the floor of Iver's bedroom, her back to the bed, and stared at the blank wall beside the door. A handful of smudges and two dents were the only decoration on the smooth surface. She imagined Iver walking his hands along the wall in the dark as he made his way to the door. Or carrying something heavy—moving a piece of furniture or a box—and knocking a corner into the paint. She studied the marks with her full attention as she pushed away the questions that spiked her blood like adrenaline and set her pulse racing, its percussion vibrating in her teeth.

Hostages. The detective had said something about hostages. She and Abby. About someone named Hudson. And Tim knew about the scars and where they had come from. What had happened to her?

The sounds of the others talking in the living room had gone quiet. There was only the occasional creak of the house settling in the cold, the distant clicking of Cal's nails on the hardwood floor. She wasn't sure how long she'd been sitting there, unmoving, when a quiet knock on the door startled her.

"Lily?" Iver entered the room and approached slowly. "Are you okay?"

Her fingers found the fresh injuries on her neck. The skin burned at her touch, a tacky sensation on her fingers.

"You're bleeding." He reached for her hand and pulled it away. "Let me get something to clean it." Without waiting for her response, he crossed to the bathroom and returned with a handful of cotton balls and a bottle of rubbing alcohol. "I don't have any hydrogen peroxide."

"It's okay," she said, the words like a dull knife in her throat.

"The cuts on your neck are bleeding, probably from—" Iver went silent.

"His hands," she whispered.

The sound that came from Iver was almost a growl as he settled onto the floor beside her. He drenched the cotton balls in alcohol, the sharp smell filling her nose as he took hold of her chin to tilt her head and dab the cuts on her neck. She felt a brief flash of cold and pain and the warmth of his fingers, and her stomach rolled as the touch brought back the moments of being on that floor with that man on top of her, his hands tight on her throat.

"Done," he said.

"Thank you."

"Are you okay?"

She met his gaze. "I'm not even sure I know what okay is."

Iver nodded. "I know that feeling."

She folded her legs up to her chest and wrapped her arms around them, pressing her cheek on one knee.

"Do you want to know about it?"

She looked up at him. "About . . . ?"

"What happened to you back then?"

Her breath caught at the back of her mouth. The van. She had crawled in to be with Abby, to calm her down. Lily, too, had been upset that night, angry at Iver. They'd had an argument, but she couldn't remember the details. She searched her memories for anything else from that time, from the months that followed. It was all blank.

Iver drew a long, slow breath and began to talk. "When I got home from Afghanistan, I couldn't remember the accident. I remembered the Humvee stopping and then nothing until I woke up in the back of a chopper. I was told that an IED had detonated and that the others had died. But I didn't know any of the details, and I couldn't remember it.

"I was a mess—the pain didn't help—but the not knowing felt worse. A couple of weeks into my stay at the veterans' hospital in Nebraska, a soldier from my unit came through. He'd taken a sniper bullet through the leg. But he knew the details. He told me about that day, about the other guys—the ones who died. As hard as it was to hear, it was a relief, too. To know."

"Iver, what happened to me?"

He looked away and drew a deep breath, as though steeling himself. Sitting down on the floor beside her, he reached for his laptop. A moment passed as he studied her face as though trying to decide. "Maybe it will be easiest if you find out by reading about it."

With a curt nod from her, Iver opened the laptop and launched a search. He shifted the computer so it sat between them, and together, they read in silence. It was like learning about a stranger. Her own abduction, her time with Derek Hudson, her escape. Details of their injuries, that she and the others had been hospitalized and received medical and mental health treatment—all of it covered in a few thousand words. The stories had been printed in a dozen papers, but the information was largely the same.

Sixteen months of her life in a prison. Because Hudson had been killed, little was known about what had actually occurred during their captivity, only what had leaked about the three surviving girls. Cuts that covered sections of their backs, small wounds that had been repeatedly opened. Lily could feel the little ridges in the dark on her right shoulder. "Like the other cuts," Tim Bailey had said, then stopped. Because she didn't like to talk about those. She didn't like to talk about them because they'd been made by a man who'd tortured her and done who knew what else.

She wanted her memories back, but did she want to remember those months? Did she want to remember exactly how those scars on her back had been made? Or the moment she'd shot the man responsible? She had survived. Wasn't that enough? But now Abby was dead. And the third girl? Where was she?

Iver beside her, Lily read everything she could find about Derek Hudson and the escape the police had called daring. She read the relieved statements from the parents—other parents. Her mother had already died, she learned from the articles. Her father—reclusive and stoic, even in light of what had happened to her—was never quoted.

When she'd read every article, scrolled through the internet trolls and their foul and often cruel commentary, Lily shut the laptop, and she and Iver spoke about their friendship. Iver told her about the church group, about their afternoons and evenings together. And then, when he brought up the night she'd been taken, he fell silent. He shook his head and went to get her a glass of water. Lily listened to the sounds of the house and waited. Because she felt certain that whatever was happening to her wasn't over. There was more coming. The universe was not done with its punishment.

Her mind spun in circles, trying to make sense of what was happening, of what she had done. She had lied to protect Iver. Why had she done that? Because he'd taken her into his home. Or let her come. Because she'd told him the truth about her amnesia. Because she had to trust someone, and his name was in her Bible.

And he hadn't told the detective about her lost memory.

A talebearer revealeth secrets: but he that is of a faithful spirit concealeth the matter. Where no counsel is, the people fall: but in the multitude of counsellors there is safety.

Iver set the water glass on the coaster on his bedside table and began to tidy his room. The slight furrow in his brow made him look thoughtful, cautious, as he folded the clothes that had been discarded on the floor and chair and returned his shoes to the closet, where the others made neat lines on the floor. She had trusted him once. He had been her best friend. What kind of man had he become?

CHAPTER 22

LILY

Lily had been certain she wouldn't sleep, not with those words in her head. But she must have, because when she opened her eyes, daylight shone through the window, and the smell of coffee wafted down the hall. She found Iver in the kitchen, and he poured her a cup of coffee, set it in front of her. She wondered if she liked coffee. Or maybe everyone was supposed to drink it, like it or not.

He stood at the refrigerator, frowning. "You want to try it with cream and sugar? Or just black?"

"This is fine," she said, though she made no move to drink it.

Iver sat beside her as though waiting. What did he expect? That she'd read those horrible articles and would break down or scream or cry? She still had no memory of any of it past the moment when she had climbed into that van with Abby. Or maybe he was waiting for something else. There was something she couldn't shake. He had been kind to her. He'd let her sleep in his room. He had saved her.

She thought about the man who had attacked her the night before. Her arms pinned by his knees, his hands on her neck. She rose from the table in a rush of emotion—anger or fear or some combination. But then she stared at the kitchen and realized there was nowhere to go. She sank again. "The man who did that—Hudson—he was killed." That one memory was clear in her mind—the man in the puddle of blood, the gun in her hand. "I killed him . . . ," she said, her voice trailing off.

"That's not your fault. You were escaping. He deserved to die, Lily."

"Then who was trying to kill me?" She turned to him. "Who killed Abby?"

Iver stood and refilled his coffee cup.

She remembered the bit of newspaper she'd found. She stood and dug into her pocket. "There was a scrap of newspaper." She could have sworn it was in her front right pocket. But there was nothing there. She searched one and then the other. All her pockets were empty. She went to the living room and looked through the pockets of her bag.

"What scrap?" Iver asked from behind her.

"It said something about a second suspect." She pressed her fingers to her forehead and tried to remember where she'd put it. "The police suspected there was someone else involved. I thought it meant me . . ."

"You? Why would you be a suspect?"

She shook her head. She couldn't explain the gun, the memory of that dead man. She had asked too much of him already. They barely knew each other now. She thought about the articles they'd read. She hadn't seen anything about a second suspect. Where had that come from?

"Like maybe Hudson had a partner the police never found?" Iver asked.

"Maybe."

But why come back now? After ten years? And why would she lose her memory on the same night that Abby was killed?

"I should probably take you home," Iver said.

And with those six words—words that should have brought comfort—a whole new wave of fear tucked her tightly in its fold.

CHAPTER 23

KYLIE

Kylie Milliard shivered in the cold air outside Skål while Hagen's amateur crime scene team swept the inside. Only the two men were allowed inside, per Vogel's orders. Kylie wondered sometimes if Vogel got his ideas from 1970s cop show reruns.

She cupped her hands around the insulated coffee mug, as though she might draw heat through the plastic. The coffee inside was still hot, but she'd already burned her tongue once. Lifting the cup, she covered her face to hide another yawn.

Stomping her feet to fight off the cold, Kylie scanned her inbox from her phone, going straight for the email from Gary Ross: information from the Hudson investigation. The email address wasn't his FBI one. Maybe he wasn't supposed to be sharing these files. Well, she wouldn't tell if he didn't.

She clicked on the email and opened the attachments. One showed the current prison record for Damian Hudson. She opened it and read the details. Derek Hudson's older brother had gone to prison in 2006 for a third-strike battery charge and had been inside ever since. She closed the file and scanned the other attachments. She clicked a zip file labeled *Scene Photos* to download and then started the file extraction. The estimated time was ten minutes. That was a lot of damn photos and a lot of data usage. She clicked it again to stop the download. It would have to wait until she was at her desk.

She wanted to get over to visit the pastor's daughter today as well. When she'd driven by after leaving Larson's, the house was dark, and waking the pastor up to tell him that his daughter had been in a bar when a woman was murdered didn't feel like a smart choice. Kylie was still turning over the conversation with Baker and Larson in her head. What were they hiding? If Larson had killed Jensen and then attacked Baker, why would she protect him? It made no sense.

Her phone buzzed in her hand, disrupting her thoughts. A call from the 584 prefix, same as the Elgin deputy she'd spoken to before. "Hello?"

"Detective Milliard, please?" came a man's voice.

"This is she," Kylie said.

"Glad to talk to you," the voice said, and Kylie always felt a moment of relief when there was no commentary on her being a detective and a woman. Maybe she'd overreacted to the whole "I am woman, hear me roar" thing. She was sure Vogel would agree. As would most of her ex-boyfriends. Okay, all of her ex-boyfriends.

"I'm Sheriff Oloff, calling from Elgin. I believe your department spoke this morning to my deputy."

Kylie stood up straighter, feeling that rush that always came with making a new contact in a case. "We did."

"Sorry I didn't call you earlier. I just got back from Florida. Got out of the cold to thaw the bones, but I came back home as soon as I heard about Abby. My current deputy doesn't know much about Derek Hudson, as he was in grade school when Jensen was taken. I was a deputy when Jensen disappeared, and I'd just been elected sheriff when they were found. Jensen and the other girls, that is."

"Jensen's family has lived in Elgin all these years, right?"

"Yes. Her mother is still here. Father passed a few years back. Tammy—that's Abby's mother—Tammy tried real hard with Abby. She was never the same after Hudson."

"Sure," Kylie said.

"There were drugs and a series of boyfriends, nasty guys. Tammy got Abby into rehab twice—once as a resident at a school in Washington that seemed promising. But when she came home, she started dating some other jerk, and pretty soon, she was back on the drugs. It was a cycle for her—the boys and the drugs. She'd get clean, and then one of those guys would come back into the picture."

"Any of them around recently?"

"Not sure," Oloff said. "Tammy thought she had a new boyfriend the past few months, but she didn't know his name. Abby had been doing better, actually." He sighed. "She was working at Resting Peak, the local nursing home. I spoke with the director over there last night. He said Abby was doing real well, was liked. But then she'd up and quit back in early December. After that, Abby sort of fell off the map."

"Did she meet someone in her job? Another of the staff there?"

"I asked, and the director didn't think so. It's mostly older ladies who work up there. Tammy reached out a few times after Abby quit her job, but Abby never responded. Tammy thought she was still in town. Truth is, Abby's second round of rehab almost bankrupted Tammy, and she had to step back. Course, she blames herself now."

Kylie knew the pattern. Tammy could no more have saved Abby Jensen than Kylie could have. "But no one knew who the new boyfriend was?"

"No," Oloff said. "And he probably didn't live in town. We're doing some rounds, talking to some of her regular crowd—kids she went to school with—but from what we've learned so far, Abby distanced herself from most of her friends right about the time this new guy came into the picture."

"If Abby quit her job, what was she doing for money?" Kylie asked.

"No idea," Oloff said. "Landlord said she paid rent for December in cash and said she'd be out by January first."

"And her mother had no idea she was leaving town?"

"None." Oloff sighed again. "If you've got more questions, I can give you Tammy's number, but you can imagine she's not in a great place."

"I don't need to bother her. But if you learn anything about the new boyfriend or what she was planning to do after January first . . ."

"You'll be my first call," he promised, and they said their goodbyes.

A moment later, the door to Skål opened, and Doug Smith emerged, carrying an ActionPacker the department used to hold collected evidence.

"Anything of interest?" she asked, nodding to the box as she followed him toward his truck.

"Not much," Smith said. "A bar glass we found in one of the desk drawers in the office." He reached into the back of the SUV and flipped open the plastic slats that formed the box's top. A moment later, he pulled out a plastic sack containing a dirty bar glass.

She was about to ask why they had collected it when she saw that the base of the glass was coated with a layer that looked like chalk. Some sort of drug residue? More likely it was something benign, undissolved antacid, perhaps. It wouldn't surprise her at all to learn that Iver Larson had digestive issues in addition to the mental ones. "That'll have to go to the crime lab in Bismarck," she said. "Can we get it out today?"

"Yep," Smith answered.

"Great," Kylie said, but she didn't feel great. She'd been antsy to get inside that bar, but maybe that had been a mistake. What had she been expecting them to find? A pair of women's shoes? A bloody shirt? For all her pushing, all they had to show for it was a single glass.

She returned to her cruiser and started the engine, shivering as the heater blew frigid air in her face. As she was putting the car in drive, her phone rang. She recognized the number as internal to the department.

"Milliard," she answered, shifting back into park.

"It's Steve," Cannon said. "Just got back from the garage."

She tilted the vent so the freezing air wasn't blowing in her face. "The garage?"

"Yeah. Davis had me pull the prints off Nolan's car, since both the crime scene guys are out at the bar."

"Did you get a match?"

Cannon let out a satisfied laugh. "As a matter of fact, I did."

CHAPTER 24

IVER

Iver had helped Lily Baker gain access to her house. Without a key, they'd had to find an unlocked window and pry it open. Once she was safely inside, he'd had felt an urge to follow, but it was a mixed desire. Part of him had also wanted to drop her off and drive away. But sitting in his bathroom with Lily, feeling her terror echoing inside him like a familiar song, he'd realized she might be the only person who knew what it felt like for him to return to Hagen after all those months in hospitals, not knowing if he would ever be the same.

How could he walk away from that? Why would he walk away?

Iver had intended to go to the bar from her house, but a voicemail had let him know the police were in the bar, exercising a warrant. The call had come in at eight, so the bar might be cleared out by now. To be safe, he'd give it another hour.

To pass the time, Iver went to the gas station and filled the truck, bought a car wash, and took his time driving through. Cal was not a fan and whined the whole way, so Iver turned up the Eric Church album and pulled Cal's head into his lap to distract him from the strange purple foam covering the windows.

The purple foam was new. Used to be plain old white. In Hagen, a new foam color in the car wash was progress. With a few layers of mud off the truck, Iver stopped by the feed shop for dog food and bought Cal a dried pig ear for being so brave. As he moved through the store, a few folks stopped to say hello, mostly old-timers who'd known his dad, many of them vets as well. More often than not, folks his own age avoided him.

Iver had never imagined he would end up back in Hagen. While he was in Afghanistan, it had made sense for Debbie to stay near her parents and the friends she'd known all her life, but they had wanted an adventure. Once he was out of the army, they'd planned to go somewhere new, where he could get his bachelor's degree, care of the US government. They would find jobs they loved, buy a little house, and start a family. A little life. That was all he'd ever wanted. Keep things simple—be happy.

But then he'd had a brain injury.

And the thing he'd wanted most after that was to find a way to stop the pain. That had become his whole life, and when his dad had passed, the bar became a natural way to afford a life filled with prescription medications and doctors' visits.

In the past six or seven years, he'd hardly thought of Lily Baker. Even when she'd returned to town after her father's death and moved into his house, they'd never spoken. So many years had passed, and their friendship had been cracked, the way a tree cracked the pavement. Other things had grown in the crevice—her abduction, most obviously, but then her move, his marriage, his time in Afghanistan, and his brain injury. They'd each had something stolen from them that they would never get back.

No. He couldn't compare the two. He had chosen to go to Afghanistan. She'd had no such choice.

Seeing her huddled in his house the night before had made him realize how her disappearance, and his part in it, had impacted him. He'd bottled the guilt and turned it into a kind of molten self-hatred that had never really left him. Then her father had died, and she'd returned to Hagen.

Spending time with her brought him back to when they were in the eighth grade. Lily had wanted to be a dancer. He'd had a dream like that once, but he couldn't remember what it was. Was that the brain injury, or was that life, saving him from the disappointment that he'd never achieve that dream?

Suddenly, he wished he hadn't left her alone at her house this morning. And he had no way to reach her. He would go by later. He considered heading that way, but where he would have turned left to head toward Lily's place, he turned right instead, toward the bar, as though the truck had a mind of its own. He would drive by, he thought. In case the police were still there.

The empty lot brought a wave of relief, which vanished almost immediately when he parked. There was a single dark sedan on the far side of the lot. As he got out, a patrol officer emerged from the car and retrieved a small toolbox from his backseat. "Hey, Iver."

Carl Gilbert. Iver recognized him now, a swagger in his step that the skinny, pimple-faced kid had never had in high school. "Hey, Carl. Thought you guys were all done here."

"I need to collect from your truck."

"My truck?"

"DA issued a warrant for it." Carl shifted the toolbox and pulled a folded paper from his inside pocket.

"That's okay," Iver said, waving it off as he helped Cal down from the cab. "Go ahead and take a look. I was just heading into the bar."

"I won't take too long," Carl said, and Iver didn't respond. Carl approached the truck. "Looks clean."

"Yeah. Took it to the car wash this morning."

Carl studied Iver with one brow raised. "You usually wash your car in the dead of winter?"

Iver stared back. "I wash it when it's dirty."

"Can't wash away everything, Iver."

135

Go to hell, Iver thought as he called out to Cal and entered the bar. He had no desire to be there, but he had enough to do for an hour while Gilbert poked around his truck. He had to reconcile the books and sign off on the payroll so that everyone got paid.

He turned his key in the lock, stepped in, and was surprised to find Mike standing behind the bar, breaking down a cardboard box. Iver looked back at the lot. "Where's your truck?"

Mike looked momentarily startled, as though he'd forgotten about his truck. "Oh," he said, turning his attention back to the box. "It's been acting up."

"Bummer," Iver said and nodded toward the parking lot. "Carl Gilbert's out there searching mine."

Mike's eyes went wide. "Really? How come?"

Iver paused. Actually, he didn't know why they were searching his truck. And if they were, why not Mike's, too? Why not everyone's? He forced a shrug. "No big deal," he said and hoped Mike couldn't hear the tremor in his voice.

"Sure," Mike said. "Just a reminder that I'm off for three days," he added as Iver started to walk away. "Leaving town this afternoon."

Iver looked at him. "Sure."

"I told you a few weeks ago. Just taking a few days off, driving down to Denver."

"Thought your truck was acting up."

Mike's face grew flushed. "It's getting fixed," he said a moment later.

Had Mike told him that he was going away? Iver couldn't remember. "What's in Denver?"

"Just going to check it out," he said.

Iver used to go to Denver once or twice a year. His ex-wife's brother lived there. "Okay," Iver said. "Anything we need to catch up on before you go?" As soon as the words were out, he regretted them. He didn't want to catch up.

There was an awkward pause. "You mean about the other night?" Mike asked.

That wasn't what Iver had meant. He'd been referring to running the bar while Mike was gone.

When Iver didn't respond, Mike went on. "We can talk about it, if you want."

"Sure," Iver said. But he was anything but sure.

"You were pretty pissed," Mike said.

His father had used that word talking about customers who were drunk. Was that what Mike meant? That Iver had been drunk? Or did he mean that Iver had been angry? "Yeah."

"Yeah," Mike repeated.

"We don't need to talk about it now, do we?" Iver's voice caught on the last word. *You should ask. Find out what you did. It's better to know.* But maybe it wasn't better to know. At least now he could honestly say he didn't know what he had done. He had no memory of it. *If* he'd done something. The image of the dead girl on Davis's phone flashed in his mind.

Mike frowned. "I guess not."

A wave of fear rose like a tsunami inside Iver's chest. "I mean, it's not life or death, right?" The words shook as they came from his lips.

"Sure," Mike said slowly, eyeing him.

Iver pressed his fingers against his temple, though he had no headache. "I'm going to take care of that paperwork and get out of here." He started for the office.

Inside, his office was a mess. The drawers stood open; the desk and floor were littered with papers. Smudges of black dust coated the windowsill and the edge of the desk. The police had done a number in there. He looked around for a blank space or a missing piece of furniture, some obvious clue that suggested they'd found the evidence they needed to convict him of murder. But there was no break in the chaos. That fact did nothing to make him feel better.

Wouldn't they have come for him already?

Again came the rush of fear.

He scooped up the scattered papers and tossed them into an empty Stoli box, then added the cash register tapes from the last few nights and the calendar on his desk. He had no plan to come back to this place today or even tomorrow. Kevin could run the bar while Mike was gone.

Or he'd close it down for a few nights. He no longer cared. It was time to sell the damn thing. It had been time for years.

There was the roar of a diesel truck in the parking lot. Out the small office window, he could see the passenger side of the cab. Mike's truck was idling in the parking lot. The horn honked, and a moment later, Mike jogged up to the truck, opened the door, and climbed into the passenger seat. In the driver's seat was a silhouette—a woman, from the narrow shoulders. Mike never let anyone drive his truck.

As Mike turned for the seat belt, Iver caught sight of the huge grin on his friend's face. Something about it made Iver feel a little sick.

CHAPTER 25

——

LILY

To gain access to her own home, Lily Baker had crawled through a window in the kitchen. Iver had helped wedge the old window open, using a box cutter to carve through the thick layers of paint that had made it stick. Once in the kitchen, she had unlocked the back door for him. But Iver hadn't entered. Instead, he'd looked around the room and said, "I should let you have some time alone."

The words had filled her with terror. *Alone.*

"Sure," she'd said, following his gaze back into the kitchen—her kitchen. A trash can overflowed. Plates were scattered across the table and in the sink. An empty bottle of Smirnoff lay on its side on the floor, and a pizza box sat half-open on the stove. It was a mess.

She'd said goodbye and started to close the back door, as though shutting it quickly enough could block out what he had already seen.

"I'll check in later," he had promised.

And then she was alone. She turned slowly in the room, wishing she could be anywhere else. How was this *her* house? How did she live like this?

In the center of the table was a small Ziploc bag, empty except for a thin film of white powder. She put a finger in the residue and brought it toward her mouth, only realizing what she was doing as her lips parted. She crossed to the sink and washed her hands, rinsed out the bag.

She paced the dirty kitchen, repeating the words *my house* in her head. Her clothes and pictures would be in other rooms, but she couldn't bring herself to leave the kitchen. She looked around for a radio, something that might fill the room with noise. But there was nothing. Other than the trash and dirty dishes, the only thing on the counter was a filthy coffee maker, an inch of dark sludge in the glass pot.

This was her life.

She fought the desire to sink onto the ground and bury her head in her hands. To walk out and never come back. Instead, she tossed the bottle and the pizza box in the trash and tied the bag closed before putting it outside the back door.

She filled the sink with soapy water and left the dishes and the coffeepot to soak, then wiped down the counters with soapy water and a dish towel. Then she faced the rest of the house, fighting off the desire to simply leave and return to Iver's.

She missed Cal. A momentary fear hit her that maybe she'd had a pet. She made a round of the house, barely looking at the spaces except to search for some living creature. But there was nothing living here.

Not even a plant.

The front bedroom was large, with a closet. Her room, she guessed from its lived-in appearance. The covers were dingy, the bed unmade, its sheets shoved to the center as though there had been occupants on both sides. Water glasses on the two bedside tables. Someone had slept beside her, but who? Surely not Tim. How would he have gotten away from his family for a whole night? Was it Abby? Like some sort of sleepover?

There were no images on the walls, no pictures. Shivering, she pulled open a dresser drawer and found underwear and bras, ugly things, utilitarian and dingy. In one corner of the drawer was a small plastic bag with two white pills in it. Nearby was an empty prescription bottle, the label pulled off. Similar bags littered the nightstand.

Moving through the rooms, she surveyed the house as though she were a guest. It was small—one story with a tight living room. What must have once been the dining room had been walled off to form a second bedroom. From the crown molding and the cracked walls, it had been done decades ago. A bed occupied the middle of the room, still made. An inexpensive-looking melamine bureau stood in one corner, its door cracked open. A small duffel sat on the floor, contents spilling onto the floor.

She sank beside it. The thin nylon bag was cheap and ripped along the zipper. Slowly, she unpacked the clothes, fighting off the sensation that she was invading someone's privacy. Did a dead woman have privacy? *This is your house,* she thought. But these weren't her things.

At the bottom of the bag was an orange prescription bottle in the name of Tammy Jensen. Abby's mother. She stared at the name. How did she remember that Tammy was Abby's mother? But she did remember. *Hydrocodone,* the side of the bottle read. It, too, was empty. She wondered if the pills in her bedroom were hydrocodone, knew as she had known how to perform CPR on Brent Nolan that hydrocodone was a painkiller and a strong one. The kind people got addicted to.

Abby's things. Abby had been staying here. And now she was dead.

Exhaustion settled over Lily as she returned to her own bedroom.

She needed a shower and sleep. Scanning the bright room, she wondered if it was safe to sleep here. Would the man from Iver's house come for her in the middle of the day? Surely it was too risky. She wished she had Cal with her, someone to alert her to trouble.

But she was alone.

She scanned the filthy surfaces, the piles of laundry, the shoes strewn everywhere. Now she noticed dirty tissues on the floor beside her bed. Who lived like this?

You do.

Lily stripped the bed and remade it with clean sheets she found in a hall closet. She started a load of laundry and forced herself into the shower, scrubbing quickly while keeping one ear out for trouble. Her fingers grazed the thin raised scars on the back of her right shoulder, and her stomach clenched as though she might be sick. She worked faster with the sensation that a threat was approaching and she had to rush before she was caught.

Emerging from the hot water, though, she felt calmer, almost sedate. She put on fresh clothes from her drawer—loose-fitting sweatpants and a long-sleeved T-shirt—and checked every door and window in the house before climbing into bed.

She wouldn't sleep. She just needed to spend some time off her ankle, rest her eyes. Her body was heavy, the bed soft and, perhaps in some recesses of her mind, also familiar.

The music had the raspy beat of a bad speaker. It came from a cell phone on the center of the kitchen table. Abby danced around the room, her head swaying and her hips cocking and her eyes already glazed and half-lidded. But it was okay because the smile on her face was real. And Lily should know. How many times had she seen the fake twist of lips that Abby had worn to appease him?

Between songs, Abby poured shots, and Lily swallowed the vodka and tried to relax into Abby's energy. Then it was time to go. Lily still felt afraid. It followed her, that fear. Abby popped two pills in her mouth as they were leaving the house, swallowed them with the last swig of vodka from the bottle. "I'll drive," Abby said, pocketing Lily's car keys. She pressed two pills into Lily's hand, and Lily swallowed them dry. Abby always laughed when Lily did that, like it was a magic trick that she could pool enough saliva in her mouth to get the pills down.

They were going to the bar, a place Lily never went, but Abby had pushed, said it would be fun. But it wasn't Abby's town. These weren't the people Abby had grown up with, who had seen her disappear, then return, changed.

Even as the bar came into sight, she knew it was a bad idea. But Abby didn't pull into the lot, parking the car on the street instead. The air was cold on Lily's face as Abby got out of the car. Lily grabbed her bag and followed.

"Hurry up," Abby shouted.

"Coming," she called back. Didn't she always follow Abby? Wasn't that how they had gotten free? There was comfort in following Abby. Only a year older, Abby was wiser, calmer, smarter. As though she heard Lily's thoughts, she spun around and grinned at her friend, reached a hand back for her. "I'm so glad we're together."

Lily took hold of Abby's hand, the long, cold fingers. Her blouse was much too thin for the temperature, but Lily didn't feel cold. The drug pressed its soft warmth into her skin, embracing her like a blanket. They were together. They should always be together, Abby always said. Abby understood like no one else. They wanted to fix Lily, to rid her of the memories of that time. But not Abby. Abby knew that to remember it was to breathe more, to breathe bigger. Because they had survived.

Abby was running now, laughing and spinning, her arms stretched out to the sides. Excited, like something good was coming. Maybe it was the idea of the high. The cold became a light touch on her skin, like someone trailing fingertips along her neck and scalp. It was sexy.

Abby led her into the woods. "Right here. Just a few more steps."

Lily followed. They were so close to the bar. The fear was gone, and now she just wanted a drink.

But then something was wrong. The dark came on fast. Around her but also inside her. Abby was begging, then shouting. The cold air burned, a pain like someone tearing out her lungs. But she had to run. Just run. Where was Abby? Lily thought to look back, but she couldn't. There was no time. Branches slapped and sliced her as she ran, stumbled, and fell, then rose and ran again.

Through the dark woods and out the other side. At the edge of the trees, she froze and listened to the silence. She scanned the darkness. Abby was gone. There was no going back now.

"Lily!" A heavy pounding sounded at a distance, then closer. Glass rattled. "Lily!"

But it wasn't Abby's voice now. It was his.

Shocked awake, Lily scanned the unfamiliar bedroom and tried to pull the fragments of the dream into her waking mind.

"Lily!" a man's voice shouted. Followed by pounding at the door. At *her* door.

He was there.

CHAPTER 26

—

KYLIE

Kylie Milliard stared up at Steve Cannon, still perched on the edge of her desk, now working that penny across his knuckles.

"You're sure the prints match Lily Baker?" she asked.

Cannon gave her that half grin. "It's not like I matched them by hand, Milliard. I pulled them off the dash of Brent Nolan's Lexus and entered them into the database. I got a hit. There's not a lot of room for error. Unless you're thinking someone entered prints into the system that aren't Baker's."

Cannon stood, pocketing his coin, and started to walk away.

"Thanks for the help," she called after him.

"Anytime," he said, and she watched him go. "Stay safe," he called over one shoulder.

Kylie returned her attention to her computer, where the crime scene photos from the original Hudson scene were still downloading. Forty-seven percent now. Brent Nolan was married. Did the presence of Baker's prints and a woman's hair in the car suggest that Brent Nolan had been having an affair with Lily Baker? Was that why she and Larson had been acting so strangely? But Baker had said she'd spent the night with Larson on Wednesday night, which would imply that Larson and Baker were together.

Kylie sat back in her desk chair. Why would Baker lie to protect Larson? Even if they were close, would she really protect a killer? After everything she'd been through?

Kylie scanned her emails for something from the highway patrol's accident investigator. She located an email from Will Merkel, selected it, and read the contents. An engineer had inspected the site and confirmed that the guardrail was compromised. The scene had been ruled an accident, and highway patrol was closing the case. The guardrails were outdated, just like Gary Ross had said. She had to give him a point for that. It never would have occurred to her that there might be a structural issue with the guardrail. It had been an accident. Ice and a weak guardrail.

Now, the question was whether Vogel and Davis knew about the matching prints. Would they want her to pursue Lily Baker as Nolan's potential mistress? To what end? The wreck had been ruled an accident— end of story.

But it was a strange coincidence that Baker was a victim of Derek Hudson and also the lover of a dead man. Not to mention the victim of an attack in Iver Larson's home, most likely by Iver himself.

A box popped up in the center of her screen. *File download complete.* One hundred and ninety-seven images. A hell of a lot fewer than they took at crime scenes these days. She double-clicked the first image: Derek Hudson lying in a pool of blood. She expanded the image to full screen and studied the scene. Hudson lay on a dirty floor in a room with no furniture. The walls were hewn logs, the windows spray-painted black.

She moved slowly through the images, staring at the rooms of the cabin. A bare-bones kitchen with a single bulb hanging from the center of the room over a table with one chair. A filthy bathroom with a cup that held seven toothbrushes and a single towel hanging over a bare curtain rod. A small bedroom with a single bed, the covers on the floor, as though Hudson had just risen from sleep.

The hardest images to look at were ones that captured a room with five child-size mattresses lined along the floor. Most were bare. One was made up, almost as though it had been vacated, and another had a pile of blankets where perhaps the girls had slept together, huddled to stay warm. The thought of it made her simultaneously sick and furious.

Later images showed the outside of the cabin, the surrounding woods, and the gravel driveway with police tape hung between two wood stakes where the drive met with a gravel road. There were no other cabins in sight, but a small group had gathered just outside the tape. Adults hung back and watched. A few children were scattered among the pictures, peering into the police vehicles or playing nearby as though the whole thing were some sort of parade rather than the scene of a murder.

A man in a gray suit stood with a notepad, talking to people. Several police officers were also visible. They seemed to be making rounds, notepads in hand, talking to the crowd. Looking for witnesses or people who had known Hudson.

She went through the images a second time, but nothing stood out to her. Seeing them hadn't solved any puzzles. And why was she surprised? If there had been something to find there, the FBI would have found it a decade ago.

She still needed to talk to Lily Baker, though she wasn't sure how best to approach her. Away from Iver Larson. Vogel and Davis had given the green light for Skål to open tonight, so Larson would be at the bar. Maybe Kylie could talk to Baker then.

As she started to make a list of questions for Baker, her cell phone rang on her desk, a number she didn't recognize.

"Detective Milliard," she said.

"Detective, this is Pete McIntosh over in Glendive."

Something about the way he said his first name made her uneasy. He had news, and she guessed it wasn't good. She cracked her knuckles and waited.

"We found Hitchcock," he said.

She sat up straighter. "You did."

"Her body was dumped in Sunset Park, right outside town. Some locals found it this morning while they were out snowshoeing."

Damn. "Any idea on time of death?"

"Her car was towed from the Walmart in Miles City on the fifth. There were two warnings on it by then, dating back to the third, so seems likely she was already dead then. But we can't say for sure. The body was frozen solid, and this time of year, there aren't a lot of visitors to the park. We had the remains expedited to Bismarck this morning. The state ME has it flagged high priority, so they're going to try to get us some initial findings in the next day."

That the ME had made the case a high priority meant that the office recognized the possible implications of the two dead women, the kidnapping victims of a man who had supposedly died ten years ago. "Any idea on cause of death?"

"Quick blood work by our coroner showed there were drugs involved, but it also looked like she was strangled. But that's not official yet."

"What about cameras at the Walmart?"

"We're working to get store footage," he told her. "I'll share anything we find."

Kylie thanked him and hung up. Then she sent a quick email to Davis and Vogel to let them know about Hitchcock. Her hands felt slightly electric with the buzz of discovery. She glanced at the calendar. Today was January 8, which meant if Jenna Hitchcock had been killed on the third when her car was first ticketed, then the killer had likely made his way from Glendive to Hagen in the past five days.

That gave her an idea. The killer would have come to Hagen along Highway 1804. About ten miles out that road lived a man named Alvin Tanner, a particularly unstable conspiracy theorist who believed the government was going to show up one day and take away his land.

Tanner had lined his house and the surrounding areas with cameras for protection.

As he was outside her jurisdiction, Tanner had only come onto her radar when Vogel had gotten a warrant for the footage to bust a company that was dumping fracking water out that way. Surely the footage could be used to identify drivers coming into Hagen, too. Over the course of a week, Highway 1804 might have carried as many as two or three hundred cars, but with a little work, she could narrow down the suspects. She logged into her police records system and started digging.

It didn't take long. Within an hour, she had enough dirt on Alvin Tanner to barter for the footage without having to go through Vogel. Cracking her knuckles, she dialed Will Merkel last. It wouldn't hurt to have a highway patrol officer with her, for the company if nothing else.

As she headed out of the department, she imagined the response if she could pull footage of the killer driving into Hagen, smiling at the camera as he passed. Case closed, their killer caught, and Kylie could write herself a ticket to that detective job in Fargo.

CHAPTER 27

—

LILY

Lily Baker lay in bed, her heart racing. For a moment, she felt like she was still in the forest, surrounded by cold air, her pulse a jackrabbit in her chest. Her hands smoothed the white sheets as her mind tried to make sense of it. Out her bedroom window, the sky still glowed bright with daylight. The darkness, the woods, the blood—all gone. A dream, but not a dream.

She fought to gather the pieces of the memory. She and Abby had been in the house—in this house—drinking and dancing. There had been pills, and then she remembered the bar. But not inside. Abby had led her into the woods near Skål. And then there had been a man. She couldn't picture his face. Had she seen him? She squeezed her eyes shut and felt her heart racing, remembered running.

Tree branches slapped at her neck and arms, stung against the cold of her skin. Running and running. And then she reached the clearing. Breathless, alone, she sprinted to the street, the bag on her back heavy as it bounced across her kidneys. Up ahead, a black car. For a moment, it looked like a police car, and she screamed out and ran straight toward it. Slipped on the curb and twisted her ankle as she hurled herself toward its headlights.

The car slowed; the window went down. "Are you all right?"

*Her hands on the slick finish of the car as she ran around and got in.
The warmth inside as she told him to drive, to hurry.*

The driver . . . that face. She'd gotten in that car to get away. Brent
Nolan had been a stranger. He'd saved her from him. From . . . the name
Derek Hudson came to her mind, like a bomb detonating.

No. It was impossible.

There was more pounding on the door. "Let me in!" a man's voice
shouted. Familiar, she thought. But not Iver. Derek Hudson. She shook
her head. "No," she said out loud, needing to hear the word.

Derek Hudson was dead.

She pushed the covers back and crept to the door of her bedroom,
peered down the hallway to the square window in the front door.

"Lily! Let me in."

Tim Bailey stood on the porch, his hands cupped against the window, face pressed close. She ducked back into the bedroom, then eased
around the corner to look again.

"Lily!" he shouted again, knocking on the door, swaying slightly on
his feet like he'd been drinking.

Lily looked around the bedroom, searching for a clock, for some
sense of the time. How long had she slept?

He slapped the window with his palm. "Let me in."

She twisted the blinds in her bedroom closed so it would be harder
to see inside if he came around the side of the house. But as she did, she
noticed a neighbor on the porch next door, watching Tim.

Tim smacked the glass harder, and she felt certain it would break.
"Let me in, baby."

Damn it. She passed into the entryway and unlocked the door.
"I was sleeping," she said, cracking the door. Tim barreled inside. She
thought immediately of the way Iver had stood on the porch, not wanting to intrude.

Tim wrapped his arms around her, lifted her up, and twirled in a circle, the front door still wide open. He smelled of cigarette smoke, and she thought of the attack at Iver's home. Had that been Tim? But it didn't seem right. Tim would have talked to her.

She wriggled free and stepped back toward the door.

Tim pulled a bag of pills from his pocket. "Brought you something."

She wrapped her arms across her body. "I need to get some rest, Tim."

"Rest? You don't need rest. You need a party." He opened the Ziploc bag and poured a handful of pills into his palm, looking around the room. "You got something we can take these with?"

She shook her head. "I don't think I can right now."

He wrapped his free arm around her, and the pills dropped and scattered across the wood floor. "Sure you can. We got all night."

She pressed herself away. "It's not a good time, Tim."

Tim held her at the waist. "Not yet, it's not. But it will be. We need to get you a buzz going." He stooped down to pick the pills off the floor, tipped, and caught himself with one hand.

Lily crossed her arms over her chest. "I don't want to, Tim."

He laughed and stood before pushing past her into the kitchen and opening cabinets. "Where's the Jack?"

"I need you to leave, Tim."

He spun around and stared at her, his head cocked sideways. His eyes narrowed. "Come on, baby. We're just about to have some fun." He opened a drawer, pulled out a picture frame, and set it on the table. There was no image in the frame. A thin layer of white dust covered the glass.

"I need you to go now."

He moved toward her, his motions slow and predatory, though he was grinning like it was all fun. "No way, baby." He took hold of her arms and unfolded them from her chest. She resisted, but he was stronger and didn't let up until her arms were at her sides. Then he stepped inside them and pulled her close, pressing his face into her neck.

In an effort to get away, she stumbled, twisting her ankle, and let out a cry. "Please, Tim. Stop."

"I'll stop when I'm done," he said, lips twisting into a smile. "Don't forget you still owe me for the last batch."

"Owe you?"

He grabbed her shoulders, fingers gripping the flesh. His mouth set in a line. "What the hell's wrong with you?"

Her pulse throbbed in her neck. "I just need some sleep." She tried to force a smile. "Maybe we could meet up later?" She took a step backward, but he tightened his grip.

His eyes narrowed. "I'm not leaving until I get my payment."

"I don't have any money, Tim. I swear. I'll get you some."

Tim reached around and cupped her bottom, gripped it hard. "That's not the kind of payment I'm talking about."

She shoved him away, stumbled backward, and landed hard on her ankle. Her knee buckled beneath her, and she fell backward into the wall. "I can't," she said, rising again.

As she stood, he grabbed hold of her hair and yanked her back. Pain scalded her scalp. His mouth was at her ear. "What the hell is going on?"

She gripped his hand, trying to loosen his fingers. Two more steps, and she'd be in the bathroom. She could lock the door.

He released her hair and spun her to face him, pulling her so that her face was inches from his. His lips twisted as he spoke. "Are you cheating on me?"

She eased backward. "What are you talking about? You have a wife, Tim." Her foot reached the threshold, and she took another step into the safety of the room.

Danielle Girard

The whump of a car door closing echoed from the street out front. Tim turned to look, and Lily hurried backward, into the bathroom, and tried to close the door. But Tim put his foot in the gap.

Lily swung the door into his foot. "Get out. Leave me alone."

Tim shoved the door open, and Lily was thrown back. Her ankle twisted, and her head struck the wall with a burst of white.

CHAPTER 28

KYLIE

Kylie drove eight miles up Highway 1804 to the address of Alvin Tanner. The sky was a broad blanket of gray, the air lit with the glitter of frost and cold. About two miles before the turnoff to Tanner's residence, she saw the highway patrol vehicle. Kylie pulled over and parked facing the patrol car. A moment later, Will Merkel emerged from the other car and walked over.

She rolled the window down and breathed in the cold air. "Thanks for your help with this," she said.

"Happy to," Merkel said, bouncing on his toes to fight the cold. "I made a few calls about this guy." He leaned against the patrol car and crossed his arms. "He's kind of an ass."

"Right." She had done her own homework and had dug up enough on Tanner to handle him on her own. But you didn't go face a potentially violent misogynist at a house in the woods on your own. Rule one of detective work. If you were a female detective, it was also rules two and three.

"He's got a pretty lengthy rap sheet, most of it nasty behavior toward women," Merkel was saying.

Kylie shrugged. "Sounds like old Tanner and me will be fast friends."

"Oh, he's going to have a problem with you," Merkel said, giving her a smile as though to remind her that he wasn't the one with the problem.

"You have a suggestion?" she asked, leaning out the window.

"Not one you're going to like."

Kylie shrugged. "Try me."

"I can go talk to Mr. Tanner on my own, get the footage."

"What if he won't give it to you?"

"I think he will."

She waited.

"Tanner's got a couple speeding tickets along this stretch," Merkel said.

"And you might be able to help him with those?"

"I could certainly imply that."

Kylie shook her head. "I'll take my chances."

Merkel shrugged. "Suit yourself."

She nodded back to the car. "I'll follow you."

Merkel drove his patrol car back onto the highway, and Kylie followed. She had Tanner's address programmed into her phone, so she anticipated Merkel's turn before it happened, which was good because he took it a little fast. Once off the highway, he made a left and then another left down a dirt road before coming to a stop in front of a small timber house with a tin roof. In front, an old Chevy truck collected dirt and snow. Nothing about the place suggested pride of ownership except for the cameras. Four were visible along the roofline: two pointed at different angles toward the driveway, two toward the bushes that lined the house. Behind the bushes stretched a chain-link fence, No Trespassing signs like red tiles along the border of his property.

She was no sooner out of her car than a man appeared on the front porch. Grizzled in flannel and denim and cowboy boots, all he was missing was the double-barreled shotgun to make him the quintessential redneck.

"What do you want?" Tanner asked, his focus on Merkel in his highway patrol uniform.

"I'd like access to the footage from one of your cameras—the one that faces the highway," Kylie said.

Turning in her direction, Tanner rocked back on his heels, as though amused by the sight of her. "And who the hell are you?"

Kylie showed her badge and introduced herself.

Tanner shook his head and made a sucking sound with his mouth, like he was trying to pull meat from between a couple of molars. "And what do you plan to give me in return for my footage?"

"A gracious thank-you."

Tanner laughed and looked at Merkel, who was raising an eyebrow at Kylie. Not the way he'd go about it, the look said. "This is private property. Get lost." Tanner turned on his heel.

Kylie stepped toward the porch. "You know a Carmen Milhouse by any chance, Mr. Tanner?"

Tanner kept one hand on the door and glanced back. "What about her?"

"We had a nice chat about an hour ago, Carmen and me."

"And what does that bitch want?"

"Not you."

He launched spit, which landed inches from her feet.

"You beat her up pretty good, Alvin?"

"I don't know what you're talking about."

"Really?" Kylie pulled her phone from her pocket. "I've got some pictures I can show you to help refresh your memory. Carmen mentioned there were others, too. Callie Roberts. Tracey Jordan. I've got names written down here somewhere. Hard to remember them all off the top of my head."

"What the hell is this?" Tanner asked, charging back to the edge of the porch.

"This is me thinking that you doing something nice for a change is a damn good idea."

Tanner stared at her, then looked to Merkel, who said nothing.

Kylie cracked her knuckles one at a time. "There's nothing I like more than to put together a case against a man who's violent with women."

"Some of those women I ain't seen in years," Tanner said, his voice suddenly breathy. "It's their word against mine."

"True," Kylie said. "But the more of them that corroborate the story, the easier it is to prove." She raised her phone. "And I've got quite a list here. Probably find a few more, if I dug around, you think?"

Tanner said nothing for a moment. "All you want's the recording from the camera?"

"That's all I want," Kylie told him.

He stared down at the worn slats of the porch. "And you'll leave this other nonsense?"

"I'll leave it behind as long as there are no new complaints," she agreed.

Tanner wiped a hand on his jeans. "You can have the damn footage."

"I need everything from the highway over the last week."

"It's going to take me some time. I got to download it from the cloud."

She almost smiled at Alvin Tanner saying "the cloud," but then she thought of Carmen and Callie and Tracey and whoever else Alvin Tanner had slapped around. She handed him a business card. "I need it now."

"I'll send over a link. Probably take an hour or so."

"Fine. An hour," she told him. "Don't make me come back out here."

Tanner said nothing in response.

"I mean for the footage or for anything else. You best keep your hands to yourself from now on."

Tanner frowned, mumbling something as he turned and disappeared back into the house.

Will slapped the top of Kylie's patrol car and let out a little whistle.

Kylie's gaze shifted from Tanner's house to Will Merkel.

"You certainly told him," Merkel said, his expression hard to read. Maybe he was impressed. Or maybe he thought she was about to fall on her face.

"Think he'll send the footage?"

Merkel glanced back to the house. "No saying with these assholes." He looked across the car at her. "If he's got any sense in his head, he'll send the footage now so he doesn't get a repeat visit."

As she returned to the warmth of the car, Kylie found herself smiling.

CHAPTER 29

IVER

Iver tried to focus on the stack of paperwork on his desk. He'd gotten behind with the record keeping. Way behind. But he couldn't stand being in this space. Everything about being in the bar made Iver feel like scratching his skin off. He'd hated the bar since he could remember, his father's place. The power that man had had over him. Still had over him even though he was dead. The very smell of the place—stale beer and dust and waitresses' stress sweat—reminded him that every decision in Iver's life had, in some way, been an effort to please his father.

His father had loved the idea of having a son who was an athlete, a soldier, a hero . . . Iver had been able to play along, checking all the boxes his dad had lined up for him.

Until the explosion.

And the hospitals. The pain. The drinking. The divorce. He thought again about Debbie. Surely she had heard about the dead woman. A year ago, he would have gone home to her. She would have been his alibi. She would have reminded him that the idea that he could have killed someone in a drunken rage was crazy. Impossible.

Iver stood from his desk, suddenly anxious to get out of the bar. Outside he pulled a Jack Daniel's box from the top of the dumpster, glancing across the inside of the metal bin and imagining the woman who had been dumped there. *You did not do that.*

Shivering, he returned to the office and collected the paperwork from his desk, adding the receipt tapes from the past few days, the unfinished invoices, and the outstanding bills to the pile in the box. He tidied the surface, then stacked a couple of glasses to take to the bar. He checked around the desk and floor for any of his meds and patted his pocket to be sure he had his phone.

As he turned for the door, he remembered arriving Thursday morning to find Mike there with Sheriff Davis and the detective. He could still feel the excruciating pain of that migraine, like a scar that still ached when the weather changed.

There had been a glass on his desk when he'd come to his office to find his medication. A dirty glass, he remembered, with some sort of white residue in its base. He opened the drawer of his desk, but the glass was gone. Hadn't he put it there? He opened the drawer above it, then the one below. The glass was gone. Its absence left a strange feeling in his gut.

He took the other glasses to the bar and left them in the sink, then returned to the office to do a final sweep. He loaded the box into the cab of the truck before helping Cal up as well.

As he started the engine, he imagined how nice it would be to walk away from the bar for the last time. Maybe his old friends like Mike wouldn't get it, but he imagined Lily would understand somehow. How good it would feel to tell her he wanted to give up the bar. Then he wondered why he felt that way.

He glanced down the street in the direction of his house but turned toward Lily's. He would check to see if she was okay. Had being in her home brought back memories? Only after leaving her there had he realized that she had no way to contact him. He would take her to get a phone, help her get settled into her unfamiliar life. He had known her well when they were younger. He could tell her about that time. Maybe it would help her memory return.

Iver thought about the smell of her when they'd been in the bathroom, the sensation of being close to her. The little jolt in his stomach when their skin had touched over the computer. How long it had been since he'd had that feeling about someone.

He'd just turned on Lily's street when his phone buzzed. He glanced down at the screen, hoping somehow it would have Lily's name. But of course it couldn't be her.

Instead, the name on his screen was *Debbie*, a little heart on either side.

He turned his gaze back to the road, wishing he could unsee his ex-wife's name. Her name with her hearts, the way she had entered herself into his phone years ago. "I'm the woman in your heart," she'd told him. The woman in his heart, the woman who had broken it to free herself. He hadn't even realized it was still written that way. Why would he? They hadn't talked in months. She'd been gone a year. More than a year now, he realized. She'd left at Thanksgiving the year before last. The marriage was over, but the damn hearts were still there. So what? He'd change it. He'd delete her from his phone.

As if it were that easy.

And why now? What did she want?

Unable to put it from his mind, Iver reached Lily's block and pulled to a stretch of empty curb. "Damn it."

He lifted the phone and read her text. Mrs. Waverly said your truck was at my house on Wednesday night. In the middle of the night.

His truck. Her house. He read the line multiple times before it made sense. The night Abigail Jensen had died. He'd gone to see Debbie.

She said you parked your truck on the curb and came to my door.

Iver searched his mind for some sliver of memory, some image of the house where she lived, the door. Had he ever been there? Yes, once. He'd come to bring her the rice cooker, of all things. He started to type, to ask her if they had spoken. Had she answered the door? But then he stopped. How could he ask that? He'd been there. He should know.

Stay away from us, Iver.

Stay away from us?

Iver stared down at the phone, at his ex-wife's name with the stupid hearts. He had pushed Debbie away with his drinking and his inability to move past the pain and the memories. How many times had he woken in the night, a strange woman's face staring at him, her neck twisted at an unnatural angle?

He had done it to save them, but then they had all died anyway. Hours later.

Everyone except him.

He glanced through the windshield and eyed the street where Lily Baker now lived. What was he thinking coming here? He couldn't help her. He couldn't even help himself. She trusted him. She believed there had been someone else in his house, that it wasn't Iver who'd attacked her. But what if it was? What if he had killed Jensen and attacked Baker?

He had no business being in her life.

He had no business being alive at all.

CHAPTER 30

LILY

Lily Baker didn't know how long she'd been on the bathroom floor. When she opened her eyes, the room seemed to swim around her. A pounding echoed—in her head or maybe from the front door.

Tim Bailey was bent over her, his fist raised. "Lily Baker!" a woman shouted.

Tim paused, hand raised, and then swung his fist backward into the mirror over the sink. The glass shattered, large shards falling to the sink and floor around them.

More pounding on the door.

Lily cowered against the wall, tears streaking her vision. Tim clenched his fingers on her face, brought his mouth to hers, and kissed her hard. "You better figure out what the fuck you want." Then he let go and slammed the bathroom door.

Lily rose again on her throbbing ankle and eased the door back open. Down the hallway, Tim stood at the door with Detective Kylie Milliard.

"This is a private residence," Tim shouted at her.

Detective Milliard stepped past him, one hand on her pistol. "It's not your residence, though, is it?" Her gaze found Lily in the hallway. "You okay?"

Lily shivered, nodding, but she wasn't okay. *Please don't leave,* she tried to tell the detective. *Don't leave me here with him.*

"Get lost," Tim told her.

The detective took a step toward Tim. He took a step back as though by instinct. "If you're not looking to get arrested today, you'd better step aside," she warned him. "I'm here to speak to Lily." She turned to Lily. "Is this the man who attacked you last night?"

"What the hell?" Tim shouted.

"No," Lily said, thinking of the feel of that man, the smell of him, a kind of earthy scent. But it wasn't just dirt. It was also sort of sweet.

"You're sure?" the detective asked.

Lily had opened her mouth to respond when Tim swung back to her. "Tell this bitch to get lost, Lily."

But Lily shook her head. Her fingers found the tender spot on her scalp where he'd gripped her hair, and she stepped across broken glass in her socks.

"I think you'd better be leaving, Bailey," the detective said.

Tim took a couple of steps back to Lily, but Lily held out a hand. "No."

Tim looked surprised. "What the fuck?"

"You should leave now," the detective repeated.

Lily nodded.

Tim halted, mouth open, as he stared at Lily. "If I go, I take—"

He glanced back at the detective and snapped his mouth closed, lips turning into a smile as though she'd tried to trick him. He swayed. Had he been drinking? Or something else? He patted his pocket. "If I go, you may not see *me* again."

"You got something in your pocket?" the detective asked, stepping between Lily and Tim.

He raised both hands and moved toward the door. "I got nothing."

"Get out of here, before I arrest you on assault."

"Assault, my ass. I didn't assault anyone. I'm here with my girlfriend."

"I am *not* your girlfriend," Lily said.

"Fine," Tim said, crossing his arms like an ump's safe sign. "Not my girlfriend." He backed onto the porch and started to turn toward the stairs.

"You better not be driving," the detective warned as Tim walked down the stairs toward the street.

"No, ma'am," he said, raising his hands to the sky. "I'm walking. It's a beautiful day for a walk." He gave Lily a last narrowed gaze and started toward town.

Lily didn't take her eyes off the doorway until Tim was out of sight. Then she hurried down the hall on her tender ankle and bolted the door.

"Are you okay?" the detective asked.

Lily nodded, but she wasn't okay. She was scared and alone. She was so alone. Had she been in a relationship with Tim Bailey? Had she let him beat her? For what? Drugs?

"Did he hurt you?" The detective set a hand on Lily's shoulder, which made her jump.

"I'm okay now. Thank you."

"Can we sit?"

Lily nodded and followed the detective to the living room, *her* living room, though it didn't feel like hers. Nothing felt like hers. Lily sank onto the couch, and the detective sat across from her.

"Are you sure that wasn't the man from last night? Your attacker?"

Lily fought chills. "Positive."

"A hundred percent?"

"It wasn't him."

Milliard studied her a moment, then said, "There's something I have to tell you, but I want to make sure you're okay first."

Lily nodded. "I'm okay."

The detective studied Lily's face as though searching for the lie. She was lying. It was all a lie. This couldn't be her life. But it was. It had to be.

Milliard sat in a chair across from her and leaned forward. "You want to tell me about Brent Nolan?"

Lily gasped, pressed a hand to her mouth. "I don't—I—" She shut her mouth. What could she say?

"Were you with him, Lily?"

She shook her head.

"We found your prints in his car. We know you were there."

Tears streamed down her cheeks. What had she done? What could she say? The truth. She could tell the truth. Someone had killed Abby and attacked Lily at Iver's home.

"Were you in his car Wednesday night, the night Abby Jensen was killed?"

Lily said nothing as the detective stared, her piercing gaze almost a physical touch. The memory of huddling with Abby in the woods circled in her head. If she shared that memory, the detective would help her find out what had happened. They could catch the man who had been coming for them, the man who must have killed Abby. She opened her mouth to start when the detective said, "You were with Brent Nolan the night you said you were with Iver?"

Iver. Her one ally. The one person she trusted. By telling the truth, she ruined his alibi. "No," she whispered.

The detective watched her, her expression tightening. "Lily?"

"No," she said again. "I was with Iver, just like I said." The lie came so easily. Because she needed it. Needed it to be true. It was all she had. She couldn't help Brent now, and he couldn't help her. But Iver was still here.

The detective leaned forward. "I need you to tell me the truth."

"I've answered this question, Detective. More than once. I'm not answering it again."

The detective sat back and nodded. "Okay."

Lily exhaled and wiped her cheeks. She wanted the detective to leave. She wanted to go to Iver, to talk this all out with him. To figure out how to stay safe, how to stop whoever was doing this. "Is that all?"

"One more thing," the detective said.

Lily waited.

"I got a call from the police over in Glendive, Montana."

Lily frowned. The town meant nothing to her. Should it?

"That's where Jenna Hitchcock had been living."

Had.

"The third survivor."

Lily's mind raced in circles. "Survivor."

Milliard nodded. "The third girl to come out of Derek Hudson's cabin ten years ago."

Right. There had been three of them. Her, Abby . . . and this woman. Jenna.

"She was found in a park."

"Found?"

"She was killed, Lily."

Lily shivered. Killed. Abby and Jenna. And her . . . she was the third.

The last.

Detective Milliard was suddenly beside her, hand on her arm. "You need to tell me what you know, Lily. Everything you know."

Never talk to the police. No. That was Derek Hudson's rule. But should she tell the police everything? Would they help her? Or would it only make matters worse?

"You're not safe, Lily. Not until we catch this guy."

Lily began to cry. Huddled, she shook and cried.

I can't remember anything. Why couldn't she say the words? Why was she so afraid to admit she'd lost her memory?

How could things get any worse?

Things could always get worse. The more she learned about herself, the more she hated who she was. What if she had done something to make this all happen? Not just Brent Nolan's car accident, but also Abby's death? And the other survivor's, too? Jenna. What if this was all her fault?

"I need your help," Milliard said.

"I can't," she said. And it was true. She couldn't help. And she could be honest. "I don't know anything."

CHAPTER 31

—

KYLIE

Kylie Milliard left Lily Baker's house as frustrated as she'd ever been. Baker hadn't told her anything. She'd answered Kylie's every question with, "I don't know. I don't know anything." And Baker had been crying and shaking so badly Kylie couldn't bring herself to push any harder. Kylie couldn't imagine what Baker had been through, how thoroughly her captivity had broken her. Kylie had noticed the scar on her left arm, the one that ran parallel to the veins in her arm. An old scar but a clear sign that Baker hadn't had things easy.

But Kylie had wanted to shake some sense into her. Baker had to know what was at stake. Two survivors of Hudson's captivity had been killed. She was the last one alive. Those were not good odds.

Kylie put a call in to Dispatch to have a patrol car stationed in front of Lily Baker's house and didn't pull away until the officer was parked. While she waited in the car, a light patter of snow collecting on the windshield, she texted Gilbert for everything he could find on Tim Bailey. Kylie knew Bailey from the hospital and around town, but she didn't trust him. She wanted to know how the hell that creep fit into all of this. Had he been at Skål on Wednesday night? More than an hour had passed since her meeting with the charming Alvin Tanner, and there was still no email footage from him.

Damn him. Was she going to have to drive all the way back out there tomorrow? The coroner's report had come in, and she was looking forward to reading that, but she felt like she had little to show for the morning's efforts. And the day was almost over. She glanced at the clock and saw it was almost four. She wondered if there was any chance she might be able to catch Sarah Ollman, the pastor's daughter.

Did pastors work banking hours? There was only one way to find out.

With Baker under surveillance, Kylie drove the four blocks to the Ollmans' house, a large Victorian with intricate woodwork and shingles of various colors. It was the kind of thing you would expect to see in a wealthy neighborhood of San Francisco, not in Hagen. The official lodging of the church's head pastor, the house was situated one block south of the church. Ollman had lived there since sometime in the nineties. A house like this, it was almost enough to make someone consider the seminary.

Not Kylie, but someone.

Kylie left her car at the curb and walked up the stone path, cautious on the ice, and rang the bell. A small dog barked, the noise growing closer, until she could imagine the pint-size thing directly behind the door. Kylie rang the bell again and stepped back to look up at the second floor. A shade shifted, and Kylie lifted a hand to wave. It was harder to avoid a guest at the door once they'd seen you. From the size of the person in the window, it was either Sarah Ollman or her mother. It would be awkward to explain why she was there to Mrs. Ollman. Kylie assumed the woman didn't know that her seventeen-year-old daughter had been in a bar on Wednesday.

Kylie rang the bell one last time and heard the sound of someone hushing the dog. The door cracked open, and a petite blonde with big blue eyes peered out, wearing enough makeup to work behind a counter in one of those Sephora places. She was beautiful and perhaps a little too thin, the kind of thin that came from not eating. Under her arm was a black-and-white dog about the size of a football.

"Yes?"

"Sarah Ollman?"

"Yes," the girl said uneasily.

Kylie introduced herself and showed her badge. "I need to ask you a few questions."

"My parents aren't home. You should probably come back w—"

"I have questions about Wednesday night, when you were at Skål. I suspect you'd rather I not ask these questions in front of your parents."

Sarah's eyes grew wide, and she shook her head. "I don't know what you're—"

"I know you were there," Kylie said.

"I'm not old eno—"

Kylie put up a hand. "I know that, too."

Sarah folded her lips into her mouth and seemed to chew on them a moment.

"Can I come in?"

Sarah hesitated. "I don't know. My mom just went to the store, and my dad usually gets home around now."

"The sooner I get my answers, the sooner I leave."

Suddenly breathless, Sarah opened the door. "Fine, but hurry."

The door closed behind them, and Sarah led Kylie to the darkened living room, where she sat in the center of a floral couch.

Kylie sat opposite her. "You want to start by telling me how you got into the bar?"

Sarah offered nothing.

"Did one of the bartenders let you in?"

Still, she said nothing.

Kylie glanced at the screen on her phone. "What time do you think your folks will be home?"

"Fine," Sarah said. "I snuck by when the bouncer was dealing with something in the parking lot."

"What was the something?" Kylie asked.

"Some guy was acting all nuts, shouting." Sarah sat upright. "But I was never there. My dad can't find out. In three months, I turn eighteen, and we'll get the hell out of here."

"'We'?" Kylie asked.

Sarah's mouth shut.

"I understand you might have some pictures from the bar last night, ones that weren't posted on social media."

"We never post bar pictures," Sarah said like Kylie was an idiot. "Obviously, we can't."

Kylie took note of the "we" again. "But you have some."

"I don't think I do."

"Really? No group shots? No selfies? No Snapchat story?"

Sarah studied the top of the dog's head.

"I know you took pictures last night, and I need them. Every single one."

The dog squirmed in Sarah's arms, but she held him tightly.

"A woman was killed."

"What will you do with the pictures?" Her voice was small, child-like.

"Look at who was in the bar, try to locate a suspect."

Sarah chewed her lips again.

"A murder suspect," Kylie said.

"I can't. If they got out . . ."

Kylie stood. "You don't have a choice. Either you give them to me willingly, or I'll come back with a warrant."

"I'll just delete them," Sarah said like it was the most obvious thing in the world.

Kylie cracked the knuckles on one hand like she had all the time in the world. When she was done, she shrugged at Sarah Ollman. "We'll retrieve them. You'd be amazed at what the tech guys can do." Kylie didn't mention that Hagen didn't have any tech guys. "And I'd have to speak to your parents, which means they would know you were at the bar. Seems like they won't be too happy—especially your dad, what with him being the head of the church and all. Might make these last months before you turn eighteen pretty rough."

The dog finally broke free and jumped off the couch. Sarah looked around as though something had been stolen from her.

Kylie gave Sarah a moment to weigh her choices. She tried to imagine Sarah and her friends in Skål. It was unlikely that none of the bartenders had noticed the underage girls, which meant the girls had probably had inside help. Kylie couldn't imagine that the bar's female servers were helping Sarah Ollman and her friends. But one of the male bartenders . . . Kylie could see that.

Sarah sat unmoving on the couch.

"I only need to see them," Kylie said. "Doesn't mean they'll get out, not if you're smart."

Sarah swiped an angry tear off her cheek. "Fine. I'll send them to you. But only you."

"The guy in the parking lot?"

"Yeah?"

"You get a picture of him?" Kylie asked.

"Maybe."

Kylie took out a business card and held it out to the girl. "Send me every single picture. Today. In the next three hours."

Instead of taking the card, Sarah smoothed her hands on her pants and nodded.

"If I find out you withheld a single picture—from your phone and from any of your friends who were there with you—if I don't get every picture, I'll make sure your father has enough evidence to send you to a nunnery. Understand?"

Tears streamed down Sarah's face, tracking little lines in her makeup.

"Sarah?"

"I understand," she said through gritted teeth before snatching the business card from Kylie. She wiped her tears and sniffed hard, lifting her little dimpled chin in defiance.

Kylie wanted to laugh but didn't. She might have been the same at seventeen. Of course cell phones hadn't been as prevalent then. Thank God.

Just then, the front door opened, and Pastor and Mrs. Ollman entered together. Mrs. Ollman, shopping bags in both arms, stopped short when she saw the two women. "What's happening? Sarah, what's wrong?"

"Nothing at all," Kylie said, walking toward the Ollmans to give Sarah an extra minute to pull herself together. "Sarah is putting together a school group to do roadside cleanup on the 1804 this spring. I was just stopping by to make sure she has my contact information so I can help her organize." Kylie smiled. "And to thank her."

"Yeah." Sarah joined them, suddenly looking more like a seventeen-year-old than the almost woman she'd been at the door.

"You've got my email address." Kylie turned to Sarah Ollman's parents. "It's great when young people get involved in the community."

"It certainly is," the pastor said proudly. "That's our girl."

"Yes," Mrs. Ollman agreed, looking almost as nervous as her daughter.

The pastor took Sarah under one arm and reached out his free hand to shake Kylie's. "Thanks for coming by, Officer."

Kylie gave them a smile and let herself out of the house. Glancing down at her phone, she saw a text from DA Vogel.

Any updates on Nolan?

She pocketed her phone and returned to her car. She hadn't done any follow-up after going to the scene of the accident with Gary Ross. Highway patrol had ruled it an accident. Maybe he'd been having an affair. What difference did it make now?

She wanted to focus on Jensen's murder.

Her phone buzzed again. Gilbert.

Vogel and Davis want an update on Nolan and Jensen. Where are we?

She longed to find a quiet place to read the coroner's preliminary autopsy report on Jensen, harass Alvin Tanner for the footage he still hadn't sent her, and wait for the photos from Sarah Ollman. But she knew better than to fight this battle over text.

Hold your damn horses, she thought.

Instead she wrote, **Be at the station in ten.**

CHAPTER 32

—

LILY

As soon as the detective was gone, Lily Baker grabbed a jacket from the hall closet and headed toward Iver's. The snow had stopped, and the sun, low in the sky, broke through a bank of clouds. The tenderness in her ankle slowed her down, while the battle in her head escalated to a new level. She should trust the detective, but what questions would follow once Lily admitted how little she remembered of her own life? She would have to confess that she'd been there when Brent had gone over the edge—that instead of staying in her seat and keeping that car on top of the overpass, she had bailed. And Brent Nolan had died.

Could she have prevented the car from going over? There was no way of knowing now. She hadn't even told Iver that piece, but she had to come clean with someone. Two survivors were dead, which meant someone was almost certainly coming after her. Maybe letting the police arrest her for fleeing the scene of an accident was the smartest thing she could do. At least she'd be safe inside the Hagen jail.

She sensed a car following her and wheeled around, terrified at the thought that it might be Tim Bailey. Instead, it was a patrol car. The officer rolled his window down. "I've got to follow you," he said, with a flash of shame. "You want a ride?"

She should have accepted the ride, given her ankle a rest, but she shook her head. "I'm just walking a few blocks."

"I still have to follow you."

She shivered and nodded. "Okay."

She kept her head down and made her way to Iver's. The cold radiated to her bones despite the jacket, which chafed against the spots on her arms that were tender from Tim's grip. She was light headed and shaky. She had used drugs with him. That much was clear. How much? How often? The hospital staff had treated her as a member of their team. Surely she wasn't an addict. But Tim, too, seemed to hold a job there, and he was clearly a regular user. Where were the drugs coming from? Did he steal them from the hospital? Did she?

Before she realized, she was standing in front of Iver's house. She started up the stairs, noticing the front door was ajar. Maybe she'd caught him coming home . . . or leaving. Cal emerged from the house, barking. She paused and called out, "Iver?"

Cal stopped barking as she reached him and made a small circle on the porch.

There was no answer from inside.

Cal began to whine. She recalled his whining from the night before, when she'd been in the bathroom, in the dark. She froze and looked into the front entryway, not daring to step inside. "Iver?"

Cal barked again, and Lily jumped, startled. Her heart was racing now, thumping in her ears and drowning out sounds. She looked back at the street. The patrol car had parked on the opposite curb.

She waved at the officer, suddenly frantic.

He cracked his door and stood.

"I think something's wrong," she told him. "The dog is whining—" She stopped, realizing she sounded insane. "Iver's not answering, but the door is open."

The patrol officer crossed the street.

"Maybe I'm wrong," she said.

"It's okay. Let me check it out."

She waited until he reached the half-open door and hovered behind him as he knocked.

"Iver?" she called.

"Mr. Larson?" the officer shouted inside.

Cal nuzzled against her leg and whined.

The officer stepped into the entryway and drew his gun, aiming the barrel down. "Mr. Larson?"

Lily took a step after him.

"Oh, shit," the officer said, holstering his gun.

Lily felt her knees buckle beneath her. Dread washed over her like a red-hot wave. Stumbling into the house, she imagined Iver dead on the floor. The officer dropped to his knees beside the couch. Lily caught up. Iver lay on the floor, not dead at all. Instead, his arms and legs thrashed, thumping against the hardwood.

He was having a seizure. His hand struck the coffee table as the officer reached for him.

"Don't," she said.

The officer looked up at her.

"I'm a nurse," she said. "Move the table so he doesn't strike it."

The officer dragged the coffee table away.

"Call for an ambulance. I've got him." She knew the rules for this. *Don't try to hold him down. Make sure he can't hurt himself. Watch for fluid in the mouth so he doesn't choke.*

Within ten or fifteen seconds, he stopped flailing. The shaking grew tighter, more controlled, and she moved instinctively. Kneeling at his side, she slid her palms under him. Her right went under his neck and her left at the bottom edge of his rib cage. With a slow heave, she rolled him gently away from her, onto his right side. She edged her knees closer, using them to help hold his body in place. Her face hovered only inches from his.

His breathing sounded labored, as though he were choking on his own tongue. She reached across and put pressure on his cheeks to try to open his mouth, careful not to get her fingers too close to his teeth.

His lips fell open, and a bit of drool slid from his mouth. Not much. Not enough to choke him.

She held tight, bowed her head, and whispered to him, "Trust in the Lord with all thine heart; and lean not unto thine own understanding. In all thy ways acknowledge him, and he shall direct thy paths."

His eyes opened. She saw fear and pain. She ran her fingers through his hair. "You're okay."

"Washum vunze," he muttered. Blood trickled from his mouth.

She pressed her shirtsleeve to the blood. "Don't try to talk. You bit your tongue."

He closed his eyes for a moment, the gentle rise and fall of his breathing the only motion now. When he opened his eyes, a single tear slid down his cheek. "Heard praying," he said.

"It's okay," she whispered. "I'm here."

"The ambulance is on the way," the police officer told her. "Is he okay?"

"Yes," she said, as Iver closed his eyes.

CHAPTER 33

KYLIE

Kylie Milliard sat in the conference room beside DA Vogel and across from Sheriff Davis and Gary Ross. Carl Gilbert was at the head of the table—or the foot. From the papers on the table and the notes on the whiteboard, they'd been there awhile. Two columns on the whiteboard, titled *Nolan* and *Jensen*, headed up a series of bullet points.

"We thought it would be smart to get our heads together and see where we are on these cases," Davis said, rubbing his palms together like a caveman starting a fire. "But I think we're damn close on Jensen."

Kylie sat up. "Close? Have we gotten lab results on the glass and the fiber back?" The state lab was remarkably efficient, but a two-day turnaround would be unusual.

"Not yet," Gilbert said. "Their office said it would be late next week at the soonest. Even later for the official autopsy report."

"Then how are we close?" she asked.

Vogel smiled. "We'll get to that. Why don't you start us off?"

Davis wasn't one to get excited over nothing. Still, she'd play it their way.

"I emailed you about Jenna Hitchcock, the third victim," she said. "Pete McIntosh, the deputy sheriff over in Glendive, will keep us apprised if they discover anything at the scene there, but so far there's nothing to help us identify a suspect."

Vogel made a note and nodded.

Kylie updated them on the Alvin Tanner footage.

"That's good thinking, Milliard," Davis said. "Have you got the footage yet?"

Kylie checked her email on her phone and sighed. "No. Tanner hasn't sent it yet." She'd thought she'd scared him enough to comply.

"Well, let's follow up with him," Davis said.

"I can do it," Gilbert offered.

"I—" Kylie started to say she would do it. But it turned out maybe Tanner wasn't going to deal with a woman after all.

"Do you have any other leads?" Davis asked Kylie.

"I do. I found out Sarah Ollman was in Skål the night that Jensen was killed. She took some pictures."

"Sarah Ollman?" Vogel asked.

Kylie nodded. "Pastor Ollman's seventeen-year-old daughter."

Sheriff Davis frowned. "How the hell did she get into the bar?"

"That's a question we need to ask Iver Larson."

"She took pictures?" Vogel asked, sitting up in his chair with some effort.

"Yes. And I should have them any minute." As though Sarah Ollman had been listening, an email popped into her inbox. "I've just got them now."

"Let's have a look," Davis said. "Can you bring them up on your computer?"

"Sure." She opened her computer screen as a text buzzed on her phone. Amber. Did u no Lily B. @ hosp Thurs am. Lkd like had accdnt.

"What is it?" Davis asked.

Kylie took a moment to decipher Amber's code. "Nothing," she lied and put the phone in her pocket, the heat rising in her face. She had believed Lily Baker when she'd said she hadn't been with Brent Nolan the night he'd died. But Baker had been at the hospital Thursday morning, looking like she'd been in an accident. Was she in the same accident as Brent Nolan? Surely, if she'd gone off the overpass, she'd be in way worse shape than she was.

"Detective?"

Kylie looked up and saw Davis watching her. He motioned to the computer. "The images?"

"Of course." Kylie keyed in her password and launched her email. She double-clicked on the email from SassySarah and waited as the images loaded. "This might take a minute." She looked up at the men. "Any other updates on Jensen?"

"Coroner's report came in," Ross commented, like he was part of the team.

"I saw it but haven't read it yet."

"Not much to learn there," Davis said. "Jensen hit her head before she was strangled."

"Glendive police said Hitchcock was strangled also," she said, thinking. "What about Derek Hudson? Did he strangle his victims?"

"Derek Hudson is dead," Vogel said.

"One of the victims ID'd the body," Ross said. "Hudson kept the girls blindfolded, and when they weren't, he wore a mask—Casper the Friendly Ghost, if you can believe it. Luckily, one of the girls had gotten a look at him, so she was able to confirm that the dead man was their captor. The monster was dead; that much we knew." Ross sounded relieved.

"But if this is someone copying his work, then maybe he's chosen strangulation to emulate Hudson." She looked to Gary Ross.

"Only one girl died in captivity in Hudson's cabin. Hudson kidnapped five in total. Another girl died during the escape, but that first one. . . I believe it might have been blunt-force trauma that killed her," Ross said. "Can't believe I don't remember."

"It's something to consider," Davis agreed.

"I can check," Ross said. "From the coroner's report, it looks like Abigail Jensen also bled a fair amount before the asphyxiation," he added.

Kylie glanced at him, then back to Davis. So they were still sharing everything with the FBI guy. "Could they get anything from the prints on her neck?" she asked.

Davis shook his head. "No. The killer wore gloves."

She would read the full report later. She glanced at her screen, where Sarah Ollman's email attachment was still opening. Wi-Fi in the department was from the Stone Age. "Any luck tracking down the caller who said she'd seen Larson driving around at two a.m.?"

"No," Davis admitted.

The call was the only real evidence they had that Iver Larson might not have been at home when Jensen was killed.

"What about the gun Sullivan collected at Larson's?" she asked.

"Some partial prints. Only ones we could identify belong to Lily Baker."

"Is the gun registered?"

Gilbert shook his head.

Maybe Baker had tried to get it away from her attacker. Or maybe it was her gun. Kylie thought about her roommate's text. Lily Baker had been in the hospital on Thursday morning. Like she'd had an accident, Amber's message said. A car accident?

"We've got the stuff we collected from Larson's truck," Gilbert said, piping up from the far end of the table. "No results yet, though."

"I didn't realize we were issuing a warrant for his truck," Kylie said, a rush of heat rising up her neck.

"We found some interesting stuff there," Davis said, nodding to Gilbert. "You collected it, Carl. Why don't you tell us?"

"First off, Larson had just washed the truck, so who knows what we might have lost." He leaned back in his chair, posing like a long, thin version of Vogel. "I collected fiber and blood from the front seat. Then I found these in the crossover toolbox in the bed of Larson's truck." Gilbert wheeled his chair until he was beside Kylie, his shoulder almost touching hers. On the screen of his phone was a pair of women's suede boots.

"Those are Abigail Jensen's?"

"Not sure yet," Gilbert said. "But they're the right size."

"He went to the trouble of washing the truck but left the victim's shoes in the truck bed," Kylie said. "That make sense to anyone?" No one responded.

Just then, the first image from Sarah Ollman filled the screen. Sarah Ollman stood beside a man in a Def Leppard T-shirt. In place of his face was a black circle.

"What the hell?" Vogel asked, looking over her shoulder.

"She's trying to hide the identity of her boyfriend," Kylie said. She scrolled to the next picture, then the next, looking for Abigail Jensen in the images. Three pictures later she saw the same T-shirt on a man at the edge of the image. She recognized him as one of the bartenders they'd interviewed after Jensen had been found.

Davis pointed to the man in the T-shirt. "This must be Sarah's boyfriend."

"He's a bartender. Kevin something," Gilbert said.

"We'll deal with Kevin later," Davis said.

They huddled around Kylie as she flipped through the images. Black circles replaced faces on the bodies of several young women Kylie assumed were Sarah's teenage friends. The bartender was in at least a half dozen of them, his face exposed. Either Sarah Ollman was an idiot or she thought Kylie was. Lucky for Sarah, Kylie had bigger fish to fry.

She kept clicking through the images until she saw one that took her breath away.

A man stood in the parking lot, his hand extended, his face twisted with anger, his right hand a bunched fist. His left held tightly to a thin female wrist. Along the edge of the image was the sliver of a woman's profile, a nose and a wave of hair—blonde hair like Abigail Jensen.

The furious face belonged to Iver Larson.

CHAPTER 34

IVER

Iver Larson opened his eyes and scanned the unfamiliar room. The smell, the sounds—he knew in a moment he was in a hospital. A sudden surge of adrenaline drew him upright. He couldn't be back in the hospital.

"You're okay."

He turned, expecting to see his ex-wife's face. But the woman beside the bed was Lily Baker. He thought immediately of the man, the attack. Had he come back? Had Iver been knocked out? He recalled waking on his floor. Lily had been there . . . and someone from high school he'd barely recognized, wearing a police uniform.

"What happened?"

"You had a seizure."

He shook his head and rubbed his face. His skull pulsed with a dull ache, like he'd hit his head on something the day before. Maybe he had.

Lily rose from the chair and sat on the edge of the bed. "Do you have seizures often?"

"Never." He adjusted the blanket around his waist, unsure exactly what he had on beneath the covers.

"The doctor should be back soon," she said. "What do you remember?"

Iver tried to think back. He'd been working on the bar receipts. There was money missing: $700 over the past five days. He'd wanted to send Mike a text about it. He'd walked out of his home office to look for his phone.

"Iver?"

"I came into the living room for my phone . . . next thing I know, I saw you and that cop. He looked familiar."

Lily shook her head. "Who?"

"The cop. He was in our class, I think. Or maybe the class behind us. Played soccer."

"I don't remember."

Iver clapped his mouth shut. "Sorry."

She started to stand, and he took her hand, then released it when she turned back. An awkward beat passed between them. "Thanks for coming to the hospital," he said.

"Of course. I wanted to—"

The door opened, and a woman in a white coat entered the room. "I'm Dr. Prescott."

Iver had thought he knew every doctor in a two-hundred-mile radius, but Prescott was not familiar.

"I joined the hospital team here a few months ago," she said, as though she'd read the confusion in his face, "but I was able to pull your chart and look at your history. How are you feeling?"

"Fine," he said. But he wasn't fine. In only a few minutes of consciousness, the hairs on his neck had stood on end. The way the doctors spoke, the patronizing looks that were both confident and worried, the clipboards, the white coats with their names stitched in blue—all of it made him crazy.

"Iver?" Lily prompted.

He shook his head. "Sorry?"

The doctor approached and used the penlight and stethoscope. She asked about his head and the seizure. "You've never had a seizure before?" she asked, though he'd already answered this question.

"Never," he repeated.

"But you live alone?"

Iver opened his mouth to reply.

"I told her," Lily said.

"Right," he confirmed. "You're saying I might be having seizures without knowing?"

"It's possible."

"Your girlfriend was able to get a list of the medications in your house."

Neither of them bothered to correct the doctor, who pulled a printed paper off her clipboard and handed it to him. "Can you confirm these medications?"

Iver scanned the list. For vision issues, for headaches and migraines, for the nausea caused by the migraines. Medications he'd been prescribed right after the accident—for cognition and memory issues, for motor-systems deficits, for pain management; he also had antipsychotics for sleep disturbances, anticonvulsants to manage the panic attacks, and antidepressants for the obvious reasons. All of them right there in black and white. He was a walking pharmacy.

"I don't take most of these anymore." He glanced sideways at Lily, who was watching him.

The doctor looked at her, too.

"Should I leave?" she asked.

He shook his head and looked to the page, pointing at the medications as he went down the list. "I still take Imitrex for the migraines when they happen and the Wellbutrin and the citalopram, and occasionally Zofran for nausea. I think that's it."

"So you're no longer suffering from sleep disturbances?"

Sleep disturbances was a mild way of describing the nightmares he'd had upon his return from Afghanistan. "Correct."

"How long ago did you stop that medication?" she asked.

"Probably almost a year. Maybe ten months."

"And there's nothing else you're taking that isn't on this list?"

"I take Advil and occasionally NyQuil, but I haven't taken either in weeks."

"That's it?" the doctor pressed.

He raised his right hand. "Scout's honor." He might have sounded sarcastic, but Prescott didn't seem to notice.

She took the list back and stared at it again. "How about recreational drugs?"

"None," he said. "Never."

"And no prior seizures," she said again.

Iver didn't answer. How many times did he have to tell her? It was like she was waiting for him to change his mind.

"What about memory loss?"

Iver froze. His eyes tracked to Lily, who seemed to flush. Her gaze shifted to the ground.

He did have memory loss. Would that be related to his seizure? But the memory loss was Wednesday night, and the seizure had happened Friday. A punch of terror struck him. What if he was developing new symptoms? The doctors had told him that his brain would change, that his pain might go away and his vision might steady, even off the meds. But what if the opposite had happened? What if his brain was getting worse?

He looked at Lily, who nodded.

"Actually, I did have some memory loss," he admitted finally.

"And when did that start?"

The room shrank, and his breathing grew rapid. "It was maybe one time for a few hours, earlier this week."

Lily watched him, but he focused on the doctor.

Prescott flipped through the pages in her file, shifting them around and making "hmm" sounds. Finally, she met his eye again. "I'm just looking at the blood work we did. The spike I'm seeing would explain the memory loss and the seizures, but it doesn't make sense with the medications that you're taking. There had to be something else . . ." She cocked her head, appearing to study him.

"Booze?"

She frowned.

"Alcohol. I had a few drinks."

She shook her head. "Even a bender wouldn't cause these tox screens." She smiled like this was a joke.

He didn't tell her that it had been a bender, that recently every night was a bender.

"And nothing else you've taken?" the doctor asked.

"Nothing else," he said firmly.

"I'm afraid that can't be the truth," the doctor said. "There has to be something else. Is it possible that you took something without knowing what it was? Did a friend give you something? A candy or piece of chocolate? Anything suspicious?"

He wasn't a damn kid. Of course he hadn't eaten candy from a stranger. He'd opened his mouth to respond when a hard knock sounded at the door.

Iver sat up with a silent prayer that his mother hadn't gotten wind of this. She'd done enough worrying about him for a lifetime. He was grateful that his mother had come down with a cold and canceled her visit. Maybe the cold would keep her in bed for a few days, prevent her from learning about the dead woman. But what then? She'd hear eventually.

The woman who entered the room was not his mother. It was Detective Kylie Milliard, followed by Carl Gilbert.

"I'm sorry to interrupt," the detective said to the doctor. She obviously didn't care that she was interrupting him in a hospital bed.

Lily stood quickly, as though she were the one being summoned.

"I'm not here for you," the detective said. "But just for the record, you lied. You came to the hospital Thursday morning looking like you'd been in an accident."

The words came out like a shot in the dark. Iver almost told the detective to leave, but he caught the fear in Lily's eyes.

"A car accident?" the detective pressed.

Lily's complexion flushed, and she gripped her hands together like she was praying. Iver tried to sit up in the bed. What the detective was saying was true. Why hadn't she told him?

"You weren't with Iver the night Abby Jensen was killed, were you?"

"I—" Lily's gaze bounced between the detective and him.

Iver started to shake his head.

"You were in the car with Brent Nolan. Were you in that car when it crashed? Did you go over that pass with him?"

What the hell was the detective talking about? Iver turned to Lily, waiting for her to tell the detective she was crazy.

"He died, you know," the detective went on.

"I tried to get him out of the car," Lily said in a rush. "I must've been knocked out, and when I came to, the car was on the edge. I tried to wake him up. I barely got out myself."

"We can talk about that later."

Lily looked confused as the detective's gaze shifted from her to him. One look at the detective's face, and a pit formed in Iver's stomach. They were coming for him. He pressed his eyes closed.

"Iver Larson, you are under arrest for the murder of Abigail Jensen."

"What?" Lily cried out. "That's impossible."

Carl Gilbert stepped forward and read Iver his rights, his words broken as though Iver's hearing was cutting out. "You have the right to remain silent . . . to an attorney . . . if you cannot afford . . ."

Iver shook his head. "I didn't. I couldn't—"

"Do you understand these rights as I've explained them?" Gilbert said, cutting him off.

"Yes, but—"

Milliard turned to the doctor. "When can he be discharged?"

"Tomorrow," she said, glancing at Iver. "Sunday at the latest."

"Fine," Milliard said. "We'll have to put a patrol officer outside the door for the remainder of his stay." She turned to Gilbert. "Gilbert, stay here until I can get someone posted to the door."

Milliard started to leave.

"Detective," Iver called out, his heart slamming against his ribs. She couldn't just arrest him and leave. He should have a chance to respond.

She looked back.

"You've made a mistake."

"It doesn't look that way," Milliard said with a shake of her head.

He licked his lips, trying to wet the desert in his mouth. "Don't I at least get to hear what evidence you have against me? So I have a chance to refute it? I'm not a killer."

Milliard crossed her arms. "For starters, we found blood in your truck. Blood that matches Abigail Jensen's blood type."

Iver felt himself panic. He wanted to get out of the bed, to cross the room and stand eye to eye with her. The words tumbled around his brain. His truck, her blood.

"It matches her blood?" Lily asked.

"Her blood type," Milliard repeated.

"What type is it?" Lily asked.

Milliard frowned.

Iver watched them. Lily was trying to make a point, but he felt as he had the first days after his head injury. He knew the words, but he couldn't make any sense of them.

"Type A positive."

Lily swung to face him. "What blood type are you?"

He shrugged.

"He's O positive," Milliard said.

Lily shook her head. "Okay, so it's not his blood. Maybe it's mine. More than thirty percent of the Caucasian population is A positive. You can't arrest him on that."

"We didn't," Gilbert said. "We arrested him because he had the victim's shoes in the bed of his truck. She was found dead without them."

Lily stepped backward as though the words had struck her physically.

The victim's shoes. In his truck? Iver shook his head. "That's not possible. I never met her." The bed of his truck was open. "Anyone could have put them there," he added. "My truck is parked outside all the time."

"They were in the lockbox," Gilbert said. "I used your keys to open it."

Panic seared his chest and throat. The lockbox. What lockbox? Then he remembered the steel box in his truck, the one he hadn't used in years. "I never use that toolbox," Iver argued. "I don't even lock it."

"Well, it was locked when I went to search it. Found the key in your ashtray."

He thought about leaving his car in his own driveway, unlocked with the keys inside. "Anyone could have done that. The key is always there, and my truck is never locked."

The room was silent.

"And what about the attack at my house? The man who tried to strangle Lily?" Iver went on, throwing things out. This was wrong. Totally wrong.

"We don't have any evidence that it wasn't you," Milliard said.

"Me?" he charged. "I saved her." He pointed to Lily. "Tell them."

"He's telling the truth," Lily said. "The man who attacked me wasn't Iver. I know it wasn't."

Gilbert aimed a finger in Iver's face. "It was you who killed that girl, Larson. We know it, and we have a picture of you grabbing her that proves it. We're going to get that footage and nail you to the wall with it."

A new pain clamped onto his skull. Picture? Footage? His head was spinning. "I don't know what you're talking about. I would never have hurt that woman." He knew that. He'd never been violent. Angry, yes. Panicked and shouting. But he'd never hurt anyone. Even in the heat of those nightmares in his first weeks back, he'd never been violent. Ever.

He closed his eyes. They had to believe him. Only it wasn't true. He had been violent with the Afghan woman. Behind his eyelids he could see the unnatural angle of her neck, the sickening crack it had made when it had broken.

All of that for nothing.

The doctor had found something in his tox screen, an unfamiliar drug that might be responsible for the seizure. Had it made him violent? Was he responsible for Abigail Jensen's death?

Oh God. What if . . . his throat clamped closed. His lungs burned as he struggled to breathe. He couldn't get air. He gripped the thin hospital sheet in both fists. The buzzing of a chainsaw filled his head, drowning out the voices around him.

A hand on his. He looked down and saw the long, thin fingers. What was happening?

"What should I do?" Lily asked.

When he looked up, the detective and the patrol officer were gone.

He felt a wave of anger at her. This had all started when she'd shown up. Then she'd lied to the police.

She took a step backward, pulling her hand away. "Iver?"

He put a shaking hand over his eyes. It wasn't her fault. His blackout had happened before she'd come to his house. The night before. She had been trying to help him. Or had she?

"Should I call someone?" she asked, keeping her distance. Was she afraid of him? For him? He wanted to reach out, to feel her hand in his, but he held himself still, focused on his breath.

"Do you have an attorney?" she asked.

He shook his head. The only attorney he knew was the one who had handled his father's estate. But he would start there. "I need my phone."

Lily pointed to the bedside tray. "It's there."

Iver grabbed the phone and texted Mike. He'd have to handle the bar. Or close it down. He paused. Mike had said something about going out of town. Hell. This trumped his vacation plans, didn't it? He asked Mike to call him, ASAP, or he'd have to put someone else in charge of the bar. Kevin, maybe.

As he searched for the attorney in his contacts, he heard the door open. He looked up. Lily was leaving. "Wait."

She looked back, her eyes glassy.

"I didn't do this," he said.

"I believe you."

He studied her face. Did she really? The evidence was damning. He couldn't worry about what Lily thought. He had bigger issues. Much bigger issues. "Will you watch Cal? Just until I can figure something else out?"

"Of course." Her eyes were clear, open, trusting. God, he hoped she trusted him. He needed her trust.

Just then, his phone buzzed in his hand. Mike. Iver answered the call and explained what had happened.

"We're not even an hour outside of town," Mike said. "We can come back. What do you need?"

Iver exhaled. Of course Mike would change his plans. They'd always have each other's backs. By the time he looked up again, the room was empty.

Lily was gone.

CHAPTER 35

KYLIE

Kylie left the inpatient corridor and returned to the hospital's main entrance. Down the other hallway—the hospital only had two—was a small empty conference room she'd noticed once or twice. She ducked inside for some privacy to contact Sheriff Davis.

While Kylie waited for Marjorie to put her through to his office, she again looked at the image of Larson they'd found in Sarah Ollman's pictures. There wasn't enough of the woman's profile in the photograph to be able to confirm that the woman whose arm Larson was gripping was actually Abigail Jensen. Her head was turned away from the camera, leaving only a section of her chin, her hair, and part of her arm. Kylie wanted to put the photo on a larger screen, zoom in to make out some detail on the woman's hand in order to confirm she was Jensen, but she hadn't had time.

As soon as Marjorie put her through to Sheriff Davis, the first sound she heard was the telltale screeching of a chair. They were in Vogel's office.

"Milliard, hi," Davis said. "You make the arrest?"

"I did, sir, but Larson's in the hospital, and his doctor wants to hold him for observation for another day or two. I've got Gilbert stationed outside his door now, and I've requested another patrol officer to relieve Gilbert. We'll have to keep an officer posted until his release."

"What the hell is he in the hospital for?" Vogel said.

"Hello, DA Vogel," Kylie said. "One of our patrol officers and Lily Baker entered Larson's home and found him in the midst of a seizure. An ambulance brought him to the hospital two hours ago."

"Christ," Vogel muttered.

"It's only a day or two," Davis said, "and as long as we've got someone posted on the door full time, we'll get him soon enough."

"Yes, sir," Kylie said.

"In the meantime, let's get this case airtight," Davis added.

"As you know, I spoke to the lab about sharpening the image of Larson in Sarah Ollman's photographs."

"The lab conclusively matched the blood type from Larson's truck to Jensen," Vogel said.

"Yes. The blood is A positive, same as Jensen," Kylie said. "I just checked with Larson's doctor, and he is O positive."

Davis made a whistling sound, and Vogel must have moved energetically because his chair let out a tremendous shriek. She paused a moment in anticipation of the break, but it didn't come.

"It turns out that A positive and O positive are the two most common blood types, representing approximately two-thirds of the Caucasian population." She didn't mention that some of the information had come from Lily Baker and not the doctor, but Kylie had confirmed it with Google. "DNA results will take weeks or longer. When I spoke to the lab, they were still processing the fiber from the truck and the glass from the bar. We're waiting for confirmation that the shoes belong to Abby. The fingerprints are smudged, but we're hoping the state lab can make the match." Kylie glanced at her phone screen. It was after seven now. "The lab's closed for the weekend now."

"Great," Davis said. "We won't see anything until Monday."

The sound of Vogel speaking reached her, but the words were muffled.

"Sorry?" she said.

"I'd like you to follow up with Pamela Nolan. Make sure she has an alibi for her husband's accident," Davis said, and she wondered if that was what Vogel had whispered.

"Right," she said. "Did you receive the highway patrol report about the accident? Everything at the scene indicates that the car hit ice and spun. Ross said the guardrails are outdated, so that's how the car was able to break through."

"He shared that with us," Davis said. "But we still need to confirm that alibi, especially if she knew her husband was with Lily Baker that night."

"She said she'd driven from home the morning after his accident," Vogel cut in. "We're crossing our t's on this one," he went on. "I don't want anyone coming back and saying that we screwed it up."

Kylie pulled out a chair and sat down. "You mean, like maybe Mrs. Nolan ran her husband off the road?"

"If he was having an affair and she found out . . . stranger things have happened," Davis said.

"But there's no evidence of another car in the accident," Kylie said. "How do we think she might have been involved?"

"She could have been standing in the road or caused some other obstruction," Vogel announced with a huff. "Is it far fetched? Yes. But it won't take much to confirm the alibi."

She thought about the hair in the passenger seat, Lily Baker's fingerprints. Baker had given her nothing, and Nolan's accident was just that, an accident. Following up on his wife's alibi was stupid busy work—busy work that could have been done by anyone. Hell, they could have Marjorie in Dispatch make the call, if they were so intent on having it be women's work. If they kept her processing traffic accidents and chasing false leads, she'd never get back to Fargo. Kylie was the detective. She needed to focus on the murder investigation.

She drew a deep breath and cracked her knuckles, one by one, feeling some of the frustration seep out with the tightness in the joints. It was just another example of Hagen's boys'-club bullshit, keeping the rising star detective in her place. But it wasn't worth a fight, not with these two. "Okay. I'll talk to Mrs. Nolan."

"Good girl," Vogel said.

Kylie took a long, slow breath before saying goodbye and ending the call. *Good girl.* She popped every knuckle on both hands, blowing out a breath as she counted to ten. If Glen Vogel called her *girl* in person, she was going to shove him out of that damn chair.

Kylie stepped out into the cold evening air and fingered her car keys. Larson would be in the hospital for another day, and the lab was still working on the evidence. Tonight, though, all she wanted was to go home and put her feet up, look more closely at the image of Iver Larson and that woman, and find something to link the picture to Jensen. It had to be there. They were so close she could taste it.

As she started for her car, a voice called to her from behind. She turned back to see Dr. Prescott.

Her stomach fell. "Did something happen with Larson?"

"No. He's fine. But if you have a minute, there's something I'd like to show you."

Kylie stepped back to the hospital entrance. "Sure."

"I'm new to Hagen," Prescott said. "And I don't know Mr. Larson from Adam, but I think you should see this."

"Sure," Kylie said again, crossing her arms as Prescott opened a manila folder and pulled out a piece of paper. The wind picked up and snapped the page in her hand. Kylie took it and walked back through the automatic doors and into the still-warm air of the hospital. How close she'd been to getting out of there. She scanned the page and frowned. "What am I looking at?"

"This is the report from Mr. Larson's blood draw. We found this compound in his blood." She pointed to a long chemical name and, below it, a weird shape that reminded Kylie of how poorly she'd done in geometry.

"What is it?"

"Flurazepam. It's a very fast-acting sedative. He says he's never taken this drug."

"He's probably lying."

"Perhaps," Prescott said. "But it's not a drug he's ever been prescribed, and he has a similar drug in his medicine cabinet to help with sleep. So why take a new drug?"

"I can't answer that, Doctor." Kylie turned to go.

"Detective, this drug also has a relatively long half-life—forty-seven to one hundred hours."

Kylie gave her a blank stare.

Prescott nodded. "Based on the concentration in his blood, if this was given to him earlier in the week as he suggested, then Mr. Larson ingested a lot of it. A much larger dose than is indicated for his insomnia."

Kylie exhaled. "I don't know what you're saying, Doctor."

"I'm saying that this drug would normally knock someone out. But with Mr. Larson's other medications, the physical reaction could have been quite unexpected."

Kylie's ears perked up at the doctor's words. "Could this drug have made him angry or violent?"

"Actually, this drug on its own should have sedated Mr. Larson."

Kylie shook her head. "We have evidence that Larson showed aggressive behavior Wednesday." She handed the paper back. "So maybe he took it Thursday." She'd certainly want to take a lot of sedative if she'd killed someone.

"Perhaps," Prescott said. "It's also possible that in combination with his regular medications, the sedative effect was mitigated. The contraindications of these drugs together—the ones he takes normally and this particular drug—have been known to cause aggressive behavior. It's not common, Detective, but it can happen."

Kylie pulled out a notebook and recorded what Prescott had said, along with her name. "That's very helpful. They teach that in med school?"

"Actually, I called a pharmaceutical rep friend to get it sorted out. But that's not all," Prescott went on with a glance over her shoulder.

Kylie held her pen poised. This was going to be great for the trial.

"While the drug interaction has been reported to cause aggressive behavior, flurazepam's side effects include blackouts and a severe lack of physical coordination. Not to mention that it's also likely behind the seizure."

Kylie stopped writing. "Severe lack of physical coordination?"

"It's not my place to speculate, Detective. But from what I have learned, this medication may have caused anger, but it would also have made it difficult to strangle someone. His strength would have been diminished and his hand-eye coordination off."

Kylie put her notebook away. "It doesn't take that much coordination to wrap your hands around someone's neck and squeeze."

Prescott closed the folder. "But it takes a lot of strength. And it requires even more to lift a hundred-and-forty-pound woman into a dumpster."

"But it's possible that he took the drug after Wednesday? Like yesterday or even earlier today?"

"Yes."

"Is there any way to isolate when the drug entered his system?"

"Not unless we know how much he took to begin with. Then we could extrapolate with the drug's half-life."

This would come up in the trial. "But what if you took another blood sample in twenty-four hours? Wouldn't the difference help you calculate how much he had to start with?"

The doctor looked momentarily flushed. "I'm not certain. It's outside my expertise. I'd have to do some research."

"Please do. And if it will allow you to identify when he took the medication, please run the blood tests as often as necessary. It could be the difference between freedom and a life in prison."

"I will," Prescott said.

"And let's keep it between us for now."

She didn't want Larson's attorney to stop the tests.

"I'll need Mr. Larson's approval."

"Well, tell him it's so we can find out when he was drugged. If he says he didn't take that stuff, then someone else gave it to him."

"I will."

Kylie turned to leave again, but as she reached the doors, she turned back. "Thank you, Dr. Prescott."

The woman smiled.

It was obvious Dr. Prescott was hoping the drug test might exonerate Larson. Fine with Kylie. She was hoping it would tighten the noose on his neck.

CHAPTER 36

—

LILY

As Lily left Iver's hospital room, it was impossible not to feel like she was the reason that he'd been arrested. But the shoes in his truck? The blood? She hadn't done that. She just didn't believe he could have killed someone.

Maybe you're not a very good judge of character.

But what if she was right? What if he was innocent? Maybe she hadn't been with him when Abby was killed, but she had been with Abby that night. Wasn't that what she remembered? The two of them standing in the snow, in the woods? That was near the bar. They'd been huddled together, shivering. She could feel the fear as intensely as in that moment. Someone was coming. He was coming. But not Iver.

She squeezed her eyes closed and tried to picture a face, but the only one she could see was Abby's—the intensity of her friend's eyes as they scanned the dark, the pupils large with terror. And then her friend lying in the snow. Not moving.

She would go to the police. She had to. Whatever memory lurked on the periphery of her mind would identify the killer and prove it wasn't Iver Larson.

Lily clenched Iver's truck keys in her fist and made her way toward the hospital exit. Walking toward the doors, she passed Dr. Prescott, who was striding down the hallway in the opposite direction. The doctor nodded without a word.

Outside, Detective Milliard was crossing the parking lot.

Lily called out, and Milliard spun around. Lily ran toward her. "Detective!"

"I can't talk about the case," the detective said, opening her car door.

"Please. I need to talk to you. There's something you need to know."

Milliard turned back, her eyes angry. "Now you want to come clean?"

"I'm sorry." Lily scanned the parking lot. They stood in the exact spot where Tim Bailey's wife had found her and Tim the morning before. One day ago. How was it possible? "I was scared."

"Fine," Milliard said. "Talk."

Lily pulled her sweatshirt down over her hands and tucked them under her arms. A heavy bank of dark clouds had rolled in, and it pressed down on her, making the open parking lot feel small. Her gaze scanned the icicles that clung to the edge of the hospital's roof, the slush that collected along the curb and at their feet. Anywhere but the detective's face, which was still hard. Confess. She just had to confess. But she was slow to speak, trying to find a way to break the seal of the secrets she'd been holding. How much did she admit? If she said the wrong thing, would she end up in jail with Iver?

Milliard sighed. "It's late, Baker, and it's been a long day."

Lily straightened her back. "I *was* in the car with Brent Nolan when he had the accident."

"No shit," Milliard said. "What caused it?"

Lily swallowed something sharp. "I don't remember."

"Christ." Milliard opened her car door again and turned to get in.

Lily grabbed hold of the door. "Please. It's the truth. I don't remember. Not the accident, not anything."

The detective stood motionless, waiting.

"I swear to you," Lily whispered. "I have no memories. I don't remember anything before waking up in that car, on the overpass. I mean, I have a few memories, but they're jumbled, like a dream."

As though against her will, Milliard's expression softened. With that bit of encouragement, Lily told Kylie Milliard about waking up, the memory of the man in the blood, the bits with Abby at her house, and then the two of them in the woods, her bag, the gun, how the hems of her jeans and her boots had been wet, how she'd pulled Brent from the car, thinking a train was coming. Then the call from the OnStar that the police were on their way, her panic, the night in the shed, and getting to town the next morning—she even mentioned the truck driver, Jim. Then the hospital, her interaction with Tim Bailey, the walk to Iver's, and the attack. Standing in the freezing air, Lily told Detective Milliard every single thing she could remember, other than stealing the money from Brent Nolan's wallet. She couldn't bring herself to admit to that.

Milliard didn't say a single word until Lily reached the moment she'd arrived at Iver's to find him having a seizure.

"That's it," Lily said, her jaw tight and shivering from the cold. "That's the whole truth."

Finally, the detective shook her head. "I'm not sure whether to thank you or arrest you. It would've been a hell of a lot easier if you'd told me everything from the start."

Lily cringed at the detective's sharp tone. She had thought—or maybe just hoped—that Milliard would feel some sympathy, but Lily had gotten herself into this mess, probably by whatever she'd been doing before she'd gotten into the car with Brent Nolan. But certainly, she'd brought it on herself when she'd lied.

"You have anything else to tell me?" Milliard asked.

"I—I didn't know who I could trust."

"So you chose Iver Larson?"

"He didn't attack me. It wasn't him. The attacker had a Taser," she said breathlessly.

"It's not hard to get a Taser," Milliard told her. "And Iver could have hidden that before he took that blanket off your head."

"It wasn't Iver," she said again. "The smell of him was so distinct." She closed her eyes and tried to bring the smell to mind. There was a hint of something minty, then spicy. Almost like a plant. "Licorice, maybe?"

"Licorice?" Milliard repeated.

That felt right. The spice, the sweet. "I think that was it. Black licorice."

"Your attacker smelled like candy?" The detective sounded doubtful.

"I'm trying to help," Lily protested.

"Well, find your memory so you can tell me what you were doing in that car. And leave the murder to me." She opened the car door and got in. "And I'd put some distance between you and Larson. He's going to jail for murder." With that, the detective closed the door, started her car, and drove off, leaving Lily shivering in the empty parking lot.

CHAPTER 37

—

IVER

A hockey game played on the small mounted TV in Iver's hospital room. He'd been watching half-heartedly, not even bothering to check who was playing, when Mike's voice echoed from the hallway. "He's got rights," Mike shouted. A man's voice responded, but Iver couldn't make out the words over the sound of Mike's fist on the door as he burst into the room.

"Asshole," Mike hissed, swinging the door closed behind him.

This was his future. Trapped, locked up, hoping for visitors. And who would come? Mike a few times. His mother.

Mike seemed momentarily surprised to find Iver sitting in the hospital bed. "Hey, man."

"Thanks for coming."

"What happened?"

"Seizure," Iver said, shifting under the sheets. He had pulled his fleece over the hospital gown, but he wasn't allowed to change out of it. Hospital rules. All the same bullshit he remembered from coming home. Back then, he hadn't been allowed to brush his own teeth or go to the bathroom or wash himself—everything had to be supervised and timed and measured, as though he was a damn science experiment. And now he felt caught in some other kind of experiment—more terrifying than the last.

"You okay?" Mike asked.

Iver met his friend's gaze, nodded.

"Seriously, man."

Something in Mike's expression set him off. He shook his head, wiped his face, surprised to find moisture in his eyes. "They think I killed that woman."

"That's impossible."

Iver studied his face, refusing to blink. He wanted to absorb his friend's expression, examine every square inch for doubt. "I've never hurt anyone."

Mike's lips shifted.

"It was a fucking war, Mike." Iver ripped the sheets back and stared down at his bare legs before realizing there was nowhere to go. He yanked the sheet back across his legs and swung his feet over the side of the bed so he didn't feel like such an invalid, such a monster.

"I didn't say anything," Mike whispered.

"You didn't have to," Iver said.

Mike opened his mouth to speak but let it fall closed again.

Even his best friend didn't believe he was innocent.

A knock on the door drew both men's stares. Finally, Iver said, "Come in."

When it cracked open, he was surprised to see his ex-wife's face. He jerked the thin blanket off the bed and wrapped it around his legs, covering the bottom half of the gown and adjusting his sweatshirt. He looked ridiculous—like he was going to a toga party in Siberia—but at least the gown was covered. Debbie had seen him in enough hospital gowns to last two lifetimes.

She stared between the two men. "I just wanted to make sure you two were okay."

Iver glanced at Mike, then at Debbie. "Why wouldn't we be?"

Debbie crossed her arms, one foot out to the side. Angry Debbie. It almost made him laugh, which almost made him cry.

"Really?" she said. "After Wednesday night?"

Wearing the blanket like a damn skirt, Iver walked to the far side of the room, if only to create distance between her and him. Wednesday night. The night that woman had been killed. The night he couldn't remember. The night . . . her message had said he'd come to her house. That he should leave them alone. Who was "them"? Had Debbie been with a girlfriend that night? Why was the whole night blank in his mind?

"You were furious, Iver."

He jumped at the proximity of her voice. When he turned, she was standing beside him. He could see the narrow birthmark on her left wrist, the one that looked like a sword.

"At us," she said, then added, "Mike and me."

"You and Mike," he repeated like an idiot, and in a flood, he knew. Mike's smile when he'd run out to his truck, the fact that he was letting someone else drive his precious rig, the reason he would be going to Denver at all. Debbie and Mike. His ex-wife and his best friend were dating.

"What? You forgot?" Debbie went on. "Even after going apeshit on Wednesday?"

"Deb," Mike said softly, pity in his eyes.

Iver stepped away and felt the wall at his back. He pressed his palms on the cool surface. He couldn't stand. His legs wouldn't hold him, so he sank until he hit the floor. "I don't remember."

"What do you mean, you don't remember?" Mike asked.

"I don't remember going there," Iver said. "Did you answer the door? Did we talk?"

"No. We never heard you," she said, shaking her head and looking at Mike. "It was two in the morning, and we were asleep."

"Did you knock?" Mike asked. "What were you doing there in the middle of the night?"

"I don't know. I don't remember," he said again, drawing out each word in the way that had driven Debbie mad when they'd been married.

"Of course you remember," she said. "Shouting at us to get the hell out of *your* bar? Threatening to punch Mike?"

The bar? Iver tried to place Mike and Debbie in the bar on Wednesday. He had no memory of seeing them there. No memory of going to her house in the middle of the night. What else had he done that night that he couldn't remember? "I swear," he said, shaking his head. "I don't remember."

"Bullshit, Iver Larson," Debbie said.

"It's not," he countered, wanting to gather his anger to fight her. All he could stir up was fear. He'd been driving in the middle of the night on Wednesday. But he usually left the bar by about ten thirty. Where had he been between leaving the bar and showing up at Debbie's house? Damn, what had he done?

"How can you not remember?" Mike asked.

Debbie knelt beside him. "Are you taking all your meds?"

He pushed her away. "I'm not a kid, Debbie. I'm fine."

"Not if you don't remember Wednesday night, you're not fine."

Iver looked to Mike, forcing himself onto his feet. "I was drugged, Mike. Someone put something in my drink. The doctor said there was something in my blood, some sedative. It's not one of my medications, and I don't take drugs, Mike. You know I don't."

Mike nodded.

Iver couldn't tell if his friend believed him. He glanced at Debbie, but he couldn't read her anymore either. Had he ever been able to read her? Once, maybe. Suddenly, he felt certain that the drug was the key to whatever had happened on Wednesday. Or he prayed it was.

If he could figure out what it was and who had given it to him, then he'd be able to save himself. Kevin brought his drinks, but usually Nate or Mike made them. A dozen of their high school friends always hung around, people who might have hated him or old-timers who had hated his father . . . or someone who wanted his ex-wife.

He looked back up at Mike and tried to speak in a calm voice. "I need to know who drugged me that night. I won't be angry." He was lying now. He would be furious, but he needed to know. He needed to know *why* he didn't remember. More than that, he needed to know *what* he didn't remember. "Did you put something in my drink? To try to calm me down, maybe?" As though that were an excuse.

"He would never," Debbie said.

"No," Mike echoed.

"I need to find out who did. Because whatever that was, it made me forget." It had to be the reason for the loss of memory. And maybe it had made him angry, too. But capable of murder? No. He couldn't believe that. He would never believe that. "They think I killed someone. Until I understand who drugged me and what it was, I can't prove that I didn't kill that girl."

"No one was even with you. You were in the office most of the night, drinking alone."

Iver rubbed his face, exhausted. "Well, someone was bringing me drinks."

Mike nodded. "I know Nate made you a couple."

"Nate," Iver repeated.

"No way Nate drugged you, Iver. We've been friends forever."

"Kevin was the one who brought them in. At least the first ones," Iver added.

Mike said nothing.

Iver didn't want to believe any of them had drugged him. Why would they? He thought about the mess of his office, the receipts and tapes he'd brought home. He rubbed his head, fighting off the escalating squeeze in his temples as he tried to remember what he'd been doing before the seizure. "Have you looked at this week's receipts? Our deposits are off."

"Do the bar books really matter right now?" Debbie asked.

Mike placed a hand on her arm, and Iver had to look away.

"Off by how much?" Mike asked.

Iver rarely let Mike work on the books. His father had always told him to keep that part of the business close to the vest. No one needed to know how much money you were making. It only caused trouble.

"Iver?"

He shook his head. "I was working on the books before the seizure, but there was money missing—like seven hundred dollars." Suddenly, he was unable to find any air in the room, like he'd been buried in a snowbank. "It might have been Wednesday night. Who did deposits on Thursday?"

"I sent Kevin. With the police there, I'd been up most of the night. I wanted to get home for a little sleep before I had to be back."

"Can you go back through the receipts and match the deposits? I think some of the tape was missing from my office." The system at the bar was old. Iver did it the same way his father had. He matched the register tape to the deposits, and he had a general feel for inventory. He should have kept a closer watch, but the bar had become just a job to him, a means to an end. "Did you check the deposit before Kevin went?" Iver asked.

"Kevin would never drug you." But even as Mike said it, something in his expression shifted. His gaze slid to Debbie.

"What?"

The two stared at each other.

"What is it?" Iver pressed.

It was Debbie who spoke first. "There's a rumor that Kevin got Sarah Ollman pregnant."

"The pastor's daughter? She's what—sixteen?"

"Seventeen," Debbie said. "She was in the bar that night, hanging all over him."

Mike sank into the chair beside Iver's hospital bed. "He said something about being under pressure. He needed money."

"For—"

Debbie stared at him, and Iver understood. Sarah Ollman wanted to terminate a pregnancy. "Would seven hundred bucks be enough?"

"Probably," Debbie said.

Kevin's dad had never been around. His mom was frail and hadn't worked since Kevin was in middle school. Kevin probably supported them both and had nothing to spare. So he needed money. "But why drug me? Why not ask for the money—an advance or something?"

Mike stared at the floor.

"Mike."

His friend shook his head, refusing to look up.

"You know something," Iver said.

Slowly, Mike raised his head. "Kevin did ask for money. Maybe two weeks ago, he asked for a thousand dollars in advance, said he'd pay it back, but it would probably take him a couple months."

"And?" Iver pressed.

Mike shook his head. "I told him I'd ask you."

"But you didn't."

"Right," Mike said.

Debbie moved closer to Mike. "Did he ask again?"

Mike rubbed his face.

"Christ, Mike, what the hell happened?" Iver asked.

"I told him you said no."

"Mike," Debbie said, his name coming out in a whisper of disappointment.

"You never even asked me. You just told him no, and he accepted that?"

Mike rubbed his hands, and Iver knew there was more. Mike had said something else, something about him. "Spit it out, Mike."

"I told him that you were a tightwad—" He raised his chin. "Actually, I told him you were a fucking asshole who wouldn't help anyone but yourself."

Debbie gasped and took a step back.

Iver held Mike's gaze until Mike looked away. Neither man spoke. His best friend thought he was an asshole and a tightwad. His best friend, who was sleeping with his ex-wife. So Kevin had drugged him to steal money. And the drug had made him aggressive. And then . . . what? Had he killed Abigail Jensen?

Maybe Detective Milliard had it right after all. Maybe he was a killer.

The room went silent. The people who knew Iver best in the whole world were here, together, and neither of them could look him in the eye.

CHAPTER 38

———

KYLIE

Kylie arrived home to find both Amber and William asleep and the house quiet. She had been looking forward to holding William, smelling the sweet scent of his baby skin. And she'd wanted to talk to Amber about Lily Baker. Amber was younger than Baker by three or four years, so it was unlikely that they had known each other growing up. Especially since Baker had been homeschooled after her ordeal and then had left town for Arizona. But Kylie needed her roommate for more than getting the latest Hagen gossip. Amber had become a sounding board for Kylie, the one person in Hagen—other than William—whom she trusted implicitly.

When had she gotten so damn dependent? She had never wanted a roommate. She thought of herself as someone who did better alone. Made her own mess and cleaned it up when she was damn ready. Didn't pick up after anyone else. Certainly not a baby. Now, though, she found herself creeping into the small den that had been converted to William's nursery and crossing on tiptoes to the crib to look down on William, splayed on his back, arms and legs spread like a tiny drunk.

Resisting the urge to reach in and touch the smooth skin of his forearm, she retreated from the room and set herself up on the living room couch with her computer and the list of follow-up items. Friday night at nine o'clock, women her age were supposed to be doing something else. Supposed to be. Kylie retrieved a beer from the fridge and popped the top with the side of a butter knife, a party trick she'd learned from her older brother when she was nine or ten before he'd headed off to college. How desperate she'd been to be as cool as her brother. There was something about the sound of the seal on the bottle breaking as she levered the butter knife upward that always made her feel momentarily invincible.

Boy, did she need that now.

On the sofa, laptop open, Kylie drank her beer and reviewed the coroner's report on Abigail Jensen. By that point, it had been in her inbox for almost twelve hours, and she was in no rush to be disappointed again. Kylie didn't have a lot of faith in Hagen's coroner. Amber joked that Milt Horchow had been burying bodies in Hagen since before the city had been incorporated. One look at him, and Kylie could almost believe it. He was barely five feet tall but at least three feet wide at his center. He wore his pants like a clown, loose at the waist with suspenders, and what little hair he had left was white and made a narrow horseshoe around his head. Quiet but opinionated, Horchow had to be in his eighties, with no signs of slowing down. But his reports were straightforward and clean, so she had to give the guy credit.

According to the report, cause of death was likely blunt-force trauma, which she already knew. Gilbert had mentioned that Jensen had hit her head, but the coroner also noted signs of petechial hemorrhage, which suggested Jensen had also been strangled. Kylie scanned the list of Jensen's belongings. Other than her clothing, the items listed among Jensen's belongings were largely what Kylie had seen herself—a leather bracelet with a metal disk and a single silver ring. Nothing in her jacket—no phone or wallet or keys. The killer had taken her shoes and likely also her wallet and phone, so why had they only found her shoes in Larson's truck?

At the end of Horchow's report, he had written that the body was in full rigor as well as frozen solid. Why would Larson have killed Abby Jensen in a drunken rage and then waited hours—four or five or six of them—to dump the body? Whoever had done it had to have broken the rigor and also lifted the woman overhead and into the dumpster. Dr. Prescott's warning came back to her: the drug in Larson's tox screen impaired strength and coordination.

She glanced at the first page of the autopsy report. Horchow had listed the deceased as weighing 137 pounds. What would it take to lift that much weight while on a drug that reduced your strength? Would adrenaline make up for the deficit? Was Larson working with someone? Or maybe the reason he'd waited to dump the body was to give the drugs a chance to metabolize out of his system so that he had the strength to lift her.

Kylie went back to her email and sorted through the long list of unread messages. Gilbert had copied her on a report to Davis and Vogel that no prisoners recently released on parole lived within thirty miles of Hagen, and no registered sex offenders resided within fifty miles. Sheriff Oloff in Elgin had forwarded Abigail Jensen's bank statements for the last three months. Back in October, she had emptied her bank account—$457—and stopped using the account. No debit card use, no deposits. Nothing. And her mother had told Sheriff Oloff that she'd stopped supporting Abigail, seeing her rarely in the months before her death. So who had been helping her?

She forwarded the message to Davis and Vogel, copying Gilbert, and requested that they obtain bank information for Iver Larson and Lily Baker. She would have liked to get it for Brent Nolan as well, but she knew how Vogel and Davis would respond to that request. God forbid they ruffle the feathers of a drilling exec—dead or not.

In an earlier email was a note from the manager at the man camp. They had only one resident who wasn't on campus Wednesday night, but they had confirmed that Benny Schade had been in Minot, North Dakota, with his family. The manager had attached a gas receipt for Wednesday evening, the night of the murder, at just past five p.m., where Schade had supposedly filled his tank as he'd arrived home to visit his family. Kylie entered Schade into the police database, but he came up clean. Not so much as a speeding ticket.

She scanned the email from the man-camp manager again. It wasn't Fort Knox over there. Surely someone could have gotten out unnoticed if he'd wanted to. She made a note on her list and told herself she'd go up there next week if she didn't find any better leads.

She opened the image of a furious Iver Larson gripping a woman's arm that had come from Sarah Ollman. The woman's thin wrist was visible, as was the edge of something dark, maybe the leather band Jensen had been wearing. Though they'd studied the images at the department, Kylie went back through them, searching for another angle of that moment or of Larson, searching for the woman whose profile might match. It could be Abigail Jensen. The waves of blonde hair were the right length and shade to be Jensen's. If only the camera had been shifted one inch to the right, they'd have been able to see her.

Her beer drained, Kylie shut down her computer. Her thoughts went to what Lily Baker had told her in the parking lot. Convenient, how she remembered nothing about the car accident or why she'd been in Brent Nolan's car. Kylie had thought it a ruse to get away with something, but the more Kylie had listened to Baker run through everything that had happened, the harder it was to hang on to her disbelief. Maybe Baker really had lost her memory.

Certainly, Baker hadn't slipped up as she recounted the story to Kylie, and she hadn't hesitated as she'd spoken, instead letting it out like one long stream of vomit.

In her notebook, Kylie jotted down a few phrases from Baker's story. *Attacker smelled like licorice*, *Tim Bailey*, and *wet shoes and pants*. That last one, she underlined twice before yawning as she rose from the couch and padded into her bedroom.

You should brush your teeth. And change your clothes. Get under the covers. Instead, she lay across the bed and pulled a throw blanket over her shoulders. As sleep drew her in, her mind drifted back to Baker's story. Nolan had been unconscious, but Baker had been able to get out. She hadn't been wearing a jacket, and it was freezing on the overpass. Her boots and the hem of her jeans were wet. Wet made Kylie think of springtime and fall. How could she have gotten wet? There was no water near the overpass where they'd gone over.

There was no water anywhere nearby. The closest rivers were miles from Hagen. Some realization drifted by, but Kylie was too exhausted to catch hold of it, so instead she let sleep take her.

CHAPTER 39

—

LILY

Lily didn't sleep. Instead, she lay in her bed, Cal beside her, and listened to the night tick by. The detective was right. Getting her memory back was about the only thing she could do to be of any help to the police.

Abby Jensen had been staying at her home, which meant she and Lily had almost certainly been together shortly before Abby was killed. Had she seen the killer? She remembered images of a dream, the woods with Abby. But she couldn't find his face in her memory. Was his name buried in her subconscious? And could she unlock that place?

Outside her window, the black sky grew inky blue and then a deep violet before Lily got out of bed. She had to get a new cell phone, but the small store in Hagen that sold them—the only store that sold them—wouldn't be open until ten a.m. It was barely seven now. She thought back to the articles she'd read at Iver's about her captivity. Only a handful had an image to go along with the story, but the ones that did had shown the same photograph—a view of the cabin where the girls were held. In Molva.

Lily made her way to the entryway. On top of the mail sat a set of car keys with a VW sign. She took them to the front door and hit the lock button. The white car on the curb chirped. Her car was here. She had driven away from the bar with Brent Nolan. But how had she gotten to the bar if not in her own car? She ferreted in her mind, searching for clues. She could remember running through the woods, getting into Nolan's car, but the time between being with Abby in her kitchen and that was blank, like a dark room with not a sliver of light.

Lily had an idea. A terrible, crazy idea. But despite her doubts, the longer the idea lingered in her mind, the more convinced she became that it was the only way. She pulled open the drawer of the entry table and searched the contents, then did the same in the kitchen drawers and finally in her bedroom. In the back of the bedside drawer, she found a credit card, wrapped in a yellow sticky note that read, *Emergencies only.*

She wanted to laugh.

She dressed quickly, fed Cal breakfast, and grabbed a handful of stale crackers from a box in the pantry for herself. The grocery store was nowhere near the top of her list, but it would have to be eventually. When Cal had finished his food, she packed a bottle of water and a bowl for Cal, pocketed her emergency credit card and car keys, and headed out with Cal loaded in the passenger seat.

Her first stop was a gas station, where she filled the tank. Inside the small convenience market, she bought two granola bars and a North Dakota road map.

"Hey, Lily," the cashier said, and Lily smiled, fighting against the urge to stare at his name tag. He lifted the road map and laughed. "Haven't sold one of these in a while."

"I know, right?" she said, sounding like an idiot as he rang her up. She slid her credit card into the reader and prayed it didn't reject her or ask for a PIN. A quick beep sounded, and a receipt slid out of the machine. The cashier handed it to her.

"Thanks," she said, grateful to return to her car.

She left the gas station and drove several blocks in what she guessed was the direction of the highway out of town before pulling over to consult the map. The crisp paper spread out before her, Lily found Molva immediately, tucked in the southwestern corner of the state, its name in tiny font. She scanned the intricate maze of roads and towns and decided it should have taken her ten minutes to locate Molva. But it was there, in her subconscious. Using her fingers to measure the inches, she figured the town was about a two-hour drive. Gathering her nerve, she switched on the radio and let the soothing voice of Waylon Jennings fill the car.

Cal settled in on the passenger seat as Lily put the car in gear and started toward the town where all her nightmares had come true.

CHAPTER 40

KYLIE

By six a.m., Kylie had finished a pot of coffee on her own and paced a new rut in the living room carpet, waiting for a response to her early-morning text to Deputy Sheriff Pete McIntosh in Glendive.

Even before falling asleep, Kylie had decided she needed to go to Glendive to meet McIntosh. The deputy sheriff was in the same position she was—with a dead body and looking for someone to put behind bars for the crime. Kylie had texted him to let him know they'd made an arrest, but she still had questions. Plus, she wanted to see the place where the third victim, Jenna Hitchcock, had been killed. She didn't know the details of Hitchcock's death or what he'd found on his end. There had to be something—some little nugget that would make it worth the drive.

McIntosh's response came in shortly after six thirty. I'm around all day if you want to come down to see the Hitchcock scene.

Two heads were better than one, and a fresh perspective would be nice, too. Hagen felt claustrophobic that way—Sheriff Davis, DA Vogel, and even Carl Gilbert seemed each to have his own personal agenda. Every interaction included an element of history, obvious or subtle. The subtext dealt with what trouble you had gotten into as a kid, if you'd been an asshole in high school, who your father was, and sometimes even who your father's father was. To close this case and walk away confident that she'd put the right man behind bars, Kylie had to clear all that away and come to the crime objectively—something that was almost impossible for folks in Hagen.

Carl Gilbert was a perfect example. He'd been so aggressive with Larson in the hospital, like the beef he had with Larson was personal. They'd gone to school together, so maybe there was some high school shit still lingering. But she didn't like how close Gilbert was to the case. And she particularly didn't like that he'd been the one to search Larson's car.

Hagen had official crime scene investigators trained in evidence collection, and Gilbert wasn't one of them. Maybe she was just sensitive to the fact that she'd been left out of the loop on the warrant for Larson's car. She was definitely bent out of shape about that.

But Pete McIntosh had no connections to Hagen. And neither did she.

Heading your way within the hour, she texted in reply to Pete McIntosh.

Forty minutes later, Kylie got into her department car with a thermos of black coffee and a piece of banana-cream pie that Amber had brought her. When she considered how many pieces of banana-cream pie she'd eaten since Wednesday, she almost felt too sick to eat it. Almost.

Unfortunately, banana cream went well with coffee. And it was all she had for breakfast as she drove out the 1804, the same road Brent Nolan had died on, and headed west toward Glendive and Billings beyond. She'd made it eight miles when she grew close to the home of Alvin Tanner. Tanner, who had footage of Highway 1804. She glanced at the clock. It was seven thirty a.m. on a Saturday morning. She'd been here less than twenty-four hours earlier, but it felt as though days had passed.

It was too early to go calling on an unsuspecting citizen, but Tanner had been warned, so Kylie didn't hesitate to pull off the highway and turn onto Tanner's creepy camera-ridden property. She'd barely made the final turn when she noticed the absence of the cameras that had lined the roof yesterday. All four were gone.

She hesitated in the driveway, waiting for Tanner to come charging out, but the house was still, quiet. Kylie gripped the radio on her dash, then let go and picked up her phone to text Sheriff Davis directly.

We ever see the footage from Alvin Tanner of the 1804? Never came to my email but maybe he sent through highway patrol? I'm at his residence now.

She made no mention of the missing cameras or the quiet eeriness of the property.

I haven't. You check with Gilbert?

Why would Gilbert have it? He hadn't even come to Tanner's. It was just Kylie and the highway patrol officer, Merkel.

No. Going to talk to Tanner now.

With that, she pocketed her phone and drew her weapon from its holster. She cracked the car door and waited for some response from Tanner. The house remained quiet. She stayed in the shelter of her car and called out, "Alvin Tanner?"

The wind picked up, shaking the evergreens and hissing through their trembling branches.

She shivered and called out again. "Mr. Tanner, it's Detective Kylie Milliard from Hagen. We spoke yesterday."

Nothing.

She took a step away from her car, crossing the yard toward Tanner's old Chevy. As she approached, she saw the driver's door hung open. A plastic grocery sack had spilled on the driver's side floor mat, a fifth of some brown liquor and several cans scattered about. A single apple had rolled out onto the ground. She reached down to touch the liquor bottle and found the glass cold.

"Mr. Tanner?" She heard the crack in her own voice.

Pausing behind the protection of Tanner's truck, she scanned the property for anything else that looked out of place. But it all looked the same—the neglected yard, a broken chair near a firepit, a handful of shingles that dotted the yard where they'd come off the roof. Where the cameras had been, the roof was slightly darker, noticeable only if you looked for it. The house remained quiet, but the groceries and the truck told her something was wrong.

Rather than walking up the front steps, she approached the side of the house.

Standing to the side of the first window, she raised her gun and edged close enough to see inside. No shades or curtains meant she had a full view of the room. It was a bedroom, the bed unmade, the sheets shoved back as though the occupant had gotten up in a hurry. She shifted across the window and looked in from the other side. A single chair sat in the corner, piled with clothes. A flannel similar to the one Tanner had been wearing yesterday and a pair of jeans lay on top.

Nothing amiss. She moved toward the back of the house, where a window looked in on a smaller room. Another bed, made hastily, a blanket lying across the foot. A cobweb stretched from the old light fixture to a corner of the window like a ghostly veil.

At the corner of the house, she listened for sounds. A motorcycle roared by along the freeway, its screaming engine adding to the thumping of her pulse.

When the cycle had passed, she glanced around the corner before creeping along the back of the house. She reached a single window just above her eye level, but all she could see was a light fixture in the center of the room, the dim bulb on. Ten steps farther was the back entrance. She paused at its edge before peering through the small window in the door.

A man lay on the floor near the table, on his side with his back to her. The man's face wasn't visible, but Kylie recognized the flannel shirt immediately—the shirt Alvin Tanner had been wearing when she'd last seen him. She twisted the doorknob, which turned easily, and stepped into the room, gun drawn.

The room smelled of sour milk and cigarette smoke. Decades of it leached from the walls and floor. Bending beside the body, she pressed her fingers to his carotid artery without looking down, her gaze scanning the doorways, her gun ready.

No pulse.

She pulled her phone from her pocket and dialed Hagen Dispatch.

"Cannon," came the response.

"It's Milliard. I'm at Alvin Tanner's, out on 1804. He's on the kitchen floor, unresponsive."

"I'll send an ambulance. You okay?"

"Yeah. Think he's been dead awhile." But even as she said it, she glanced down and saw Tanner's outstretched hand. A deep groove ran along the wrist where he'd clearly been bound, though the restraint was gone now. Small cuts covered the bare arm, horizontal slices, as though he'd been grazed by some sort of fine rake with razor points. "Jesus," she whispered, leaning in.

Beneath his hand was a pool of blood. Only then did she notice he was missing two fingers—his pinkie and his pointer.

She stood and backed away from the body. Heat pooled in her gut. What had happened? Had he had some sort of accident? But there were no weapons nearby, no drops of blood on the floor around him. Plus, he hadn't bound his own wrists. She scanned the kitchen surfaces and bit back the sound at the back of her throat.

In the center of the kitchen table was an ashtray, almost full. Lying among the ash and butts were the two severed fingers.

CHAPTER 41

—

Lily

Lily arrived in Molva and drove slowly down Main Street, past a handful of shops and a delicatessen. She studied the buildings, scoured their facades, willing herself to remember something. A woman walked out of the deli, a white bag in her hand. Her gaze fixed on Lily's car and followed it as she drove down the street. Lily was panting, her breaths coming shallow and too fast. In her rearview mirror, the woman still watched as Lily went by.

The whole of Molva was about seven blocks long before Main Street reached the river and the road curved to the left. Lily found herself crossing the bridge and following Main Street as it wound out of town. As she drove, she studied the flat landscape, the low brush that grew thicker at the water's edge. A mile passed and then another, the road winding left and then right along the river. She pulled out at the first turnoff and put her car in park.

She had no idea where that cabin was and no way to find it. No phone to use Google Earth and search for it. She had gas and a map. Beside her, Cal rose on the seat, and Lily shut the engine off. She opened her door and braced herself against the cold wind as she rounded the car and let Cal out. He walked slowly to the edge of the gravel turnoff and did his business while she stood and stared back at town.

She hadn't seen a single car since she'd crossed the bridge. As soon as the thought entered her head, a brown sheriff's car came around the bend and pulled into the turnoff. The window went down, and the officer called out to her, "Everything okay?"

She forced a smile and nodded. "Thanks."

As the window started to roll up again, she put out a hand. "Wait." She approached the car and leaned down so she could see the deputy. About her age, he looked kind, his gaze steady and cautious. "I'm actually trying to find a cabin," she said.

"In Molva?"

"I believe so."

He glanced beyond her at the dog. "You have an address?"

She swallowed, hesitating, and shook her head.

"Hard to find a place without an address."

She forced a smile. Feeling unbidden tears fill her eyes, she blinked hard to send them back. "I'm looking for the house where Derek Hudson held his captives."

The deputy narrowed his eyes. "You a reporter?"

"No," she said firmly. "A nurse, actually."

He studied her face without speaking.

The urge to turn away was so strong she had to clench her fists to remain facing him. Finally, she said, "I was one of them." And with the words, the ground seemed to pull her gaze.

"One of—" His voice halted, and she could hear the shock in the hard stop.

Several beats passed, and she was gathering her courage to stand up straight and walk away when he asked, "Why now?"

She met his gaze, her heart a thrumming beat in her neck and chest. "Because I need to."

"I'll take you there," he said. "But I need to see ID first. You understand?"

She exhaled, half in relief and half in terror that she was actually going to face the place where she'd been held for sixteen months. The deputy's engine went quiet, and he stepped out and followed her to her car as she pulled her Arizona ID from her wallet and handed it over.

"You have a driver's license?"

Lily froze. Where was her driver's license? Did she have one? All she had found in her wallet was the Arizona ID, no driver's license at all. But she could hardly tell the deputy that. "I left it at home accidentally," she lied as he looked up and down between her and the image on the ID.

The deputy frowned. "What about registration on the car?"

She had no idea. She'd come down to get closure, and she was going to end up getting arrested for driving without a license. As she opened the glove box and rooted around for a registration, Cal nuzzled against her leg as though to offer support. She located it and checked the date. It wasn't even expired. The deputy studied it, then returned both registration and ID.

"The cabin is about three miles out of town to the north. You want to follow me?"

She nodded, unable to find words.

He started to turn but stopped and turned back. "There's not much to see there. The cabin's been empty for a decade, and it's likely been taken over by varmints. I think the family tried to sell it, but there were no buyers."

What was she expecting? That it would look as it had the day she had escaped? That seeing it would bring back her memory in full? Suddenly, she couldn't even remember why she'd come here.

"My great-aunt knew the family," the deputy said. "Hudson's family, I mean. If you wanted to talk to someone, Mindy might be willing to answer some questions."

Lily studied his face. He looked as uncomfortable as she felt. Did he know what had happened to them in that cabin? There'd been no mention in the articles of sexual assault, but maybe the press hadn't printed that because they were children and it was too horrific.

"It might be more helpful than seeing the place," he said. "I know she's got some pictures of that day, ones her son took."

Almost without thinking, she nodded.

He exhaled, a small smile curving his lips as though her answer was a relief. "Let me give her a call." The deputy returned to his car. Lily knelt down to pet Cal, focusing her nervous energy on the dog while she waited. It seemed far too long had passed when she heard the deputy's voice, still on the phone. "We'll be there in about ten minutes. Thanks, Mindy."

Lily rose slowly and turned to face him.

"She says she'd be happy to speak to you," he said. "Her name is Melinda Danson, and she lives right off Main Street. You can follow me." He pulled his badge and drew out a business card. "Then, if you still want to see the cabin, give me a call, and I'll take you there."

"Thank you," she said, though what she felt was regret. Why had she thought this was a good idea? Because she had to know. Because she had to save herself. To find out what had happened to Abby. And maybe help Iver. Because she believed that the root of her lost memory, the root of all the bad decisions she'd made for who knew how long—all of it had started here, in Molva.

With Cal loaded, Lily climbed into the car and secured her seat belt. The deputy's car was at the edge of the turnout, waiting for her, as she started her car and put it in gear.

This was the right decision. *You have to know.*

Aunt Mindy. As she started forward, she had the thought that it seemed odd that she would get such gruesome news from someone with such a light, happy name.

CHAPTER 42

KYLIE

Kylie paced outside Alvin Tanner's home, waiting for the coroner while Smith and Sullivan collected evidence. The snow fell in whispers from the tall pines around the property as a light breeze trembled in the air. The sky, which had been blue when Kylie had left her house, was darker now and increasingly gray.

Her fingers searched for knuckles left to crack, but there were none. She'd been cracking her knuckles for two hours. Sheriff Davis had been on the phone since he'd arrived at the scene, and Gary Ross had gone inside and returned looking a little sick to his stomach. "Been a long time since I've seen one like that," he'd said when he'd passed her. From where she stood leaned up against his car, it looked like Ross was on the phone as well.

Kylie was still anxious to talk to Pete McIntosh about the scene of Jenna Hitchcock's murder. Despite the fact that Hitchcock's murder had occurred in Glendive, it seemed more obvious than ever that Hagen was at the center of these crimes. Or at least that their killer was close by.

She thought again about the footage Alvin Tanner had on those cameras—footage that would have helped them identify a killer. Davis had confirmed that no one in the department had ever received the footage from Tanner. All of it was gone now, along with the monitoring computer and the backups.

Judging from the severed fingers sitting in the ashtray and the amount of blood on the floor, Kylie suspected that whoever had killed Tanner had tortured him first. Tanner had likely put up a fight over giving up his precious cameras. The killer got what he wanted—the cameras and footage were gone. There was no computer in the house either. If a digital backup had existed, it was gone, too.

Why hadn't she insisted on taking the footage when she was here yesterday? Would she have been more demanding if the highway patrol officer hadn't been with her? And how had the killer found out that they were collecting footage? She'd told Gilbert, Davis, and Vogel. But Will Merkel might have mentioned it to someone else.

Davis approached, muttering a curse and pocketing his phone.

Kylie waited for him to explain.

"There was a call to the man camp last night. Big fight, supposedly."

"Supposedly?"

"According to the Dispatch call, they requested all available cars, so we sent over everyone." Davis shook his head. "Took forever to get access to the camp because it was after midnight, when the gates are closed. When they finally got in, there was no fight. Call was fake."

This had to relate back to Tanner. "Larson," she whispered.

"We pulled the guard off his room last night to deal with the man-camp situation. Gilbert's over there now. Seems Larson might have left his room."

"Might have?"

"One nurse thought she saw him outside his room. She isn't sure."

Kylie looked back at the house. "So Larson could be good for Tanner." Then she remembered the way Gilbert had threatened Iver Larson. Everyone in Hagen knew about Tanner, how he recorded every living thing within a hundred yards of his house. When Gilbert had spouted off about the footage that would prove Iver had killed Jensen,

Iver would've known Gilbert was referring to Tanner's cameras. She told Davis, who nodded.

"Gilbert remembered the same thing. He's on his way to interview Larson." Her phone buzzed at the same time as Davis's. They stared at their individual screens. A text from Gilbert. At first, she wasn't sure what she was looking at, but soon she made out the profile of a tennis shoe, its sole muddy. Another image showed dirt on a linoleum floor and Gilbert's note. Larson's. It looked like fresh dirt.

"I'll have Smith and Sullivan document any tread marks around and inside the house," Kylie said. "Maybe we can match Larson's shoes."

Davis pressed thumb and index finger to the bridge of his nose. "I'm going to have to deal with the mayor on this."

"I haven't had a chance to follow up on Pamela Nolan's alibi," Kylie said.

"I think that can wait a day or two," Davis told her. "We've got to close this case."

Kylie sensed that Davis was getting pressure from the mayor, maybe even someone in the state building. Either way, she was grateful not to have to argue the importance of solving the murder over some crazy theory that a woman had run her husband's car off the road. "Have you seen any results from the state crime lab yet?"

Davis shook his head. "No, but I can give them a call, see if we can speed things along," he offered, nodding toward the house. "Especially in light of this."

"That would be great," she said.

"Absolutely," Davis said. "I'll call up there as soon as I'm off with the mayor."

She thanked him and went to check on the scene, where Smith and Sullivan were still collecting evidence. Sullivan was printing around the table and body while Smith searched the living room for anything that might have remained of the cameras and recording devices.

"I think the perp got it all," Smith said.

She'd figured as much. She told them about the muddy tennis shoes in Larson's hospital room and requested they document anything they found, but she didn't notice many footprints as she walked back to her car. Not much mud either. There wasn't a lot about these past few days that made her feel lucky. She only hoped that her trip to Glendive brought some answers.

Back in her car, Kylie texted Pete McIntosh, telling him she'd been delayed but was on her way. As she pulled back onto the 1804, she found herself puzzling over the muddy shoes in Larson's hospital room. Pausing at a stop sign, she brought up the images again. In the second one, mud appeared right beside the small locker where Larson's personal items were stored, but nowhere else.

If Larson had left the hospital and returned with muddy shoes, wouldn't there be tracks all the way back to his room as well as by the locker? And if he'd gone to all the trouble to sneak out and then torture and kill Alvin Tanner to destroy the footage of the highway, wouldn't he have been smarter about the mud on his shoes? It reminded her of Abigail Jensen's boots. Larson had gone to the effort of getting his truck washed, but he'd left her boots in the truck's lockbox.

Her phone buzzed with a text from Gilbert. Larson's guilty.

Again, Kylie found herself wondering about Carl Gilbert's motives. Was he working in the best interest of the case, or was there something else at play?

She thought about responding but decided against it. Instead, she set her phone on the seat and pulled onto the highway, hoping that some discovery in Glendive would clarify Jensen's death and put an end to her doubts.

CHAPTER 43

IVER

Iver woke to the sounds of voices in the hospital corridor, and within seconds, his door opened and two police officers stormed in, followed by a nurse. At the front of the herd, a red-faced and breathless Gilbert went straight to the corner of the room where the small melamine locker contained Iver's clothes, the ones he'd been wearing when he'd been admitted yesterday.

Against a pounding in his skull, Iver pushed himself up in the bed. "What the hell is going on?"

Gilbert was pulling the stuff out of his locker and going through his clothes.

"Hey," Iver called out, but the officers ignored him.

"I tried to stop them," the nurse said. "Should I call someone?"

Iver watched them, only then realizing they were here because something had changed. This was not good news. He grabbed his cell phone off the bedside stand and texted Mike.

Hospital asap.

He waited a beat and added, Please.

"No car keys," Gilbert announced to the other officer. "Someone picked him up."

"What are you talking about?" Iver called to Gilbert, but the officer didn't even look up at him. Iver turned to the nurse. "Could you try to get hold of Henry Cooper? He's an—"

"Sure," she interrupted. "I know Mr. Cooper. I'll call over to his house."

Iver almost grabbed her hand, he was so grateful. "Can you ask him to hurry?"

She nodded with a look at the officers, still rummaging through Iver's things. "You bet I will."

His phone pinged. As he read Mike's message, a rush of relief hit him.

There in ten.

The nurse left, and Iver gripped his phone, waiting for Gilbert to tell him what the hell was going on.

"Look at his shoes," Gilbert said, then swung around to face Iver. "We've got you now, asshole."

Iver followed his gaze to his tennis shoes, which Gilbert held in the air. Bits of dirt and mud dropped from the soles. "What happened to those?"

Gilbert narrowed his eyes, and Iver shut his mouth. He'd seen enough television to know that now was the time to shut the hell up. He gathered the awkward skirt of his hospital gown and walked toward the bathroom, bringing his phone with him.

"Where the hell do you think you're going?"

"To take a piss," Iver said, closing the door behind him. He jabbed the lock and then looked around the tiny space. The bathroom was barely the size of a linen closet, covered in railings and a cord that he could pull if he needed assistance. It would almost be funny . . . but it was not funny. His heart pounding, he drew a breath and reminded himself that the nurse was calling Henry Cooper, and Mike was on his way. He just had to wait.

There was no toilet seat to sit on, so he pulled the single thin towel off the rack and spread it on the cold tile floor before sitting down. His thoughts drifted to Cal. They hadn't been apart even a night since Debbie had brought the dog home. He'd forgotten to tell Mike to pick him up. He'd been so shocked about their news. His ex-wife and his best friend were together. A month ago, it might have derailed him, but compared to everything else going on right now, he didn't even care.

Or maybe some part of him had known, even before Wednesday.

Someone pounded on the door. "Larson." Carl Gilbert.

He didn't answer. Let Carl Gilbert scream himself hoarse.

"Mr. Larson?" a woman's voice called. "It's Dr. Prescott. Are you all right?"

"I'm fine," he called back. "But I'm not coming out until my attorney arrives."

Gilbert's loud voice bled through the door as he issued some invective, and Iver leaned his head back against the bathroom wall, a pulse of satisfaction in his sternum. But it was short lived. Gilbert had been saying something about no car keys, that someone else had driven him. Driven him where?

And what was with the mud on his shoes? He'd been in his living room when the seizure had started. He shouldn't have had mud on his shoes. He dropped his face on his folded arms, closing his eyes against the escalating pain in his head. Why was the pain back?

"You're going to have to discharge him," Gilbert announced. "Because we're booking him today. Soon as he comes out of the damn bathroom."

Iver strained to hear Dr. Prescott's response.

"I do have a good reason," Gilbert shouted loudly enough to be heard clearly through the bathroom door. "He killed another man last night. Those shoes prove it."

Iver froze. Killed someone last night? He shook his head. No. He remembered last night. He'd slept well, soundly. At one point, he had woken to the sounds of sirens, followed by noise in the corridor, people shouting. But he hadn't been awake long. And then he remembered going to the bathroom at some point. But he remembered the whole night. There were no gaps. He couldn't have killed someone.

The room had long gone quiet when a gentle knocking reached him. "Iver? It's Henry Cooper. And your friend Mike is here, too. Will you come out and speak to us?"

Iver rose slowly, his joints achy from the cramped position. He opened the door slowly and scanned the room. Gilbert and the other officer were gone.

"I've asked them to wait outside," Cooper said.

"Thank you."

Cooper glanced at Mike, but Iver shook his head. "It's okay. Mike can stay."

As Cooper told him about the man who'd been killed, Iver felt the first rush of true relief he'd experienced since arriving at the bar on Thursday morning.

"I was here, all night," Iver said, making his way to sit on the bed. "I never left this room."

"And your shoes?" Cooper asked.

"No idea. They weren't muddy when I came to the hospital, and I haven't left."

Cooper nodded. "We need to find you a criminal lawyer, Iver. This is way outside my area of expertise. I'll get working on that. In the meantime, Officer Gilbert has an image of you attacking a woman at the bar on Wednesday. From what I can gather, that is their primary evidence against you."

"An image?" Mike asked. "Like a picture?"

"Yes," Cooper said, still talking to Iver. "It's you grabbing hold of a woman."

"In the bar?" Mike asked.

"Officer Gilbert said *at* the bar, not necessarily *in* the bar."

Iver looked at Mike, who was frowning. "What are you thinking?"

Mike looked at Cooper. "We need to see that picture. Is that possible?"

"It should be. Let me see what I can do." Cooper moved to the door. Carl Gilbert was hovering in the hallway, hands on his hips.

Cooper's voice was soft as he spoke.

Gilbert shook his head.

Cooper kept speaking.

Iver glanced at Mike, who watched the scene as well.

"I think you'd better defer that decision to Sheriff Davis," Cooper said, raising his own phone. "Either you can call him or I can."

Gilbert's expression went tight, and Iver would have felt joy if he weren't still so afraid. Gilbert stepped out of view, and a minute later, he returned and spoke softly to Cooper, his head bowed. Whatever happened, Cooper had won.

A minute later, the attorney returned to the hospital room and shut the door behind him, leaving the frowning Gilbert outside.

"What did you find out?" Mike asked.

"I got the picture they have of you and the woman."

Iver felt his heart sink. There *was* real evidence against him.

Cooper handed Iver his phone. An image filled the screen: Iver's own face, pinched in rage. The sight of it made him sick. His outstretched hand held on to a thin arm. His field of vision started to go black, his right eye losing focus. He had a migraine coming on fast.

"Can I see that?" Mike asked, and Iver passed him the phone.

"Are you okay?" Cooper asked.

"It's my head," Iver said, the words hammering. "Migraine."

Cooper reached past him, and the nurse call button pinged softly in the quiet room.

"Iver," Mike said. "Look at this."

Iver squinted, trying to focus on the phone Mike now held.

Mike zoomed in on the image until the woman's hand and forearm filled the screen.

There, just above the wrist, was a small mark. "Sword," Iver whispered.

"Yes," Mike said.

"What do you see?" Cooper asked.

Iver studied the image of the birthmark on his ex-wife's wrist. "Debbie's birthmark," he said as a nurse entered the room, Carl Gilbert on her tail.

"Please move aside, gentlemen," the nurse directed.

"I see the birthmark," Cooper said as Carl Gilbert peered over his shoulder. "What does it mean?"

"It means the woman Iver is grabbing here isn't the victim. It's his ex-wife, Debbie Wilson," Mike said. "That picture was taken Wednesday night at the bar, right? Debbie and I were there."

Carl Gilbert looked frantically between Iver and Mike.

"It's true," Iver said, leaning back and closing his eyes against the pain. "I recognize the birthmark."

"That's not a birthmark," Gilbert countered. "It's just dirt."

"It's a birthmark," Mike said. "Here, I can show you another picture of it."

Iver opened one eye to see Mike scrolling through his phone.

"There," Mike announced, turning the phone so Gilbert could see the screen.

Iver let his eyes fall closed again. He definitely didn't need to see Mike's pictures of his ex-wife.

Someone patted his arm gently. "We've got some meds on board," the nurse said. "Pain should be better momentarily."

"It still doesn't prove anything," Gilbert argued.

"I disagree," Cooper said calmly. "This photograph is no longer evidence of contact between my client and the victim."

"We don't need it," Gilbert said. "There's other evidence. The mud on his shoes proves he was outside last night."

"Nurse? Does the staff check on patients overnight?" Cooper asked.

"Yes," the nurse said. "Normally. But we did have an active night. Fridays are usually pretty busy, so some of our nurses may have been pulled off their normal rounds."

"There was someone in here," Iver said. "A custodian, I think."

"A custodian?" the nurse repeated.

Iver opened one eye and nodded. "Emptying the trash, I think."

The room was quiet.

"Is the pain improving?"

Iver opened his eyes to see Dr. Prescott standing above him. "A little," he said.

"Dr. Prescott, was Iver given something last night to help him rest?" Gilbert asked.

"She can't tell you that," Cooper cut in. "It's a violation of patient confidentiality."

"We'll just get a warrant," Gilbert said.

"Then you should do that," Cooper countered.

The pounding in his head lightened to a gentle ache as he pushed himself up on one elbow. "I'm telling you, you should talk to that custodian. He was here—middle of the night."

The nurse watched him, then glanced at Dr. Prescott, who was checking his vitals on the screen.

When no one answered, Iver went on, "I'm sure you can find out who that guy was."

"What guy?" Gilbert asked.

"The custodian—the janitor." Iver sat upright. "He wheeled his garbage can in and emptied the trash can—the one right there, in that corner." Iver pointed to the far corner of the room, just past the locker that Gilbert and the other officer had emptied. But the corner was empty. There was no trash can there. As he scanned the room, he saw no trash can anywhere.

"Iver?" Mike said softly.

But Iver was still searching the room for the trash can. "He was wearing a dark uniform, like a one-piece thing. Navy, I think."

No one spoke.

"We'll need to speak to this janitor," Gilbert said.

"Yeah. Talk to him." But when Iver looked back at the group huddled by his bed, they were all looking at him. "What?"

The nurse shook her head. "We don't have night janitors," she said. "The cleaning staff comes in during the day. And I believe they're all female."

After a moment, Dr. Prescott cleared her throat. "I need to examine Mr. Larson, if everyone could leave the room for a few minutes."

Gilbert started to argue. "He's—"

"I'm not discharging him until I've done an examination," Prescott said, gaze on Gilbert.

Slowly, the room emptied. Iver kept his eye on the door until it had closed. Then he looked to the doctor. "Do you think I'm hallucinating?"

Prescott shook her head. "It's very unlikely that the dose of sedative you're on could cause hallucinations."

"But not impossible," he said.

Prescott didn't answer him as she shone her penlight into his eyes, left and then right. He imagined that picture, the sliver of his wife's arm, his own face frozen in rage. But Debbie was alive. If he had any reason to kill a woman, it would be her.

He drew a slow breath as the doctor turned off the light and made a note on his chart. She flipped it closed and headed for the door. As he watched her leave, the pressure seemed to ebb from his chest. For the first time in a long time, the voice in his head grew quiet, and he closed his eyes to the blissful silence.

CHAPTER 44

—

LILY

Lily followed the deputy back through Molva's small downtown, turning south for a few blocks before stopping in front of a squat yellow house with chipping paint. A makeshift ramp led from the driveway to the front door. The porch sagged slightly in the middle, barely supported by two stacked cinder blocks.

Hesitating, Lily scanned the neighborhood. The other houses looked a lot like Melinda Danson's, tired homes built when someone had thought Molva would be an economic center. Or perhaps it had been, though any evidence of a boom was gone now. On the other side of the street sat a house with its door and front windows boarded. Neon spray paint marked the large slabs of particleboard covering the openings. Around them, the black tongue of flames scarred the house's facade. In the driveway a sad-looking red tricycle lay on its side.

When she turned back to Danson's house, the deputy was standing on the front walkway, waiting for her. She left the window down for Cal and got out of the car.

"Mindy's real friendly."

She nodded and followed him up the makeshift ramp, which squawked beneath their weight. The sound only added to the chill that Lily carried as she walked toward the door.

"Come on in, Andy," came a frail voice even before he could ring the doorbell. The ramp made its own announcement.

"Hey, Aunt Mindy," the deputy said, pulling back the screen door and letting himself in.

Lily followed a few steps behind. The first thing she noticed was the smell—cooked beans and the sweet, pungent sweat of the old. Ms. Danson sat in a wheelchair parked beside a small TV tray. On it were a pair of reading glasses and three remote controls. Andy greeted his aunt and motioned for Lily to sit before explaining to his aunt that he had to get back to work. Before he left, Danson directed him to the back bedroom. "It's the shoebox on the desk there."

He returned a moment later, carrying a worn blue box, its color faded to white in places from years of handling. He set the box carefully on the small coffee table and glanced at Lily. "You okay?"

She nodded. "Thank you."

And with that, Andy was out the door. The screen door slammed behind him, giving her a little start. The town of Molva made her uncomfortable. Lily wanted to ask her questions and get out.

"Can I get you some water or tea?" Ms. Danson asked.

"I'm fine, thank you." Lily noticed Danson's empty glass, its bent straw dangling over the rim. "Would you like something?"

"Oh, thank you, dear. If you would just fill this with water . . ." The old woman lifted the glass in a trembling hand, and Lily took it from her. "The kitchen is just through there."

"Of course. Can I get you anything else?"

"Oh, no. I've got someone coming with lunch in a bit," she answered, twisting a watch around her tiny wrist, though she made no move to look at it.

Lily filled the water glass, noticing the general dinginess of the kitchen, how its surfaces had yellowed with age. A few dishes sat in the sink, and a sticky residue on the floor clung to her shoes as she walked.

She set the glass on Danson's tray and settled onto the couch across from the wheelchair. "Thank you for meeting with me."

Danson seemed to sense Lily's hesitation. "Andy said you wanted to hear about Derek Hudson."

Did she want to learn about the monster who'd held her captive for sixteen months? Her fingers found the seams of her pants and gripped the hard denim. Had Andy told his aunt that she was one of Hudson's victims? A survivor? But why else had she come here if not to learn about Hudson?

"I would like to hear about him," Lily said, the words accompanied by a wave of hot nausea.

Danson grasped her hands together and made little circles with her thumbs, the crepe-like skin folding over on itself as she moved. "Well, we may as well start with Derek's mother, Stephanie. She was just a few years younger than me, no family nearby." The way Danson talked was comforting, her relaxed manner of speaking and the soft smile on her lips.

"Was Derek an only child?"

Danson's mouth thinned as she shook her head. "There was an older boy, a real troublemaker. He's been in prison most of his life. That's where he was when Hudson took those girls. The police checked that first. I suspect he's still in prison."

"But Mr. Hudson is deceased?"

"The boys' father? Oh yes. Frank Hudson died fifteen years ago, maybe longer now. He was a nasty fellow. Came to Molva from somewhere down south, wanting to live off the land. Mostly he drank and hunted. Back then, there were a few of them like that—maybe five or six families in all. They all set up on a big parcel of land just past mile marker nineteen. Place had been a campground—KOA-like—that they'd bought from the owners, cheap because there wasn't much to the land. Hudson got the idea that they'd build a few cabins up there, create some kind of commune.

"Stephanie was all for it. Not too bright, that one. She was pregnant before she ever finished high school. The commune never got off the ground. Most of the families moved within a year or two. The kids who stayed never went to school past about fifth grade. After that, they were supposedly homeschooled, but we all got the idea that they just ran around like animals, that bunch."

Lily listened. "Ten years ago, was the commune still running?"

"I don't think so. Most of the kids who grew up there were long gone. I don't know that anyone knew exactly who was living up there all those years. The residents didn't take too kindly to visitors, and the Hudsons were the only ones we ever saw in town, even when the commune was larger. Stephanie and Frank did all the shopping and selling for the commune. They sold whatever they grew and also some crafts and things that the women and children must have made. None of it very good quality."

"And after Frank died? Stephanie still came to town?"

"Less and less after that. There was some disagreement with the man who owns our local mercantile, so they started heading over to other towns to do their business. Occasionally we'd see one of them—boys, mostly—driving through town for one thing or another."

Other boys. Something uncomfortable edged down her spine—something with legs. "But the others were gone ten years ago?"

"That I don't know," Danson said. "There were at least three or four boys up there for a decade or more. I believe there might have been another boy or two up there for longer. Hard to know for sure when the last of them left. Course, they were all long gone when Derek kidnapped those girls. The police checked for others living up there then."

"Do you know who any of the other families were?" Lily asked.

"I knew one of the other families," Danson said. "They had a boy about Hudson's age, and the mother was close with Stephanie, but they've been gone for years."

247

"When Derek Hudson took those girls, he was up there alone?" He had taken five girls and held them for sixteen months without help? The words came back to her. *Always take what's easy. Quick. Then you get back home. Don't help nobody. Don't stop for nothing. You don't come back, you know what happens.*

Hudson must have sent them out for things, threatening to hurt the others if they didn't return quickly or if they spoke to anyone.

"That's what the police told us—that Derek Hudson kidnapped those girls and held them all on his own," Danson confirmed. "I barely knew anything about him before those girls escaped. Couldn't have picked him out of a lineup. Not sure many of us in town could. Course, there was a lot of talk after that."

"What kind of talk?"

"Well, the police spent a lot of time looking for an accomplice. It didn't seem likely that little Derek Hudson could do all that on his own. According to the people who knew him, he was a gentle kid, much more like Stephanie than Frank and the older boy. Used to babysit, of all things."

Shudders raced along her shoulders and buzzed into her fingertips. "Babysit?"

"The commune hadn't been around more than a couple of years when Stephanie started teaching ballet. They probably needed the money. She rented a little studio right in downtown Molva. Derek used to come and entertain the younger ones while his mom taught the older ones. People said he was great with the kids. You can imagine the shock when people found out what he'd done."

"Why would he take those girls?" The words slipped from her mouth.

"Later on, we all heard some stories about what young Derek went through. Some of them would turn your stomach."

Lily waited. *This was what you came for. To understand.*

Danson took her silence as a cue to continue. "Derek was a skinny kid—tall and lean like Stephanie. He was quite a bit younger than his brother, who was thick and bullying like his father. I guess there was a time when Derek was nine or ten that his father sent him out to the barn with a knife to slaughter one of the pigs to prepare for Christmas dinner." At this point in her story, Danson looked up. "You raise animals? 4-H or anything?"

Lily shook her head, though she wasn't totally sure.

"Well, pigs are no joke. The breeds most commonly raised for their meat aren't as big as boars, but they get up to a couple hundred pounds, and they're amazingly strong animals. A bite from a pig can easily cut to the bone. They are not to be messed with. And you certainly don't send an eighty-pound kid to take down a two-hundred-pound pig. With a knife," she added, her voice pitched high with alarm.

"The story goes that Derek didn't have much luck even getting at the pig, let alone killing it. Every time he came inside unsuccessful, his father sent him back out. That went on well past dark. I guess his father eventually said, 'You either kill that pig, or you live outside until you do.' Of course, this is December, so it's freezing cold.

"Middle of the night, the older boy came out. Maybe he was taking pity on his brother, or maybe his father sent him out there. He shot the pig with a handgun, then slit the pig open with the long knife. Derek thought it meant he could come inside now, but his brother said, 'No. Because you didn't kill it, you have to stay out here for the night.' Like I said, it was December. He'd have frozen to death." Danson shivered, her hands no longer fidgeting as she gripped them together.

"What happened?"

"Early the next morning, the sheriff's department got a call about possible child abuse up there. People think it might've been Stephanie who made the call. The deputy who went up there said he'd never recover from what he saw."

Lily waited, gooseflesh trailing her arms like something sticky.

Danson's gaze settled on a far wall. "Sometime in the night, Derek Hudson had cut out the pig's entrails and climbed inside the cavity to stay warm. They found him half-frozen and covered in pig's blood."

Lily didn't need to close her eyes to picture a skinny boy inside the body of a pig. Was it any wonder that Hudson had grown into a monster?

CHAPTER 45

KYLIE

By the time she was nearing Glendive, Kylie had started to doubt the intelligence of coming. She should have been at the scene of Tanner's death when the coroner arrived, and she wanted to be the one to arrest Larson. Instead, she was on a rough two-lane highway, driving fifty behind some idiot in a diesel truck, while someone else—probably Carl Gilbert—made the arrest and met the coroner.

The entire drive she'd been making phone calls and leaving messages. Ten minutes outside of Glendive, her phone rang with a Bismarck exchange.

"Milliard," she answered, unsure who would be calling her on a Saturday morning.

"This is Dr. Sarah Glanzer. I'm a senior criminalist up in the state lab. I got a call from your sheriff to touch base on the evidence on the Abigail Jensen case."

"In on a Saturday?"

Glanzer let out a short laugh. "Yep. Most of them, actually. We've got a huge backlog, and thankfully the state compensates us for the extra hours—to a point, anyway."

Milliard wished she were getting overtime, especially on this case. Since this whole thing had started, she'd done nothing but work, and she didn't see an end in sight. "Do you have news for me?"

"Actually, I do. I just called your department, and your dispatch gave me your number. Are you the right one to talk to?"

"Yes. I'm the lead detective."

"That's what Dispatch told me, but I had a different name written down. C. Gilbert?"

"He's in our office, but I'm the person you want." Kylie felt the edge creep into her voice and forced a smile, even though Dr. Glanzer couldn't see her. "I'm point on this one."

"Sure," she said. "I'm just following up a couple of pieces of evidence that came in from the Jensen case."

"What did you find?" Kylie asked. Grateful that the diesel truck had turned off the highway, she sped up.

"There was a glass in the bar's office. According to the collection notes, they found it in a desk drawer. It had two sets of prints. Iver Larson's and prints of someone by the name of Kevin Clouse. He's in our system for an old D and D."

Drunk and disorderly. "Makes sense," Kylie said. "Clouse is one of the bartenders."

"That glass contained a residue of a drug—flurazepam."

"Huh," Kylie said.

"That mean something to you?" Glanzer asked.

Kylie checked her rearview mirror. "That same compound was present in a suspect's toxicology screen."

"An unusual choice for a party drug," Glanzer commented.

"How do you mean?" Kylie asked.

"Side effects are impaired motor coordination and severe sedation. It's what you give someone who has anxiety about being in the hospital before minor procedures. Some dentists administer it, too. But a patient is never allowed to drive afterward. It's not quick to wear off."

Almost exactly what the doctor had said. Prescott. "Anything else?" Kylie asked.

"We've got two fibers we're studying, but they're from different sources."

An old Ram truck roared by with a blast of thick black smoke. Kylie glanced at her speedometer. She was going sixty, which meant that asshole was going eighty-five or more. She brought her attention back to the call. "Fiber, right. One was found in a truck?"

"Yes. The other came from the victim's blouse."

"And they don't match?"

"No. Similar color, but that's about all. The one from the woman's blouse is PET, or polyethylene terephthalate—otherwise known as polyester. The one from the truck is a cotton-wool blend. The two are actually almost nothing alike."

That meant no good connection existed between Iver Larson and the victims. Except the boots in his truck. "What about the victim's shoes?"

Glanzer was quiet a moment.

"The ones that were found in the truck toolbox," Kylie added.

"Yeah, I remember those," Glanzer said. "Hang on."

Another moment passed, and Kylie sensed that something was wrong.

"Detective, we sent those findings in our preliminary report."

Kylie sat upright in the seat. "Preliminary report?"

"It was sent to your office yesterday before noon. Went to Deputy Gilbert." Glanzer paused. "Oh, C. Gilbert."

"Before noon?" When she'd met with Gilbert and the others yesterday afternoon, Gilbert had said he didn't expect the report until Monday, at the earliest. "When did the shoes make it to your lab?"

"Friday, around ten a.m. The preliminary report only takes a few hours. I finished it before lunch."

Heat seared Kylie's chest. Gilbert had sat in that meeting yesterday afternoon and lied right to her face. He'd already gotten Glanzer's report, but he'd told her it would take at least two more days before they'd know anything. Which meant he *was* keeping her out of the loop.

The sound of papers shuffling filtered through the line. "They were processed first thing Friday—priority for the double homicide."

Double homicide. Abigail Jensen and Jenna Hitchcock? Of course, she suspected that the two murders had been committed by the same person, but she wouldn't have called it a double homicide. "Can you send me that initial report? I never got it."

"Sure. I'll email it to you now, and my number will be in the email, so call if you have any questions. What's your email address?"

Kylie gave Glanzer her email address and listened as she repeated it back. "That's it."

"Sending it now. And sorry about that. Hope it wasn't a screwup on our end," Glanzer added.

"No. I'm guessing it wasn't," Kylie said, wondering why Gilbert would have intentionally held back the report. It was possible he'd been busy with other things yesterday and hadn't checked his email. Unless he'd hoped to present it privately to Vogel and Davis himself and, what, try to steal the limelight?

"I can tell you we didn't find anything useful on the shoes," Glanzer said. "They were really wet, so the partial prints on the soles and the heels were too compromised to make a match, and we didn't find any fibers. We swabbed them for DNA, but—"

Heart pounding, Kylie jerked the car onto the shoulder of the road. A car blared its horn and swerved around her. "Wait. You said the shoes were wet?"

"Oh yeah. Soaked."

Abigail Jensen's shoes had been soaked.

"How about her pants?"

"She was probably lying in the snow before the killer dumped her," Glanzer said as though it was obvious.

"But when you say her shoes were wet, you mean all the way up? Or just at the bottom, near the ground?"

"Hang on. Let me pull up the images."

There were several moments of silence, the only sound the clicking of a keyboard. "Looking at pictures, the boots look soaked. The suede—or fake-suede material—is saturated front and back, almost to the top of the boot." Another click, then a few more, and she said, "It's hard to tell from the images, but it looks like the bottoms of her jeans were also wet—not just up the back where she'd been lying in the snow but all the way around the bottom."

"Like she'd been walking through the snow," Kylie said.

"That would match the findings."

Abigail Jensen had been walking in the snow and gotten her shoes and pants wet. When Lily Baker had woken in Brent Nolan's car, she'd noticed her shoes and the bottoms of her pants, near the hems, were wet. Kylie had remembered thinking there was no running water near the site of the accident. And no snow.

But there was standing snow behind Skål, lots of it.

Kylie gripped the steering wheel. Lily Baker had been in the same place as Jensen. They'd been together at the bar. But then, somehow, Baker had gotten in Brent Nolan's car.

Why would she have done that? Had she been running from something? Or toward it?

And if Lily Baker couldn't remember that night, how could Kylie figure out what had happened?

CHAPTER 46

—

LILY

The image of a skinny boy frozen inside a dead pig was as clear in Lily's head as any image she'd seen since her arrival in Molva.

"It's a terrible thing to imagine," Melinda Danson said.

Lily only nodded. She wanted to get up and leave, go back to Hagen and bury herself in a normal life. Her job at the hospital . . . but that was all she had. There were no friends, no family.

"Before you go, you ought to look at those." Ms. Danson pointed to the shoebox Andy had set on the low coffee table. "Those are my son's pictures."

"Pictures?" Lily reached for the box, then hesitated. The boy in the dead pig still lingered in her mind.

"My boy Matty took those before he died. Pictures of Molva," she added, waving at Lily to open the box. "Matty loved taking pictures," she said, her eyes glazed and soft. "There are some from that day. It was quite an event here in Molva, as you can imagine."

The words buzzed in Lily's head. Her escape from sixteen months of captivity had been "quite an event."

"Go ahead and look, dear," Ms. Danson urged, and Lily lifted the box, surprised by its weight. With the box in her lap, she removed the lid and stared down at hundreds of photos. "These are all from that day?"

"No, no. Those are all the pictures he took his last couple of years of high school. They're pretty well organized, though." She shifted forward in her chair, her motions shaky and unstable. "I think you'll find the ones from Hudson's death right at the front, separated by a marker. There might be a few more after that first marker. A bunch were real out of focus, but I never could bring myself to throw them out. Can't seem to get myself to throw out anything of his."

"I'm sorry," Lily said.

Ms. Danson waved a shaky hand through the air. "Don't you worry about me, dear."

Returning her attention to the box of photographs, Lily located the thin white divider and pulled out the images ahead of it. She recognized the cabin in the first pictures from the newspaper stories. Unlike the chilling, empty black-and-white photographs that had accompanied the news articles, Matt Danson's were filled with people who moved around the cabin. She scanned them, her heart trilling in her ears as she looked for her own face. But the faces were unfamiliar.

"You find them?"

"Yes," Lily said, forcing her fingers to shuffle to the next image. She moved through them slowly, fighting against tremors in her hands. She had survived. Escaped. She was no longer that girl. And the more images she saw, the more that terrifying place looked like a normal cabin. Mostly. The dark windows, which were spray-painted or hung with heavy curtains, would have cast the interior in absolute darkness. She shivered as though remembering something, but then it was gone. It didn't have the texture of memory. Maybe it was no memory at all but her imagination filling in the terror of the dark.

But you were held in the dark, even if you can't remember.

Slowly the images lessened their hold, and her breathing grew easier as the cabin vanished, and instead she was staring at the photographs of people. Several were local police officers, identifiable by the same brown uniforms that Andy had worn today. A couple of others wore suits, and Matt Danson had captured them as they interviewed people in the crowd. Likely state investigators or perhaps FBI, though it was hard to imagine the FBI in a town like Molva. But that case surely had brought the FBI.

Several pictures in a row featured a man in a suit, who appeared to be interviewing a number of the people in the crowd, a notebook in his hand. Then Lily came upon a dozen images of the surrounding woods, empty and dark. Matt Danson must have found them especially interesting, because he'd taken a number of photographs that were almost identical, variations of a clump of trees, thick with undergrowth. It was only in the last images that Lily noticed the shape of a person standing among the trees.

Lily brought the photograph closer. The shape was lean and tall, a young man from the look of it. She wished there were a way to zoom in. She flipped to the next picture and found herself staring at the same patch of trees, close up. She scanned for someone hiding there, but it was just trees and shrubs. The next image showed more trees, but the one after that was mostly black, a thin patch of light in one corner.

"You find something, dear?" Danson asked.

"Oh, I don't know." Lily shook off the chill she felt. It wasn't so strange to think some kid had hidden among the trees to watch the police investigate a murder. What did she expect to find in these pictures? These were not people she'd known. She'd never lived in Molva.

Studying the dark and light shadows, Lily flipped the photograph over, wondering why Matt Danson would have kept it.

When she turned it upright again, the image changed for her. She saw that the black was something over the lens, the light filtering in where it wasn't covered. A hand, she thought.

The next image showed fingers, the hand coming off the lens. The next showed a section of wrist, the skin still blurry. Then the last one of the group had captured a close-up of an arm, a section of forearm that was, like the others, mostly out of focus.

She puzzled over it, squinting to try to bring the fuzzy image into focus. There was something there, across the skin. She shuffled the pictures, returning to the man in the woods, and studied them side by side. The fuzzy images were part of the same series—blown-up sections of the picture of the man in the woods. Matt Danson must have seen something there, and the man had tried to stop him. She shivered at an invisible draft as she circled back through the images slowly. She studied each, stopping at the one filled with forearm. The trees made a green haze around the focus on Matt Danson's image.

A gasp caught at the back of her throat.

There, on the surface of the man's skin, was what Matt Danson must have seen.

"Are you all right?" Ms. Danson asked.

But Lily couldn't answer. She was staring at a full-frame image of forearm. Even out of focus, the horizontal lines that crossed the skin were now recognizable.

They were tiny slices as though made by a light touch with a scalpel. She felt a blindfold slip away.

Her eyes watered from so many days without light. His bulk pressed behind her as she hunkered down, knees to her chest. Then a motion flashed in front of her eyes, the sensation of sight overwhelming. In the shadowed room, a man's arm passed through her vision. His hands grabbed the blindfold and lifted it to her face.

She put the photograph down, her hands shaking.

Because she remembered.

Cuts, hundreds of them. Cuts lined his left forearm, identical to the ones she'd felt on her back.

CHAPTER 47

KYLIE

Five miles outside of Glendive, Kylie called Pete McIntosh, who gave her directions to the park where Hitchcock's body had been found. As she pulled into the semicircle parking area, her head swam with thoughts of Lily Baker's wet shoes, of the preliminary evidence report that she'd never received from Gilbert.

From the raised lot, the recreation area—a large frozen meadow—was visible below. Tall grasses stood in frozen clumps, interspersed by a handful of small fishing ponds, currently solid sheets of ice. A winding trail system stretched out for acres, dirt trails that ran through the brush. She left the engine running, comfortable behind the steady stream of warm air as she opened the mail app on her phone and looked for Glanzer's email.

As promised, Glanzer had sent it while they'd still been on the phone. She clicked on the attachment just as a gray Silverado pulled in beside her. The man in the driver's seat raised a hand. In it was a deputy's badge. Kylie nodded and pulled on a hat and gloves before shutting off the engine. Already she could feel the outside air leach into the car.

Zipping up her coat under her chin, she climbed out into the cold. "Detective Milliard?"

"That's me," she said, extending a hand to the deputy. "You must be Pete McIntosh."

"One and the same," he said. McIntosh had a firm handshake and a full head of red hair that ran down the sides of his face into a neatly trimmed beard. He wore no hat and no gloves and didn't look the least bit uncomfortable with the freezing temperatures. Beneath one arm he'd tucked an accordion folder, probably images and reports on the scene.

"Thanks for coming down." He nodded to the park. "I thought we'd take a walk down to where we found Hitchcock. Then I can show you what we've found." He studied the park in silence a moment as though it were a friend who'd disappointed him greatly. "I don't know if it'll help any," he added, returning his gaze to Kylie. "You said you have a suspect in custody?"

She nodded. "We do. I can tell you about him, but the case doesn't feel solid yet. You know what I mean?"

"Absolutely. Let's go have a look, then."

McIntosh glanced at Kylie's shoes as though wondering if they were appropriate for walking. They weren't hiking boots but sturdy street shoes, and he didn't comment as he started for the park. Kylie followed, and they made their way down a series of switchbacks to arrive at the trail entrance. A map of the area hung on a wide board along with information about trail maintenance and cleaning up after pets. The walk to the scene took about ten minutes, and as they went, McIntosh asked questions about Jensen's death and how the Hagen police had come across a suspect.

"Shoes in his toolbox," McIntosh repeated when she told him about the evidence.

"Seems like a pretty big oversight on his part to leave them there, right?" Kylie asked.

McIntosh looked back with a slow nod. "It does. Especially after going to the car wash and all." He paused. "I've seen stupider, though."

That was true for her, too. Only Iver Larson didn't strike her as stupid. Maybe that was what was bothering her.

Around a bend, they came across an area cordoned off with crime scene tape hanging on a number of boundary stakes. Bits of it flew loose now, probably from the wind, but it was conceivable that someone had come looking around. It was nearly impossible to keep curious people away from the scene of a crime. The grislier the crime, the more they flocked.

The two stopped as Kylie studied the area of flattened grass at the center of the taped-off area.

"Body was there," McIntosh said. "ME ruled COD asphyxiation by strangulation, but she had a lot of drugs on board, too. Made it easier to kill her. Report said killer wore gloves, so we can't tell anything about the killer's hands. Could've been a woman that done it, according to the report."

According to Hagen's coroner, Abigail Jensen had also been strangled. What had the state medical examiner's office ruled for Jensen's cause of death? The report was in her inbox, and its presence made Kylie feel antsy to sit down with it. But she was here now, so she needed to learn what she could about Hitchcock. "Any idea what the drugs were?"

"Opioids."

"No flurazepam?"

"Don't think so. I could check."

Kylie nodded. "Hitchcock was seen in a Walmart up in Miles City with another woman, right?"

"Yes. Just got the store security images about an hour ago," he said, opening up the accordion file he'd been carrying under one arm. "Had to jump through a bunch of hoops for these." He slid a stack of images into his hand and righted them so Kylie could see. Blown up to eight-by-ten prints, the images were grainy and pixelated.

Kylie recognized the two women immediately. "That's Abigail Jensen," she said, pointing to the woman beside Hitchcock.

McIntosh nodded. "I figured."

"You mind?" Kylie asked, reaching for the stack.

"Be my guest," McIntosh said, handing her the photos.

One at a time, Kylie examined the images, looking for other faces nearby, any sign of a third party with Hitchcock and Jensen. There were several customers caught in the periphery, coming or going at the same time as the two women, but no one caught her eye. No sign of Lily Baker at all. The two women appeared to be alone. Kylie went through the images three times, starting to shiver in the cold, still air, but nothing struck her. She handed the images back. "Any cameras in the parking lot?"

He shook his head.

"And this was the last time anyone saw her?"

"Yes. This was taken January second, about ten a.m., and her body was found Thursday afternoon, the seventh. Medical examiner figures she'd been dead at least four or five days by then. The freezing temps made it hard to nail down an exact time of death, but she's in different clothes than she was wearing in the Walmart footage."

"So she was alive after the trip to Walmart, but she'd left her car there."

"Right," McIntosh confirmed.

"What was found with her?" Kylie asked.

"No phone or wallet. We still haven't turned up those items."

Just like with Abigail Jensen. "Shoes?"

McIntosh narrowed his eyes at her. "She had her shoes on and a jacket, real old one, though—same one she's wearing in those surveillance pictures. Other than that, there wasn't much with her. A soda bottle and some food wrappers. Those are over in Bismarck, but no results yet. We're hoping for DNA, but it's a long shot."

"Anything in her car?"

"Nope. Not a print on it other than the guy who did the tow. Whoever he is, he's being careful."

"But she was on a lot of drugs, right? So maybe Jensen killed her?" Kylie said.

McIntosh shook his head slowly. "But she wasn't killed out here. At least not according to the ME. Livor mortis showed she'd been moved. Now, she wasn't a large lady, but she weighed one fifty, plus or minus."

"That's more than Jensen," Kylie said, recalling Jensen herself had weighed just under 140 pounds.

"Right," McIntosh said. "You get what I'm saying."

"It probably wasn't Jensen. At least not acting alone."

"Right."

McIntosh nodded to a path she hadn't noticed. "Let's walk the rest of the loop. I'll show you where I found the other thing yesterday."

"Other thing?"

McIntosh nodded and kept walking without offering an answer.

Kylie's teeth had started chattering, and she was grateful to get moving. As they walked, McIntosh explained how the local Eagles club led a biannual cleanup effort in the twenty-acre park in May and in October. "These trails aren't used much during the winter. We don't get enough snow in this area for cross-country skiers, so it's mostly a handful of snowshoers and an occasional hiker."

McIntosh referenced an image on his phone as he slowed to a stop. Pointing back to the lot, he said, "Folks can walk the path in either direction, from the right or from the left; it's just a circle, but if I was going to dump a body, I don't think I'd make the whole loop."

Kylie puzzled on it a minute. "You're thinking the killer entered the loop from the left side."

McIntosh nodded. "Where the body was found is just about halfway around the loop. He might have had a sled, pulled her or something. No way to know now."

He stopped and pointed to a spot just off the trail. "Found it right there," he said. "Temps warmed up the last couple of days, so I came back up after lunch yesterday, and there it was." He handed her a phone, and she looked down at an image of a carabiner. "It's an old thing, paint coming off."

Kylie studied the image, unable to tell the dimensions. "Is it large? Like for climbing?"

"This one's smaller, the kind of thing you might hang keys on," he said. "The lever on it was broken off, and I haven't found that piece yet, so it might just be more trash, but like I said, we did a cleanup effort just a few months back. And if it had been right there, beside the trail, I can't see how they would have missed it. But it could have come off someone working the cleanup. Or our killer might've lost it. I'm sending it all to the state lab, but who knows when we'll hear back."

Kylie stared at the picture. With gloved hands, she tried and failed to zoom in on the image.

McIntosh reached over and expanded the image so that it filled the screen. A scratched-up metal carabiner lay on the snow, its clip missing, chipped green paint still visible, though most of it had been worn off. Along the side were words Kylie couldn't make out. "What does it say?"

"Green Bay Packers."

Some memory bobbed near the surface of her brain, but she couldn't reach it.

Her phone buzzed in her pocket. Sheriff Davis's line. "I need to take this."

"We just finished processing the Tanner scene," Davis told her.

"You find anything?"

"Just a lot of Tanner's prints. Didn't look like he had many guests, and whoever killed him didn't leave any that we can find. How's it going down there?"

"Here with Deputy Sheriff McIntosh. I'll head back up there when we're done. What's the status with Larson?"

"The hospital discharged him, so he's in the courthouse now. Arraignment is scheduled for Monday."

"We get a warrant for his house?"

"Vogel's working on it."

"I want to be there for that. I'm on my way back."

"See you soon. Careful on the roads," Davis said. "There's a big storm heading in."

She ended the call and walked the remainder of the loop with McIntosh before they went their separate ways, promising to be in touch if either learned something useful.

Sitting in the car with the heat on, Kylie cracked her knuckles before shifting into reverse to head back to Hagen. Something hovered just outside her grasp. She felt confident that if she could put the pieces together, she'd have her answer. But whenever she tried to grip it in her hand, it escaped through her fingers like smoke.

CHAPTER 48

—

IVER

Iver lay across the single narrow cot in the small jail cell, his hands under his head. Eyes closed, he tried to tell himself that he was back in Afghanistan, that the cot was his bunk at the base. That his platoon was nearby and the enemy outside the gate. Over there, he'd trained his body to sleep in any position—on the ground or in the back of the Humvee when he needed to catch a few hours between patrols. Back then, he could sleep anywhere, shut out the heat or the freeze and sink his mind to an empty, quiet place.

But that skill was long gone.

Instead, he stared at the concrete ceiling, its single bulb enclosed in a cage, just like him, and waited for something to happen. Carl Gilbert had been all too happy to put him behind bars, refusing his repeated requests to talk to Detective Milliard. Henry Cooper, his father's attorney, was supposedly working on finding a criminal lawyer from Fargo to take his case, and Mike was out enlisting Donnie and Nate to help him drag Kevin into the station to make a full confession about drugging him. Whatever good that would do.

All of that had been hours ago.

Since then, he'd been left with only quiet. There were no windows, not even a clock in this place, so he had no idea what time it was.

His mind spun questions and theories that tumbled over one another. He felt twitchy, both his mind and body restless. To pass the time, he had been doing sit-ups, push-ups, and air squats until his muscles trembled. Then he'd rest ten or fifteen minutes and start them again. The act of exhausting his body helped slow his mind, even if he couldn't sleep.

He went back through the past few days. The loss of his memory Wednesday night, the realization that he'd gone to Debbie's house in the middle of the night, the headaches and seizure that he now believed had been caused by some drug put in his drink. Had Kevin really drugged him for money? In light of the dead woman and the man who'd been killed last night, the money felt so stupid. Hell, he'd happily give Kevin the $700 to make this all go away.

But the fact that someone he'd known since grade school, a supposed friend, had drugged him . . . it was disconcerting, to say the least. And not only was the bar short $700, a few register tapes were missing. Was Kevin stupid enough to think that taking the tapes would hide the fact that he'd stolen from the bar?

They wanted him for murder.

Murder.

The fear of possibility, of not remembering, was eating him alive.

Iver hadn't hurt that woman. He knew he hadn't. No, he told himself, he *thought* he hadn't. He believed that he wasn't capable of killing a stranger.

But that was the problem. He *was* capable of killing a stranger.

He closed his eyes and pictured their Afghanistan home, what the army called a containerized housing unit, what the soldiers called the CHU. From the outside, the CHU looked like an oversize shipping container, and at first glance, Iver had been certain that they'd boil alive in that thing. But the inside was surprisingly comfortable—a window and venting, a power cable, and an air-conditioning unit. A wet CHU in their case because they were one of the lucky ones to have a latrine inside. It was supposed to house four, but theirs had five—Brolyard a late addition. What he wouldn't do to go back there now, change the outcome of that day.

The end of his army career had been brutally abrupt. The five had gone out on an easy recon mission, a quick trip away from the base to a burned-out building in their area. They were there to take a look inside and check for signs the locals were using it as a base for something.

They'd only been inside for a few minutes when an RPG hit the building next door. The walls around them trembled. A group of insurgents appeared about a block away—three or maybe four of them. The back door of the building where Iver and the others were hiding led to a dead-end alley. Their only way out was through the front, which meant they would have to take down the Afghan with the RPG as well as any others in order to make it to the vehicle.

And that was if the enemy didn't figure out where they were. Brolyard was less than a month from heading home, Sanchez still a little green. Wykstra held it together, but it was Garabrant, twitchy and loud as he peered out the front window, who made Iver especially nervous. To take out the Afghan with the RPG and escape, they had to remain unseen, unheard.

Iver had just crouched by the rear door, huddled behind what had once been a small counter, when the insurgents splintered off to search the surrounding buildings. He had a good angle out a blown-out window on the side of the building. He'd have a clear shot in less than a minute if the men continued on the same path. Take out the RPG, fire at the group to make them scatter, then go for the Humvee.

That was the plan.

A sound from behind. Shoes on dirt. He swung his gun around and aimed. An Afghan woman had come in through the back door, alarm in her wide brown eyes. She might have been his age—maybe even a little younger. She wore a traditional tunbaan, a dress with blousy pants that reached her sandals. A magenta chador fell loosely around her head, all of her covered in a layer of dust.

He'd had no choice.

At least that was what he told himself.

CHAPTER 49

—

LILY

Lily shook Ms. Danson's hand and thanked her. Her mind was numb, the image of a bloody boy inside a dead pig occupying the full screen in her head. Still holding the pictures Matt Danson had taken of the woods and the fuzzy images of the scarred forearm, Lily half stumbled down the ramp. She had promised Ms. Danson that she would return the photos as soon as she could, but she needed to take them to Detective Milliard. While Derek Hudson had lain in a pool of his own blood, this man had been alive in the woods. Danson had captured the image of him that day, hiding.

He had been in that cabin with her. He'd blindfolded her. Cut her.

Whoever she'd shot that day was not her abductor—or not the only one. Had Abby discovered him somehow? Was that why she and Lily had gone to the bar that night? To confront him? Jenna Hitchcock was dead, too. Was he finally cleaning up the girls who had gotten away? Why now?

Lily ran to her car, fumbling with the keys. She had to get back to Hagen. Or stay away. No, she had to get to Iver. And she could trust Milliard.

A few blocks from the house, Lily realized that she should have asked to use Danson's phone to call Detective Milliard. She glanced in her rearview mirror, considering turning back. The road was quiet and empty. She could have turned around right there, but she didn't want to waste the time. She'd go straight to the police department.

After a couple of miles on the two-lane highway outside of Molva, Cal began to whine on the seat beside her. Of course. He'd been cooped up in the car for over an hour while she'd spoken to Melinda Danson. No water, no place to relieve himself. A minute later, he began to bark. "Okay, buddy," she said, scanning the road for a turnoff. "Hang on." Behind her was a brown sedan, so she signaled to pull off the road.

She approached a gravel road, turned off, and drove a few feet before pulling to the side. The brown sedan turned behind her. Only now did she notice the single police light on the roof, its red color dull. Was she being pulled over? It wasn't the same car as the deputy's. She cracked her door and looked back at the sedan as a man stood up. He wore street clothes.

"Is everything all right?" she asked.

"I was about to ask you the same thing," he said with a smile, glancing into her car.

"I'm just letting my dog out for a few minutes before the drive," she said, hesitating to get out. "Am I in your way?"

"Not at all. I'm just making my way upstate."

She watched him a moment, then noticed the phone on his belt, in a holster like a gun. He was some sort of government worker or something. "Would you mind if I used your phone? I'm afraid mine's out of juice," she lied, wondering what it was that had her so nervous. But of course she was nervous. She'd seen those pictures, heard about Derek Hudson.

"No problem at all."

He pulled the phone from his waistband and typed something in before handing it over to her. "Should be unlocked for you."

"Thank you." Without moving from the front seat, she searched for the nonemergency number for the Hagen police department and pressed the number to dial. As soon as the phone started ringing, she felt a wave of relief.

"Hagen Dispatch. This is Marjorie."

"Hello," Lily said. "My name is Lily Baker, and I'm trying to reach Detective Milliard."

"Sure thing, Miss Baker. Hang on just one minute."

Beside her, Cal whined again. She reached across the car and released the passenger door, but Cal just stared out at the gravel road without getting out of the car. "Go on, buddy," she urged.

Cal didn't move.

Lily glanced back to the government man, leaning against his sedan, arms crossed. He was whistling.

Come on, Detective Milliard. Where was she?

Cal barked—once, then twice—before he started the high whine again.

Lily hurried around the car, the phone to her ear, and opened the passenger door and helped Cal down onto the ground. Once there, he walked slowly away to find a place to do his business, stepping gingerly on the snow-crusted grass.

"Miss Baker?" The voice was the woman from Dispatch again.

"Yes?"

"I'm afraid I'm not able to reach Detective Milliard. I'm going to put you through to another officer."

Lily hesitated. She only knew Milliard, but of course. Anyone there should be able to help her. "Okay."

"One moment, please."

The cold penetrated the down of her coat, and she exhaled, her breath clouding the air.

"Hagen Police Department. How can I help you, Lily Baker?"

Lily froze at the sound of the voice. That voice. His voice. She felt the dark, the fear. The warnings about hurrying back and not talking to anyone.

Derek Hudson was on the phone.

"You still there, Lily?"

Hands shaking, she whispered into the phone, "Who are you?"

"What? You don't recognize me?" he asked, lowering his voice into a hiss. "It's your old friend Derek."

No. It was impossible. Fingers trembling, she ended the call. Her heart pulsed in her ears, her legs weak beneath her as she doubled over. But that voice belonged to Derek Hudson. It was the voice of her nightmares. But that meant he wasn't dead. Worse, he worked with the police. He'd been there in Hagen all along. How had she never seen Hudson in Hagen? Or maybe she had. His face was unfamiliar to her. It was his voice that she knew.

But if he was alive, then who was the man she'd shot at the cabin?

She stood up and stared at the phone, wondering if she should call back. She needed to speak to Detective Milliard and only Milliard. Or else go back to Molva, explain it all to the deputy there. Andy. He'd felt safe. But if a Hagen police officer was involved, then couldn't one in Molva be as well?

No. She had to find Milliard, which meant getting back to Hagen. Suddenly, she wished she hadn't stopped for Cal. But then she wouldn't have known Hudson was alive and in Hagen.

Cal.

Where was Cal? She turned to look for the dog and sensed something behind her. She spun around to face the man from the car. "Oh, you scared me," she said, pressing a hand to her chest.

"I'm going to have to take that picture," he said, pointing at the image on the passenger seat, the one she'd taken from Danson's house.

"What?"

But even as she said the word, his hand connected to her neck with a buzzing sound. White-hot pain shot through her, the piercing shriek of electricity. She tried to take a step, to run, but she dropped to the icy gravel.

He was there, on top of her, the Taser to her back. Electricity shot through her again. "You don't remember?" he asked with a shake of his head. "I wish I could believe you."

Remember. She ought to remember. She held that thought as she tried to study his face, but every muscle was firing, then failing. And suddenly, the word was there. Abby had said it, that night in the woods. Lily opened her lips and let out the monster's name.

"You *do* remember." He clenched his teeth as he pressed the Taser to her, the smell of burning flesh in her nose. "This whole thing's your damn fault," he said, the buzz finally dying.

Her fault. It was her fault. What was? Abby?

If Derek Hudson had been on the phone in Hagen, then who was this man?

His beady eyes were so familiar. He looked like someone else, but who?

As the black descended, she knew. He looked like the man in the photo, the police officer who'd been interviewing people in Danson's photographs.

Oh God. He *was* that man.

CHAPTER 50

Kylie

Twenty minutes outside of Glendive, Kylie pulled over in a spot with decent cell service and launched the email app on her phone. Then she tried to download the state lab report on Abigail Jensen. She waited five, then ten minutes while the little wheel spun on her screen.

This was Carl Gilbert's fault. She could have reviewed this report last night. Giving up on her email, she dialed Gilbert directly.

"Detective," he said. "You still in Glendive?"

"On my way back," she said.

"You learn anything?"

"Actually, I'm calling about Jensen's autopsy report."

"Oh?"

Something haughty in Gilbert's tone made her want to slap him. If only she were a little closer. "The report came in yesterday?"

"Did it?"

"Gilbert," she snapped. "It went to your email. Why the hell didn't you forward it?"

"I haven't seen it," he said. "I've been a little busy up here."

Kylie gripped the wheel. "I need to know what the report says, Carl. Can you walk me through the findings?"

"I don't need to see the findings to know what they'll say. They'll say that Iver Larson killed her, then left the hospital and killed Alvin Tanner."

"You find a witness who saw him leave?"

"I'm working on it." A faint shout leaked through the phone, somewhere on Gilbert's end. "I've got to go, Detective. We'll see you when you're back."

Kylie started to say something, but Gilbert had hung up. Fury burned through her. That asshole . . . she drew a slow breath. Gilbert was right to try to locate a witness who'd seen Larson leave the hospital. Without prints at Tanner's, there was no way they could prove Larson had killed him.

She thought about Iver Larson, the strange way he'd been with Lily Baker that first night—so protective and yet so distant, like she was a piece of china that might break if he held on. Then she remembered the sight of Alvin Tanner's butchered hand. Iver was guilty. The pieces fit, didn't they?

Kylie found Dr. Glanzer's phone number in her email and dialed it. Inside two rings, her voice came on the line. "Glanzer."

"This is Kylie Milliard. We spoke earlier."

"Sure. What can I do for you?"

Kylie explained her trouble opening the autopsy report and asked if Glanzer would be willing to give her a five-minute summary. "I wouldn't ask, but we've got another victim this morning, and . . ."

"Alvin Tanner. Heard about that one."

"I'm just trying to get a handle on the evidence on the off chance that something clicks," Kylie explained. "Was the ME able to determine time of death on Jensen?"

"Actually, that was kind of my doing," Glanzer said. "Well, mine and the victim's watch."

Kylie shook her head. "I don't think Jensen was wearing a watch, only a wide red leather bracelet with a silver disk. It had snaps," Kylie added, then realized how dumb that sounded.

"Right," Glanzer agreed. "That disk was actually a watch. Not sure why it was turned inward—if it was a style or she just wore it that way—but that disk was a thin children's watch, mounted with the glass face against the leather. The snaps allowed her to flip the watch and see the time. Like I said, I'm not sure why it was like that. The watch was Mickey Mouse. My lab identified it as something made in the mid- to late nineties, mass produced and sold on a black plastic band for about ten dollars. I can text pictures, if that helps."

"It might," Kylie said. "But tell me how the watch determined time of death."

"Our state ME, Dr. Nelson, reached out to the Hagen coroner to talk about time of death. Your coroner suggested the victim had likely died between ten p.m. and one a.m., but Dr. Nelson thought the watch told a different story, so he sent it to our lab. The watch has a single dent in the back casing—the part that would have been facing outward, considering how she wore it. The dent looks to have separated the gears, which stopped the watch," Glanzer continued. "Dr. Nelson asked me to determine if the watch had stopped earlier or if the dent had happened that night."

Kylie sat up straight in her seat. "And could you figure that out?"

"Yes. As it turns out, whatever blow caused the dent in the watch also cracked the face. We found trace glass in the leather. Had the victim removed the bracelet after the blow—or even opened it to check the time—the glass would have fallen free. Instead, it was trapped between the glass face and the leather, which was tight against her arm. Means she hadn't removed the bracelet since the blow that caused the dent and separated the gears. And the leather wasn't wet and showed no signs of being submerged in water."

"So she didn't shower or bathe in it," Kylie said.

"Exactly."

"Which means the watch probably broke during the struggle that night."

"Almost certainly. Dr. Nelson had called your coroner to check if he had considered the bracelet in his initial autopsy findings, but he hadn't.

Dr. Nelson had the impression that the local coroner didn't realize that the silver disk was actually the backside of a watch. He was probably more focused on the body."

Kylie took a moment to process what Glanzer was saying. "But isn't it possible that the blow happened some hours before her actual death?"

"Dr. Nelson doesn't think so. There were only minimal signs of hemorrhaging on her arm—bruising—so she likely died within an hour or so of the blow."

"But this assumes that the watch was working, right?"

"Yes," Glanzer confirmed. "It appeared to be. Battery power was good, and the gears were clean."

Kylie felt like she was holding her breath. Letting it out, she asked, "So we know exact time of death?"

"Well, we know the exact time when she was attacked."

"And what time was that?"

"If we believe the watch, it was eight forty-three p.m."

"Eight forty-three p.m.," Kylie repeated, needing to hear the words out loud, let them echo in her mind. Not even nine o'clock. "Which meant she died some time before ten."

"Yes. Those were Dr. Nelson's findings."

Iver Larson had been in the bar until ten thirty. No one had seen him go outside except for a few minutes in the parking lot.

Iver Larson wasn't the killer.

He couldn't be.

Had they missed something? Could he have sneaked out a different way? But his guilt had been based on the fact that he'd been seen driving in the middle of the night, that maybe he'd met the victim later in the evening. But she'd been dead by ten thirty. Unless the watch was wrong. The lab thought it had probably been working, but maybe the time hadn't been set correctly?

"Detective?"

"Thank you," Kylie said.

"Not what you were expecting," Glanzer guessed.

Kylie's phone buzzed with an unfamiliar number. "No," she admitted to Glanzer. "But it was very helpful. I've got another call coming in. Thanks for the help."

Head spinning, Kylie ended the call with Glanzer and accepted the incoming call. "Detective Milliard."

A man's voice. *Deputy . . . Molva . . . Lily Baker.* He was talking too fast.

"Whoa," she said. "Slow down. I can't understand you."

The man on the line seemed to be hyperventilating. "I'm a deputy in Molva. Lily Baker was here this morning. She wanted to see the cabin—"

The line went silent. "Deputy?"

"Yes," he said as though he'd been holding his breath. "She wanted to see the cabin where she was . . ."

"Held," Kylie finished.

"Yes."

Her pulse was like a hiccup in her temple, and she pressed her fingers against it. "And? Did she remember something?"

The man on the other end of the phone went quiet.

"Hello?"

"I'm here, Detective. I don't know yet," he admitted, sounding distraught. "See, I took her to see my aunt, Melinda. Mindy's been in Molva for her whole life—almost eight decades. She knew the Hudsons and all of them, so I thought she might be able to help."

"Where is Lily Baker now? Has she left town?"

"Well, that's why I'm calling."

Every part of Kylie tensed. She imagined Alvin Tanner, his missing fingers, lying in a pool of blood. "Has something happened?"

"Maybe."

"Tell me what the hell is going on!" Kylie said, shouting now.

"The other deputy—there are two of us here in Molva—was driving out 171; that's the road out of town. And he found Ms. Baker's car."

"Her car." Kylie pressed her eyes closed. "But not her?"

"No."

"You sure it was her car? Maybe he's mistaken."

"No, ma'am. I saw that car this morning, Ms. Baker in it, along with her dog. She followed me to Mindy's house. I know it's her car."

"Maybe she had car trouble?" Kylie said. "If her car had broken down, would she have come back to Molva, or was there somewhere else she might have gone?"

"I thought of that, but her keys were right there in the car, and the engine turned over, no problem."

The air was swept from her lungs.

"Plus," the deputy added, "I don't think she would've left her dog."

The dog. Iver Larson's dog, it had to be. "The dog was still in the car?"

"Outside the car, curled up under one of the wheels, trying to stay warm, I think."

Larson was in jail. But according to the watch, Larson hadn't killed Jensen. And there was no way he'd kidnapped Lily Baker from Molva.

So who the hell had her? And where had they gone?

CHAPTER 51

—

LILY

Lily followed Abby into the woods, scanning for whatever her friend saw there. But it was all shadows and cold to Lily.

"Abby?"

"Almost," she said. "Just a little farther."

"I thought we were going to the bar," Lily said, trying to sound carefree. Abby had only been in town a few hours, but already her presence unnerved Lily. It had been Lily's idea for Abby to come. The transition back to life in Elgin after the years at the school up in Washington had been hard for Abby. After Hudson, the school was all she had known, and Elgin no longer felt like home.

During those first months away from the cabin, Lily had longed for Abby. So many days spent feeling the older girl at her side, feeding off her strength to go on. But Abby had been distant after their escape. She'd settled in a new place, while Lily had returned to a home that no longer felt like home. And then her father had decided she should go to Arizona and live with his sister, who had never married. She was married to Jesus, she'd said. Although she wasn't technically part of the church, she was one of its most dedicated attendants. Soon Lily had been, too.

When her father had died and Lily had returned to Hagen, she'd gotten a note from Abby. At first, she hadn't replied, but several months later, there'd been another. Abby had been back in Elgin and struggling. A month later, another letter came. Letters arrived every month or two for almost two years, as though they were her own private journal entries. The words in the letters had felt like the closest thing to a home that Lily could remember.

And then Abby had written her longest letter. She was happy. At her job in a nursing home, she'd met a man, the son of a woman Abby was caring for. "Meeting him was like coming home," Abby wrote. "I want to come visit. I need to see you, Lily."

And two days later, she called.

A week passed, and now Abby was here, leading her into the dark. Why did she follow?

Abby turned back as though sensing Lily's hesitation and stepped back to her friend. She wrapped her arms around Lily and whispered, "I'm so glad we're together again."

And then she pulled Lily into the woods.

Lily felt the darkness drag across her like a thick fabric screen.

"I want us to be together," Abby said. "Like before."

Abby was still walking, Lily following. The words danced around like fireflies, and she tried to track them. They lined up momentarily, and she halted. "What?"

Abby looked around carefully, then turned to Lily, dropping her hand and taking hold of her shoulders. "I want you to come live with me. We will be together, like before." Her hand touched Lily's cheek, then trailed over her shoulder to her back, where Abby's fingers pressed into the soft skin below her shoulder blade. Abby stared at her, rubbing a small circle on the place where she'd been cut, the place where he had focused his knife in her soft skin.

Abby's expression shifted, becoming full of ownership and pride. Those moments being cut in that cabin. Silence, the gentle pressure of the slice. The words in her ear, Abby's words. "Don't move, or the knife will slip and you'll die. Please don't move, Lily."

Then came the brief sensation of something thick and warm against her skin. A lapping sensation, like a tongue. The memory brought a wave of shudders. That had been Hudson. Abby had been there to keep her safe, to protect her.

Abby's hand continued its circles.

Lily stepped back. "Abby?"

Abby tilted her head, offered a sideways smile as she tugged at the sleeve of her jacket, raising it to her elbow. Dozens of tiny cuts marred the skin. Abby focused on one, using her fingers to spread the skin, tear the wound.

Lily gasped as a drop of blood oozed up from the angry red line on Abby's arm.

Ducking her head, Abby flicked out her tongue and lapped up the bead of blood.

Lily froze in place, trying to make sense of what she was seeing. They'd been captives together. They'd helped each other, protected each other.

"Abby, that's over. We're free."

Abby's head rolled up, a small dot of blood at the corner of her mouth. She reached into her pocket and pulled out a thin scrap of newspaper, held it up in the darkness.

Lily shook her head. "I can't read it. What does it say?"

"It says it's not over," Abby said, reaching out to hand her the clipping.

Lily stepped backward. "I don't want it."

Abby took hold of her arm and shoved the newspaper clipping into Lily's front pocket. "Read it," she said, a growl in her voice. "It means we can go back, go home."

Lily pulled her arm free. "We were prisoners, Abby."

"No." Abby's voice was sharp as she waved her hands through the cold night air, the wound on her arm still leaking blood as she yanked her jacket sleeve down. "This is the prison, this life. That life was perfect . . . and now we can go back, the three of us."

Only then did Lily hear the footsteps approaching, the crunch of snow. He was coming for her.

CHAPTER 52

KYLIE

Kylie was breathing hard and driving like a madwoman. Police lights flashing, she sped along the highway toward Hagen. The Molva police were searching for Lily Baker there, but Kylie's gut told her that the key to all of this was in Hagen. She'd tried to reach Davis, but he hadn't called her back. She tried Vogel, too, and then, desperate, she'd called Gary Ross.

Where the hell was everyone? Gilbert had turned his phone off completely—or the battery had died. Calls to him went straight to voicemail. Only Steve Cannon was answering his phone, and he gave her the one piece of information she needed—the location of the man she now thought was behind all of this.

She was only thirty minutes outside Glendive when she called Pete McIntosh and told him what had happened.

"I could use your help." She explained the call from Molva, Gilbert's reaction to her questions about the autopsy, and her mad rush to get back to Hagen. Maybe Carl Gilbert was working some sort of power play, but she didn't trust him. What she needed right now was a guarantee—someone whose motive she trusted 100 percent.

"Not sure who you can trust?"

The words were like a trigger. "Yes."

"I'm on my way," McIntosh told her. "I'll call when I'm close."

Ending the call, Kylie dropped the phone on the passenger seat and gripped the wheel with both hands. Her focus on the road, she replayed the first conversation she'd had with Glanzer. The drug in the glass found in Larson's office had been a strong sedative. Glanzer had made it sound like Larson had been drugged. And wasn't that what Dr. Prescott had implied as well? But if someone had wanted to set him up for murder, why sedate him? Why not give him a drug that would simply erase his memory? Or was that what they *thought* they'd done?

The only other possibility was that Larson had been drugged for some reason other than to be framed for murder. But then why had he been drugged? She thought about the fingerprints. Kevin Clouse. Gilbert had interviewed the bartenders. Clouse was dating the pastor's daughter. Would that give him reason to drug Larson? Could Larson's blackout possibly have nothing to do with Jensen's death?

Who was responsible for her murder, then? All the evidence pointed to Larson.

Evidence that could have been planted.

Gilbert had found Jensen's shoes in Iver Larson's truck. Gilbert, who hadn't gotten her the autopsy report, who had turned off his phone. Gilbert, who had volunteered to arrest Iver Larson. Carl Gilbert? Baker said her attacker had used a Taser. Like what police officers carried.

She shook her head. Gilbert, with his lanky awkwardness and his fat wad of keys. The carabiner. She felt suddenly sick, picturing the green-and-yellow mug in Gilbert's hand. Some sort of team. Green Bay Packers. The Packers' colors were yellow and green. Suddenly, despite the stream of hot air blowing from the vents, she was freezing.

Gilbert had startled her in those woods. Why hadn't she heard the jangling of his keys then?

And how had he found her? The woods had been dark, and she'd been in there long before he'd come. Unless he'd known exactly where the crime had happened. Because he'd been there before.

The night he killed Abigail Jensen.

CHAPTER 53

LILY

Lily came to in the darkness, a steady thrumming behind her eyes. She tried to shift, but the space was tight, her legs and hands immobile. Instantly, she recalled the car on the overpass, tipping toward the edge. She tried to curl her fingers, remembered the numbness.

No. There was no chill now. Her fingers moved easily. There was no seat belt across her chest and no rustle of the airbag. She was not in a car. Where . . . then she remembered stopping outside Molva, the man in the government car. The Taser.

Shifting in the darkness, she felt bindings on her wrists and twisted against the tape but was unable to break free. Her fingers skimmed across wool-like material on the hard surface below her. Fresh terror rolled across her shoulders. She was in the trunk of a car. She shut out the image of the car on a ledge, ready to tip. She couldn't think that way.

Get out.

Blinking against the darkness, she willed her eyes to adjust. Her breathing was ragged, her pulse racing. She closed her eyes, forced a slow breath. With a rasp in her throat, it sounded like she was choking. "Stop," she commanded, pulling herself together.

Before she could make a plan, the trunk opened.

Light blinded her. The man. She tried to shift away from him, but there was nowhere to go. A large hand gripped her thigh, pressing her down even as she tried to pull her knees to her chest and kick. He moved quickly, his left arm blocking her feet and his right swinging toward her. Too late, she spotted the needle in his fist as it stabbed her leg. The sharp bite of the injection was followed by a sting at the site, then heat as the drug traveled through her leg.

She clenched her muscles in a futile effort to drive the drug out. "Who are you? Why are you doing this?"

He stared at her without answering. With the light behind him, his face was shadowed, his eyes empty sockets. He blinked, and she started as the flash of skin covered the black holes.

"Why would you help him?" she asked.

"'Cause he's family, and you take care of family," the man said, resigned.

As her eyes adjusted to the light, she studied his face. There was something familiar about it. Within moments, his face grew fuzzy. Her skin flushed with warmth, and her eyelids grew heavy.

Focused on breathing, she fought the cloud of drug settling over her.

"A few more hours, and this will all be over, God willing."

Her throat closed, and tears welled in her eyes. She pressed her eyes closed and fought back the fear. *Be angry. Be smart.* She couldn't give in. It wasn't over yet. She was still here. Alive.

She could still get away. God willing.

But the fearful, and unbelieving, and the abominable, and murderers, and whoremongers, and sorcerers, and idolaters, and all liars, shall have their part in the lake which burneth with fire and brimstone: which is the second death.

The warm wave of drowsiness yanked her under. She fought against it, but the drug was stronger than her fight, and she was dragged back into the darkness.

CHAPTER 54

IVER

Drops of sweat hit the concrete floor as Iver took a break from his exercise routine. His thoughts circled between the woman in Afghanistan and what had happened at the bar on Wednesday. He hadn't been angry at the Afghan woman. He hadn't feared her. What he had feared was that Garabrant would shoot, that the noise would kill them all. He hadn't been violent in anger. He had been violent in fear.

And he hadn't been afraid on Wednesday, had he? His reaction to his best friend and his ex-wife dating was not fear. At first pass, their relationship had seemed like a violation, of course. He and Mike had been best friends forever. But Iver and Debbie weren't going to be together again—that had been crystal clear from the time she'd moved out. They were done. She was done.

And Iver had been done, too. Their marriage had become a routine that no longer served either of them. He needed to recreate himself with new limitations—headaches and pain, but also a new understanding of what there was to lose. He'd wasted a year living in that old rut, working at a job he hated, drinking himself in and out of pain, and ignoring the blatant signs that he was screwing up his life.

He pictured the photograph of him gripping Debbie's arm, and a wave of shame washed over him. Yes. He had been rough with her—or it looked that way from the picture. But he wasn't a violent person.

Debbie had left. She was moving on. He wanted to be happy for her. And for Mike. He would be, eventually. That burst of anger at her—at them—had been wounded pride, humiliation at what others would think when they found out Debbie had left him and was now with his oldest friend.

Closing his eyes, he rolled onto his back and started sit-ups, telling himself that this time he would change. He'd said it before, but it felt real now. He lowered himself again and crunched back up. The only chance he had at a future was to prove that he hadn't killed Abigail Jensen.

How did he do that when he didn't even remember seeing her that night?

Halfway through the next sit-up, he halted. Put his hands on the cold floor. Behind his ugly, angry face in that picture was the parking lot. He closed his eyes and pictured the regular assortment of cars— mostly pickup trucks—that filled the lot each night. Beyond the lot was the street that ran along the bar. No one ever parked there. Why would they? The bar's lot was plenty big.

But in the picture Henry Cooper had shown him, there'd been a car on the road. Not a pickup but a small white car, and someone sitting inside. Two people? He stood, realizing he'd seen the car before. He wiped the sweat from his face with his forearm. That was Lily Baker's car. Had there been someone else in the car with her? Had the faces been caught in that photograph?

He needed to talk to Cooper again, have the police blow up that image. Iver gripped the iron bars of his cell. He hadn't used his phone call yet.

"Hey, I want to make my phone call," he shouted. "I have the right to a phone call. Hello!"

Several moments later, footsteps came down the hall.

"I get a phone call!" Iver called out.

Carl Gilbert appeared in the doorway, a smirk on his face. "You're making quite a racket in here, Larson. You best sit down and shut up."

"I get a phone call, Gilbert. The law requires that you let me make a phone call."

"Of course," Gilbert said, the smile widening into a grin. "I'll get right on that." He drew a gun from his hip, and Iver moved away from the bars.

"What the hell are you doing, Gilbert?"

"Taser," Gilbert said. "For my own protection if you try to escape."

But the expression on Gilbert's face read entirely different. No fear. Only a perverse sort of anticipation. "You sure you want to make that call now?"

And suddenly, Iver wasn't sure he'd have a future after all.

CHAPTER 55

KYLIE

Kylie tried to reach Sheriff Davis a half dozen more times, then spoke to the weekend Dispatch officer, who tried Sullivan and Smith and a couple of other officers. No one knew where Davis was. Vogel wasn't reachable either—he never was on the weekends—and Gilbert's phone was shut off. The drive from Glendive felt interminable, and as she sped past the turnoff for Alvin Tanner's house, it seemed impossible that only seven hours had passed since she'd found him dead.

As she drove into Hagen, the wind was blowing hard, a constant pressure nudging the car toward the centerline. The sky was quickly growing dark, turning the afternoon as black as nighttime. It was going to storm, and from the look of the sky, it was going to be a nasty one.

Kylie sped through downtown, scanning the streets, nagged by the unrelenting sense that something would jump out, that the chaos in her head would be mirrored in town. But the streets looked like they always did—quiet and peaceful.

She drove into the station parking lot and didn't bother to pull into a spot, instead leaving the department car in front of the building. As she ran for the front entrance, a strong gust whipped her hair against her face, and she had to fight to open the door against the pressure of the wind. She stepped into the quiet vacuum of the lobby in time to notice the first snowflakes fall.

The receptionist's desk was empty on a Saturday, so Kylie blew past, using her key card to get into the main office. She scanned the bullpen, but it was quiet, so she ran straight to the jail.

The low voices of men talking drifted down the hall, and she slowed down to listen.

"I get to make a phone call, Carl."

"I think we'll just have to wait." Gilbert's voice.

Kylie drew her weapon and opened the door slowly, moving heel to toe until she was in the doorway. Carl Gilbert stood with his back to her.

"Keep your hands where I can see them," Kylie said.

Larson's hands shot into the air. "Don't shoot."

Gilbert spun around. "What the—" He saw the gun, and his mouth snapped shut.

Larson finally noticed the gun wasn't aimed at him and moved to the far side of the cell.

Gilbert slowly lifted his hands. "What are you doing?"

"Take the gun from your holster and lower it to the floor. Slowly."

Gilbert looked behind him as though she might have been speaking to someone else.

"You, Gilbert," she said.

"What the hell?"

"I'm not screwing around. Do it now."

"I'll let him make the damn phone call. You don't need the gun."

"Nice try."

Carl Gilbert looked nervous now. Something clinked between his teeth. A hard candy.

"Gun," she repeated. "Now."

Gilbert kept his right hand in the air and removed the gun with his left. The movement sparked a memory. Pete McIntosh had said that some people walked the Glendive park loop from the right and others from the left. It had looked like Jenna Hitchcock's killer came from the left. She watched Gilbert's left hand, his dominant hand. Were left-handed people more likely to walk left to right? Gilbert set the gun on the floor, and she moved toward him. "Where is Lily Baker? What did you do with her?"

"What are you talking about?" Larson asked from the cell, his voice pitched high. "What's happened to her?"

Gilbert shook his head. "You're confused, Kylie. I haven't seen Lily Baker since . . . not since the hospital room yesterday."

"Give me the Taser, too," Kylie said. Lily Baker had been tased at Larson's house. Maybe they could get DNA off Gilbert's Taser. Get him locked up first. Then she'd get him to talk. "The Taser," she repeated.

Gilbert passed it to her.

She set it on the desk behind her without looking away. "Now, where are the keys to the jail?"

"What? You're going to bust him out?"

"Where are the keys, Carl?" She edged her finger toward the trigger. "I swear to God I'll shoot."

"They're on my belt. Left side."

"Take them off and hand them to Larson. Slowly."

Larson stood frozen in the corner of the cell.

Gilbert pulled a ring of keys off his belt and dangled them from one finger. The keys hung on several individual key rings, but the bundle was looped on a silver carabiner. Shiny and new.

"Nice carabiner, Carl. You break your other one?"

"What are you talking about?" His eyes went wide, and he looked genuinely terrified.

She shook her head. She wasn't buying it. "Come on, Iver. Take the keys and unlock that cell."

"Wh—what's happening?" Larson asked, his gaze moving between the two of them.

"You're innocent, aren't you?" she asked without taking her eyes off Gilbert.

"Yes, but—" Larson stuttered.

"Then let's go."

Larson grabbed the keys from Gilbert and fumbled with them.

"Kylie, what is going on? Explain to me what you're doing." Gilbert stared at the gun as he spoke.

She moved closer, keeping the gun close to her body. If he reached for it, she'd shoot. Center mass. He'd be dead. She halted two feet away. That smell. "What are you eating?"

"It's just a candy."

"What kind?"

"Uh." Gilbert closed his mouth as though he didn't know what the candy was. But she did.

The jail door swung open, and Larson stepped out. "Inside," she said to Gilbert.

He shook his head. "What? Me? No way."

But Larson took hold of Gilbert and shoved him into the cell. "Where the hell is Lily?"

Gilbert stumbled into the concrete box, and Larson slammed the door and locked it.

"Give me the keys," she said, and Larson handed them to her. Without looking, she hooked the carabiner onto her belt and squatted down to retrieve Gilbert's gun.

She shoved the gun beneath her waistband at the back of her pants and holstered her own weapon.

Gilbert clung to the bars. "You can't lock me in here. You're going to lose your job, you crazy bitch."

"Where is Lily Baker?" she repeated.

"I don't know what the hell you're talking about."

Kylie shook her head. "If something happens to her, I swear—"

"I don't have Lily Baker. I didn't do anything."

Kylie halted, the department parking lot coming back into her mind. Gilbert's cruiser hadn't been there. "Where's your patrol car?"

"I'm not telling you a goddamn thing until you let me out of here!"

Just then, the jail door opened again. Steve Cannon peered into the room. "What's going on?"

Kylie turned to Cannon. "There's a way to track the patrol cars, right?"

He glanced at her gun and took a step backward. "What's he doing in the cell? And why—" He pointed toward Larson.

"Not now, Cannon," Kylie snapped. "I need to find Gilbert's cruiser. You have a way to track them?"

"She's crazy!" Gilbert screamed. "Cannon, get me out of here."

"Don't you dare," she said to Cannon, who looked momentarily afraid. "Tell me how to track the cars."

"It's an online system," he said with a furtive glance at Gilbert. "Standard for police vehicles."

"I need you to track Gilbert's cruiser and call me with its whereabouts."

"My car's there!" Gilbert shouted. "Parked in the lot."

Kylie ignored him. She had to find Lily Baker. "Can you do it?" she asked Cannon.

"Sure," Cannon said, nodding toward the jail cell. "But Gilbert? Don't you think—"

"If you let him out of there, I will personally kick your ass. Are we clear?"

Cannon looked between her and Gilbert and nodded slowly.

"Now, how soon can you get me the location?" she asked.

Cannon took a step away from her. "Five minutes?"

"Do it, and call my cell the second you find that car." She stabbed his chest with her finger. "And no one lets Gilbert out of there until I say so."

"Wait!" Gilbert cried out. "I think my car's parked on the street."

Kylie wished Davis were there. Or even Ross. With no options left, she pointed to Larson. "You come with me." She started for the door and turned back to Gilbert. "And the candy you're eating—it's black licorice. Same thing that Lily Baker smelled when you attacked her on Thursday."

Gilbert's eyes narrowed. "What? You're insane. You're screwing this up. We had the right guy."

But Kylie wasn't listening anymore. She was already halfway out the door.

CHAPTER 56

LILY

Lily stared at the gun in Abby's hands, aimed in her direction.

"Why do you have that?"

"It's his."

Lily said nothing as Abby took Lily's hand. "You'll come?" Abby asked, eyes wide and hopeful.

Lily forced herself to nod. "Of course," she said, the words a hoarse whisper. Her ragged breathing might have given her away, but Abby shoved the gun into her pocket and threw her arms around Lily.

"Oh, thank you. Thank you, Lily. I need this so much."

Lily held Abby with one arm as her other hand snaked around to reach for the gun. Get the gun away, then get Abby out of these woods, into the bar. Her fingers reached the zipper of the coat, but Abby pulled back, hand fumbling in her pocket to bring the gun back out. Her eyes narrowed at Lily.

"You lied to me," Abby shouted. "You lied about wanting to come. You're just trying to escape."

Lily shook her head. "Please."

But Abby was distraught now. Tears streamed down her cheeks as she aimed the gun. "I should never have trusted you."

Lily took a step back as Abby wailed on, her voice rising.

"I needed you," Abby shouted through the sobs. "Someone we could trust. I said it had to be you."

Without shifting her head, Lily scanned the woods. We? Where was the man? Or was there a man at all?

Abby stopped crying and leveled the gun, taking a deep breath, as though regaining control. "You don't have a choice, Lily. You'll do what I say, just like I did for him."

"Why are you doing this?"

But Abby didn't answer. "You'll help me find the new girls, the same way I helped back then."

The way she had . . . back then.

"You?"

Abby smiled. "Me."

But it made no sense. They'd been prisoners together. Abby had been kidnapped just like Lily.

Lily's body and mind warred in opposite directions. She needed to get away, to run. To get hold of Abby's gun. At the same time, she was desperate to know the truth. What had Abby done? Was this the alcohol talking? The drugs? Who knew what sort of drugs Abby had been taking. Was she simply delusional? The victim of some sort of psychosis? The kind of trauma they'd experienced could do that. It could literally make them insane. Lily had felt that insanity.

"You'll do what I say," Abby said, jamming the gun into the soft flesh under Lily's ribs.

Lily lost her breath, doubling over. As she fought to draw air into her lungs, the soft crunch of boots in the snow filled the small clearing. She froze, listening, but it was Abby, looking around. Looking for him.

"You there?" Abby called.

When Lily raised her head, Abby had turned away, putting her back to Lily. Escape. With a painful breath, Lily gathered her strength and drove her elbow into Abby's side.

But it wasn't Abby's side anymore, because Abby had turned back to face her again. Lily's elbow struck Abby in the chest, and the gun went off. Lily waited for the tearing sensation, for the pain. But none came. Instead, she saw the dark form of the gun drop into the snow and sink down.

Abby was off balance as Lily rose to her full height. The sound that came from Lily was more animal than human as she gripped Abby's shoulders and shoved with every bit of strength she had.

Abby swung out an arm in an effort to regain her balance, and her wrist struck a tree with a thwack. But she didn't catch herself. Instead, Abby fell backward, her blonde hair swinging into her face as she dropped. There was a crack, and Lily ducked, thinking it was another gunshot. But the sound was low and muffled. Abby lay in the snow, eyes and mouth open as though stunned. There was the sound of boots in the snow, and Lily snatched the gun from the ground. She stood and froze, listening. Abby's breath stuttered, and Lily bent to her. Only then did she see the rock beneath Abby's head. And then the blood.

Lily opened her eyes with a start. She was still in the trunk, but somehow the cold air burned her cheeks as the wind howled around her. The feel of Abby's shoulders in her grip, the tension in her arms as she'd pushed her friend. The crack of Abby's head on that rock and the realization that Lily *had* been there, in the woods. She'd shoved Abby. She recalled the panic and heat as she'd run, his gun tight in her fist. The struggle to be fast in the snow, the voice calling out to her. Him. The same man she'd heard in her nightmares, the voice on the phone.

She stilled, listening. The engine was off, the car cold. A howling wind screamed, and the car rocked from its force. *Get out now.* She kicked at the trunk lid, but it was solid and unyielding. How did you get out of a trunk? Kick out the lights and wave her hand out the back of the car. Someone might see her. If they were driving. But they were not driving.

A release. Some cars had a trunk release. She blinked, willing her eyes to adjust to the dark, but it was penetrating, blindingly dark. She closed her eyes, drew a breath, and rolled onto her side, facing the back of the car.

Forcing herself to move slowly, she walked her fingers along the surfaces, the process awkward with her hands bound. She covered one strip, then moved closer to the bumper. Tears burned her eyes. It was taking too long. He would come back. He would kill her.

Shaking, she kept searching. Her breathing hurried, she wanted to scream, to cry out. And then her left index finger caught on something. A lever or a clip. She gasped and worked her fingers around it, pulling and turning and twisting.

It clicked, and the trunk popped open, the wind suddenly sharp and painful on her cheeks. And she'd never been more relieved.

"Oh, good. You're awake."

Her relief burned into a fiery coal of dread.

CHAPTER 57

——

KYLIE

Even with the wipers working full speed, snow collected on the windshield almost immediately. Kylie gripped the steering wheel while Iver sat at the edge of the passenger seat, alternately peering into the storm and studying the screenshot Steve Cannon had sent them. "There should be a bend up here," he told her.

They had driven north past the man camp and the fracking sites, then turned off the main highway. Now they were navigating a series of dirt roads.

She'd sent a copy of the map and their destination to McIntosh as well as to Davis. There had still been no word from Davis. Not in hours. Where the hell was he? That wasn't like him.

McIntosh had texted that he was about thirty minutes out. That was ten minutes ago.

Kylie rarely traveled north of Hagen this way. Technically, this area of town was within the jurisdiction of the Hagen police, but the drilling companies kept a tight watch on their territory. If there were crimes up here, the Hagen police never found out. "Where the hell are we going?"

Larson looked down again. "This is the right way. You've got a straight shot before the road bends to the left."

"How much farther?"

"Looks like it's another couple miles up this road."

The car bumped down the road, across potholes and ice and snow. "What the hell is even out here?"

"Mostly oil fields," Iver said. "Growing up, I had some friends who lived out this way."

She took the next bump slowly, glancing at Larson. "Was Carl Gilbert one of them?"

"I was never friends with Carl Gilbert," Larson said. "I have no idea where he lived." With that, he rolled down his window and stood on the floor to lean out of the car.

"What are you doing?"

Gripping the edge of the windowsill, Larson swept his arm across the windshield, pushing the snow off the glass. Then he got back in the car and rolled the window up, shivering.

For a moment, the windshield was clear, giving them a full view into the blizzardy darkness. Visibility was as bad as she'd ever seen it. The road curved in an endless series of lefts and rights, following the path some ancient river had cut into the low hillside. They were only traveling at twenty miles per hour, and still Kylie had to resist the urge to brake around the turns. There was no way to see what was coming.

The snow had begun to accumulate on the edges of the windshield again. Damn this storm.

"There should be a road up to the left," Iver said.

Kylie focused through the windshield, gripping and twisting the leather on the steering wheel until it was painful on her hands.

"She's going to be okay," Iver said.

Kylie nodded, unable to bring herself to speak. She had to remind herself that she couldn't have saved Abigail Jensen or Jenna Hitchcock. But Lily Baker . . . she'd had a chance to keep her safe, and she had failed. She hoped that mistake wasn't fatal for Baker.

As she crested a small hill on the gravel road, her cell phone rang. Davis.

"I've been trying to call you all day," she said.

"I'm out . . . Jensen . . . family."

She shook her head. "You're breaking up, Sheriff. Did you get the map I sent? Lily Baker has gone missing. I think Gilbert is involved."

". . . town . . . past . . . four . . . two miles . . ."

She put the call on speaker. "Say that again?"

Davis repeated the words, but she couldn't understand. She looked to Iver, who shook his head. "I'm surprised there's any service out here."

Without any idea if Davis could hear her, Kylie spoke directly into the phone. "I can't hear you, Sheriff. I sent you a screenshot. If you get it, meet us there." Then she ended the call, dread hot in her chest.

Neither spoke for a full minute. As they came around another bend, Iver looked up from the map on the screen and pointed through the windshield. "There's a spur road there. Looks like it leads to a small parking area. Maybe a drilling site."

Kylie peered out into the driving snow, the muscles in her back aching from the drive. The headlights illuminated the clumps so that they looked like stars falling from the sky. As she edged forward, she spotted a lane where the snow level was lower. It had to be the turnoff. "Maybe this is it."

"I think so. Pull up a little bit, and you should be there."

Kylie moved slowly down the road, the car bumping and sliding on the snow. About thirty yards later, the road ended in a flat parking area, big enough for a half dozen cars or an oil truck.

Iver glanced down at the screen again. "This has to be it."

There were no buildings visible. No other cars. As Kylie shifted the car into park, she realized that she was going to be searching blind.

Iver unfastened his seat belt, hand on the door.

"No," she said. "You have to stay in the car."

"I'm trained. I can help."

"You're a civilian here. Stay."

"You shouldn't go alone," Iver said.

"I'm not going to argue," she continued. "Stay here until Davis and Pete McIntosh arrive; then tell them which way I went." She grabbed Gilbert's gun off the floor where she'd put it for the drive and opened the glove box to stash it. She paused, her hand halfway there. Iver Larson wasn't guilty of killing Abigail Jensen, but she wasn't going to leave him with a loaded gun.

It was obvious that Larson wanted to say something else, but he only nodded as she rose from the car, shoving Gilbert's gun down the back of her pants. She started walking through the open lot to the far side. There had to be something out there. For some minutes, she just walked, listening for sounds to guide her.

Soon the silence was cut by the creak of a drilling rig as it rose and fell and the gentle hiss of a flare growing louder. Now she wished she'd worn better shoes and a warmer coat. She lifted her hand to her chest, a rush of dread running through her. She'd left the patrol car without her vest. Damn it. Only ten or fifteen feet from the rig, she turned back. She had to have her vest.

A woman cried out.

Kylie faced the sound and aimed her weapon, squinting through the driving snow. She came through a patch of trees and hesitated, scanning the white expanse. As the grasshopper rig's giant head lowered, Lily Baker appeared. Lily's hands clawed at her throat, as though someone was choking her from behind. As her head lifted, the band of an arm across Baker's neck came into view.

Then the steel head reared higher into the air, and her captor's face became visible through the driving snow. The smile on his lips twisted upright as he dragged Lily Baker by the neck.

Kylie froze in place, hidden behind a narrow pine tree. Glen Vogel. What the hell was the DA doing? Even from a distance, Kylie could read the terror on Lily Baker's face. Glen Vogel was dragging Baker through the snow. An arm against her neck, a gun in one hand. Why was he holding her?

They knew Lily Baker was innocent. She was a victim.

Unless she was a threat to Vogel. Unless he was somehow involved. Kylie thought about how Vogel had sent her to the scene of Brent Nolan's accident rather than to Skål, how he had delayed the search for evidence at the bar, how he'd let Gilbert search Larson's truck.

Had Vogel been planting evidence? Were he and Gilbert in this together? But why? How? Kylie wanted to turn around and call for backup. But who could she call? McIntosh knew where she was. And Davis, too, if he'd gotten her screenshot. Plus, Steve Cannon knew where she'd been going.

She couldn't wait for backup. She wouldn't forgive herself if something happened to Baker while she was twiddling her thumbs.

As she watched, Vogel struck Lily in the head with the gun, and she dropped to the snow.

Kylie bit back a cry. She had no choice but to pursue them, to stop Vogel.

And yet she had no protection. Her Kevlar was in the trunk of her patrol car. She was alone with no backup. That was her fault. Because she'd thought Gilbert was working alone.

She'd been so sure that Carl Gilbert was the only guilty one. She'd never considered that there could be two of them.

CHAPTER 58

IVER

The detective hadn't been gone two minutes when falling snow made it impossible to see out the windows or the windshield. Milliard had left the engine running for the heat, but the noise of it, along with the blinding-white haze over the windows, made Iver feel like a sitting duck. He shut off the engine and cracked his door to listen. The wind whistled around the car, whipping snow across the dash and seats. The temperature had dropped since his ride from the hospital to the police station, and now the air was bitter, the kind of cold that cut straight through the layers until it was an ache in your spine.

Beyond the wind was the rhythmic groaning of a drill, its metal head rising and falling somewhere in the storm. The grasshopper sounded close, but the snow fell too thickly to see the beast. The flare, which would light up a clear sky for miles, was barely a dull glow in the white.

But Iver was grateful for the dim light. Without it, he wouldn't have known which way was up.

Standing from the car, he made a small circle, listening. The detective had told him to stay, but knowing Lily was out there, he couldn't just sit.

He wished he had Gilbert's gun, but Milliard had taken it, tucked it in her pants. Gilbert. The idea that Carl Gilbert was guilty of killing

Abigail Jensen came as a hell of a shock. Iver couldn't wrap his head around the idea.

Shivering in the storm, Iver noticed the sheriff's emblem on the passenger-side door. It gave him pause. She'd taken the handguns, but there might be something useful squirreled away somewhere else. Snow pelting his hands and face, he popped the trunk, wincing at the beep it made.

A bulletproof vest lay in the trunk, along with a police jacket and a Remington 870 shotgun. Behind those was a black Easton baseball bat. Iver pulled the vest over his shoulders, though it was too small to zip, then grabbed the police jacket to layer on top. As he lifted the jacket, he spotted a long black gun box at the back of the trunk.

With a glance over his shoulder, he slid the box forward, unfastened the locks, and flipped up the lid. Inside was a Colt M4 carbine. Without hesitating, he lifted the rifle into his arms, the weight comforting and terrifying at once.

His fingers knew this gun from Afghanistan. Muscle memory took over as he checked the clip for rounds and snapped it into place. The familiar sound, the weight of the weapon, and suddenly Iver was back in that building. It smelled of gunpowder and dust and something burning in the distance. All five of them huddled in one room, waiting to take out the insurgents and make a run for the Humvee.

Brolyard positioned himself at the west-facing window while Sanchez and Wykstra covered the north side of the room. Iver and Garabrant stuck to the east side—Garabrant closest to the street and Iver with a better angle to take a long shot.

A scraping sound reached his ears, sandals on gravel. Iver spun and faced an Afghan woman who had entered the back door. Terror made her eyes black. She opened her mouth to scream. Garabrant pivoted, aimed his weapon at her.

"No," Iver hissed, dropping his own weapon.

Gunfire would announce their position. Then they'd all be dead.

The woman turned to run, but Iver grabbed hold of her, clapping a hand on her mouth, his arm across her neck.

She kicked and screamed into his palm, her teeth snapping at the skin of his hand.

Outside the insurgents grew closer. Another ten yards, and her voice would be audible, maybe even the noise of her struggle. Iver was their best shot. He needed to be ready to take out the insurgents. He couldn't stand there and fight her.

"End her," Garabrant hissed, his gun still aimed at them. His eyes were wide, their focus twitchy.

Fear pulsed like a hammer in Iver's throat and lungs. The woman thrashed against him as he tried to hold her quiet. The insurgents were too close now.

Iver saw no other option. He had no doubt Garabrant would shoot, and they'd all die.

He took two steps toward the back door, whispering in her ear. "Shhh," he said. "Shh."

Her struggles paused for a moment, her gaze darting toward the exit to the alley. "Yes," he told her. "I'm going to let you go."

He started to set her feet on the ground, and she calmed. Her motions halted, though her pulse raced like a rabbit's under his arm. "It's okay," he whispered again, and then, with her feet only inches from the floor, he reached his hand across her face and gripped her jaw between his palms.

Closing his eyes, he wrenched her neck with a brutal twist. There was a sickening crack as she slumped in his arms, and he lowered her to the ground. Her eyes were open, her mouth flexed in terror.

"Is she dead?" Garabrant asked. "Make sure she's dead."

"Look at her neck, Kenny," Wykstra said to Garabrant. "She's dead."

Iver looked over to see Sanchez wipe his mouth with the back of his hand, vomit sprayed across his feet. Sanchez didn't meet his eye. Brolyard made a sign that the insurgents were close.

With the dead woman on the floor a few feet away, Iver took up his rifle and positioned himself for the shoot, a numbing calm swimming through him. His fingers tingled, and a strange taste filled his mouth. It took him a moment to recognize it as blood, to realize that in the struggle he'd bitten the inside of his cheek so hard it was bleeding. He swallowed and shifted his full focus to the target. Brolyard counted down, and they all took aim and fired. The insurgents dropped and fled, and the men made it safely to the Humvee. Iver climbed into the back.

The realization of what he had done struck him as the Humvee pulled out in a cloud of dust. Iver was sobbing silently when they hit that IED.

He'd had no choice. It was what Brolyard and Wykstra and Sanchez would have told him that night, when they were safe in their CHU. Garabrant, too, once he had calmed the hell down.

He had done what he had to do. Her death would have been worth it, her life a fair trade for his brothers', if those four men hadn't died on the three-mile trip back to base.

The wind rattled the open trunk lid of the sheriff's car and stung the wet skin of his cheeks. He jolted, scanning the area around him as he returned from the nightmare. *Move,* he commanded himself. *Go find Lily, the detective.*

He focused on the remaining equipment in the trunk and grabbed the shotgun, too, leaving the bat before lowering the trunk's lid until it was almost closed. Orienting himself by the dull orange flare, Iver headed out in the snow, his breathing rapid. Despite the frigid air, sweat pooled at the small of his back.

He clenched his jaw and blew out the stale breath in his lungs, focusing on a plan for approach. He didn't want to startle anyone, which was an easy way to get shot. But if the detective and Lily were in trouble, he also needed the element of surprise. He took ten steps and stopped to listen. The snow blew from the north, coming straight from the direction of the flare. The wind should have carried voices, too, but

Iver heard only the wind, the drill, and, as he moved closer, the snickering of the flare as it burned.

Rather than continuing north to the spot where Gilbert's car appeared on the map, Iver cut east fifty yards before turning north. The storm raged now, and visibility was maybe twelve or fifteen feet. Then, he shifted his course to head north, taking one step due west for every ten north in an effort to counteract the natural curve of his gait. When left in a place with no markers, humans naturally walked in circles, even if they thought they were going straight. Iver had enough experience walking through blinding sandstorms to know his own directional bias.

In the distance an engine's growl cut through the storm. Not the groaning mechanics of the pump but something small, like a car. Iver stopped to listen. The engine shut off, close to where Milliard had parked. A door closed lightly. The wind buffeting it? Or someone trying to be quiet?

After the metal sound of the door, nothing. One person. He considered the silence. If someone had come to help Milliard, why not call out? It would be standard protocol to announce yourself, wouldn't it? But maybe they wanted to retain the element of surprise, too.

Or maybe whoever had arrived was not a friend.

The wind changed, and now the snow blew from the east, pellets hard against his neck and the right side of his face. Iver lowered the shotgun to the ground and abandoned it there. He would need both hands on the rifle to shoot accurately. He trudged forward slowly, snow sliding into his boots with every step. As he lifted the rifle to a ready position, the bulk of the grasshopper rig appeared like a ghost against the white, startling him.

But it was comforting to know it was there. Orienting.

Hunching to make himself a smaller target, Iver continued north. By his estimation, Gilbert's car should have been close. The hissing of the flare grew steadily louder and, with it, the snapping sounds of the hard pellets of snow striking the flame. Iver ducked around the back of the grasshopper and slowed. Once he passed the massive steel structure, there would be no cover.

But there was no car. Where the hell was Gilbert's car?

And where the hell was Milliard? If she'd found Lily, she should have been back at the cruiser by now. She would have seen that he was gone and called out. Or Lily would have called for him.

He should have heard something. It was too damn quiet.

CHAPTER 59

LILY

The arm across her neck made it hard to breathe. Her shoes slipped in the snow as the man dragged her backward. This man. Had he been the man in the woods with Abby? The memories flooded her, and her heart stuttered. But he hadn't killed Abby. Her legs buckled beneath her, and his forearm locked around her throat.

Lily squeezed her eyes closed, struggling to draw air into her lungs. The image of Abby bleeding in the snow was crystal in her mind. Abby's gun in Lily's hand.

She tried to push away the memories of lifting that gun, aiming at Abby.

Her friend's eyes wide and scared. Terrified. Abby's expression was a blade that had cut through her. How many moments of pure terror had they suffered together? Afraid of that man, of the darkness, the pain, the seemingly endless screams before the first girl had disappeared. She'd been buried in the grounds around the cabin, Lily had read in one of the articles Iver found.

But in the woods, Abby's terror had been directed at Lily. Because Lily was ready to kill her rather than be taken again.

Had any of Abby's terror been real during the months they were held? Or was Abby a part of it from the start? Abby was there the night Lily was taken, had lured Lily with her tears.

Her teeth chattering, Lily tried to make sense of the memories. The months still blended together in a vague sense of darkness and fear. But the rituals, those had been intense. Every two or three nights? More? Less? The time ran together. So much blackness and sleep. The juice he'd given them had made them sleep and forget.

Lily could still feel that blade slicing her skin, the heat of the pain followed by the soft feel of a tongue. His tongue.

Of course it had been his tongue, hadn't it?

The forearm at her throat tightened. As she struggled for breath, the truth of that night in the woods rushed over her. Two or three times each week for sixteen months, someone had cut her. But it hadn't been Derek Hudson.

It had been Abby. Abby's voice in her ear. Abby's tongue soaking up her blood.

The fear of those memories was so intense that Lily had exploded, knocking Abby backward and wrestling the gun from her hands.

And then she'd heard the sound of someone coming, so she had taken a last look at her friend, and she'd run. The woods rose up, sharp and clear in her memories now, the branches rough on her bare skin as she sprinted through the snow, the sounds of him close behind her. She'd reached the street, breathless and panicked, and a man had stopped and offered her a ride.

"Are you all right?"

"I just need to get out of town. As far as possible."

Why hadn't she gone to the police that night?

He was heading back to Fargo, he'd told her. He hadn't asked any questions. She could ride along with him. It would give her time to make a plan, to figure out how to talk to the police, to tell them what she knew. And time to wrap her head around Abby. The betrayal.

But they'd never made it to Fargo. Lily couldn't remember the accident, whether it was a patch of ice or an animal that had caused him to swerve and crash through the guardrail.

If only she had gotten away, made it to Fargo.

Tears burned on her cheeks, warm against the bitter cold. She longed to lie down in the snow, to quit. She stopped moving her feet. The end was near now. It had to be.

The man stumbled, and the gun struck her temple. Her vision went white and she cried out.

"Move," he hissed, shoving her.

She took a small step, then slid and stopped again. Why shouldn't she die, too? Abby was dead because of her. The driver of that car, Brent Nolan, was dead because of her. She had failed to get him out of that car before it went off the overpass.

Not just that. She had stolen from him first. Taken cash from his wallet.

It was an instinct.

No. It was who she was. The relationship with Tim, whatever drugs she'd been taking, her house . . . all were signs of who she really was.

"I said move," the man hissed.

"Just shoot me," she said.

"I'll shoot you when I'm good and ready." He shoved her again, the arm on her neck guiding her forward and also choking her.

Momentum carried her a few steps before she stopped. Done. She let her body weight drop, fell against the pressure of his arm. The tears froze on her cheeks; the chattering of her teeth stilled. If he killed her, it would be over. All of it. His victims would be dead.

Some part of her brain struggled against acceptance. He would get away with it. There would be no justice. But who was she to claim justice?

She was as bad as he was.

Her dead weight pulled on him, and he loosened his arm, let her fall to the snow.

"Get up!" he shouted, but she turned away from his voice. Her pulse still thundered as she imagined the moment the bullet would fire from the gun and enter her flesh.

Was that a sign she should fight?

He grabbed a fistful of her hair and wrenched her head upright, the gun in her face. "Get on your feet."

She searched his eyes, looking for something familiar. "Who are you? Why are you doing this?"

"I swear to God, if you don't stand up . . ."

She closed her eyes again.

A short whistle of sound was followed by an explosion in her ear as metal struck her temple. Pain rocketed through her skull, crimson and orange behind her eyelids. She pitched forward and vomited.

She struggled against the inclination to stand again, to do what he said. Death was coming, one way or another.

Another whistle sounded, and she flinched.

But there was no pain other than the dull pulsing from his first strike.

From somewhere in the distance came the crunch of boots in the snow. She opened her eyes and squinted.

A dark shape moved through the storm.

"Vogel!" a woman shouted.

Lily sat upright. The detective.

"Damn it," the man cursed beside her.

Snow clung to Lily's face and hair as she watched the shape move closer.

"Vogel. Wait!" the detective shouted again.

The man—Vogel—raised his gun and aimed it at the detective in the distance. Lily froze at the shift of his hand, anticipating the explosion even before it happened.

"No!" she screamed.

The roar of gunfire cut through the hum of the storm. She flinched and covered her ears as he fired a second, third, fourth time.

The wind shifted direction, and she searched for the detective through the falling snow. Something on the ground in the distance shifted. The detective. Had she been hit? Lily lunged toward her. She had to help.

The hand in her hair wrenched her back, and she cried out.

"You make this hard on me, and I'll go out there and finish her off right now."

Lily studied the shape, the movements. Maybe the detective could get away, get help. Maybe Kylie Milliard didn't have to die, too. If Lily let this man take her, maybe she could save one life.

Her head throbbing, she lifted her hands into the air slowly.

"That's a good girl," he said, yanking her to her feet.

She shivered against the cold wind, something shifting in her chest. Purpose. If she could get free of him, if she could get his gun . . .

"Back up, nice and slow," he hissed, tightening the arm on her neck. He yanked her backward, and she stepped tentatively, studying the sensation of him behind her. His bulk, the arm at her neck, the way it shifted up and down as he moved. The feel of his jacket—canvas, she guessed. Could she sink her teeth through it and bite hard enough to get him to release the gun?

He'd fired four bullets. How many did the gun hold? A magazine could hold more bullets—a dozen, she thought. Maybe more. But his gun was a revolver, not a pistol.

A few hollow notes traveled across the field, like a voice. Vogel froze, and she tried to turn her head, to search for the voice. But there was only whiteness around them. The wind howled from the line of trees, and Lily felt the stabbing pain of disappointment. Not a voice. Just the wind.

She was alone with him.

The arm hitched tighter on her throat as he yanked her backward. Over her shoulder a shed loomed like a gallows.

The detective was no longer visible, and Lily pressed her eyes closed and prayed Milliard was okay, that the bullets had missed.

CHAPTER 60

IVER

Iver took another half dozen steps before the profound white quiet exploded in gunfire. Iver dropped for cover, face in the snow, the rifle under his right arm ready for the counterattack.

The tattoo of four bullets in rapid succession gave way to total silence.

Lifting his head, he listened for the sounds of someone dying. Dying people were loud. Even a bullet to the head made a distinct sound, both a wet noise and a hard, dry crack. Perhaps he was too far away to hear anything. Most likely, someone out there was dead. Maybe more than one.

His heart drilled against the cold earth. *Not Lily. Please, not Lily.*

He fought the rush of rage, the impulse to spring up and attack. Instead, he forced himself to wait. If someone was alive, they needed him to stay alive. When he reached the count of twenty, he rose to his knees, gripping the rifle as he stood.

He replayed the noise in his head. Four bullets were fired, but it had sounded like a single weapon. He moved forward, focused on awareness. He recalled his time in Afghanistan, the moments when he'd sworn he could sense the bead of the laser on his head. *Keep moving.*

He stepped lightly, scanning, on high alert. He'd taken a half dozen steps when he spotted a figure stooped over something on the ground. The figure was broad, too large to be Lily. A man.

Iver took a slow step forward, the rifle at chin level, ready to fire.

The man grabbed at something, and Iver made out a second figure, a woman on the ground. Her dark hair in his hand, the profile of her face. He knew her immediately.

Lily.

He wanted to cry out to her, tell her he was there. Instead, he raised the rifle to his eye and searched through the scope for the man. Snow covered the glass immediately, and Iver reached to brush it off.

He took aim again and found the man's hulking form. Drew a breath. The wind blew the snow across the right side of his face. He shifted his aim an inch to the right to make up for the wind, then another half inch. It was a long shot, too far to be accurate. But if he moved any closer, he'd be seen.

He lifted his head. What if he missed and the man shot Lily? What if he didn't shoot and she died anyway?

He brushed the snow off the scope and barrel and took aim again. Sucked air into his lungs and paused, waiting for a moment of stillness. The wind howled. He released the air slowly, then inhaled again, watching. The man was trying to pull her up. It was now or never.

He drew air through his teeth, found the figure of the man in the scope, and laid his finger on the trigger.

Then he shouted, "On the ground, Lily!"

Lily's face appeared to shift toward him. Did she see him?

The man reared up.

Iver took his shot. The rifle kicked against him. Then a second explosion, something internal. No. Something from behind. Another bullet, this one to his back.

Unable to breathe, Iver dropped to the snow.

He never saw the shooter.

CHAPTER 61

KYLIE

A shot echoed in the blizzard, then a second. *Baker.*

Kylie tried to lift her head, but the searing heat in her shoulder kept her pinned to the ground. She'd been shot. Vogel had aimed that gun and fired four bullets, and one of them had hit her. She would die here. Gilbert was in jail, and Vogel would get away, make up some story about how Lily Baker tried to shoot him and he'd fired in self-defense. How Kylie was already dead.

He'd spin it so that he was a hero.

She opened her eyes and stared up at the falling snow. What fell were no longer flakes but quarter-size clumps. If she closed her eyes and lay there another fifteen or twenty minutes, she might be invisible under a drift. She could die of hypothermia rather than bleed out. Or maybe the blood leaching from her body would freeze up. All her blood would eventually freeze. A giant bloody popsicle.

Screw that, she thought. She drew a breath, filling her lungs as much as she could. *You're not dead yet. Get the hell up.*

She shifted in the snow, wincing at the pain. It hurt like hell. Setting her gun across her chest so as not to lose it in all the whiteness, she reached her right hand under her coat and pressed gently on her shirt. When she removed her hand, blood tinted her fingers. "Shit." Vomit rose in her throat, and she swallowed it back. Closed her eyes. It wasn't that much blood.

If the bullet had hit a vessel, her hand would be covered in blood. She wasn't dying. She reached back, pressed again, walking her fingers under the shirt to feel the skin. The shirt felt moist but not saturated. She was bleeding, but not bleeding to death. Not yet anyway.

Pinning her left elbow to her side, she gripped the gun, rolled over, and pushed herself onto her knees with one hand. She drew a shallow breath and stood, staring into the storm. The dark figures had disappeared. All she saw now was white.

She felt the swell of panic and pressed it down. She turned back to study the snow where she'd been lying, trying to discern where the bullet had come from. In every direction, there was only snow.

She squinted as though she might sense something even if she couldn't see it. Then, by some chance, the wind shifted, and she could make out the dark form of a shed. A moment later, a light shone through the narrow slit of a window. Bingo.

She started in that direction, taking slow steps and studying the growing darkness for signs of anyone else.

She thought of Iver Larson. Was he still waiting in the car? Had he heard the shots? Would he come to find her?

There was no depending on anyone now. She shifted her grip on the gun and moved forward, the shed looming ahead.

She was almost there when she heard noise over her shoulder.

"Thank God I found you. It's a whiteout."

She turned back. Iver Larson was her first guess, but the voice was wrong. She held the gun and watched as the shape grew closer.

"Kylie? You okay?"

She blinked, and Steve Cannon's features came into focus. She cried out in relief. "Glen Vogel's in there. He's got Lily Baker." She shifted toward him. "He shot me."

Cannon furrowed his brow. "Jesus," he whispered. "Are you all right?"

"Hurts like hell." She drew a breath. "Is there more backup coming? Did you get in touch with Davis?"

"No. Afraid it's just me," he said. "Let's take a look at that wound."

She shook her head. "It'll wait. Let's get Baker out of there."

Cannon nodded, but instead of moving toward the shed, he gripped Kylie's injured shoulder. A strange smile twisted on his lips as he clenched down on the place where the bullet had entered.

Kylie screamed out and dropped to her knees. Reflexively, she dropped the gun and pushed him away. "What the hell?"

Cannon stooped to retrieve her gun, shoving it into his jacket pocket.

"Shit," she cursed, pressing her palm to the pulsing ache in her arm. But there was something unfamiliar in Cannon's expression. She'd always thought he had kind eyes, but now they were hard and flat. "Steve?"

"Let's go," he said, motioning to her with his gun.

Kylie didn't move, her mind spinning. Was Steve Cannon Derek Hudson's accomplice? But . . . what about Vogel? And Gilbert?

"Stand up," Cannon directed.

She didn't move. "Steve, what is going on?"

"Get the fuck up before I shoot you in the head." He clenched his jaw and shook his head. "Christ."

Kylie did the only thing she could. She stood.

Cannon shoved her toward the shed, the barrel of a gun pressed between her shoulder blades. When they reached the door, Cannon knocked. "Glen, it's me. I've got Milliard."

The shed was silent.

Cannon pounded again. "Uncle Glen?"

Uncle?

Cannon reached around her and twisted the door handle. The door fell open, and he shoved her inside.

Across the shed, Lily Baker was huddled against the wall. Glen Vogel stood, a gun aimed at Baker. When the shed door slammed closed, Vogel looked up.

Glen Vogel was Cannon's uncle.

But what did that have to do with Hudson and Carl Gilbert? Was Cannon protecting him? But from what? When Hudson had kidnapped those girls, Vogel had already been in Hagen, working for the old district attorney. He couldn't have been Hudson's partner.

The gun trembled in his hand, and Vogel looked unsteady on his feet.

"What happened?" Cannon started across the room before swinging back to face Kylie. "Sit over there." He pointed to the floor beside Baker.

Kylie moved slowly, studying Glen Vogel, still trying to process what was happening. Vogel looked sick. His skin was a pale yellow, and sweat dripped down his face, the hair at his temples damp. His breath came in shallow pants, his free hand pressed against his chest, the fingers like red sausages against his coat.

He was having a heart attack.

Cannon shoved her. "Sit."

Kylie sank onto the cement, using the wall to guide herself down. She grabbed hold of Baker's hand, the fingers icy to the touch. "It's going to be okay," she whispered.

Cannon spun toward them, his gun in his fist. "He's been shot. Who shot him?"

Kylie realized that Carl Gilbert wasn't guilty at all. It had been Steven Cannon all along. She watched as he cocked the hammer and stretched the gun toward them.

"One of you had better start talking."

CHAPTER 62

——

LILY

Every word from Derek Hudson's lips was a shock of electricity, a burning pain in Lily's spine. This man had kept her prisoner for sixteen months. He was supposed to be dead. All these years, she'd thought he was dead. Who was the man she'd shot at the cabin? Abby's voice in her ear. "It's over," she had said. "You saved us."

Had Lily even been the one to pull that trigger? Had she killed that man? And if it was her, who exactly had she saved? Herself and Abby and Jenna? Yes. They had escaped. But was that what Abby had meant? Or had she meant that Lily had saved Derek Hudson? That shooting the other man had enabled Hudson to escape? To live like a free man until . . .

"What is happening to him?" Hudson shouted.

Lily trembled, and the detective squeezed her hand. Lily had wanted to save the detective. Here she was, alive. But now they were both going to die.

Hudson spun back to them. "Did you shoot him?" he said, aiming the gun in Lily's face.

"No." The word caught in her throat.

"Then what happened?"

"We didn't shoot him," the detective said. "Lily doesn't have a weapon, and I never fired mine."

His gaze shifted to the door of the shed. "Larson," he whispered. "Damn it."

"Iver." The name escaped Lily's mouth without thought. Iver was here.

Vogel gripped Hudson's pant leg. "Can't. Breathe."

Hudson crouched by his uncle. "I didn't think he hit you. He was so far away."

Relief flooded her. They weren't alone. Iver had come to help them. He'd found her.

Hudson looked frantic. His uncle was tachypneic, his breathing abnormally rapid, the pallor of his skin more pronounced with every minute. There was no sign that he was actively bleeding. She wasn't even sure he'd been shot. It could have easily been a coronary event. Something was definitely wrong, but without being able to examine him, Lily had no idea what it was.

Hudson slid his jacket off his shoulders and pushed his sleeves up. An intricate tattoo wrapped around his right forearm, a lattice of vines with purple-black flowers. As he twisted his hands together, Lily saw the scars beneath the art—the short, thin ridges. Like the ones on her shoulder.

In a wave of panic, she closed her eyes and recalled the texture she'd felt when she was attacked in Iver's home. A strange ridged material, like soft rubber. Skin with old scars. Derek Hudson's arm.

"Kill," Vogel whispered. His lips parted, and red bubbles formed in the corner of his mouth.

Hudson lowered himself to the floor. He still held the gun, but with his free hand, he wiped the blood from his uncle's lips and dabbed the sweat from the old man's skin with his sleeve. Then he wrapped his jacket across his uncle's shoulders. "I shot him, Uncle Glen. I shot him right in the back."

The scream caught in Lily's throat as the detective gripped her hand. Nails dug into her skin. Iver. Shot. She shook her head. She was propelled forward onto her knees. The detective yanked her back, shaking her head.

Iver was here. He'd come for her. He'd been shot. She yanked herself free of the detective's grip. "Your uncle's going to die," she spat at Hudson. "Look at him. The pale, sweaty skin, the hemoptysis."

Hudson sat back on his heels. His mouth fell open. "Hemo-what?"

"Hemoptysis," she said. "The blood. He's coughing up blood."

"How do I save him?"

"You can't."

Hudson panicked, his focus bouncing around the room. His motions were rapid, disjointed.

Lily let the tears stream down her cheeks, pressing her hands to her face. The room was suddenly freezing, her insides hollowed out. The one person she had trusted—trusted completely—was dead. Let Hudson watch his uncle die. She would enjoy that.

Hudson pressed his face to Vogel's. "Stay with me."

Lily snickered.

Hudson glared at her, patting his pockets and pulling out a phone.

He set the gun down momentarily so he could use both hands to cradle the phone. Lily watched the gun, ready to pounce. She wanted to press that gun to Hudson's head and pull the trigger. She wanted to watch his brains spray across the room and then empty the chamber into his chest.

Hudson stared at the screen of his phone and cursed. Then he shook it as though that might fix it. After another glance at the screen, Hudson spun and hurled it at the wall. The device exploded against the concrete.

A sob escaped her throat. An image of Iver's face, his smile. The gentle way he had spoken to her in the bathroom. She leaned forward, eyes on that gun. If she tackled Hudson, the detective could get the gun. She just had to make sure Hudson didn't get it.

Before she could move, Hudson snatched up the gun and aimed it directly at Lily. "You. You're a nurse."

Lily said nothing. She shook her head.

"Don't lie," Hudson shouted, spit flying from his lips. "I know you're a nurse. Abby told me." He glanced at his uncle, then back to her. "Get over here and help him."

Lily shook her head. "I'm not helping you."

"I'll shoot you in the head right now."

Lily was about to speak when the detective grabbed her elbow and squeezed.

"You can do it," the detective whispered. From her peripheral vision, Lily could feel the weight of the detective's stare. Lily felt certain she was issuing some hidden message, trying to give her an idea. But Lily couldn't think. Iver was dead. Hudson was going to get away with murder. He'd already gotten away with kidnapping and torture and . . . all she wanted to do was kill him.

"Now!" Hudson shouted, his voice echoing through her, setting every nerve on fire.

The detective nudged again, and Lily relented, crawling slowly across the concrete floor to the injured man. The rage suppressed thoughts of Iver, and she focused on Vogel. "We need to see the wound."

Hudson nodded, waving the gun at her in warning. "Do it."

Vogel's eyes flashed open, his gaze flickering across her face as she grew close.

She squeezed her hands into fists, fighting off the shaking, then unbuttoned his coat. He cried out, and she froze.

Hudson studied his uncle.

"It's going to hurt him to move," she said.

Hudson licked his lips, his gaze bouncing between her and his uncle. "And if we don't move him?"

Lily glanced at the detective, who nodded.

"He'll die," she said with a little satisfaction. She wanted him to die.

"Then do it," Hudson said. He placed his hand on her shoulder and squeezed, the tips of his fingers biting her skin along the old scars. "If he dies, you know what happens."

His voice carved like a blade on her skin. The words so familiar. *Don't help nobody. Don't stop for nothing. You don't come back, you know what happens.*

Hudson slammed the gun into her ribs. "He can't die."

Lily was thrown sideways, the air forced from her lungs.

"He can't die," Hudson said again.

Lily tried to push herself up.

"Steve, stop," the detective warned. "If you hurt her, Glen dies. Give her some space so she can save him."

Hudson shifted away from Lily. She unzipped Vogel's jacket and started to unbutton his shirt. Vogel sagged forward, wincing with his inhales. She pushed the shirt across his shoulders and partway down his arms, looking for the source of the pain. Her eye caught a bloodstain on the fabric at his right side. At the center was a hole. Palpating his skin where the shirt had been, she located a corresponding entry wound.

Vogel cried out in pain.

She pressed a little harder.

He'd been shot, and there was no exit wound. The bullet was in his chest cavity.

She squeezed her eyes closed. This man was going to die.

And when he did, Derek Hudson would kill them both.

CHAPTER 63

LILY

Lily studied the dying man's face. His breathing was shallow. She pressed her ear to his chest and listened. She couldn't make out any breath sounds at all on his right side, but he was a big man, and she obviously didn't have a stethoscope.

She listened to the left side, which rattled with each inhale. She tried to remember the exact anatomy of the right side and adjusted for his bulk. Any number of organs might have been hit—liver, kidney, intestines. She tapped against the front right side of his abdomen. The sound was dull and flat. She tapped the other side and heard the normal deep sound of healthy lung.

"What is it?"

"I think his chest cavity is filling with blood," Lily said. "It's called a hemothorax."

Hudson punched Lily in the stomach with the gun.

She cried out, hunching over and gripping her belly.

"Do something!" Hudson screamed.

Lily sat up, hands trembling, and leaned into Vogel. The man was wheezing heavily now.

"You can do this, Lily," the detective said. "Just tell us what you need. How can you help him?"

"I have to relieve the pressure," Lily said. Her fingers were tacky with his blood. She wiped it on her pants. "I need a knife."

"Fuck you," Hudson snarled at her. "I'm not giving you a fucking knife."

"Fine," Lily said, sitting back on her heels. "His chest is filling with blood. Eventually, the blood will fill the entire chest cavity, and the pressure will compress his lungs."

Suddenly more alert, Vogel grabbed Hudson's hand, his eyes wide.

"When that happens," Lily continued, "he won't be able to draw air at all. He'll stop breathing and die."

Vogel opened his lips to say something. Blood trickled down his chin. He shook his head and made a rolling motion with his hand.

"I'm not sure how fast the blood is pooling in his chest cavity," Lily went on, enjoying the small satisfaction of watching the two men panic. "But if I don't relieve the pressure, he dies. To do that, I have to cut an opening between the ribs."

Hudson looked between his uncle and Lily.

"He doesn't have long, Steve," Kylie said. "Look at him."

Hudson cursed, moving the gun to his left hand, then reaching into his right front pocket. The detective shifted slightly against the wall, and Hudson spun toward her. "What are you doing?"

"It's a hard floor, Steve," she said, lifting her hands. "My ass was numb."

Hudson motioned with the gun. "Keep your hands in front of you, where I can see them."

"Of course," the detective said, placing her palms on the concrete floor.

Lily noticed the detective didn't meet her eye. She *had* been doing something. What was she planning?

Hudson pinned his gaze on the detective as he pulled a pocketknife from his pocket and slid it toward Lily. Before it was close enough to reach, Hudson had the revolver tight in the grip of his right hand again. "One wrong move with that, and I'll put a bullet in each of you, whether he dies or not."

Lily stared at the knife.

"Hurry up and do it already!" Hudson shouted.

Lily picked up the knife and tried to pull the blade out.

"The button," Hudson shouted. "Press the damn button."

Lily pushed, and the blade extended. She shifted it, catching the dull light of the single overhead bulb against the steel blade.

As she leaned forward, Vogel shivered and gasped.

Hudson looked away.

The light was too dim, and Vogel was slumped against the wall, making it almost impossible to get a clear view of the wound. But Hudson had thrown his phone against the wall, and if the detective still had hers, Lily didn't want Hudson to know about it.

Using touch, Lily worked blindly to locate the entry wound, counting along Vogel's ribs. She'd never placed a chest tube to treat a hemothorax before. And if she had, it would certainly not have been with a pocketknife and a gun to her head. She tried to remember which intercostal space was ideal. Placement for maximum drainage should be at the posterior axillary line. That much she remembered, but between which ribs?

She walked her fingers along Vogel's ribs, counting. She stopped, shook her head, and went back, did it again. Was it between fifth and sixth? Sixth and seventh?

"You can do this," the detective whispered.

Lily said nothing. She couldn't let Hudson know that she wasn't certain. That there was a chance she might make an incision and kill Vogel faster.

"Go on," Hudson hissed. "Get it done."

"You're doing great, Lily," the detective said. "You can do this."

"Shut up," Hudson barked, and the detective went silent.

Lily closed her eyes, took a breath, and pressed the knife into Vogel's skin.

He cried out and struggled to roll away.

"Someone has to hold him down," Lily said to Hudson. "I have to get this just right."

Hudson nodded to the detective. "Go on, Milliard. But no funny stuff. You move one finger the wrong way, and I'll shoot it off."

The detective nodded, standing and crossing to the far side of Lily. There, she knelt and pressed both hands down on Vogel's shoulders.

Lily drew a breath and slid the knife between her two fingers, applying additional pressure as the layers of muscle resisted the blade.

Vogel screamed, the sound emerging from his lips in a spray of blood. He fought the detective's hold.

Hudson looked like he might be sick. He sat back, his gun aimed at them. A flick of his wrist and two twitches of his index finger, and they'd both be dead.

Lily pushed the thought from her mind as she forced the tip of the knife deeper between Hudson's ribs. After a moment of tension, the blade slid in. Vogel moaned.

Lily levered the blade to one side to create a small opening in the wound. Seconds later, blood flooded around the blade of the knife and trickled down Vogel's side.

"What the hell?" Hudson shouted. "Why is there so much blood?"

"It's good," Lily said, twisting the knife to allow more blood to escape the chest cavity. "Watch."

Vogel gasped a full breath. He coughed and drew another while Lily held the knife steady. Within a minute, some color had returned to his cheeks, and his chest rose and fell in deep motions as he drew air into both lungs.

Hudson reached a hand toward Vogel. "Thank God. You're okay, Uncle Glen."

Vogel closed his eyes, pushing his nephew's hand away.

Lily held the knife at an angle. This was as much as she could do. They'd need a tube of some sort to hold the wound open. A straw or something.

"Uncle Glen," Hudson whispered. "We did it. We're going to clean up the mess. I'm going to clean it up, just like you told me." Hudson choked on a sob. "I'm making it right. I took care of Abby, just like you told me." Hudson glanced up at the women, and she knew what he was thinking. He'd kill them next.

He turned back to his uncle. "You're going to be okay. It's all going to be okay." Hudson used the sleeve of his shirt to wipe Vogel's face.

Lily sensed the detective shift away from the men.

Vogel shook off his nephew's pampering. "Enough." He nodded to the women. "Take care of the girls first." Vogel said, his voice hoarse and labored. "No more witnesses."

Hudson nodded like an eager puppy, still wiping the blood off his uncle's face. His right sleeve. The gun was in his left hand again. "Sure thing," Hudson said. "Then we'll get you to the hospital, get you fixed up."

He rubbed at a thin streak of blood on Vogel's face, but his attention started to shift toward them. The girls, as Vogel called them. They would end up frozen to death and buried under the snow—disposable—like the girl who'd disappeared while she was Hudson's captive.

They were about to die.

As Hudson started to swing the gun in the detective's direction, Lily yanked the knife from Vogel's chest. Vogel's head reared up, his mouth forming a small, tight O. He tried to speak but couldn't get a word out.

Lily didn't hesitate even a second. She swung the blade in a short arc, out and down. There, she buried it in the meaty flesh of Derek Hudson's thigh.

Hudson roared and fell sideways. The revolver slipped from his grip as he grabbed for the knife, hands trembling as they danced around the wound. "Help me. Uncle Glen, help. What do I do?"

Vogel lunged upright and grabbed for the fallen revolver. "You fucking bitch!"

But the detective was already on her feet. She drew a gun from behind her as Glen Vogel's hand reached the barrel. Before Vogel could get the gun into his fat hand, the detective fired four bullets into his chest.

Then the detective aimed the weapon at Hudson, who had scurried backward, dragging his left leg. He pressed himself against the wall, his hand still hovering over the blade.

"I wouldn't pull that out if I were you," Lily said. "If it hit the femoral artery, you'll bleed out in less than a minute." The blade was nowhere near Hudson's femoral artery, but he didn't need to know that.

In the distance, Lily heard the whine of police cars.

Vogel's eyes were open, unmoving. Already death had flattened their gleam, drained the hate.

Hudson grabbed hold of Vogel's face. "No!" he roared as he cradled Vogel's head in his lap, resting it on the leg without the knife in it. "Uncle Glen," Hudson whispered to the dead man. "Oh God. Please, no."

Lily stood and moved toward the door.

The detective didn't flinch, holding the gun aimed at the two men until the sirens shrieked outside the door. "Nicely done," the detective said.

Lily nodded.

As voices in the storm called out to them, the detective shook her head. "I always fucking hated it when he called me 'girl.'"

Someone pounded on the door. "Police!" a voice shouted, and Lily had never been so grateful.

CHAPTER 64

IVER

Iver felt hands on his arms and back, a light in his eyes. It hurt to breathe. He opened his eyes and stared up at the night sky. The snowfall had ceased, and the thick bank of gray clouds moved across the sky, the storm retreating.

"Are you hurt?" an unfamiliar voice asked.

Iver took in the paramedic's jacket, the young face. He closed his eyes and took stock of his body. His back felt broken. He'd been shot, close range. He'd aimed the rifle at the man holding Lily, and then he'd felt the impact.

The paramedic called out to someone, "Some help over here?"

Iver shook his head and pushed himself up off the snow. "I'm okay." Hands helped him stand. The blanket of gray sky made everything feel eerily still.

He'd barely pulled himself upright when he spotted Lily running toward him. She came straight into his arms, and he had to brace himself for the impact. The pain in his back rocketed up his neck and down his spine. He grunted.

She scanned his face. "He said he shot you." She stood back and touched his face and arms, ran her hands over him in a hunt for injuries.

He laughed, the pain cutting it short. "I'm okay." He shook the police jacket off his shoulders, snow tumbling off the fabric and onto the ground. His breath billowed in thick white clouds as he peeled away the Kevlar vest, coughing, arms pressed to his ribs.

"You were wearing a vest." She took it from him and turned it over. In the center of the Kevlar was a massive twisted dent, as though the vest had collapsed around the bullet. She lifted his shirt and ran her hands across his back.

Iver flinched at her touch, bending over to gasp.

Gently, she wrapped an arm across his shoulders. "You probably have some broken ribs."

"I thought the bullet went through," he confessed, fear rising in his throat. He'd been sure he was dead.

She took his hand and held it tight. He wrapped an arm around her, shifting himself carefully to hold her. He wanted to lock her in his arms. He was okay. She was okay.

Lily leaned in and pressed a kiss to his wet cheek, her lips cold against his skin. The paramedics trudged through the snow, carrying a gurney between them. A man lay moaning, a knife in his thigh.

"Who is that guy?"

She shuddered against him, and he regretted the question. "That's Derek Hudson."

But Derek Hudson was dead. He'd been shot. According to the articles they'd read, he had been shot by one of the girls. Iver had so many questions, but he held them in. Lily's gaze trailed Hudson as he passed.

"You're safe now," he whispered.

"Stay here," she told him, and he watched as she followed the paramedics to the ambulance. At first, he thought she was going to help them with Hudson, but she returned almost immediately. In her hand was a small penlight. She shone it in his eyes, left and then right.

"Am I okay, Doc?" he asked, teasing.

"We're going to the hospital. You need x-rays and a full workup."

"I'm fine," he said, but she shook her head.

"We are going." She pushed on his ribs gently, and he winced at the pain.

"I hate hospitals."

She nodded. "I know." She took hold of his hand. "But I'll be there." She turned back toward the ambulance, and her gaze froze. "That man held me hostage for sixteen months."

"I want to kill him."

She was quiet a moment. "I stabbed him with a knife."

"Good for you. But it looks like he'll survive."

"He will."

Iver started to say something else, but they were interrupted by the arrival of more vehicles—a truck and a police car. The vehicles drove along the road that had been nearly invisible in the storm, parked only meters from where Iver had been shot. As the others approached, Iver placed a hand on her back protectively, nodding toward the man who approached. "Sheriff Davis," Iver said.

Davis ran toward them, another unfamiliar man beside him. "What the hell happened here?"

Detective Milliard approached, left arm in a sling and a paramedic trailing her. "It's a long story," she said, tilting her head as she eyed him. "Where were you all day?"

"In Elgin with Ross. Cannon jammed my cell signal. Didn't realize it until about an hour ago." Davis had been looking at the detective but now shifted his focus to Iver.

Instinctively Iver took a step back, still shielding Lily.

"I'm sorry I doubted you, Iver," Davis said.

Iver nodded. He was sorry, too.

"We need to get you to the hospital. Get checked out." Davis turned to the man beside him. "This is Deputy Sheriff Pete McIntosh from Glendive. Pete, can you get them to the hospital?"

"Happy to," McIntosh agreed.

"I'll go, too," Detective Milliard offered.

Despite the cold and the snow, there was a lightness in the air, a sense of relief, but Lily felt hesitant, stiff. Iver turned to her. "What's wrong?"

Lily scanned the group. "Can we go to the hospital on our own? Just Iver and me?"

"Why?" Milliard asked.

"Why not?" Iver countered. "It's been a long day."

Milliard motioned to the third man. "Pete's a good guy, I promise. He's not part of this."

But McIntosh only nodded. "I get it." He pulled his truck keys from his pocket and handed them to her. "You drive, though," he said to Lily. "Till someone checks him out."

Lily nodded, the tension in her shoulders softening. "Promise."

"I'm the Silverado," he said, pointing to a gray truck.

Iver thanked him, and he and Lily moved away from the group.

The paramedics had loaded Derek Hudson into the ambulance and were closing up the doors. Hudson was making a hell of a racket. Iver pulled Lily a little closer, ignoring the way the motion shot pain through his back and ribs.

"We'll see you at the hospital," the detective called after them.

Iver opened the driver's door for Lily and rounded the truck as she climbed in. He was about to close the door but then stood on the running board and called out to Milliard. "Hey, Detective, what about Carl Gilbert?"

The detective's mouth dropped open. "Shit," she called back. "I forgot all about him."

Iver was laughing when he got back into the truck.

"Gilbert?" Lily asked, starting up the truck and turning the heat to full blast. "What was that about?"

"Long story," he said. "It'll make you laugh."

She put the truck in drive. As they lurched forward, Lily seemed to fold into herself. "Lily?" Iver whispered.

She shook her head, swiping at her cheeks, struggling not to cry.

Iver shifted into the middle seat to be close and buckled himself in. He laid a hand gently on her leg. "You're okay, Lily. It's over now. You're safe." He had failed her once. It would not happen again.

She shook her head. "You don't understand, Iver. You don't know what I've done."

Swiping her tears, she pulled onto the road and started down the hill. The clouds were breaking up, and a few stars were visible in the patches of black sky.

Iver pushed a piece of hair off her face and tucked it behind her ear. "You can tell me. You can tell me everything."

Her shoulders shook with the sobs. "No. I can't."

He took hold of her leg and pressed his fingers firmly into the skin. "I'm not going anywhere. Not unless you tell me to leave. And even then, I'm going to fight you. Nothing you've done can change that."

She studied his face, scanning it as though searching for the doubt. But he didn't have any doubt.

"I'm a killer," she whispered.

"That was self-defense. That man was holding you hostage."

She shook her head, strands of hair falling across her eyes. "Not him. I don't even know if I did that. I don't remember shooting him. I only remember holding the gun, Abby telling me it was over. That I had saved them," she added, choking on the last few words.

He thought of the dead Afghan woman. Would he ever be able to tell her what he'd done? He pushed the thoughts away. "Maybe you did shoot him, and maybe you didn't. If you shot him, you did it to escape. He was keeping you prisoner."

She shook her head. "That's not what I'm talking about."

He ran a finger across her cheek, catching the tears as they fell. She didn't shy from his touch. But she was in shock. He was so messed up. What could he possibly offer her? But he would offer her whatever he could. He'd do that much. "What are you talking about, Lily?"

"Abby."

"What about her?"

Lily looked over at him, her eyes swollen with fear. "I killed her, Iver." She watched him, hesitant.

"You can tell me," he said.

As they made their way across the uneven road, Lily told Iver about the letters with Abby, about her visit, being in the woods, the moment when Lily had learned who Abby was, what she'd done.

Iver listened without a word, nodding to her that he was on her side, that she was safe with him.

When she was done, he took hold of her hand and gripped it tight. "Everything you did, you did to save yourself, Lily. And I'm so thankful that you did."

The truck slowed as Lily turned to look at him. He held her gaze. "You did the right thing," he said.

She looked back through the windshield and picked up speed as they neared the main highway. "I don't know if I can forgive myself."

"I understand that, too." He had yet to forgive himself. "I understand it too well."

She looked over at him, a furrow in her brow.

He shook his head. "It's a story for another time."

Turning onto the freeway, she asked, "Like Gilbert?"

He smiled softly. "Not a funny story. A story from Afghanistan, my story."

She reached out and intertwined her fingers with his.

"We're going to be okay," he whispered. "Both of us."

The look in her eyes shifted. The fear was still there, wide and glossy, but there was something else, too. He wanted to say it was hope. And maybe it was.

CHAPTER 65

KYLIE

Kylie wore a sling on her arm, a bag of frozen peas under her shirt against the place where the bullet had torn through her shoulder. Despite the initial pain, she had been lucky—the bullet wound was a clean through and through. Medicated with regular doses of ibuprofen, Kylie spent Saturday night and all of Sunday in the police department conference room with McIntosh, Davis, Sheriff Oloff from Elgin, Gary Ross, and a very cranky Carl Gilbert. She'd apologized a dozen times, but Carl was clinging to his grudge like a kid with a sandbox toy.

Davis had taken to making jokes, jabs like, "Gilbert, I think orange might be your color"—and that was not helping the situation. The truth was, Steve Cannon and Glen Vogel had done a hell of a job setting up Gilbert. Once the possibility of Gilbert's guilt had entered Kylie's head, everything seemed to point to him. First, the preliminary autopsy report on Jensen had been sent to Gilbert but never made it to Kylie. Then Gilbert was the one to find Jensen's shoes in a lockbox on Iver's truck—a lockbox that Iver swore he never used or locked. Gilbert hadn't done himself any favors with how he'd treated Iver in the hospital, and his attitude with Kylie on the phone when she'd called from Glendive had only cemented her suspicions.

But Cannon had also played his part well. A receipt on Cannon's work computer showed the purchase of the Green Bay Packers carabiner, which he'd distressed to look old. When he attacked Lily Baker, he'd made sure to have black licorice on his breath. Gilbert finding Kylie in the woods behind Skål had been dumb luck, but it had made her suspect him, too.

Cannon and Vogel had also manipulated Sheriff Davis like a pro. By planting a cell phone jammer on Davis's truck, Cannon had prevented Davis from getting any of Kylie's calls. Vogel, meanwhile, had convinced Davis to take Ross and go down to Elgin to talk to the sheriff there in search of Abby Jensen's mysterious new boyfriend. All the while, Vogel had followed Lily to Molva, and Cannon stuck close to the police station to keep the rest of the department in the dark.

After a day and a half of living on take-out pizza and the stale air of the department's tiny conference room, they'd been able to fit together the pieces of the puzzle—at least most of them. The DNA found under Abby's nails was a match to Baker. But Baker wasn't the one who strangled Abby while she was bleeding out. The bruises on her neck were from someone with much larger hands—undoubtedly Steve Cannon's, though the bruising wasn't clear enough to make a positive fingerprint ID.

Baker admitted her involvement in Abby's death in the woods that night. She'd been emotional when she confessed to pushing Abby down, to seeing her head hit the rock before she fled. But Kylie didn't blame her one bit. And the new DA wasn't going to touch Lily Baker, not after what she'd been through.

As the state lab had confirmed, the fibers found in Iver's truck and his office at the bar weren't a match to Abigail Jensen's blouse, though they were similar in appearance. Those fibers had come off a fringed purse that Iver's ex-wife, Debbie Wilson, had been carrying the night she and Iver argued, the same night Jensen was killed.

As far as Jensen's shoes in the crossover toolbox in Iver's truck, they might never know whether Cannon or Vogel had planted those. They'd located a burner phone in Cannon's house, used to alert the police of the attack on Lily Baker at Iver's home. A second burner phone had been used to alert the police that Iver was seen driving in the middle of the night. Kylie suspected that was Debbie Wilson's doing, but it didn't much matter now.

There was no question that both Cannon and Vogel played a part in covering up for Cannon. Certainly, DA Vogel had pushed everyone in the right direction, including encouraging Gary Ross to go to the scene of Brent Nolan's car accident. Anything to keep them all away from the murder investigation until they could be certain that there was no evidence pointing to Cannon.

They were confident that Tanner's death had also been Cannon's work. They'd discussed Tanner's cameras and the footage in their meeting, where Vogel was present. He could have easily shared that information with his nephew. Exactly what happened at Tanner's the night he'd been killed was unknown. Cannon was in the hospital, and who knew if he would ever talk.

When it came to the question of why Jenna Hitchcock had to die, no one on the team was able to come up with a decent theory. What threat had she posed? Did Jensen and Cannon try to lure her back into the fold, and she rejected them? Or were they cleaning up loose ends before starting again with Lily Baker? Kylie couldn't imagine she'd ever find out. Or maybe Cannon would be one of those criminals who suddenly got a conscience and wanted to make a deathbed confession. Kylie also didn't know exactly why Cannon had lured them up to the place where Vogel was holding Lily Baker. Sheriff Davis suggested that Cannon saw her and Iver as more loose ends to be tied up, a theory that Kylie knew would keep her up nights wondering.

As Kylie left the conference room for a breath of fresh, cold air outside, she found herself thinking back on all the clues that might have helped her if she'd seen them more clearly at the time. The gun that Gilbert collected at Larson's house—the one Lily Baker had taken from Abigail Jensen in the woods—was missing its serial number, so there was no way to know if it had been Cannon's or come from somewhere else.

Glen Vogel had done everything in his power to protect his sister, Stephanie, and her monster son. Vogel might have gotten away with it. If they had succeeded in killing Lily Baker, no one would have known that Vogel was a criminal. Cannon might have gone on to kill again, and Kylie would have worked alongside him for years, maybe, and never known. She took one last inhale of cold air, shivered, and made her way back inside the warm station.

Sunday afternoon, the mayor arrived in his church suit. Kylie didn't think the man knew her name, but he came right up to her and congratulated her on the fine detective work. "Hagen is honored to have you, Detective Milliard." The mayor stayed long enough to hear where they were on the investigation, then left before they got back to work.

He wasn't gone ten minutes when Glen Vogel's wife, Wanda, arrived at the station. She wore a black wool dress and flat boots and carried a large Tupperware container of her scones, which she handed to Kylie without meeting her gaze. Wanda Vogel held her back straight, but her cheery expression was absent.

"Thank you for coming," Davis said.

Kylie led Mrs. Vogel to the conference room and offered her a cup of coffee.

"Please. Decaf with milk if you have it."

When Kylie returned with the coffee, the men stood awkwardly around the table. Kylie set the cup in front of Mrs. Vogel, and Davis pulled out a chair.

Mrs. Vogel sank into it slowly, as though the process of sitting was painful.

Davis motioned to the scones. "You didn't have to bring—"

"I had to do something," she interrupted. "I couldn't sleep." She covered her mouth as the tears streamed down her cheeks.

"I'm so sorry," Kylie said and passed her a box of tissues.

Mrs. Vogel waved a hand through the air and took the box, inhaling deeply. "Baking helps when I'm upset," she said, then shook her head. "Usually." She paused to take another breath, appearing to push away that last thought. "I always knew that boy was trouble. His mother, too," she added, taking a tissue from the box. "I thought it would be better after Stephanie died. I thought Derek might leave North Dakota, finally. Leave us alone." She frowned. "But the sicker she got, the less stable Derek became."

"What did Glen say about Steve?" Davis asked. "About Derek Hudson?"

"Oh, Glen wouldn't say. He never talked about things that worried him. But I could tell." She touched the tissue to her nose. "And he was right to be worried. Derek went off the deep end after his mother died," she said, blinking back her tears. "And he dragged my Glen down with him."

They did not tell Wanda Vogel that her husband had almost killed a detective and an innocent woman—and possibly others. With the mayor's blessing, they had decided to keep the details from the public. No need to announce that their district attorney was a killer and his nephew the man who had kidnapped those girls. There was a chance that Hudson would try to implicate his uncle at his trial if he lived to stand trial. They would prepare for that, too.

Kylie had wondered about the timing—ten years almost exactly. But these were no anniversary killings. It had all started again after Hudson's mother's death, triggered by grief. They asked Mrs. Vogel to tell them about her husband's family so that they could better understand Derek Hudson, a.k.a. Steve Cannon. Much of what she knew they'd already heard—his father's antigovernment leanings, the commune. As for the real Steve Cannon, according to public records, he had never existed in North Dakota. The real Steve Cannon had a South Carolina driver's license, issued sixteen years earlier. His younger brother had been looking for him for ten years. According to the brother, Steve Cannon had left home and headed west toward Vegas or maybe Los Angeles, working along the way. Cannon's brother said Steve used to call him every few weeks to check in. Then, ten years ago, the calls just stopped.

Steve Cannon's brother thought Steve was in Montana when he disappeared, and the brother had traveled to Montana a half dozen times in the following decade to search for Steve, extending the search west into Idaho and Nevada. But no missing person report had been issued in North Dakota, so no one ever discovered the man living as Steve Cannon in North Dakota. Dark hair and a fuzzy driver's license photo had made it easy enough for Derek Hudson to use Cannon's ID and adopt his identity.

For a few years after the girls escaped, Hudson had lived off the grid, working odd construction jobs, mostly for cash. Then he'd taken Steve Cannon's driver's license to a motor vehicle office in Linton, North Dakota, about a hundred miles east of Molva, and renewed it with his own picture three years later. After that, Derek Hudson officially became Steve Cannon.

It was hard to know if the real Cannon had ever been involved in the kidnappings. There was also no way to know if Lily Baker had shot the real Steve Cannon in a genuine effort to escape or if Cannon's shooting had been Hudson's doing. Perhaps Lily had seen the shooting and taken the opportunity to make a run for it. Maybe the sight of Cannon's death had made Lily believe that she was somehow responsible. After all, another girl had died while they were in captivity. Who could say what that had done to Lily.

And there was no doubt in Kylie's mind that Abby would have twisted Lily's memory of events where she could. It left Kylie wondering if Abby had run after Lily to change her mind about escaping. Or in order to control the narrative with the police.

For her part, Kylie wanted to believe that Steve Cannon had actually been shot by Hudson himself, a victim of being in the wrong place at the wrong time. Perhaps he'd come across the cabin where Hudson was holding the girls and had given Lily the window she needed to escape. While that scenario didn't explain why Lily remembered holding the gun over the dead body, memory was a tricky thing. Since Derek Hudson was refusing to say anything to the police, they might never know. Maybe someday.

According to Wanda Vogel, her husband had told her Derek had changed his name to Steve Cannon in order to get a fresh start. Wanda had never known that there was another Steve Cannon. From how Wanda spoke, Glen Vogel had done his best to keep her out of his family's business.

"But Glen didn't want anyone to know that Steve was his nephew?" Davis asked.

"No, no. Glen made me promise not to tell anyone. And Steve"— she stopped and shook her head—"Derek, I mean . . . he was always trouble, so I thought it made sense to keep their relationship private, especially with Glen's job. I figured Glen was worried about what would happen when Steve messed up again."

The room fell quiet a moment.

Davis asked a few more questions and thanked Wanda Vogel for coming in.

Hudson's condition was stable. Soon enough, he'd be transferred to the state penitentiary in Bismarck. Hudson might not provide them any help in the case against him, but they didn't need his help to send him to prison for the rest of his natural life. North Dakota had abolished the death penalty in 1915, but there were strong feelings about men who abused children. While Derek Hudson might not get the death penalty, he would likely live behind bars the rest of his life, and that was enough for Kylie.

As she was heading out of the department, half-dead on her feet and on her way home to get some sleep, she passed Gilbert in the kitchen, holding the Green Bay Packers mug and staring into space.

"Hey."

He spun around, and she put her hands up.

"I'm really sorry about everything that happened."

He nodded.

"We going to be okay?" she asked.

He was quiet a moment, then said, "I heard a couple of the Patrol guys talking. Sounds like Davis might resign."

She didn't know what to say to that. Looking back, it was clear that Vogel had manipulated the sheriff, pushed Davis to run the investigation in a way that benefited him and Hudson. But Kylie wasn't sure how Davis could have known what Vogel was really up to.

"You could throw your name in the hat," Gilbert said.

She frowned.

"For sheriff . . . ," he said.

Sheriff Milliard. It had a ring to it. She shook her head. "It's not for me."

Gilbert shrugged. "Just a thought."

"See you tomorrow?" she asked.

"I'll be here," he said.

Sheriff Milliard. She repeated the words in her head. It *did* have a ring to it. But she enjoyed the hunt too much. She didn't want to sit at a desk or kiss the mayor's ass. She *definitely* didn't want to kiss the mayor's ass.

She wanted to kick ass and take prisoners.

And she would.

CHAPTER 66

LILY

Three months later

Lily sat in the shade of the house, a red-handled trowel in her hand and Cal at her feet. Her fingers and palms were covered in dirt, lines of black beneath her nails. Along with the new trowel, Iver had bought her a pair of blue gardening gloves, but she found the feel of dirt on her skin comforting. She dug a small pit in the earth six inches in front of the row of blue delphiniums she'd planted earlier. Gently turning over the thin plastic container of a brilliant pink zinnia, she coaxed the flower into her open palm and set it in the divot, then gathered the dirt around the roots and used the watering can to saturate the soil. Moving down the row, she planted a yellow one next, then an orange. Every few minutes, she glanced up at the street. Iver had come by earlier for coffee before his meeting. He would be home soon.

For almost two weeks after she had escaped that shed and Derek Hudson, Iver had slept on the couch in her living room. Lying under the thick down comforter, with only a wall between them, she could feel the energy of him so close. She knew he felt it, too. Night sounds came from the floorboards as he shifted on the couch. Even Cal paced restlessly, the click of his toenails on her wood floor lulling her into a dreamless sleep.

She wanted him to be in bed with her. She wanted him to kiss her, not just on the temple or the cheek or the top of the head. To really kiss her. He wanted the same. In three months, she'd come to know him better than she knew herself. She'd told him everything. And learned everything about him.

But they had yet to take that last step. At the first AA meeting Iver had attended, the Sunday after they almost died, Iver had come back more than just sober. He had looked distraught.

"What is it?" she asked him as he came in the door, the worry etched in his expression.

"They say the worst thing you can do in recovery is to start a new relationship."

They stood in silence, her mind spinning. What was he saying? What did he want? Finally, she said, "So we won't start."

His gaze swept across her face.

She saw the fear in his eyes and grabbed his hand, interlacing her fingers with his. "I mean, we won't start yet."

"You mean, like, wait?"

She nodded, swallowing the fear that he would reject the idea, reject her.

"Like a while? A few months?"

"Sure," she agreed. "Whatever you think."

"Three months," he said.

She nodded. "Three months."

They stared down at their hands, the grip of their fingers, and slowly let go. So they kept their relationship platonic, waiting for Iver's ninety-day chip. While she was desperate to be with him in every way, there was something comforting in the absence of physical intimacy. Instead, they found every other type. They were inseparable.

He was with her when Detective Milliard came by to tell her that they'd found her phone near the scene of the accident. Showed her the small plastic piece on the back that stored her credit card and driver's license, though she'd gotten a new one by then. He held her hand while the detective explained what they thought had happened after she'd gotten into the car with Brent Nolan, how Hudson had strangled Abby, then returned Lily's car to her house before doubling back later to dispose of Abby's body in the dumpster. Iver had held her afterward while she cried.

She had gone with Iver to confront Kevin, who admitted to drugging him that night at the bar and seemed to think it was no big deal. "I was desperate," he'd said. In the end, Kevin returned the cash, and Iver agreed not to press charges. Iver seemed fine with putting the incident behind him.

Together Iver and Lily moved forward and made plans. She was beside him when he called his attorney to draft the paperwork to sell Skål to Mike Hammond, then met him for dinner to celebrate the sale. They sat on the couch in his house as he navigated the unexpected emotions that came with ending the relationship with his father's business, with burying that part of his dad at last.

Each day she shared the memories she gained as pieces of her old life flittered down with the inconsistency of Hagen weather—some days like drips of rain and others like fat clumps of snow. Some memories arrived in a hailstorm. But the memories did return to her—most of them. What remained a void was the period when she'd been held hostage.

Instead, she had what might have been memories but felt like strange dreams—huddling with a crying girl, being stabbed, a man with blood running down his face. She might never remember the period between getting into the van with Abby Jensen and waving down that truck driver sixteen months later. Iver urged her to try not to worry about remembering, and she was trying.

What became obvious to both of them was how much they cared for each other. Sex was not love. And while she wanted to share that with him, he already had her love. They had unknowingly—or maybe not unknowingly at all—gone headfirst into a relationship.

Now, Cal laid his muzzle on her thigh, and she patted his head. "He'll be here soon," she told him.

She lifted a fuchsia zinnia from the cardboard pallet, shook it free gently from the plastic, and set it down in the earth. Digging with her fingers to deepen the hole, she nestled the flower into its new home and patted the cool soil across its thready roots.

She glanced up at the house she'd grown up in. The shutters were absent, currently on sawhorses in the garage, sanded and freshly painted charcoal gray. The siding on the front left of the house was a patchwork as they replaced the pieces that were rotting and too far gone to sand and repaint. It all felt like they were building something together.

Maybe the relationship wouldn't make it. Maybe they ought to have been more vigilant about keeping their distance. They'd talked about this, too, and she'd come to see the idea of their recovery in broader terms than simply Iver's sobriety. With their pasts—her imprisonment, the things that Iver had seen and done in Afghanistan, all that had happened to him—life would be about recovery for a very long time. Maybe, in some part, forever. AA only gave shape to one piece of that.

With all of the things they had to wade through, why deny each other a partner to gather strength from along the way? How could they deny it?

Iver was more the straight shooter. "We're not really starting a new relationship," he said one night when they were cuddled, talking on the couch in the middle of the night.

"We're not?" she asked.

"No," he said. "After all, our first kiss was almost twelve years ago."

She smiled at him. "Always the pragmatist."

An engine roared in the distance, and Cal rose on stiff hips and began to bark. She turned to see Iver's truck pull to the curb. Something hot rolled around in her chest as he climbed out of the cab. He walked toward her, a sideways smile on his lips, and leaned down to pat Cal's head.

Lily rose and brushed her dirty hands across her jeans. "How was your meeting?"

His lips broke into a smile, and he pulled a shiny gold coin from his pocket, settling it into his palm. The outer edge read, *To thine own self be true.* In the center was a 3.

When she looked up, he was staring at her. His gaze held her, swept across her lips in the way that gave her a bump deep in her gut. She smiled up at him. "Iver?"

He nodded, leaning toward her.

"Ninety days," she whispered.

"Three months," he whispered back, his lips brushing hers. "We waited."

She let out a nervous laugh. "That's it?"

He shifted back, touching his nose to hers. "If you want it to be."

She nodded slowly.

"You're sure?" he asked, the words cracking in his throat.

"So sure," she whispered.

And he leaned in and kissed her. She pressed her dirty palms to his cheeks and kissed him back, holding him against her. And then he lifted her up and carried her up the front porch steps into the house. He paused at the threshold and studied her face. "What are you thinking?" he whispered.

"That you're a much better kisser than you were in the eighth grade."

He dropped his head back and laughed, and she laughed, too. Then he whistled to Cal. As soon as Cal made his way slowly up the steps and into the house, Iver kicked the door closed and carried her toward the bedroom.

AUTHOR'S NOTE

I would not be pursuing this dream if it were not for you, the reader. It is only fitting, then, that my first gratitude goes to you. Thank you for reading this book, for following me to the tiny town of Hagen, North Dakota, and following Lily and Iver in their adventure. While we're at it, thank you for every book you've ever read. It is the greatest gift you can give an author.

Next, my sincere respect and gratitude go to the men and women who devote their lives to the pursuit of justice. As an author, I aim for a realistic portrayal of crimes and their investigation, but I certainly don't always get it right. Any errors and poetic license are my responsibility entirely.

For research, I am, as always, indebted to the people at the San Francisco Police Department, who have been answering strange questions since book one. Dr. Craig Nelson, associate chief medical examiner, North Carolina Office of the Chief Medical Examiner, has become absolutely invaluable in an accurate portrayal of death and death investigation—or as accurately as the story will allow. Thank you, Dr. Nelson.

The team at Jane Rotrosen Agency continues to blow me away. I am so lucky to call myself one of their authors. Thank you to all and especially to Meg Ruley, Rebecca Scherer, Michael Conway, Sabrina Prestia, and Hannah Rody-Wright. Thank you also to my fabulous editor, Jessica Tribble; to Sarah Shaw, who makes sure we're always having fun (we are!), and the incredible team at Thomas & Mercer; to Leslie

Lutz for bringing out the best in the book; to Riam Griswold and Rachel Norfleet for the thorough edit; and to Shasti O'Leary Soudant for the fabulous cover art.

I am hugely grateful to those who support the process of writing a book and especially to fellow authors J. T. Ellison, D. J. Palmer, Barbara Nickless, Jason Backlund, Randle Bitnar, and Shawnee Spitler and to the eagle-eyed proofreaders: Albee Willett, Christy Delger, Dani Wanderer, and Whitney Pritham.

Finally, I'm grateful to my family for supporting this crazy dream from the early days. Above all, this book is for the ones who make my life complete: Chris, Claire, and Jack. Because of you three, I am the luckiest lady in the world.

If you enjoyed this book, please leave a review on Goodreads, Bookbub, Amazon, and the like so that others might discover *White Out* as well.

Sincerely,
Danielle

ABOUT THE AUTHOR

Photo © 2018 Mallory Regan, 40 Watt Photo

Danielle Girard is the *USA Today* and Amazon #1 bestselling author of *Chasing Darkness*, the Rookie Club series, and the Dr. Schwartzman series—*Exhume*, *Excise*, *Expose*, and *Expire*, featuring San Francisco medical examiner Dr. Annabelle Schwartzman. Danielle's books have won the Barry Award and the RT Reviewers' Choice Award, and two of her titles have been optioned for movies. A graduate of Cornell University, Danielle received her MFA at Queens University in Charlotte, North Carolina. She, her husband, and their two children split their time between San Francisco and the Northern Rockies. Visit her at www.daniellegirard.com.